The Corrupted

By

Dennis Lewis

Published by Accent Press Ltd – 2006
ISBN 190517036X
Copyright © Dennis Lewis 2006

Printed and bound in the UK by
Cox & Wyman Ltd., Reading

Cover Design by Emma Barnes

The publisher acknowledges the financial support
of the Welsh Books Council

To the men of Tower Colliery, for saving a nation
from victimhood

Foreword

Despite what I write here, you should know that the city of Cardiff still enchants me, still holds me in its immoderate thrall. Especially 'The Bay' area, with its paradoxes of architectural thought; the sternness of Victorian red-brick, the bright shock of modernism; the Pharaonic, the phallic, the mighty curve of a bronzed roof humped like a satyr's back. (O, Reader, Dear Reader…the opportunities that were missed!)

From where I sit I can see tourists tumbling from a fume-snorting tour-bus, emerging blinking like surprised country bumpkins, they gawp at the glittering buildings then shockingly indulge themselves in a normally un-American activity. They walk (yes, I said walk) to the railed-in waters, and stare at the quicksilver wavelets heaving and fluttering like a distressed mind. Behind them, a group of school children are organising themselves into a ragged queue like a cowed gang of supplicant asylum seekers. The children are queuing to inspect that brand-spanking, high-souled Shangri-la of the Welsh Opera; the gleaming sixty-five million pounds worth of upturned bathtub the Tourist Office prefers to call – Millennium Centre. Sydney got its billowing sails, one of the most popular, iconic buildings in the world; we got an upturned bathtub. Fair enough. (What can you get for a mere sixty-five million these days? A triumph of modern architecture, a priceless tourist attraction, a much loved cultural centre? Oh come on…come on!) Each compliant child clutches at its hat and cranes its neck, eyes flinching at the bruised copper on the sun-reflecting roof: each infant nose is crinkled up, already learning how to sneer.

For many years I knew Cardiff like an old friend: an old friend that whenever I met I said, "Hi, it's good to see you. Boy, you look great."

And the city always said, "Hey, it's good to see you too. I'm just going down the pub, want to come along?" I always went along. And it was there, in the smoke gullied striations of the ancient bars that all my unuttered miseries would pour out; and a gallon of Brain's Dark and gossipy humanity would pour in. Oddly enough, Cardiff and I remained friends on the sound basis of expediency; because we felt we needed each other. I brought real discernity to the city: a cultural person, with my mantle of pretensions, my opera season ticket and knowing ovations. The upwardly mobile city happily wrapped me in its sycophantic arms. We were really, really good friends.

I kept up a friendship with this fraternal town for a long time, but now it's broken. Everything is gone. The newly regenerated waterfront is a monument over the grave of in situ communities and cultural diversity. The waterfront was once Tiger Bay, but no one calls it 'Tiger' anymore; now it's just 'The Bay'. I suppose 'The Bay' sounds more moneymaking, more mendaciously marketable than, 'Tyger, Tyger, burning bright…' From Tiger Bay to Protean Bay to Smugly Bay – a foul-weathered Riviera of bleak skies and gooseflesh, reeking with the hot breath of avarice and self-interest (I exaggerate only a little).

Yes, it's true. The amiable city I was born in seems to have undergone a voodoo transformation: it has none of the deep familiarity and reassuring safety I used to enjoy. It seems our Welsh capital, this once friendly city of rain, salty winds and multi-cultural accents, has been fragmented and dislocated, its flummoxed inhabitants emerging from a centrifuge of change to a crushing horizon of Gothamite architecture. Now I understand how city planning can be seen as a displacement of sexual energies (I'm convinced that the City Fathers are all worried about the size of their penises.) Perhaps someone should tell them that it's not the size of the building that matters, it's what you do with it that counts.

The city's nighttime intemperance and its rampant steel and concrete tumescences have distorted its once trustable face into a grimace of fierce misanthropy. In the twenty-first century Welsh capital, the twin prurience's of gigantism and awe-inspiring drunkenness rule: urbaness without the urbanity. I no longer feel at home here: I feel old while the city feels young, I am slow while the city is fast, I am nostalgic while the city is go-gettingly anticipative. The city I knew seems to have been uprooted and dislocated; it seems as though our skittish capital is merely making a brief pit stop on its way to somewhere else.

Now, sadly, I'm willing to admit a physical repellence for the city, especially its nighttime feuds and antipathies. The city centre attracts too many tribes of noisy drunks and boorish adolescents, all mindlessly pissed or doped-up on illegal substances; all eager to assault innocent passers-by with the ferocity of recently de-institutionalised psychotics. When visiting the city at the night you avoid everyone's eyes: lest they see the fear, lest they implicate you in their wars.

I worked in the city as a newspaper hack for the South Wales Mail. Oh yes, I am a fully trained-up impresario of gossip: I understand the entertainment value of disgrace and ruin. We are now so used to human tragedies being handed over to the newspapers and television to be turned into entertainment that we hardly notice it. We live in a democracy of gossip; it has become the national faith. This book, this memoir of gossip and innuendo, is a novel; for the most part it contains the shimmer and invention of my imagination, but it is based entirely on the story as told to me by my oldest friend Sweep: another newspaper hack, another mindless drunk.

We became friends partly because we were both enmeshed in the same demoniacal game: the boozing game. Oh, don't get me wrong; we weren't helpless alcoholics, at least not yet. At that time we were a pair of ambitious young journos; we both admired the life-skills of the Mail's pinstriped strivers, the successful young executives. But Sweep and I admired much more the rarer life-skills of the drunk in the park, wearing his scarecrow clothes and his impassive look. How much more of a life-expert is the hopeless drunk! It is he who unmasks life's desolation; it is he who reminds us of life's betrayals. Both Sweep and I knew in our booze-thirsty hearts, that it is the successful executive that is one of life's deviations, one of life's atonal wrong notes. As all the best writers say at the start of their gossipy novels, I have changed the names of the characters enclosed within these pages: to protect the guilty.

DL. Cardiff 2006

Part One

1

Why is it that our bad dreams are so life-like?

Well…why? Why are our nightmares so very like life?

Is it because, as in life, we have to suffer them alone?

The Viennese drug addict, Freud, knew a lot about nightmares. But in his own, personal nightmares, the genius psychoanalyst was still a lone-creature, feeble and separated from the flock. Even Freud, the expert on dreams, had to suffer his bad dreams alone, lying in the dark.

Shit!" says Motley, waking suddenly, still full of yearning, apology and vast contrition. Before his eyes can grow used to the gloom, they play a cruel trick on him: "Boys?" he says hopefully, "…Boys? Where are you?"

Alas, Staff Sergeant Motley's boys can't hear him anymore; they're all gone. And he's calling out in his dreams again. It makes sense to Motley to cry out in pain every night. His unconscious struggles cover him in a cold lather; the rumpled sheets of his bed are soaked with sweat. He stares groggily into the darkness for a few more seconds, then says, "They're gone…all gone."

The nightmares happen a lot lately: those uninvited deliverers of toxic memory. Motley's dreams flare and burn with liability and shame. This is one of the ways the past finds him out, the spilt-milk past. The past likes to find him in his sleep; it comes to get him, bringing with it his forgotten wrongs. He just can't stop the past; he just can't keep it out of his dreams. Motley's past is full of smoke and screams and the sound of the sky cracking open. Sometimes he wakes up in the night and his mind isn't his any more, it just isn't working for him anymore. In his dreams, Motley's mind is working for the other side, the side that says he should have got it right: "Oh Mother! Lord! Anyone! –No more dreams!"

Motley longs for amnesia, that long, cradling, melancholic sleep. But Motley's past is still out there, the straight-line past that runs right through the heart of his present like a castigating spear. Most men of Motley's age dream of naked women, but on these misshapen nights, he isn't that blessed. Motley doesn't have the peace of mind for that kind of raison d'être horniness any more.

2

Motley's nightmares are the detritus of Iraq: the renascent shock of seeing his men blown to pieces less than ten yards away. The veteran NCOs' inexperienced Second Lieutenant had sent three of his troopers out from behind their sandbag wall to stop traffic and search cars. Motley remained behind the wall, covering his men with a GPMG. He'd already warned his officer that the guys were too exposed. He tenaciously told the young Lieutenant three times that only one guy should be out front stopping the cars. But the greenhorn Sandhurst graduate wouldn't listen.

"I've had enough of this Staff. Whose patrol is it, mine or yours?"

"Yours, sir, but…"

"Quite. Then we'll do things my way. Is that alright with you?"

"Yes sir, but…"

Then the sudden flash of light, bright as a giant red jewel. The street-shattering concussion tore through the thin membranes of Motley's eardrums like a giant fist punching holes through cobwebs. His whole body warped and quaked from the tremendous blast; even his bowels churned convulsively. From the seething inferno of smoke and flame tumbled strips of uniformed flesh and the broken arcs of white ribs, falling like stripped bark from a dead tree. An obscene shower of flesh and bone, red and black snowflakes of blood and gore fell from the frightened sky. In those terrible moments Motley saw the real colours of his men: their foaming veins, their innermost voices, the stain of their souls. The explosion's barbaric spectacle made public the men's underlying animality; the pale vertebra, the lengths of femora, all the scattered teeth and strange fragmented things that were moments ago friends and comrades, men who drank and smoked and loved and joked. Now their sundered molecules seeded the dusty ground.

A pico-second after the car bomb went off, the mass of blood in Motley's forebrain had tried to swarm to the back of his skull. He had almost passed out, lurching and swaying behind the sandbag wall, but somehow he'd remained on his feet. The skin was peeled from Motley's face in raw, agonising strips. His scorched cheeks bubbled and percolated. Only the combat gloves he wore had saved his hands from the same pain-shrieking treatment. String-like filaments of blood began to trickle from his ears and nose. As eddies of searing wind subsided, a silence descended over him like a pacifying drug. Then he realised that the sudden tranquillity was due to his post-concussion deafness.

Now he began shivering and trembling uncontrollably. A tsunami of adrenaline surged through his dilated, fear-decoding veins. Trying desperately to blink away the dirt from his eyes, Motley gave up in despair: there was too much of the road's abrasive dust and cataracting granulate. He squeezed his eyes shut, praying that the scene before him would go away and his men would still be standing there. He remembered turning around and seeing the dazed officer picking himself up from the ground. Motley glared savagely at him. He couldn't hear what the Lieutenant was saying through the ringing in his ears but from the movement of the man's lips, he could make out: "What…what happened?" The headstrong young officer's tactical dispositions had

3

been badly flawed; three of Motley's friends were dead, that was the flaw. The next thing Motley recalled was punching the Lieutenant in the face.

All around the roadblock, the strong bones of fit young men lay shattered, broken, splintered like thoughts in a disordered mind; their heedless spirits drifted through the flux of smoke and flames, their buckled souls transcendent amongst the hot human mulch. On a cloudy, overcast morning outside the faction-riven city of Basra, the lives of Motley's three friends were suddenly and grievously ended, their vigorous husks undone and streaming everywhere. Pools of human blood, black as oil, boiled in the sand under Iraq's furious and unstable sky. In those brief moments, Motley felt a whole Mahabharata of emotions, an entire Mabinogion of loss and pain.

Of course, soldiers know all about the risk of reduced life expectancy; they know all about the ins-and-outs of not living very long; they've learned the tumultuous lessons of sudden death. The veteran soldier has an overview of the shorter life span, the condensed and the heroic-but-brief. Though nothing equips them for the awfulness, the repulsion and the razor-cutting agony of seeing their friends tugged into oblivion before their very eyes. Just imagine, the last time you saw your mates they were a few feet off the ground, and in flames.

On that fearful roadblock, Motley learned something about the myths of death; which meant that what he'd really learned about were the half-truths of life. He had unwillingly tuned into that great misery – the chaos and pitilessness, the wonder of roaring violence; and then, after that, after that…the vortex of post traumatic shock.

4

Much later, Motley recalled that he was looking into a medic's calm but insistent eyes. The mouth in that concerned face was moving soundlessly. Then Motley found he was lying on a bed in a hospital, crying like a baby. He lay on that bed for a long time, paralysed with shock. He couldn't wipe from his mind the excruciating image of those brave men corrupted into a sizzling, tattered scandal of bloody, high-protein wreckage. For three days, the tears were unstoppable, swarming down his burned and feverish face. He got tired of trying to furtively wipe them away so he let them run, sticky and fat, down his raw cheeks. For three days, there was nothing he could do to stop the flow of scolding, unforgiving tears. Motley was ashamed of himself for what had happened to his men. The death of his comrades was constantly searing through his mind like white-hot shrapnel; his sense of guilt was killing him. In fact, during one vast, terrifying night of accusing introversion, Motley had even considered the ultimate in self-criticism. But he decided that he wasn't deferential enough for suicide. Staff Motley only kept going because he wasn't certain that his entire life had just turned to shit: he only guessed that it had. Okay, he had lived through a tragedy, but tragedy is always manageable. Look how we all live through it.

So what had happened to Motley's friends? Where did they go? They had just been standing there, but then they were chased away by the ruthless, violent cloud that had instantaneously enveloped them; turned them into ghastly loose strips of red and black carrion. Death's split second of nothingness had carried them away; the split second of nothingness that lasts for eternity. Death...the most powerful Black Hole in the universe, nothing escapes its gravitational pull.

Terrifying isn't it, and life's full of terrifying tricks like that. You're young, fit, and some mother's pride and joy, and a split second later you're snatched into eternity. For a time back there, Motley was no great pal of life. Life's terrifying tricks made him nervous, its random sharp-practices gave him palpitations.

Motley's bad dreams kept on prompting him like an angry whine, "Gone," he grieved, "Gone." He repeated that word over and over as if the word was a malevolent mantra; as if he were muttering the foulest, most defiling swear word that he could possibly conceive…"Gone." The insistent word sought Motley out, tearing at his self-control like a wild animal, dissolving him into rivulets of stinging tears. It broke his heart to know that his boys wanted to say something before they went: because they always want to say something before they go. Usually they just cry out for their mothers, or sometimes their dads; but they never scream, "I'm hit! I'm hit!" like they do in the movies. They cry out for their mums and dads because they are boys in uniform, because they're soldiers, and they want recognition for going down in the line of duty. "Mum! Dad! I'm going down!" they cry, looking for their mums and dads, and recognition.

For Motley, those hospital tears had represented a profound emotional experience; he'd never cried in public before. Strangely enough, just a few years later he fervently believed that public displays of emotion were not only vulgar, but a crime against true grief. He hated seeing those clichéd sprays of flowers and the mawkish cards left at the scenes of deadly crimes or fatal accidents. The war veteran had seen a great deal of grief in Iraq; he knew that true grief knocks the breath from your lungs and pins you to the ground; true grief is tragic-comic; turning you into an absurd and ridiculous figure. Because true grief is like true love: it debases you, completely and utterly.

4

The trick-cyclists believe that there are two kinds of memory: one when the mind skilfully recreates an emotional reaction (the feelings of the event), and the other when the mind evokes an absolutely accurate optical replica (a video-ghost of DVD quality). How Motley loathed both kinds of memory; how he agonised over how easily memory found every half-hidden crack in space and time. Sometimes not even near-fatal doses of drink and drugs could thwart his clawing memory. Again and again Motley's dreams leafed through the pages of his past, trying to analyse motives, actions, alternatives, each alternative forking and re-forking without end. He was convinced that he felt his dead comrades floating through his dreams, their incarnations nervously asking through the dark: "What happened Sarge? What's happened to us?" And then he would start trembling and twitching in his sleep, his body an overflowing spring of acrid sweat.

Why had his friends been taken on that particular day and not him? How had he avoided death? Was it luck? Fate? He knew that his death was already out there, waiting. His ending already had its own place, its own chosen hour. His final minute already existed, when all the time he'd had would telescope back into itself, leaving behind only the vehement, confiscatory darkness.

5

He was angry and disappointed with himself. But worse than that, Motley felt sorry for his vanished friends. He felt sorry too for all the other poor, put-upon bastards that he knew served in every fighting army in every part of the world. He felt a crushing responsibility for what had happened to his men. In fact, at that moment, Motley's well-developed conscience felt a crushing responsibility for all the remorseless inhumanity in the entire mortified, desecrated world. ...Well? Why the hell not? Motley was a soldier wasn't he? And didn't the very fact that he was a soldier, skilled in the arts of killing, encompass all the wincing, nightmarish acts of inhumanity?

During one sleepless, angst-ridden night, he couldn't stop himself from wondering – is there any equivalence of cruelty between terrorists and soldiers, any kind of broad parity? Are there any deterministic loops of inordinate injury, any regrettable cobwebs of killing that link them together? He sagged under the weight of his karmic scrutiny. Technically, he reassured himself, a soldier is of a different moral order than a terrorist. But to hell with all that – Motley still couldn't stop himself from wondering where he fitted in with the murderers, with the world's indignant, blood-spattered purveyors of killing.

Of course, Motley didn't really think of himself as a life-taker; he'd never actually killed anyone. And naturally, he didn't really think of himself as one of the bad guys. There were worst killers, and much, much badder guys. So who are the worst killers, where are the much badder guys? There, on the intimate flight deck of an airliner, for example, holding a blade to the throat of a wailing air-stewardess. The minds on those worst guys – the hateful minds in their hateful universes. No. Taff Motley wasn't that bad. He didn't hate the people he'd been trained to kill. When the time came, he would have to kill thoughtlessly, helplessly, acting on orders from above. In a self-righteous sense, his orders would be the things that redeemed him – God bless those orders from above, God bless em all.

*   *   *

Even as a soldier in Iraq, Motley's humanity had never deserted him. In the battle-disordered, ramshackle surroundings of Basra, amongst the weird and strange perspectives, he'd been deeply moved by the sickly-faced children who had watched him walk by, tight-lipped and tense on his nerve-punishing patrols. Wearing thin, tattered tee shirts and no shoes, the kids sat dumbly on the kerbs in the raw winter rain, admonishing him with big, sad, catatonic eyes. He felt crushed by their dogged and hungry stares. What a warrior he was! What a real hero! His breached soul writhed and cracked under the weight of the children's unappeasable stares. What a shitty country! What a shitty war! He wanted to bomb the whole feculent place to smithereens, bomb it out of existence, smash it out of his mind, then he wouldn't have to look into those pale, sad, sickly faces any more. Walking past those afflicted, war-haunted kids, Motley wondered how many children were destitute in his own prosperous country. How many drunken fathers would be arriving home from the pub that night and beating up their wives and kids? How many uncomprehending children were being bullied and abused, were going hungry or having their hearts gleefully broken?

6

When the Military Policewoman marched onto Motley's ward, she had been greeted with a chorus of wolf-whistles. A new female face entering the ward, even the stern face of an officer from the Provost Marshall's office, was like the effulgent light of dawn lighting up the room with its hopeful rays. For more time than they could bear thinking about, the sex lives of the men on the ward had been entirely conversational. Risking a charge of showing disrespect to an officer, one of the youngest and most desperate soldiers shouted: "Excuse me Ma'am, are you married?"

Some tacky cynic instantly replied in a low growl, "She's Military Police, dickhead. Who's going to fall in love with one of those?"

"But that's the sort of woman I should be associating with," the sex-starved voice chimed in again, "She looks so…clean."

All the men could tell instantly that the immaculately uniformed female officer had class. They didn't know what class was, exactly, but whatever it was, they knew that she had it. Even through the woollen serge of her tailored jacket, the appreciative audience of libidinous soldiery could tell that the officer's breasts were large and pointed. Her enticing hips flowed smoothly as her heels clip-clopped attractively across the parquet floor. Fifteen wounded men simultaneously wondered what kind of underwear she was wearing beneath her figure-hugging uniform, and whether military policewomen were interested in fornication.

Motley's eyes had flipped open when the banter had started. He saw the Redcap march purposefully to the bottom of his bed and stand to attention. Her eyes were large and white with tension as she stared down at him. Motley's eardrums had healed a few days ago, and his hearing had only just returned. Now, almost the very first words he heard came from the absurdly thin, salmon-coloured lips of this female Military Police officer: "Staff Sergeant Motley, you're under arrest."

The policewoman had spoken the egregious, truncheon-weighted words as quickly as they would leave her efficient mouth; then she lowered her eyes in embarrassment from Motley's scorched and flame-blackened face.

One of the guys leaned up on his elbows to get a better view, "Jesus, she thinks she a cop." The MP hadn't even bothered to ask Motley how he was feeling. Without further comment, she moved around the bed and handed him a fat, official looking document.

"Yes, Ma'am. That's fine," was all Motley could think to say. The policewoman looked irritated by his sanctioning reply. It wasn't the inflammatory reaction she'd expected from the hard-bitten, battle-scarred paratrooper, who'd been charged with assaulting his superior officer.

Surreally, Motley couldn't stop himself from thinking that the Redcap officer standing next to his bed looked like a five-foot-four matchstick with spindly arms and legs. He suddenly realised that Military Policewomen were the only females he could look at without thinking about sex.

"It's the officer he thumped you should be arresting!"

"Shame on you!"

"The guy's a hero!"

"You should give him a bloody medal!"

"It's bullshit!"

"Bloody crap-hats!"

A furious wave of howls and jeers of disapproval started up. The other wounded men in the ward were incensed at the exemplary justice being pushed through by the Ministry of Defence. The unnerved policewoman hysterically shouted something about an ill-disciplined rabble; then she fled from the chaotic ward like a victim from a roomful of rapists. Motley watched the syncopating curves of her backside go, blinking at the onset of a headache and wondering what kind of underwear she was wearing. There didn't seem to be room for any under that tight-fitting uniform.

"Don't go! Are you married?" cried the fastidious eighteen-year-old who admired the dishwasher-clean officer, and desperately wanted to get to know her.

"Good riddance to bad rubbish," yelled the tacky cynic.

"Don't say that about her. I wanted her to stay," whined the youngster with carbolic sex on his mind.

"She wasn't even pretty."

"But I'm madly in love with her!" A well-laundered woman, who showered every day, was the closest thing to paradise that this near-Brahminically clean soldier could imagine.

"You're too young to know what love is," the foul cynic persisted, "and anyway, she didn't even look clean."

"You bastard, you're only saying that because you know it hurts me."

"She's a dirty Redcap bitch, for Chrissakes!" the misogynistic cynic insisted.

"I don't care, you don't know anything about her. And I don't want you talking like that about the girl I'm going to marry." Risking the brand-new epiderma that was forming on his lips and faltering cheeks, Motley couldn't help smiling at the madcap exchange. "That's rich. Falling in love with an MP? That's really rich," he chuckled.

When the sound of the policewoman's clip-clopping heels had retreated down the hospital corridor, a cold, belligerent silence drifted over the ward like a creeping sea mist. The antiseptic air crackled and flinched under the weight of repressed rage. Then a calm, concerned voice asked, "You okay, Taff?"

Motley raised his hand from the bedclothes, his thumb up.

"Fuck `em. Eh mate?" the calm voice intoned, "Fuck `em all."

For a moment, all sixteen wounded men in the ward shared that one, single, impenitent thought.

"What the hell are you lot getting so upset about?" piped a pathetic voice from its bed-bound ghetto in the corner. It came from the despondent mouth of the poor bastard with both his legs blown off. He had arrived a week ago from the intensive care unit. "Things could be a lot worse, you know. At least you've got your legs and your balls."

The ward-full of wounded men lay mutely on their beds, surrounded by a fog of body-mutilating possibilities. Finally, the contrite voice of the guy that had fallen in love

12

with the squeaky-clean MP said, "Sorry mate," then he chirruped, "Hey, at least you're still alive!"

"Alive? Look what they've done to me!"

Another thoughtful silence descended upon the room. Finally, the silence was broken. "Oh, Christ. Oh, merciful Christ," whimpered the tremulous voice from the corner bed. A few seconds later, fifteen condolent men were wilting to the sound of the dismantled man's sobbing. In a mood of stupefying melancholy, everyone in the room inwardly wept.

A few minutes later, the well meaning but hapless Chaplain poked his bald, bespectacled head around the door and cheerfully asked, "How's it going in here then. Everyone on the mend are we?"

The men's impassioned reply came as one single voice. "Piss off, Padre!"

7

The men talked and joked about the female MP for days afterwards. But Motley remained silent. He detested all MPs, and people like them. They were the capitulators, he thought, the incorrigible chastisers. They were history's hangers and drawers, the Army's equivalent of Torquemada's Inquisition scourgers. Military police were the conformist, well-inclined soldiers who combed their hair with a parting and grew dapper moustaches. Unforgivably, to Motley, they stopped boozed-up squaddies in the street and ordered them back to barracks; they became profoundly upset with un-soldierly behaviour and pounced exasperatedly on any commotion caused by some battered fighting regiment's combat-numbed misbehaviour. And, worst of all, Motley knew that the crap-hats loathed the Parachute Regiment's aggressive men of action. To the letter-of-the-law Military Policemen, the Paras were a mystic phenomenon, a brutal, exalted misfortune: an abysmal riddle of military creation. To a Military Policeman, Motley himself was the heretical apotheosis of all that was unrighteous and ignoble. The Redcaps desperately wanted to see him safely locked up in a military-prison cell. Motley fervently believed that it was a Roman military policeman who had stood on the benighted hill at Golgotha, and pierced the ancient demi-god with a mortifying spear.

Three weeks after the MP officer had arrived on the ward to formally arrest Motley, the Surgeon Major who was treating him informed him that he had been medically cleared to return to the UK. A week after that, he was given a date for his repatriation to a military prison back in England. On the afternoon two Redcaps were due to arrive to escort Motley to the airport, all the men on the ward held a tactical conference and decided to swap Motley's medical bed-charts with those of the legless guy in the corner. One of the fitter guys then borrowed a doctor's white coat from the medical-staff changing rooms and hung around the ward with a stethoscope dangling around his neck.

When the two policemen strode onto the ward they were greeted by the white-coated soldier who demanded, "What do you men think you're doing walking onto a surgical ward without theatre masks? Where do you think you are, in a bloody butchers shop?"

"Sorry sir," the Redcap corporal in charge apologised, "We're supposed to pick up a prisoner for escort to the airport."

"What's the man's name?" barked the phoney doctor.

"Motley, sir. Staff Sergeant Motley."

"Well that's Motley in the corner bed. Now get him out of here before you two spread your germs amongst these brave men."

"Yes sir." The corporal quickly glanced at the name on the chart dangling at the bottom of the bed and then looked up at the guy lying in front of him, "Come on Motley, get a bloody move on."

The legless guy threw back the bedclothes, revealing his bandaged stumps. Then the he happily declared, "I'm not going anywhere without a wheelchair, am I?"

The MP corporal's mouth was dangling open with amazement. The private standing beside him couldn't stop himself from saying, "Jesus Christ Corp! He's got no bloody legs!"

"I haven't got any balls either," the guy in the bed pugilistically informed the Redcap private, "so what's it to you?"

"Bloody hell," the corporal intoned, pushing back his cap and scratching his chin. He began steadfastly rifling through the documentation he'd brought with him.

"Hang on a bloody second. It says here that you've been charged with assaulting an officer."

"Yeah, that's right. I punched the bastard in the nuts," replied the legless guy, "And you bastards will get the same treatment if you're thinking of pissing me off."

"Fetch a wheelchair," the acquiescing MP corporal ordered.

The legless man was finally wheeled out of the ward to a pandemonium of cheers and uncontrolled laughter, escorted by the two nonplussed military policemen.

An hour later, a puce-faced Redcap corporal burst onto the ward, followed by his traumatised, wheelchair pushing colleague, "Right, you smart-arsed buggers. Which one of you is Motley?"

It wasn't until the corporal had found the Surgeon Major that Motley was finally identified. "Staff Sergeant Motley, these men are here to escort you to the airport. Get dressed please," ordered the medical officer. "I'm sorry, Sergeant," he quickly added, "But there's nothing I can do about it." The medical officer had mistaken the tears of mirth that were streaming down Motley's cheeks for a different kind of tears. When he was dressed, Motley walked across to the dismantled soldier now sitting beaming in his wheelchair. He shook the grinning man's hand warmly.

"Thanks, mate. That was bloody brilliant. If I had balls as big as yours, they'd break my bloody spine." The wounded man smiled a regenerated smile at Motley. The tough sergeant bent forward to within a few inches of the legless man's face.

"Now, I'm going to say something to you that I want you to remember. I want you to remember this when you think that you've got no more excuses for staying alive." Motley leaned forward and pulled the terribly mutilated man even closer to his own ravaged face, "Listen, you've got to find a new kind of courage now. I know you can do it. You've already shown me that you've got the biggest balls of anyone I've ever served with in this fucked-up army. So remember this, I'd be happy to serve with you anywhere, anytime, and in any fucked-up war you want to fight. Okay?"

As he looked into the paratrooper's scrupulous, combat-scarred face, the traumatised soldier could see that the veteran sergeant's eyes were gleaming with sincerity. The man in the wheelchair gave a concordant nod, "Okay, Sarge. Thanks."

Motley had spoken loud enough for everyone on the ward to hear, and now the entire room erupted into a cacophony of loud cheers and handclaps. The two bungling Redcaps suddenly grabbed the distracted Motley by each arm and dragged him towards the door, "Hang on you crap-hat bastards, I haven't said goodbye to my mates yet." Motley began to struggle with the uncompromising MPs.

"I think you should leave now, Sergeant Motley, you're upsetting the men," pleaded the medical officer. As Motley disappeared through the doors, the Surgeon Major enthusiastically called after him, "Good luck to you, Staff.

Bloody good luck to you!" Another sympathetic wit cried, "Off to the Stalag Taff!"

8

Sitting in the back of the Land Rover on the way to the airport, Motley suddenly felt alone. A nagging doubt about his court martial burrowed like a painful worm inside his conscience; he could get five years with labour for striking an officer. He raised his hand to wipe his itching cheeks; his face still felt grimy from the afternoon's tears of laughter. The MP beside him suddenly began slapping his palm with his nightstick in an attempt to intimidate him. "So, why did you chuck a mental with your officer, Motley?" he asked, "gave you an order you didn't like did he? I guess a guy like you doesn't like taking orders, do you?"

Motley just ignored him.

"What I'd like to know, is how the hell did a hopeless dead-beat like you get promoted to Staff, eh? You know what, I'd like to know how the hell a dud like you ever became a soldier in the first place, let alone Airborne? Smacking your officer! Jesus, how dumb can you get?"

Motley stayed silent for a minute, then he finally replied, "Well, I'll tell you something, Corp. I've loved being a Para. In fact, I've loved being a combat soldier for the last thirteen years, taking fire, fighting my country's enemies. How about you, eh? How many poor pissed-up squaddies have you arrested in the last thirteen years?"

"Don't push it, Motley," retorted the venomous MP, his clipped moustache pinching and twitching like an epileptic caterpillar. "When you're in shit up to your nostrils it's best to keep your fucking mouth shut."

"Hey, you asked for the conversation, Corp," Motley grunted.

Staff Motley hated the army now, but he could remember a time when he loved it. It was true, he had loved being para, and he loved being a senior NCO too. He got a satisfying kick from training his boys up to the regiment's exacting standards. But, since he came to Iraq, soldiering hadn't been much fun at all. It wasn't like real war any more. He and his battlefield-trained boys kept running into unconquerable, shadowy insurgents who wanted to kill everyone, so the army were constantly having to take a crack at killing them first. Now, Motley was tired of the all the venomous stalking and killing. In fact, Motley was remorsefully tired with everything that his occupying army stood for.

Squirming in his seat, he looked out at the crepuscular nighttime streets of Basra spinning past the vehicle's window. Slivers of light swam languorously out of the dark and then submerged again into the primeval darkness. Everything looked mysterious and illicit, imbued with the colour of festering puke. The squalid daytime streets of the city were chaotic and ungovernable, but after the curfew the streets became fearful and apathetic. A shiver of alarm passed through Motley's nervous system; he realised that he was feeling exactly the same mea culpa contrition as the blood-guilty streets of Basra.

At that moment, the usually uber-confident Motley was feeling as vulnerable and insubstantial as an atom in a particle accelerator; in the very near future, he suspected, he was going to be hit very hard and very fast by something that would knock bits off him. Then a single thought began to burn in Motley's mind like a timid flame. The thought ignited into a raging brush-fire and spread turbulently through his body in all directions until finally it wracked and scorched in the depths of his stomach – he was beginning to realise that he had been tricked.

Bingo! – with a sickening shock, Motley realised that he had been lulled, lured and trapped into fighting a war that he didn't believe in.

"Get out, prick," the MP corporal was yelling at Motley. They had arrived at the airport without him realising it. "Move it!" cried the vengeful policeman, jabbing his handcuffed prisoner in the back with his stick, "I'm going to make sure my mates back in Colchester are ready with a proper welcoming committee. They just love getting their hands on shabby smart-arses like you."

After stretching and filling his lungs with the warm night air, Motley sank his elbow sharply into the corporal's stomach, and then raised his knee swiftly into the winded man's groin. The flabbergasted MP private looked down at his corporal, now moaning and writhing on the tarmac in a tight foetal curl. The private gasped in surprise, "He's just made it worse for himself, hasn't he, Corp?" A moment later, the private was on his knees beside his incapacitated NCO, clutching blindly at his own roaring and painful gonads.

9

Three years later: Arriving drunk in a city is hard on the nerves, even if it is your hometown. A strange sense of paranoia and alienation descended upon Motley, a creeping feeling that something was wrong. It was a feeling that put him on the defensive. He hadn't set foot in his hometown for more than five years, and it made him feel like he was losing his grip.

Even before the train had come to a stop at Cardiff Central, he had already noticed the new buildings that had sprung up like an uncontrolled rash on the city's horizon. Disconcertingly 'modern' architecture seemed to be spreading across the city like a sexually transmitted disease. The City Fathers were obviously aiming to make Cardiff's new-century skyline the acme of architectural avant-garde. Oh-so-up-to-date glass and steel-legged structures dominated the cityscape, making the once beautiful capital look like a seventies style dining-room suite that was too bloody scary to sit on. Motley would happily have taken a bet that, out in the city's periphery, on the neglected council estates, you couldn't get a new tile fitted on your leaking roof if you waited a lifetime. He knew that for the hubristic politicos, there was no prestige in keeping their tenants warm and dry. Building badly needed council houses doesn't get near to a figurehead architectural design project.

It was getting late in the afternoon, and Motley was just starting to feel better; warm and secure inside – molecules of alcohol were tickling the stress-loaded synapses of his cerebral cortex. These were feelings he hadn't had for more than three years: the loose, confident kind of feeling that comes to a man when the drink moves in and he knows he's headed on a straight line to a bloody good booze-up. He began to feel more relaxed, chilled-out, and best of all, TOTALLY FREE!

10

Ex-Staff Sergeant Taff Motley of the Parachute Regiment was flushed with alcohol and excitement. He was thoroughly enjoying his first day on the outside after being banged up in Colchester Military Prison for the last three years; he had paid the army's price for punching his platoon officer. The court martial decided to strip him of his sergeant's stripes, and send him to the glasshouse for three long ones. That officer had killed his men, and they had put him away! Jesus Christ, those court- martial duffers weren't paying attention. He was right. He'd kept his men alive for the first three months; through the toughest fighting – with all their limbs and their dicks intact – do they know what that took? But that arsehole officer wouldn't listen. Motley knew things, but the officer had turned his back on him. He hadn't given Motley any credit, and that's what got his men killed, blown to hell because that officer wouldn't listen. And they put him away!

Then last week, they had walked into his cell and told him that they'd finally kicked him out of Her Majesty's army. Motley didn't show them any reaction. He thought – hey, no fucking problem! He had hated what the army was doing in Iraq anyway. Those three troopers he'd lost to the suicide bomber at the roadblock in Basra didn't stand a chance. If that officer had listened to what Motley had been telling him, two of his friends would still be alive today. How the hell did that pin-brain get into the Paras anyway?

11

The fighting in Iraq and his time in prison had changed Motley. He'd seen with his own eyes that every human being is a culprit, every human being a victim. Motley ecclesiastically reasoned that human beings should stand up and take the blame for imperilling humanity with their own inhumanity. He marvelled that humanity could take such relentless inhumanity for so long. Why do they take it, he wondered, why is humanity so stoic with itself? Perhaps humanity enjoys its inhumanity. That's it! – Motley guessed. Humanity enjoys its own inhumanity!

Despite the danger from the murderous fedayeen, Motley had developed an enduring affection for the long-suffering people of Iraq. When Motley was 'in country', he'd become fascinated with Iraq's culture and its long and tortured history. His column had stopped one afternoon at ancient Babylon: "It's real, it still exists – bloody Babylon!"

Motley had dismounted from his Land Rover and touched the ancient stones. He couldn't help thinking that from this land, now overrun with foreign armies and a dictator's infamy, great chieftains once marched and their names grew huge. Where shepherds once sang wild praises to Alexander, cement factories and oil wells now marred the lean geology: "This fucked-up country has forgotten its legends." But Motley hadn't. Motley thrived on legends. "What else has the entirety of human history given us but a bunch of dead heroes?"

12

Glugging down can after can of cider on the train, Motley had been constantly laughing at himself: "Well, you've got to laugh haven't you? It's cruelly funny, isn't it?" He'd got back from Iraq in handcuffs and went straight into the slammer. No parades, no medals, none of the uniformed pageantry, no nothing. Yet just two months before the disaster at the roadblock, and with considerable risk to his own life, Motley had helped to drag several wounded troopers from a burning APC. His CO told him afterwards that he was putting him in for an award. If Motley had been blown to bits with his friends, he'd have got the lot – medals, glory, a full military honours funeral. And to top it off, his sister would now have been picking up a handsome pension, while at the same time telling the TV crews that: "They should never have sent our boys over there." Motley violently cursed himself for his gullibility.

Stepping out into the chaos and ozone-scorching traffic of St Mary Street brought back feelings of disorientation. He watched the lax-jawed shoppers browsing the shops in their bovine clusters, fingering their platinum-powered credit cards like supplicatory intemperates. You could take the scene as a symbol of the futility at the heart of western capitalism: people working hard to buy things they don't really need to keep themselves in jobs so that they can buy things they don't really need. And, of course, the city being Cardiff, it was bucketing down with rain. This wasn't the itty-bitty, Lilliputian kind of rain that falls everywhere else. This was Welsh rain, that heavy, familiar, tea-coloured deluge that has never gone pitter-patter in its entire life.

Cardiff rain always hits the pavements with a nasty 'Blat-Blat-Blat,' sounding like a .50 cal. machine-gun letting rip with a full belt of ammo. Getting caught in a shower in this town means a pounding to the head like going a few rounds with a pro boxer. An old army friend of Motley's used to say that visiting Cardiff was like dating a fashion model – dim, wet and miserable. Motley agreed that the rain and the dimness of the light were there to provide a commentary on the city, but was also there to tell visitors something about themselves. The rain and dimness was just the city letting them know where they stood: Cardiff doesn't take any shit.

13

But never mind the rain; it gave Motley an excuse to dive into the nearest bar. It turned out to be a wine-bar. Everything was dark-oak, shining brass, and leatherette stools. There was sawdust sprinkled across the floor.

"Jesus. Are they expecting a machete-wielding bloodbath?" Motley sniffed to himself. He walked up to the bar and stood there staring down at his worn-out trainers, already soaked through by the rain. After drinking solidly on the train for three hours, it looked to his addled brain like he was wearing more than one pair of sorry looking shoes.

Motley sent his restless senses out on patrol. He checked out his surroundings, peering into the shadowy corners and dimly lit cubicles. The place showed every sign of being a pretentious big city watering-hole. There were a dozen or so people scattered around the place, eating snacks, drinking and talking, or just staring silently at the walls. Most of the men wore suits and ties. The women chatting with them looked hyper and brittle. All of them attractive and blonde, most of them wearing the mandatory office uniform of white blouse and dark slacks.

Although this was a public bar, it purposefully gave out the innuendo, the emanation, of being a private club; its members luxuriating in spluttered conversations about money and gossipy business deals. He glanced down at his own clothes and realised that he looked like something that had crawled out of the tide-less, oxygen-starved waters of Cardiff Bay; where the avidly clued-up post-80s yuppies now lived, nursing their permanent panic-attacks of acquisitiveness. For most of his life, Motley had suffered from a form of reverse acquisitiveness; he had an embarrassing fear of owning things. For him, ownership meant responsibility: he was so un-twenty first century.

Motley once had lots of friends who lived in the pre-development Butetown area, friends who now dreamed only of escaping from their council tower-blocks; those eyries of the underclass, with their slice of cloud instead of a garden. A corporation high-rise block of flats is unlike an office block of similar height and bulk: a high-rise is much more tentative, less sure of its gravitational pull. Motley was all too aware that some of the city's high-rise blocks came under the heading of tragic-comedy – the low-budget 'sink estates' and the high-rises; explicit urban-horror, cheaply lit, oppressive and hair-on-end.

The rumpled duffel coat he was wearing was more than ten years old, and his exhausted, too-long jeans were frayed at their wet bottoms. Motley was obviously out of place in this yuppie-haunted bar. Trying to be a pretender, he ordered a bottle of Beck's instead of his usual pint of cider. The unsmiling, jelly-haired barmaid wore a face like a cat licking shit off a thistle. Her hair looked as though it had been cut with an old-fashioned tin-opener; the irregular hanks were stiffened with gel and shot out from her head at peculiar angles. In her late-twenties, she had the tired Gothic look of a too-long-on-the-shelf Metallica groupie.

Motley knew the reason for her sullen looks of disdain. He looked poor. No doubt he had the mark of a bad apple in this highly paid barrel of class-A fruit. In this high-earning, monied milieu, he felt about as welcome as an income tax form.

14

In a world where celebrity and wealth are the only virtues, Motley supposed that most people have to resign themselves to failure. Most people are made painfully aware that they lack the moneymaking aplomb and ridiculously optimistic savoir-faire that enables so many aggressive ladder-climbers and loud talkers to get ahead. The unwelcome, subtopian truth is that most people are not equipped to excel – though they struggle heroically to ignore that unpalatable fact.

Motley agreed with the philosophers on the epistemological dilemma that there is no way of really knowing anything; and yet most people know, for sure, that honesty and kindness will get them nowhere. Which meant, to Motley, that the good are never without misery, and never without hope. Which in turn means that the good are either stupid or blessed, unseeing freaks or blue-eyed angels. The good can take their pick.

15

Glancing around at the excessively motivated sharpsters as they shrieked and brayed and downed their expense-account-driven drinks, Motley couldn't help wondering: what is it with those super-phallic elbowers anyway? You know the ones, the ones whose humility gene is entirely absent from their genomes. Those aggressive bastards who always push and shove their way to the front? How do they always manage to climb to the top of the pile? Are their minds never in a shambles; is their unshakeable belief in themselves never tested? The recently dishonourably discharged soldier jealously supposed that for the successful, their lives are endless supernatural acts of achievement and profit: that they are totally immersed in their depthless, tragedy-muffling egos. No 'dark night of the soul' cataclysm will ever befall them: their souls are too massive, unmoving, and unshakeable.

Without a shave and some new clothes, Motley knew that he would never make it in the wine-bar. He'd already decided to forget about chatting up the haughty barmaid, and after three silent, elbow-leaning beers, he shouldered his dilapidated rucksack and slipped out of the cold-shouldering boozer. Outside, the clouds that had hovered over the city like a grey wash had blown away. The rain had stopped and the evening sky was darkening; it looked cool and graceful – something Motley had just been reminded he was not. He retreated down the traffic-humming street, away from the city centre, heading out towards the Ninian Park area, where the footy club lives, and Motley's kind of people.

16

The first time Motley walked through the new 'café' area of the city, he quickly realised that his hometown had undergone a drastic makeover; and it wasn't just a skin-job, either. The designer reconstruction was a bionic rebuild, starting with the fact that the make-over artists obviously had a love affair with Paris's left bank. But Motley guessed that they had reckoned without the ever-lurking Welsh rain. Oh yeah, Paris has its fair share of rain too. But Parisian rain is more feminine, gentle and blameless. Cardiff rain is booby-trapped, testosterone hefted and onerously butch. A brief hugging from Cardiff rain leaves you smelling like a wet jockstrap.

But what really stopped Motley in his tracks were the women. Beautiful city girls were sitting alone under the sweating umbrellas, nursing their campari and sodas or warming their hands on cups of expensive froth. What's all that about? – Motley thought. Who told those chicks they could haunt the city's pavement bars with their civilized pleasures and soothing relaxations? But the swish, clothes-conscious babes didn't have him fooled. After six or seven hopeful, "Hey doll, you waiting for me?" and then several, "Hey, buy you a drink?" Motley suddenly realised that for him, the game was up. As the ladies tapped their feet and clicked their tongues and after three or four venomous 'Piss offs', he realised that in the re-modelled Cardiff, the skirts had taken over the streets. How the hell did that happen? Some weasel town-planning bastard certainly had a lot of fucking explaining to do.

After ten minutes walking, he had crossed the Taff bridge, chuckling as he passed the steel-webbed, horizon-violating edifice of the Millennium Stadium. Getting into his stride, Motley put his head down and arse up towards Canton. Then a bus going in the right direction halted to let some people off, so he leapt on board. The bus ground slowly down the middle of the double-parked streets. Away to his left was the new waterfront where the city's digital hipsters paid out funny-money prices for mouse-mat sized apartments, handing over bundles of tax-avoided cash and telling the mickey-taking estate agents to "keep the change." The original communities down there had been destroyed not by Nazi bombs or terrible tsunami, or any natural disaster; but by a construction company. The new waterfront had been turned into a kind of Utopia; cleansed of incident, conflict and drama. Cleansed of life too.

Over to his right, beyond the rooftops and businesses of Canton's main drag, were the sprawling council estates, where the streets heaved and reverberated to the thumping of ear-blistering, boom-box car-stereos and people yelled and screamed spectacularly, and shook their fists at each other, "C'mon 'en. You want some of this?" And yes, most of them did want some of this. In fact, they couldn't get enough of it.

It was on these forgotten estates that the disadvantaged of Cardiff – the lost, the broken and the effaced – struggled to keep on the surface. It was too easy to go under on these minatory streets, and too hard to rise up again. Motley remembered, as a kid, going fishing along the banks of the River Ely. He didn't need any money for expensive fishing gear in those days. All he needed was a long stick, which he would use to beat the shit out of the rich kids who had the expensive fishing gear, and then steal their fish.

The bus had pulled up at a stop. The faces outside the window had the doughy, stoic look of the people Motley had grown up with. Those distant days came rushing back; childhood days of twilight playing on the volatile streets of the estates, the parents' calls to return home hooting like paroxitic owls in the urban gloaming. The unregulated enjoyment of kids running wild, the mixed-sex gang of tireless bodies unconstrained, the confusion of girl/boy prowess not yet registered. It all came flooding back like a great river of nostalgia. He felt as though he had reached the end of a long and wearisome journey.

Motley suddenly succumbed to the strange feeling that comes over you when gazing out of a bus window – it's as if your life is passing you by, as mercury-slick as the fizzing streets. It's called anachronism – something that's out of keeping with time. It wasn't slow either; he got the feeling that his life was rocketing by with a terrifying roar. Hey, Motley, remember when you were a kid; when you were all ribcage and sweet-toothed innocence…that was only three stops back. Now look at you. You're all gut and ball-scratch; you're all burger-sponge and couch-ache. What the fuck happened, son? You look as damaged and shagged-over as an Amsterdam weekend. You're a mad looking, shot-eyed, Methuselah. But, hey, don't worry Taff – who the fuck isn't?

Just then, a metal-crunching bang came from the rear of Motley's bus. Looking down he saw a beaten-up Volkswagen had slammed into the back of the double-decker. Three young guys had jumped out of the crumpled motor and legged it down the road. The bus-driver hopped down from his cab and was checking out the steaming wreckage. "What the hell happened?" Motley could hear him saying. The driver gazed down the road at the disappearing kids. "They're a menace. The bastards should be locked up."

Locked up? For bending some metal? Motley wondered what the driver thought being locked up was like. When he realised that the wounded bus wasn't going anywhere for a while, he got down and started off again on foot. Motley was heading for his sister's house; she had written to him that when he got out he could stay with her and her partner Dave, until he got on his feet. He rummaged in one of the deep pockets of his rucksack and rescued another can of Bow from its damp nest. He popped its ring-pull and took a couple of heavy glugs. After suffering the class-ridden invariability of Army justice, it definitely felt good to be a civvy again – and back in his hometown. Motley had forgotten how much he loved the histrionic, rip-roaring streets that surrounded the wind-buffeted arena of the Ninian Park footy ground.

17

Life had been rough for Motley from the start; he'd always had a meagre time of it. But in between the low points of his being born and seeing his mates blown to bits, Motley had achieved a degree of success in the Army. Among the hard men of Three Para, Motley had stood out as a hard man. Although physically he was unprepossessing – five-ten and medium build – his nitro-glycerine temper and his phenomenally fast fists would floor an opponent before the poor shmuck new what was happening to him. He was attractively good-looking and unattractively conceited. With his chiselled chin, his swashbuckling charm and sociable smile, Motley could win over a woman as easily as falling into bed.

While in the forces, he had developed the habit of measuring his worth against the progress of others. That day in Hereford, when he'd been badged into the SAS, had been the happiest, most fulfilling day of his life. He gloated at the fact that thousands of good men had agonised at their failure to meet the stratospheric standards that the shadowy but famous Regiment demanded. But even though he had joined the elite of the fighting elite, Motley was no 'death or glory' seeker: "I want to die in my sleep like my granddad did, not screaming and yelling like the passengers in his car."

At his sister's that night, Motley enjoyed a slap up Chinese take-away. When they were kids, the Motley family had been the typical care-worn, joyless social hub dominated by an unemployed despot who browbeat his subordinate wife and drunkenly thrashed his deficient, good-for-nothing children. The youthful Motley had bided his time growing up, until he was old enough to spot where the true power in the household lay: in the strength of his young arms and in the warp-speed striking power of his fists. Even as a teenager, Motley was very good at fighting: when he outfought someone, they stayed outfought. He knew that he already had three strikes against him: his father, his temper, and his arrogant self-assurance. At seventeen, Motley had finally decked his cruel old man with a flurry of punches: he had never forgotten the strength he'd felt in his arms as he beat his father down. It was the first time he'd seen his old man cry, sitting there on the floor with his hand to his bloodied nose. Motley believed that if time travel were suddenly made possible, most people would go no further back than their own childhood. And they would travel back with just one thing on their minds – Payback. At seventeen

30

and a half, he'd gone off to join the British Parachute Regiment: "The best fighting men in the whole damned world. Bar none."

Many years later, the death of his father, whom he did not love, shocked Motley for the very reason that he realised that he did not love him. It was then that he understood for the first time that his life flowed like a zigzag. The first bend had been passed when he had closed his teenaged fists and turned them on his father. At the funeral, Motley had tried to catch a whiff of posthumous tenderness from the old man; but all he could feel was the full force of a slapping hand. Even now, if a floorboard creaks in the middle of the night, Motley responds with a flat: "Fuck off, Dad."

But tonight, the two siblings have enjoyed themselves. They managed to destroy all the booze they had in the house. Then Dave had to nip down to the offy to buy some more cans and bottles: "...and don't forget the salted nuts!" They had a good night: a very good night.

The next morning morning, over a couple of fags and a pot of brew, Motley's sister started telling him about the Government trying to ban smoking in pubs. Apparently, they'd already done it in Ireland. Then she told him that over there, people would go and stand outside the pub to have a smoko. Of course, they'd get chatting and then end up going home with each other. They reckoned that cigarette sales had fallen by fifteen percent; but condom sales were up by twenty: "So, fewer fags but more sex, eh?" Motley reflected. It sounded like a bloody good deal to him.

Despite all the exhilaration and hilarity of his homecoming, the future looked ugly for Motley. He realised that his impenitent drinking and uranium-depleted temper only gave him a couple of months before his sister would come to him with a polite request: "Get the fuck out of my house you noxious bum." He reckoned he'd probably end up sacking-out in some grotty little attic flat, fighting off the illegal immigrants to do twelve-hour shifts in hot and sweaty below minimum-wage dead-enders. But to his surprise, after he'd made some phone calls to one or two ex-comrades-in-arms, an old mate put him on to an ex-Royal Marine SBS guy who worked for the South Wales Mail. Within a week, Motley was driving a delivery van for the newspaper. And that's where he met his new friend Sweep. (No – he wasn't Sooty's little friend.)

18

It turned out that Motley's newest friend happened to be my oldest friend. When we were schoolboys we had both played for the same valley's rugby team, and then, years later, we worked on the same newspaper. So, I knew all about my mate Sweep's exposures to life's little difficulties, if you know what I mean. Now I'm sitting here telling you the story exactly as he told it to me. Of course, there were many gaps in his rambling, whisky-induced telling of the tale, and there is much here that was most likely to have happened. But the bare facts of the story are as they were given to me by my old, booze-soaked, Grub Street friend.

19

When he first met Motley, Sweep was the manqué sports journalist at the Mail, and a raving piss-head He'd been given his nickname when he first joined the newspaper because he organised the news-office's sweepstakes for the big races. Even though he was only in his mid-forties, my friend felt that life had already punched him too many times below the belt, and way too hard. In his early twenties, he'd fallen poignantly in love with a sixteen-year-old girl, who was looking to find her way out of an unhappy home-life. They seemed fair-matched, so Sweep fell like a dropped anchor, singing on its departing chain as it sank into the ooze. But in her scabrous heart, the young girl he had married secretly despised him.

The marriage ended a few years ago, its migrating anchor dragged by treacherous tides. Sweep had almost got used to the strange phone calls – the curious hang-up calls. No sweat, no big deal; just some whacko. Then his wife buggered off one ego-drubbing Friday with the horny deadbeat who emptied their rubbish bins. During the final degrading scolding, his departing wife had accused him of only being faithful to her because he couldn't find another woman who would let him fuck her.

"You can't find another sucker who wants what you've got," she'd said. And Sweep's embezzled heart knew that she was right about one thing: he was way past the point where a woman would want to go to bed with him. For the last two-and-a-bit years Sweep's sex life had comprised nothing more than forlorn and scowling hand-jobs. For the last two-and-a-bit years Sweep had scored nothing but his meaty palm; he'd been wandering around like a shagged-out ghost, his face shining with that sweaty wanker's glow, his tense fingertips shuffling the paper tissues stuffed in his trouser pockets.

As a blind man suddenly made to see, Sweep was grief-struck that what he had thought was a marital garden – something that he had cultivated and nurtured – was, in reality, a putrescent graveyard. Then he had suddenly found himself in a courtroom, his eyes washed clean by lies and ancillary loss: a forensic featherweight, outlawed by badly loaded scales. The lawyers had crept up on him like vampires; then came a judge's simple condition to parting – he lost almost everything he owned.

It's a common story. You hear about a guy whose marriage ends, and he comes roaring out of his divorce behind the wheel of a newly acquired ten-year-old Porsche. Another takes himself off to Africa, and yet another takes to cultivating roses – the real saddos take to writing novels. Sweep took to the bottle. But all those guys were left staring down the toilets of their lives, afraid of the future, and what the future held for them.

Sweep held love to blame; lapping at his blood, striving to eat his soul like a demon on his grave. It was as if his entire life had suddenly decided to take a shit, so he started hitting the bottle – big-time. Sweep had always been a heavy drinker, but, in a nation of heavy drinkers, he began to set a new standard for glugging. Sweep's teenaged daughter had decided to stay with her booze-helpless, whipped-dog father.

You could tell that Sweep was an alcoholic from a mile off; the ghost-of-a-living-thing eyes, the nerveless, sweating face, the flamboyant lava-red veins in the nose. We know that some people try to fight their alcoholism, but Sweep had long ago declared it a no-contest: he had no intention of fighting it. It seemed sensible to him never to fight any battles he didn't think he could win. So he enjoyed the slummy routine of being an alcoholic; the exit-less visits to the pub, the hourly wrestling with recalcitrant corks and ring pulls, the disgraceful, unfatherly felonies of bed-wetting and shitting in his pants: "Oh, Dad! Not again! You're doing the washing this week."

Sweep knew that that there's no such thing as a recovering alcoholic; there are only drunk alcoholics or sober alcoholics. That's it: "For an alcy, it's meths, turpentine and paint remover, or pure sobriety. Utter desecration, or dignity." He was a good alcoholic, a talented alcoholic; an alcoholic's alcoholic. Why fight it?

For good reasons, Sweep had come to believe that Life really hated him, and so his ashen face was now set into immutable lines of fearful hostility. He saw his whole bevvied-up life as a billowing cloud of darkness and disappointment, occasionally pierced by tiny beams of light. The impious sports reporter wasn't one of those who

34

thought that Life was some kind of supernatural miracle, benevolently created by some omnipotent, anthropomorphic god. Sweep didn't believe in any kind of miracles, or gods. He believed that Life was an accidental misfortune, stamped with brutality, decay and corruption. He'd come to the conclusion that Life itself was a grotesque, immoral blunder; its unpredictable, heartbreaking vagaries terrified and bewildered him. So he had one middle finger permanently held up at it.

Sweep was convinced that Michelangelo had been taking the piss when he painted that Sistine finger pointing at God. According to Sweep, Michel had been taking the Michael; Adam was pointing at the bearded old man and saying, "Who's that mad fuck?" The embittered ex-rugby player had never, even in his most sententious moments, considered the existence of an irreproachable Creator Spiritus. But, if he had, he would have instantly accused HIM of staggering incompetence, if not outright malevolence – and then piously kicked HIM in the bollocks.

"You think you've been in a war zone?" he once said to Motley over a few beers, "You should have my life. That's a fucking war zone!"

The pot-bellied, shaggy-bearded Welshman had broad shoulders with no neck and a large head adorned with close-cropped brown hair that was greying at the sides. His large pouting lips hung limply on his face; giving him the appearance of a disgruntled, genetically enhanced cherub. As a young man he had been a promising hooker for a league-topping rugby team, but now he was grossly unfit and in the overheated news-office, sweat constantly formed glistening beads on his calorific forehead and stained the armpits of his shirt. Except in the very coldest weather, Sweep's ferocious BO made him smell like an elongated dog's fart. If Sweep had soaked his rancid body in the shower four times a day, he would have still smelled like a cross between a brewery and an Augean stable.

After entering his forties with a casualty ward of medical problems, Sweep had been worryingly diagnosed as a diabetic and had recently spent some time undergoing tests at the University Hospital. Trying to pin down some of the irredeemable damage Sweep's alcoholism had done to his vital organs, the doctors had wheeled in a complicated looking machine and started enthusiastically scanning his abdomen. Staring at the oscillating pictures on the machine's video screen, the doctors shook their worthy heads and tut-tutted like a couple of garage mechanics examining an old car's clapped-out engine; "My God! This man hasn't got any kidneys!"

"Yes he has, there, look."

"But those things are only the size of walnuts," said the flabbergasted medic.

"And his liver is the size of an over-ripe pumpkin," said the other.

Sweep gazed up at the two Hippocratic heroes and smiled wanly, "Hell, you guys make it sound like I've set up a market-stall in there." he joked, guiltily.

He hated doctors even more than he hated the Greeks. (He never forgave them for inventing algebra). "They were still wiping their arses with vine leaves and they invented algebra! What the fuck were those people thinking of? The bastards ruined the lives of twenty million school kids!"

When his GP had talked to him about 'recommended units of alcohol', Sweep had looked at her with uncomprehending, lachrymose eyes, his bottom lip trembling like a child's after it had been smacked for doing no wrong. Few aspects of life made as little sense to Sweep as alcoholics trying to give up the booze. For him, there were only two choices for anyone addicted to alcohol: to drink themselves to death slowly, or as quickly as possible. As Sweep's mind pondered the unenviable choices, his abused sweat-shimmering body waited for his decision. 'Oh my God! Can you believe this? The mad fuck's going to kill me', his body fretted, 'I'm going to die. Die I tell you!' But despite its eagerness for self-preservation, Sweep's body was already working up an appetite for the next drink. The truth was that Sweep's body had already surrendered; it wasn't even trying any more.

One of the still tut-tutting hospital doctors was saying, sternly, "If you carry on drinking like this, you know you're going to kill yourself, don't you? And I can tell you that liver failure is a very unpleasant way to go."

The many millions of unpleasant, horrible ways that he could 'go' crackled across Sweep's cerebral cortex at the speed of light. Apart from his fanaticism for the booze, there were too many unpleasant ways to 'go' to count. There were knife wielding psychos and suicidal terrorists, various violators and murderers, delinquents and squalid monsters of depravity, devils incarnate and public enemy number ones – all of them to worry about. They all, almost certainly, wanted him dead. And Sweep's fevered brain couldn't even begin to count the millions of bugs and germs and viruses that day and night unrelentingly incubated and diligently went about their business of trying to do him in. It would take a truly diseased mind to even try to think of all the shameful, disgusting ways a man might 'unpleasantly go'. Then there were the cannibalistic traitors within, the ever hungry, body-eating tumours. Despondently, Sweep raised himself up on one elbow, and asked the doctor caustically, "So what is a pleasant way to go, Doc? Writhing in agony with cancer until you've been doped stupid with morphine?"

The doctor's eyebrows shot up in surprise at his patient's belligerent question. The determinedly bibulous Sweep just smiled sweetly up at him. After achieving his desired effect, the befuddled word-monger helped his oversized liver carefully back down onto the examination couch; and tried to remember how many R's there were in 'cirrhosis'. Only once during his adult life to date, had Sweep tried out a full day of sobriety, and he'd hated it. He had suffered a complete and total acquisition of compos mentis. Hey, you know what…I'm getting pretty tired of making excuses for Sweep. We've all got our reasons for our addictions, right? Sweep had a wayward wife; I had a dipso dad. So, shit happens…live with it. (Thanks Dad. No, really, thanks. What the fuck would I have done without the bottle to lean on?)

20

In his own drink-stupefied mind, Sweep was still the youthful, dazzlingly aggressive rugby player he used to be, with his masculine physique and his highly polished hooking skills. For the last fifteen years his favourite song had been Bruce Springsteen's 'Glory Days'. He would inevitably end up crying into his beer whenever he heard those melancholic, laurel-revoking lyrics. At nine years old, Sweep's classmates had called him 'Bunter'. At thirteen, he was first choice for the school's rugby team hooker; and everyone called him by his proper name. At thirteen, Sweep was punching out twenty-year-olds.

If Sweep happened to find himself in the presence of young rugby players, he would tell interminable, valorous stories of hard-won games and treasured schoolboy caps. But now he cut a pathetic figure. The girls in the office would entertain themselves by lining the windows each morning as Sweep arrived late. They'd laugh helplessly as the big hairy guy fulminated and struggled to free himself from the claustrophobic grasp of his tiny, battered Clio. Someone once said that he looked like a raging mastodon trying to fight itself free from a block of ice.

Every morning, when the Mail's editor handed Sweep his daily assignment, he would struggle to choke back a sob of indignation, and later throw the damn thing in the waste-bin. Unwittingly, Sweep had discovered deep within himself an aptitude for avoiding any form of real work. He 'worked' only to provide the money for his prodigious alcohol intake. And when he said 'worked,' that meant he hung around the office for a couple of hours each day, then the rest of the time he was 'doing research' propping up a bar in the city's rugby or footy clubs. He was constantly running up intemperate booze-bills that he would have to flee from until his quarterly bonus provided a solution to his humiliating 'persona-non-grata' status.

On one busy morning in the news-office, Motley had made the mistake of picking up the framed photograph that Sweep kept on his desk. "Is this your daughter, Rachel?" he asked, "Nice looker." Sweep had viciously snatched the frame from Motley's hand.

"Don't even think about it!" he growled. "She's only sixteen. She's still in bloody school."

Motley held his hands out towards his friend, palms up in supplication.

"Hey, hey, me looking at Rachel isn't going to harm her. Is it?"

"I know you army types," Sweep had snarled, looking Motley directly in the eyes, "You lot can shag a girl at three hundred yards without her even knowing she's been had." Motley just laughed, and patted the concerned father on the shoulder. But he'd already made up his mind: he was going to get to know his friend's daughter, whether he liked it or not.

21

The Mail was a great place to sell your time and meet all kinds of people. It was a clearing-house for every vagrant chancer and semi-literate journo who happened to be out of work in the Welsh capital. Sweep was an integral part of its dipsomanic and ill-tempered milieu. Over the following months, Motley learned a lot from Sweep, including the introductory importance of presenting a business card. In an effort to impress women he met in bars, Motley had some cards printed with the Mail's logo on the top, and underneath, where his name appeared, was…'Foreign Affairs Desk Chief.' Sweep agreed to let Motley put his desk phone number on the cards so girls could leave messages when they rang. Motley knew, that when you're out to impress women, 'Van Driver,' to their minds, interprets as 'No-Hope-Fucking-Loser.' A tag like, 'Foreign Affairs Desk Chief' could get you half way into their beds before they even realised it was happening. It's a sad truth, but universally acknowledged, that when chasing women, perceptions are everything. Anyway, the whole idea sort of fizzled out when Motley became bored with prefacing every dirty joke he told with, "And I got this one from a very highly placed diplomatic source."

The big problem for Sweep was, that he made just enough money to get himself shit-faced most nights, but he was perennially broke. Sports writing barely made him enough loot to survive. And then, one munificent, sunny-skied day, a wild-eyed young Turk, fresh out of Journo College tripped into the news-office as a junior reporter. It turned out that Toby was a genuinely talented writer. But even more importantly, to Motley's and Sweep's futures, he was also utterly dishonest, a loon and a total fucking degenerate, but he knew how to make money – lots of it. And best of all, he needed a couple of allies for his money making schemes.

22

When Motley drove to work through the urban badlands of the Ely estates, he couldn't get over how shabby it all looked. The wide main drag with its boarded-up windows, the girls looking tough, the old men tired; the young guys with their half-hearted snarls of fury, sweatshirt hoods permanently pulled up. And everyone with the compressed, sooty look of living under a stone that there's no getting out from under, their genetic pool shrinking in the darkness. Failure was everywhere; employment, opportunity and hope shrivelled and left behind, like afterbirth.

It would seem there's an unpalatable truth hunched at the heart of the capitalist ethic of avidity and profit – a kind of queered, fuck-em-all Darwinism that favours the few over the majority. Now Motley had no problem with that, in fact he'd be first in line with a bucket and ladder, ready to wash the glittering windows of resolute twenty-first century self-interest. The fact was that he'd done his bit to rescue humanity from its own savage misanthropy in Iraq, and now he felt it was time he showed some compassion for his own venality. So, he became a drug dealer.

To be more precise, he became a franchised drug dealer, delivering all sorts of chemicals around the city for Toby, who guaranteed his customers that within twenty minutes of calling him he would have the drugs at their door. Twenty minutes and you were released from your tiresome bondage. Neat that.

After a suggestion from Motley, Toby then recruited Sweep to troll the sports bars and the rugby and footy clubs; using his contacts to drum up business…besides the usual recreational stuff, those pumped-up athletic types are into all sorts of performance-enhancing shit. And Toby was eager to sell it to them. Within a short while, Motley and Sweep were doing some very good business, and Motley was soon in the process of buying a flat down in Yuppyville Bay. The redeveloped Cardiff Bay was no longer marked by its industrial burdens, dumbly and filthily borne. The Bay had gone up in the world, and the old Butetown community didn't like it. They wanted everything to stay down in the world – with them. But now the Bay, with its Millennium

Centre's 'high insolent dome' refracting the grey light from its coppered roof, symbolised the triumph of a demanding future over a weary past. Envy and insidiousness: they arise from the fear of being left behind, of being deserted by the agreeable future.

23

After just six months of dealing, Motley felt they like he had it made. Of course, feeling like you've got it made is arrogant. And for a drug dealer, arrogance is very BAD news. Motley and Sweep would get dressed up in their designer suits and hang out in the inhospitable wine-bar that Motley had fallen into when he first got off the train. He would lean against the bar, lording it over the haughty jelly-haired barmaid who resolutely failed to recognise him. Motley's favourite gag was to order a couple of ferociously expensive pink and green cocktails, remove the umbrella and sparkling fire-work, take one sip, wrinkle his nose up, and then pushing the drink away from him and shaking his head, he'd declare unhappily. "Not good enough…Not good enough. You'll have to learn to make a decent cocktail if you want to keep your job miss." Motley loved her grimaces of contempt; they were like salvage from his former life. Pissing off the morose barmaid became pure masturbation for him.

Sweep was doing very nicely for himself from the dealing game too; he'd never had so much boodle in his life. He finally managed to pay off all his bar debts, with appropriately handsome tips for the bar-staff. But things weren't all beer and skittles for the old rugger-bugger. He walked into the wine-bar one afternoon with a face like a smacked arse.

"What's up Sweep? You okay? Jesus, you look as miserable as a shag in the nettles." Motley noticed that his friend's eyes were moist. He was hoping that nothing was wrong with his mate's daughter.

"I had a date…last night," Sweep spluttered.

"Good on yer, mate!" Motley slapped him on the back, "So why the long face, Arkle?"

"This one is special," Sweep moaned.

"So what's the problem? Doesn't she drink?" Motley chuckled.

Sweep gave him a hurt look, and then whispered, "I couldn't get it up for her. The little sod let me down." The confession left him wounded and speechless.

"Shit, Sweep. Is that all?" Motley couldn't stop himself from smirking, "Hell man, we all know that our willies have a mind of their own. The schizophrenic bastards stand up when you don't need them and lose their enthusiasm when you do. It happens to us all, mate. Don't worry about it."

Leaning on the bar with both elbows, Sweep held his head in his hands.

"It's more than that Taff. I can't remember the last time I had a hard-on." His voice almost cracked as he spoke, "It's been years."

"Jesus, Sweep. What's the problem?"

Sweep's voice stuttered and broke as he forced the words from his lips, "Thirty years of boozing is the problem."

"Fuck. Did you try popping it in her mouth?" Motley asked, "That always seems to work for me."

Sweep just looked up at him helplessly. Tears were starting to brim in his doleful eyes. "This one is special," he said, softly.

Motley didn't have the heart to tell him that's exactly how he felt about his daughter. Instead, he pulled Sweep towards him and spoke into his ear.

"Listen, my friend. I can get my hands on some Viagra. For a boozer like you, that stuff is the best invention since the ring-pull. I've tried it myself."

Sweep's eyes lit up like a couple of super-novas on a power surge.

"Does it work?" he asked, his eyes brimming with hope.

"Like a dream."

"Really? That stuff actually works?"

"Sweep. I once popped one of those little blue miracle workers after eight pints of Bow. Two days later I had to beat the shit out of my prong with a stick to get rid of the boner. That stuff works, trust me."

Sweep was suddenly waving his empty glass in the air, trying to catch the eye of one of the barmaids. "Have another drink, Taff!" he laughed ecstatically, "Have anything you bloody want!"

For the last couple of years, Sweep had been painfully aware that nobody in the world loved him, save for his long-suffering daughter. Most of the women he had drunkenly tried to chat-up in the pubs and clubs that he frequented had responded by swearing at him, or just sullenly glaring at him with rising resentment. He'd finally given up trying to pull any women at all, fearful that they might respond by hitting him over the head with a stiletto heel. He couldn't believe his luck when the large and jolly sixty-year-old barmaid at the Sportsman's Club had suggested that they go out to a country pub for a meal one night. Gastro-pubs! The whole concept was anathema to our ex-rugby-playing dipso-romantic. In his mind, gastro-pubs, like gastro-enteritis, rarely proved to be a good combination.

The idea of going out for a meal was an entirely novel one to Sweep; he was never convinced by the idea that food was an essential part of a balanced diet. Food made Sweep belch uncontrollably, like most people belch after eating cucumber. And that's another thing he wouldn't dream of eating, cucumber. Sweep thought that the overgrown courgette was nothing more than a sex-toy for the porn industry. Every porn movie he'd ever seen had featured a bored housewife in a romantic encounter with a cucumber: "Haven't those one-track-minded buggers ever heard of a banana, for Chrissakes!" The bar-lady was more than fifteen years older than Sweep, but to his female-parched, company-deprived eyes, she looked sexier than a teenage pole dancer.

In the bar the following day, Motley slipped two boxes of hard-on pills into his friend's jacket pocket. Sweep gave him a kind of un-expressible look, a look that went way beyond gratefulness; he looked at Motley like he had just stepped in front of a bullet that was meant for him. "Thanks mate, yer blood's worth fucking bottling." he said, downing his double Islay malt and patting his pocket, "Hey. I've gotta go."

Sweep ran from the bar like someone had just pulled the pin from a grenade. Motley noticed that his friend was dragging his mobile from his pocket as he left: he guessed that, somewhere in the city, a woman was about to take her second shower of the day, and would perhaps be slipping into some sexy lingerie. Soon she would be singing happily and offering up pious hosannas to the beneficent gods of pharmacology: "Party on, big guy. Party on," Motley intoned, jealously.

He didn't see Sweep again for five days. When he finally surfaced, it looked like the once burly guy had run a hundred marathons. He must have lost a couple of stones in weight. Motley thought for a second that he might have given Sweep slimming tablets by mistake. Then he noticed his friend's permanent, self-satisfied grin. "Smug bastard," Motley greeted his revivified, satiated friend.

24

The two men began spending a lot of time in the wine bar. Sweep enjoyed the huge selection of rare and exotic drinks there, and liked to try liver-eating concoctions that would make most imbibers' stomachs explode. Motley got to like the place so much that he even began doing a little dealing of his own there. He started cutting the cocaine that Toby gave him for his customers and selling it on to his own. Of, course Toby knew nothing of his little enterprise. Motley's overripe arrogance got to the point that he'd pull up outside the wine-bar with a throaty roar from his newly-bought slate-grey Z4 Beemer and park it on double yellows. Inside the bar, he'd buy all the barmaids a drink – except of course for old Jelly-Hair – and then sell all the dope he had on him. He'd then proceed to get shit-faced and leave the motor on double-yellows all night. Booze and drug addled, Motley didn't give a fuck about anything, but there again, prodigal arrogance was always his imprudent forte.

On an average weekend, Motley was doing nearly a grand's worth of business in the wine-bar. And when Toby's customers finally complained about all the talcum powder they were snorting Toby asked him to go round to his place to sort things out. Motley thought that the evil sod might have arranged a kicking for him from some hired help, so he dropped some speed before going over. Motley barged through Toby's door with a fist-full of change in both hands, ready for a fight. But all he found was the twenty-three year-old newspaper reporter and a young guy naked on the living room rug. Toby was dovetailing some spotty under-aged rent-boy he must have picked up on the street.

25

Now Motley had nothing against alternative lifestyles; he held no stern views about the pride thing – in fact, some of the toughest, most reliable soldiers he had met in the mob had been secretly gay – but he knew that Toby was a total sleaze-bag. He knew that his supplier was turning the neglected street-kids into dope-fiends just so he could get control over them. Now I know you might say that Motley was just as bad, considering all the mind-altering gear he was selling to the college kids, but his customers weren't street-unfortunates that didn't have a chance or a clue or a crust in their pockets. Motley and Sweep were only selling dope to spoiled rich-kids and thirty-something money-suckers. In Motley's mind, a drug habit was God's way of telling those privileged rich bastards that they had too much money to spend.

"Get your kit on sunshine. And get the fuck out of here." Motley yelled at the startled youth. He grabbed up a pair of scurfy looking jeans off the floor and flung them at the kid. Then he turned to Toby and growled, "Give him some money and get rid of him. You and me need to talk business."

"Excuse me!" Toby whined, "This is my apartment and this is my friend!"

Motley felt like beating the crap out of the gut-cringing little bastard, but fighting with Toby wouldn't be fighting – it would be like hitting a woman: he'd just be doing harm, doing damage. "Look shit-head, I don't give a monkey's toss about you going with under-aged kids, but I do mind about you shovelling coke into them like it's bloody sherbet. Now get rid of the little sod or I'll give you a slapping and throw both of you off that balcony."

For a moment, Motley had a horrible thought that was just what Toby wanted: he was looking forward to the high of some 'rough stuff.' The pervy bastard had a wistful look in his eye. But one look into Motley's eyes told Toby that the ex-Para was hyped up enough to beat the living shit out him.

Motley's composure slowly started to trickle back, though he still gazed down at the two naked bodies with a disgusted frown. "Why do you want underage kids like that?" he asked, pointing at the teenaged boy, "You can go to jail for that, you bloody idiot."

"I can't help it," Toby whined, hiding his face in his hands.

"If the cops find out, it's you who's going to get fucked," Motley warned.

"You won't tell anyone, will you? If my family find out I'll cut my throat."

Huge, corpulent tears began to fall from Toby's eyes. "Please don't tell anyone."

Motley let out a weary sigh and dropped into one of the fat leather armchairs. Slowly shaking his head from side to side, he wanted to spit to clear the foul taste from his mouth. "I'd only tell on you in extreme circumstances," he finally announced, "Now get dressed and get rid of the kid. We've got to talk business."

Later, after pouring most of a bottle of cognac into two huge snifters, Toby began telling Motley how disappointed in him he was for cutting his cocaine. Then after some half-hearted wrangling, they reached a workable agreement. Toby would sell Motley the junk wholesale, as long as he confined his activities to the wine-bar and didn't poach any of Toby's customers.

"Fair enough," Motley agreed. He wasn't interested in starting a turf war with Toby. There was enough action out there for both of them.

Pretty soon, after his meeting, Motley was making more money than he knew what to do with: "There must be a million ways to get rich in this world," he said to Sweep, "but selling drugs must be one of the quickest."

26

The thought of being rich sat comfortably with Motley's socialist principles. He'd spent most of his life being unhappily skint, suffering an extreme shortage of pecunia. As a kid he'd even thought that the monied folks were fundamentally different from himself. He thought perhaps that the rich had different souls, that they went to a different heaven from poor people – their heaven was better decorated, with nicer food, and they only served bottled water and champagne.

"Okay, you can say that I was pretty dumb," Motley admitted, but whatever else you might have said about him, nobody ever accused him of being modest; and this new, money-grabbing life-style was pure balm to his long-abused ego. It felt like all the money he was now making was a long overdue confirmation of what Motley had always suspected: that he was born to be rich. Of course he felt he was smarter than most rich people; Motley was going to be a rich person who knew how to enjoy himself.

27

As I've already said, Motley and Sweep's customers weren't street-trash. They had an upmarket clientele, and they didn't sell any of that killer main-lining shit like heroin or crack. That kind of fearsome gear is the last place of boredom. When the world has bored you flat, you come to smack and crack; and they bore you straight off to death. Coke, Speed and Weed were the main gigs Motley and Sweep dealt in, but on a Friday night good Doves (Ecstasy) would fly off the shelf like you wouldn't believe.

One night in the wine bar, a drunken insight told Motley that he had the solution to the drug problem: "Not less drugs – more drugs. But what we need to do is give drugs to the right people."

To Motley's dismay, every time you read about somebody OD-ing it was always somebody talented, like Joplin, Hendrix or Belushi: "And yet the useless, pain-in-the-arse bastards that you pray will OD, never do."

Before the dope-dealing business started, both Sweep and Motley had been going through 'a terminal financial embarrassment.' Sweep had spent all his money on booze and Motley had got bugger all out of his misguided career as a paid killer for Her Majesty's Government – his Audie Murphy years, as he liked to call them.

"When you think about it, it's a strange job, being a soldier, isn't it?" Motley once reflected to his friend, "You can hardly call it 'trying to make a living'. In fact, the exact opposite is true."

He had gone into the army skint, with a bad haircut and whistling along to U2. Fourteen years later, he came out skint with a bad haircut and whistling along to Dido.

" Fat lot of fucking good that did me."

The Army had even robbed him of his pension when they threw him out. But at least Motley didn't kill anybody, either fighting in Iraq nor in Northern Ireland.

"Although, at that roadblock in Basra, I did get very close to slotting that no-hope Lieutenant."

So anyway, there Motley and Sweep were, living high off the hog and sitting mighty prettily, thank you very much. Motley had all the money and drugs he needed, and Sweep was drinking as lavishly as he liked, and humping his new girlfriend like there was no tomorrow. Money and glamour had suddenly appeared in their lives like a pair of beneficent, compassionate angels. The scouring self-pity that the two friends had so recently wallowed in seemed incomprehensible to them now.

"Bloody hell. What happened, Taff?" Sweep kept asking his new partner in crime, "Did we suddenly do something right?"

"Don't keep asking those kind of questions, Sweep, you might scare it away. Anyway, maybe it's just our turn for the good times."

Just a few months ago, both men were suffering bitterly at the hands of life. On the bad days, Motley and Sweep's lives were interchangeable. Those were the days when Motley was feeling boxed in with tormenting rage. They were the days when he couldn't control himself or anything else, his newspaper, his cigarette, his cup of coffee. Those were the days when all Motley wanted, all he could think about, was forgiveness. Just a few short months ago both men had been wondering what was the point of life. But now, they knew; they knew the point of it. For the two friends, life had suddenly become superabundant. You want to know what superabundance is like? Ask the billionaires sunbathing on their yachts about superabundance. They'll tell you, from the peace and freedom of their heavenly sanctuaries, that the great thing about superabundance is there's always room for more. Oh yeah, that's the point about superabundance: there's always room for more inside.

28

"Yes please," Rachel had said when Motley had asked her out on a date. But even as she said it, she didn't hold out much hope. After witnessing her parents' fights and acrimonious marital breakdown, Rachel didn't have much hope for love. The idea of a man and woman really loving each other was obviously impossible. Despite her youth, Rachel had already recognised the fact that being in love means entirely different things for a man and a woman. When love appears in a man's life with its wash of cool air, its soul-in-bliss pleasing and surprising, love accelerates his life, extends it. And the man who is falling in love thinks that love will last indefinitely. But when love arrives in a woman's life, she places her hands over her eyes and moans with confusion and distress. Because women know things about love that men don't know; they know what love means. And they know that they can't prevent what's going to happen.

Love looms into a woman's life with its velocity and noise, with its defencelessness and apologies; and women can't stand it coming because they can't stand the absence of power, they can't stand the pain that they know is coming. They know that love can die in a blink of an eye, because someone decided to throw it away; and what's worse, is that when love's utopianism is humbled and destroyed, it replaces itself with fury and anger, with callousness and shame. But the most frightening thing for women is that they know men think that love is about ownership; they know that to men, love is just a pissy little word that means ownership.

"Why do men want to possess women?" Rachel had once asked her dad. "Why do they think they can own them like their pets?"

"That's not true," Sweep had replied, indignantly, "Although, I once knew a guy who went to his wife's funeral in the morning, and then went back to work in the afternoon."

"Yeah, well? That just proves he didn't have much love for his wife. Doesn't it?" Rachel sniffed.

"Mmm...maybe. But the point is, when his dog died he had to take a week's sick leave. The poor old bugger couldn't stop crying."

Rachel had smiled at the simple irony of the story; she thought that in some way it proved her point. "But that's just what I'm saying, isn't it? He obviously loved his dog more than his wife, but he probably felt ownership of them both in exactly the same way."

Sweep was shaking his head, " No. I just think he thought that his wife was better off dead. But he could never think that about his dog, could he?"

Sweep's daughter now shook her head at her father's interpretation of the story. "You're embarrassing Dad. That's sooo sad."

"Oh, I didn't make that story up, sweetheart," Sweep insisted, "I wouldn't make up a story like that."

Although Sweep had taught his daughter many things about how to navigate life, she realised that it was now the right time to cast off from his legacy, to make her own way towards womanhood. She still loved her dad, but she also realised that she was out there, alone with her newly forming discernment.

"When you were married to Mum," Rachel suddenly asked, "Did you love her?" The teenager had asked the question ungrudgingly, without blame or accusation. Sweep's clammy face took on a despairing look. He nodded slowly, distractedly, his chin sinking to the barrel of his chest.

"Mmm…yeah. I loved your mum a lot. As much as a man can love, I think."

…Wow! Did you hear that!

You don't get many parents who let their children know what's going on inside their heads do you? I mean, not like that, not with that kind of honesty. But Sweep was an open book for his daughter to browse.

"So what went wrong then Dad? Why did you two end up fighting so much?"

Sweep looked at his daughter with weighted eyes, tears were beginning to flourish behind their glistening orbs. "Don't know, sweetheart. I just screwed it all up, I guess. It was probably my fault."

Rachel crossed the room to her father, wrapped in the outstretched arms of his battered old armchair, his usual tumbler of scotch clutched in his right fist. She patted the back of his left hand. "No Dad. It wasn't your fault. Mum just wasn't your type, that's all."

"I don't expect you'll know what the hell I'm talking about, Rache, but it seems that our marriage was like a cricket ball that had been given a bloody good whack." Rachel looked puzzled by her father's simile. "Zooom…It took off at a hundred miles an hour." Sweep's hand shot out, stabbing at the air in front of him. "…Up and up it went, looking like it was headed for heaven. But…" Sweep's hand fell limply into his lap, "After ten years or so, the whole bloody trajectory changed. It was like some force had grabbed hold of it, like gravity or something, dragging it down. And down and down it went, until finally it plopped into a bloody great cow-pat, burying itself under all sorts of bullshit."

Sweep suddenly felt the taint of theatricality in what he was saying. He looked up at his attentive daughter, "Does that sound daft to you, love?"

"No Dad. It's just you being you." Rachel said, softly, her arm crawling reassuringly around her father's shoulder as she perched on the arm of his chair.

29

As far as falling in love was concerned, Rachel knew that she was going to be very easy to bruise, so she had decided that she would walk amongst love with an effaced and ginger shuffle, hoping that love wouldn't notice her, wouldn't pick her out. Even as a teenager Rachel thought that, for women, love arrived in their lives with smiling eyes and flying fists. Love dropped into a woman's life like a raptor from a clear blue sky, all talons and ripping beak. She was just seventeen, and knew all she needed to know about love – renunciation and relinquishment, the ruthless giving it to the defenceless. That's it. That's the whole deal. She'd already decided that she wasn't going to diminish herself with love; she wasn't going to let herself fall for that one.

30

If you asked Rachel when she fell in love with Motley, she'd say it happened at first sight. But it isn't true. Well, it is, in a way. If you asked Motley when it happened he'd say at first sight. And it's true, in every way. He loved everything about her at first sight, her crow-black hair and sea-grey eyes, the flicker of a smile that constantly tugged at the corners of her mouth. He loved the way she kept saying yes and nodding when he was speaking to her, the way she laughed at all his corny jokes – Rachel had the loud, head-back laugh of someone who'd already had a few drinks. But most of all, he loved the way she unselfishly gave him her time. And Motley thought about Rachel all the time. She broke his heart whenever she left a room. "Don't break!" He'd have to say to his fragile heart, "Just don't break!"

Rachel was already becoming the dark matter of Motley's universe; giving it the gravity it needed to exist. But despite his bright-eyed optimism over being in love, Motley was soon to discover that being in love isn't as easy as it looks.

31

Rachel had known that Motley was interested in her from the very first moment they met, because he suddenly went stupid on her. It was as though a mist of adolescent shyness descended upon the normally confident man, turning his tongue into a clunky and awkward piece of meat in his mouth. When Motley first saw Rachel, he suddenly felt as naked and defenceless as a newborn chick. With her heart-catching smile, she kept flipping back her long black hair – the graphite colour reminded Motley of pencil tips. He noticed that her hips were much wider than the tops of her thighs – unusual for a seventeen-year-old girl, he thought. They were hips that were obviously made for childbearing: for bearing his children.

As a fresh-from-jail marauder, Motley was grateful to have been granted access to such female splendour. As Rachel ducked into Motley's car on their first date, in her glass-scratching Cardiff accent she'd said, "Promise me that you're not going to try to get me drunk or anything. You're not going to try anything on are you?"

An hour later she was lying in Motley's narrow single bed at his sister's house. He remembered thinking that Rachel's seventeen-year-old skin was as smooth as warm butter, and her eagerness to please naked and absolute. Motley had instantly recognised that she was the gentlest, sweetest creature that he'd ever hopped in a sack with. When Rachel had stood before him wearing just her thong (those metamorphic flip-flops for the female arse) he almost came in his pants.

After kissing and stroking each other's naked bodies, Rachel had started in on the oral thing. Motley gratefully realised that her sexual power lay in her lightness of touch. For Motley, getting his first oral sex from Rachel was just one long sigh of gut-wrenching pleasure. There was none of that admonitive slurping and gurgling that he was used to from the more experienced, lets-get-it-over-with-quick brigade.

Unfortunately, Motley failed to control his explosively infatuated, hair-triggered weapon, and climaxed even more rapidly than his customary, full-on selfishness usually called for. After kissing the still-hot semen from Rachel's lips, he placed a finger under her chin and swivelled her head around to face his. He looked at her for a long time with an evaluating frown.

"You know, maybe I'm not in your class..." He went on staring at her for a few more seconds, then closed his eyes and shook his head. "Nah," he said. "I'm definitely not."

Rachel looked up at him with yearning and tentativeness, "Don't be daft," she said, and then squashed his lips with her own.

The second time they did it was half-an-hour after the first time. It wasn't so much making love; it was more like unarmed combat. They did everything but eat each other. After bouncing around like lunatics on each other for over an hour, both of them reached shattering and simultaneous orgasms. Afterwards, Motley had rolled over and lit up a spliff, just to slow things down a bit and catch some air. Rachel had her head snuggled into his neck.

"You didn't cry," she said.

"What? What do you mean…cry?" he asked, stupidly.

"Well, my ex-boyfriend used to cry after we did it."

"Who did?"

"The last guy I did it with."

Motley almost fell out of bed laughing. Finally, when he'd laughed himself almost to tears, he said. "Bloody hell, Rache, I might weep because I'm NOT making love to you, but you'll never see me cry because I've just shagged your brains out. What the hell was the wimpy jerk crying about?"

"Never mind. You probably wouldn't understand," was all she said, sniffily.

"Jesus, what's been going on around here? Who was it you were shagging before me, Dale-Fucking-Winton?"

When Rachel stopped giggling, she did try to explain to Motley the benefits of a good cry – the redemptive release of tension, the propitiation of pity it generated.

"Yeah, well," Motley groaned, "Me Tarzan, you Jane. Okay?"

"Chauvinist Pig!" the black-haired teenager cried, thumping Motley's hairy chest lightly. The satiated Rachel whimpered softly, cuddled up with her head on her boyfriend's chest, and threw her leg over his belly.

"Anyway," Motley said, arrogantly, "If I cried every time we made love, I'd be fatally dehydrated in one afternoon. I'd have to come to bed with a bloody saline drip hanging from my arm." But the more Motley thought about the crying game, the more he thought that there might be something in it. Crying always seems to get you what you want (it especially works for women). Perhaps that's why women think that crying is such a good idea; perhaps that's why women cry so beautifully. Perhaps that's why, Motley thought, women are so good at it.

32

Before he'd started dating Rachel, Motley had been trolling the city's nightclubs almost every night. He'd also tried his hand at the internet dating game, but he soon realised that the women who inhabited the internet dating scene were just like the internet itself – shared access, open to all.

A few weeks ago, he'd been drunkenly lurching across the beer stained carpet of a seething nightclub, fumbling his way towards the reeking dolour of the men's toilets. As he swam through the agitated crowd, pawing his way through the pulsating, hedonistic bedlam, he stroked and squeezed the haunchy backsides of two heavily sweating girls as they thrashed and flailed to the ear-drum-blistering music. Moving through the eddies of noise and the flickering lights, the human shrieks and jerking bodies, was like moving across a battlefield. The reverberating hard-core 'garage' thumped and howled, curving the air into vast waves of injurious sound, sucking tremulous gouts of breath from his lungs, making his whole body shiver and shrink with alarm. Even though he was totally shit-faced on booze, adrenaline and 'E', there didn't seem to be any logic behind the scary punishment being meted out.

One of the prancing girls suddenly grabbed Motley; her lips quickly found his own. She licked his lips lightly then clamped her mouth against his mouth, nuzzling the tip of her taste organ at his lips until they parted wide enough to let her tongue inside, to entwine with his. They began mimicking the sex act with their tongues. Motley's prong was already writhing and squirming, uncurling itself expectantly in the encompassing nest of his Calvin Kleins. Naturally, Motley's sexual animus would not allow him to pass up such a gloriously coital opportunity.

Cardiff's genito-urinary clinic is housed in a satellite building across the road from the old Royal Infirmary in a

Gothicy pile that looks like an old chapel. Over the previous year, Motley had been a frequent visitor to the windy, antiquated structure built of powdery grey stone: the receptionist had even begun making egregious and hurtful jokes about 'season tickets' and 'invites to the staff Christmas party'. All Motley could do was to shrink beneath her excoriating wit and smile wanly. And today he is back. This morning, there aren't as many people sitting or standing around in the clinic as there usually were. Motley relaxed; all he had to do was offer up his love-wand for five minutes of humiliation and pain and then undertake a course of broad-spectrum anti-biotics. After refraining from sex for at least ten days, he could carry on as usual. As he made himself comfortable on one of the hard benches in the waiting room, he reflected happily on the fact that he'd managed to avoid picking up any of the mainline diseases: gonorrhoea, syphilis, malaria, Ebola. But he knew it was only a matter of time – there were too many dangers to think of in the fornication game, and in the fornication game everybody gets what he deserves. Motley just wished that all those nightclub fornicators would keep their punishments to themselves. He knew in his heart that he was going to have to tell Rachel that he'd probably passed on an STD to her, and she would have to call the clinic to be tested.

As he sat waiting his turn for an examination cubicle, Motley couldn't help thinking that there were not nearly so many diseased people inside the clinic as there were outside the clinic. And at least the people who were inside the clinic knew a lot more about sexually transmitted diseases than the people outside it. The staff at the clinic couldn't keep disease outside, but they made sure it behaved itself when it got inside. And maybe that's why some of the diseased boys and girls swapped telephone numbers while they waited. Doubtless some of them would swap their diseases too, but they probably thought that another dose of clap was a small price to pay for a good night's entertainment. All things considered, and even though the clinic had its faults, meeting up with the lively young crowd that cluttered the waiting room was almost as much fun as a couple of hours down at the pub. The only people who didn't mix, the ones who took themselves off to the farthest recesses of the waiting room, were the poor unfortunates who arrived with scabrous sores on their faces, their ragged lips roaring and dripping as they walked, stooped and hunched into their ghetto. These people skulked in dark corners, talking in offended undertones, reviling the ghastly imposition visited upon them for their love of oral giving and receiving. Their flayed and ragged facial cavities were a dreadful reminder that a mouth can be kept spick-and-span with a toothbrush, but the herpes virus cannot be brushed away.

So now he sits at home with a cup of steaming coffee in his hand, squirming with pain and indignity and wondering what he will say to Rachel. He is thinking that the mating game all boils down to the same thing – fornication: dogs sniffing at each other's bums, cats yowling in the night. It's just an animal thing. Then Motley suddenly realises that there is a difference between Rachel and those girls in the nightclubs. He understands with a sore heart that those nightclub girls can have unfeeling, sardonic sex with a guy and never think about him again, not even to fantasise. Because those girls never have sexual fantasies, they have sexual experiences instead.

Motley's heart whimpers and squirms in his chest; he understands with alarm that those nightclub wraiths freely offer their belligerent sex because it isn't about sex at all; it's about something else. He tries ineffectually to work out what that something else is, but only his piqued and writhing heart has an inkling of that dark secret: and his heart is feeling too crushed to say anything.

Motley was a person who had never prayed in his life (to avoid disappointment) but on this particular morning he got down on his knees and prayed: "Dear Lord, help me to tell Rachel. Put the right words into my mouth so that she doesn't just run off and dump me." Motley was determined to tell Rachel that very night, so he ended his prayer with the customary ritual obeisance, "So God, let me know what you think by tonight, okay."

Rachel stood before him, silent, head bowed. She stood that way for five excruciating minutes. Motley stood too, fidgeting and swaying on restless legs. Then, finally, Rachel looked up. "You say this night club thing happened weeks ago, before you asked me out, right?"

"Yes. Yes…of course it did. I would never go to a place like that after asking you out," Motley whined.

"And this will never happen again, yeah?"

"No…No, never, of course not. I swear it." A very relieved Motley placed his hand over his heart as he faithfully swore his oath of allegiance.

"Okay. But you're coming to the clinic with me. All right?"

Motley took Rachel in his arms, "I'll look after you, don't worry," he sighed gratefully, "And after that, I promise there'll be no more visits to the clinic. Ever. Honest to God."

33

Despite their recent glitch, the teenaged Rachel was still happy to have met Motley and his projection of maleness. Even as a budding feminist, she had already tired of the younger boys' feminisation and timidity. All of them now appeared to her to be revoltingly earnest and emasculated, bragging about their 'sensitivity' and fifty-fifty sharing. Rachel was intelligent and sexy (boy, she was truly sexy). If you ever saw this girl Rachel walking down the street, you would think, 'That's a class act', you would think, 'That's something off the Chanel cat-walk.' Then, instantly descending into a deep and hapless sulk, you would decide that she is hopelessly remote and unattainable, just as Motley had the first time he met her. And now she had met some marvellously stimulating man who wasn't afraid of his vain, muscled, heterosexual power. A languid, "Wow! You look bloody great!" and a friendly pat on the bum had poignantly signalled to her that Motley was sexually savvy in ways that younger men wouldn't understand. Her guess was that this tough guy had had one eye on the bed since the very first moment he saw her. Of course, Rachel was wrong: he'd had all three of his eyes on the bed.

Through the prism of his memory, Motley would often recall the first night they ever slept together. He'd been astonished when Rachel had prayed out loud before going to sleep. First came a rapid rendering of 'Our Father', followed by a more personal prayer that included fervent invocations regarding her father's drinking. Rachel prayed, and Motley listened, gazing at his child/woman with a melting heart; smiling unbelievingly at where his very own rainbow met the ground.

34

So, Rachel was now the succulent icing on Motley's luscious cake. He'd taken his new car around to Sweep's on the pretence of showing it off to his best friend. Instead, he'd taken his daughter on a quick drive around the city in his new BMW ragtop and then asked her out. Motley had started dating Rachel without her father knowing; old Sweep was too busy shagging his new girlfriend and keeping his fat lips soaked with rare malts to have noticed anything anyway. When Sweep did finally find out, it was because someone had said something to him at the office. That night, Motley had dropped Rachel off around the corner from their house, and when she'd got in Sweep was standing in the middle of the kitchen. His normally ruddy cheeks were glowing like a Chernobyl nuclear reactor; his angry face was redder than a Ferrari. "Right. From now on you're grounded young lady."

A tearful Rachel told Motley later that she was getting fed up of perjuring herself to her father every night anyway.

Rachel's relationship with her Dad had been formed out of commonality of interest. She had formed an Electra alliance with him against a common enemy: her mother. Sweep's ex-wife would start off berating him for all the things he did that annoyed her, then, little by little, she'd turn her vituperative tongue on her daughter, and start going on about all the things that she did to get on her nerves. As it turned out, Rachel hated her mother, and Sweep had grown to hate his cruel, bullying wife; her favoured form of communication was throwing a cup at Sweep's head. Crouching low, he would usually be yelling, "For Christ's sake, what have I done now?"

And then, one day, Sweep confronted his wife with the rumour of her infidelity with their bin-man. He came home from work the next day and – poof! She was gone. And she'd cleaned out the house. She'd taken everything, including the toilet seats and light-fittings. Of course, a few months later she went to court and hammered Sweep on the ancillary settlement, taking half the value of the house and a slice of his pension. Two years later she rang, asking to speak to Rachel.

"I never, ever want to speak to her again!" Rachel had shouted down the stairs. There were no more phone calls to the house after that.

Had the circumstances been different, and Rachel was Motley's daughter, he'd have skinned alive any little toe-rag that dared to try and take her away from him. He did feel bad about coming between father and daughter; he realised that Sweep depended upon his daughter for some stability in his life. But Motley wasn't about to give her up for anything. Sweep could have beaten the shit out of him if he liked, and Motley wouldn't have lifted a finger. After all, taking a pounding from his best friend would have been like taking "friendly fire."

35

A Cardiff girl through and through, the teenager loved living in the fast-moving city. There were lots of opportunities for work, entertainment and culture: Cardiff has all of that good stuff and much, much more. Within a forty-five minute drive you can be walking in the mountains or lolling on some of the finest beaches around. But when the city started to make Motley feel anxious or just plain crazy, Rachel and him would take a drive up into the Brecon Beacons. When he'd joined the Parachute Regiment, he used to tab up and down Pen-y-Fan mountain with a rucksack the size and weight of a small family car, so he knew his way around the rugged and beautiful hills of the Welsh hinterland. In summer, the couple would take a picnic and lie by a deep pool on the Mellte riverbank, drinking wine and smoking weed. Motley loved the wild places. He had once read somewhere that nature was a chain of life. If that's true, he reasoned, then a city must be one of nature's broken links: with its anaemic air, botched dawns and limpid sunsets. (There is never enough air in the city to go around.)

Motley would entertain Rachel with stories from Iraq; she especially liked to hear about the ancient history of that unhappy country. He told her he had once stopped at antique Babylon, and that every brick of the rebuilt walls of the city had Saddam's name imprinted on them. (It's true!) But she liked to hear the funny stories most. Motley kidded her that the best selling sex-toy in Baghdad was a peek-a-boo burka, the second-best sex-aid was an airline ticket to Amsterdam, that kind of stuff.

Rachel would giggle uncontrollably at the lame Iraqi police jokes he'd picked up. She liked the light-hearted

64

stuff, knowing that he'd get morose if he thought too much about the fighting. Those stupid jokes were a bigger hit with Rachel than with the Army lads. She especially liked the one about the Iraqi cop who stopped a battered old Volkswagen Beetle at a roadblock. The cop ordered the driver to get out and open the boot for a search. When the driver got out and moved to the front of the car, "No!' says the cop, "I said open the luggage compartment."

The driver pointed at the front of the car. "This is the luggage compartment."

"You think I'm an idiot?" says the cop, pointing at the back of the car.

So the driver does as he's told and opens up the back engine compartment.

"Aha, Ali Baba!" declares the cop, "You've stolen an engine, and you've only just done it because it's still running!"

After the stories, the couple would strip off their clothes and stretch out on a rug amongst the ferns, lying side by side, kissing and touching each other's bodies. As Motley closed his eyes, he would still see his seventeen-year-old girlfriend's dawn-coloured skin shimmering and blushing, her seal-grey eyes and the curve of her hips.

Soon he would feel her cool hands on his genitals, and then his blood-packed penis would be sliding gently into her wet mouth. When she was lubricated and ready, Rachel would guide the head of his zealously willing cock into the cusped and moistened part of herself. Motley would make love to the moaning Rachel, sucking and tonguing her nipples until she let out a deep animal sough as they both reached shuddering climaxes. And Rachel knew, even while she was moaning, that it's this that's making Motley fall in love with her. And it's so easy. It's so easy to make a man fall in love – at least any man with a prick. And some men know it; the ceaseless men who've had seven thousand fucks and ten thousand blow jobs. That's why those guys don't flirt anymore: they don't have time for all those inane acts of decency, like falling in love. They go straight to the raw thing, because they can't love anymore; they can't sustain it. They can't justify love's grandiosity, its sentimentality. No, you have to be tragic to love Love. And those guys are just too hard-hearted, too durable: love is just pussy-fodder for them.

36

After the languorous lovemaking, butterflies the size of pterodactyls fluttered in Motley's stomach. He felt hugely privileged and favoured to be making love to this wonderful girl. (All men know it's a shoddy fact of life that some female blessings are withheld forever.) Recovering from the trajectories of their orgasms, Rachel would lie there for ages without moving, shimmering and glowing in the miracle of her smile. Her arms and legs were always wrapped tightly around him as she whispered huskily in his ear, "I'll never let you go. Never!" At that moment, deep in the throbbing runnels of Motley's heart, he felt promoted, flattered and of course, infinitely tender.

Lying on his back, with Rachel's head resting in the crook of his neck, Motley would gaze up at the ragged quilt of cumulus cloud nosing about above, the white lumpiness being swiped and torn by the wind. The changing clouds reminded him of something, and it was something he didn't want to be reminded about: change. Everything changes, he was being reminded, sometimes things change for you, and sometimes they change against you. But for the first time in his life, Motley realised that he was afraid of change. He wanted time to move forward slowly, walking a narrow gangplank. He wanted time to stop so that he could suck every second dry, he wanted nothing to change, nothing at all.

Feeling like some lustered god had taken him into his hands, he felt like the Olympian Titans had elected him Zeus – and who could profane him now? Sharing a bottle of wine with a beautiful, naked woman in the middle of the day, the sun sitting high in the sky, the lover's love being spilt, is without a doubt the closest a man can get to heaven on this earth. Those outdoor lovemaking sessions gave him so much zest, so much joie de vivre, that it rivalled any dope that Motley had ever smoked, bettered any mind-appeasing coke that he had ever snorted…"Mmm. Jesus, Rache. That was good."

He would get an instantaneous erection just thinking about those long hours lying amongst the tumbling, scented ferns of the Mellte riverbank. Motley still didn't believe that there was a God; but when he was with Rachel, he knew for sure that there was a Heaven. When he looked down at the naked, smiling Rachel, Motley saw heaven. He could hold heaven in his hands, kiss it and taste it. Oh man, did heaven taste good. You want to know what heaven tastes like? It tastes of salt on the hot cheek of a beautiful girl.

After the joys of their al fresco lovemaking, he would take a skinny dip in the icy river to wash away the sweat of their sexual gymnastics and the city's cloying mental grime. Motley was so sublimely happy that it seemed as though every wish he had ever made had suddenly come true. And that's the trouble with all your wishes coming true at once: it can only go downhill from there.

37

So, Motley and Rachel…Motley and Rachel? 'Motley and Rachel!' – assimilating, reciprocating, vice-versing. Well, Ladies and Gentlemen, boys and girls, revered readers – how would you rate their chances? Personally, I didn't think their hook up was a good idea for either of them, not really. Yes, I know that they were desperately in love with each other, fabulously, dazzlingly, prodigiously in love with each other. But where does love take you, eh, to a happy Nirvana, or a snug desideratum? Christ no! Are you kidding me? NO WAY, JOSE! Hey, no fucking day, Ray! Love takes you down terrifying paths and desperate alleyways. Trust me on this.

Hey, Motley, better look out, cos I know what's coming. I've been there, pal. You see, the problem with love is that it makes you start to give a Fuck: and you, my prototypical adolescent friend, my ferocious, dark-glassed ornery ex-Die Hard, you've never given a Fuck in your life.

"Oh yeah, I know what love is," you once said to Sweep and me in the wine-bar, "I read about it in a book."

Remember that? Then came, "But the best thing is not to love, not to give a fuck about anything. That way, nothing ever gets to you, nothing can mess with your head. You know what I mean?"

And remember what Sweep said?

"So, my emotionally crippled mucker – no love, and no hate, eh? So how about a full lobotomy? How about living the rest of your lopped and nearly life in a darkened room? What are you trying to do chicken-shit, make your excuses and leave? You just don't get it do you? You just don't get it; we LIKE our heads being messed with. We poor misguided bastards just can't get efuckingnough of it!"

And, dear reader, don't forget; it wasn't just Motley now, there were other people to consider too; family, and friends, for example. But for now, summer or winter, sunshine or snow-showers, Motley and Rachel were always having a great time. In the winter months, they'd wrap up in their warmest gear and head out west, driving over to the Gower. They would walk for miles on the deserted beaches, carving their names in the sand with their heels like a couple of teenagers. (Hell, Rachel was a teenager!)

Even though he loved those cold-weather trips with his girlfriend, Motley hated the demented winter skies; their frowning voluminousness their incredible crying jags. In winter the sky always looks like weak electric light, and the darkness…well, the darkness is something else; in winter the devouring darkness never gets ripped, never gets torn. It's in winter, when the sky is boiling and shuddering and full of alchemy, when the frigid air is suffused with lost things; it's in winter that Motley can feel his own ghost travelling through the cold, dark days.

Don't let it in Motley, whatever you do; don't let your hungry-for-forgiveness ghost in. Remember, ghosts don't only come from what has gone. The futuristic ghosts come from what lies ahead. These are the knowing ghosts, flustered and blinking and hoping to impress. But the future-ghosts are never quite true, with their tiptoeing connections and predictions. How else would you explain the vagaries, the equivocal and the arbitrary? The future is habitually infidelitous – as is the past.

As they walked along the Mumbles seafront through a flurry of unexpected April snow, Motley said to Rachel: "I still can't believe that I've met you."

Rachel leaned her head into his shoulder. "Me too," she replied, brushing the snow from her hair. Motley moaned as they ducked their heads against the windblown flakes. "I can't believe this, snow. In bloody April!"

"The snow's okay. It's melting as soon as it hits the ground," Rachel reassured him. Then she said thoughtfully, "Hope our love lasts longer than the snowflakes."

Motley raised her chin to look at her face. "Stop it Rache. Don't talk like that." Then he squeezed her hand and added quickly, "Please."

After their walk, they would find their way back to the Italian café at the end of the Mumbles promenade and sip frothy cappuccino with brandy chasers. On another of their long beach-walks, Rachel had said to him gently but accusingly, "You know, some people think that selling drugs is a disgusting and vicious thing to do."

It stopped Motley in his tracks. He was flabbergasted, stunned and disappointed. "Christ Rache! Where the fuck did that come from?" he snapped. However much he lied to himself about his new profession, he'd never lied to Rachel about it. The aura of his anger had dilated the tiny blood vessels in her cheeks; the sharp edge to his voice made her face glow. Her hurt was so palpable and definitive that there was no need to enhance it with her tears. She stared at him for several seconds then turned away. Motley looked at the back of his girlfriend's loveable, snow-garlanded head and sinking shoulders.

"So, disgusting and vicious, eh? That's what they say they, do they? So what are you saying Rache, scratch a drug-dealer and you get a murderer, is that it? Okay, so how does bombing and shooting innocent women and kids stand up against drug dealing? Is soldiering such a noble and wonderful thing to do? Is killing people with a bullet better than selling them the chemical means to kill themselves?"

While Motley was a soldier, he had tried to be a good soldier; the best soldier he could possibly be. But now he'd stopped trying to be good at all. Well, it's hardly a staggering move is it, considering where trying to be good had got him: being a good soldier had made him gag on life, and had very nearly driven him out of his mind.

"Anyway, I see the drug profits as a kind of tip for doing my duty…for doing my patriotic duty."

Dear me, did you hear that? Those exorbitant prices for patriotism! Still, I suppose we all have our price lists for loyalty and duty. But what about the millions of dead soldiers lying in the ground, what about the thousands of war widows living on a beggar's pension: did they have their price lists? No. I don't think so. There isn't enough currency in the world to pay those men and women the price of their loyalty.

"It's not the only way to make money," Rachel moaned, "there are other ways. You're intelligent, you could earn money in lots of ways." Rachel's naiveté riled Motley; he tried to control his anger but couldn't stop his voice from rising.

"What if it isn't about the money, Rache? What if it's just about me showing the world the finger, eh? Have you thought about that?"

"It's the money," Rachel insisted.

Motley grabbed Rachel by the arm and spun her around to face him.

"Listen, there's only two things I know about money. One of them is that if you can count your money, you don't have enough. The other is that money means you can tell any arsehole in the world to go fuck himself. That's all I know about money and all I need to know. So it isn't just the money, okay."

"You're hurting me," Rachel whined. Motley realised that he was squeezing his girlfriend's arm with a vice-like grip.

"Sorry," he apologised, opening his hand. "What do you want from me Rache? Tell me. You want the truth? I've told you the truth, and you won't believe me. Is it because I'm an ex-con? You can't trust me, yeah. Is that it?" Motley realised that he was shouting; he lowered his voice. "I'm not the enemy Rache. I'm not the one responsible for killing thousands of people illegally."

Rachel didn't answer. She was now staring at a distant point in the fulminating, snow-filled sky.

"Why do you have to use those stupid drugs, anyway? Don't I make you happy enough?" she asked, her voice trembling.

Not only did she not understand Motley's need to sell drugs, Rachel couldn't understand his need to use them.

When he smoked marijuana, the mind-rescuing weed turned him introverted and sleepy. What was the point of entering that padded nullity? Why did he need to seek out that kind of limbo? Was it a summons from the pandemonium perhaps, a desire to retreat to childlike unknowing, a means of escaping his purgatorial conscience? What Rachel didn't know was that smoking dope was the nearest Motley could get to being someone else. The ganja took him to another place, beyond the grasp of the flame-blackened past.

38

As a part of the generation who are proud of their shallowness, Rachel's unblemished and youthful mind did not have the breadth of knowledge, the acuity of experience to resolve the questions that bothered her. Now she started to feel bad; they had just had their first cross words. Their first cross words! When even a frown from Motley hurt her like smoke in her eyes, can you imagine how BAD Rachel now felt?

You know what I wish? I wish Rachel had known more about love. Because love takes time to learn. It's the one thing you can't rush: it's the one thing you can't learn without time. Poor Rachel, she felt BAD because as a young girl she loved the way everybody else loves, with total passion; but she loved without the experience. She didn't know that love always makes you feel BAD.

There's another reason I feel sorry about Rachel's lack of life-experience. When she had heard the simple message that all drugs are a catastrophe, Rachel had believed it. And when she heard that drug dealers are all vicious, death-dealing demons, she believed that too. But no one had explained to her about the fireball of flame and fizzing metal that was now wriggling its way over Iraq's vast distances. The embattled country seemed to be sprouting flame all the time now, in the form of murderous terror. Liberty and democracy, the things that Motley and his men had fought for, couldn't stop the fires, couldn't extinguish the terror. How lucky Rachel was; she only had to worry about what people said about drug dealers, and not about the simmering fires and the inexhaustible terror. You can see that gaining life experience is going to be hard on Rachel, because gaining life experience is always particularly hard on young women. Always. It must be tough, the realisation that half the world's population want to do what the hell they like with you. It must be hard on a poor girl knowing that half the pleasure-loving world is watching, itching, swelling.

The couple's thirteen-year age-gap brought the only other difference between them: it was their polar-opposite tastes in music. Motley preferred chilling out to Cold Play or Dido, while Rachel seemed to enjoy getting her ear-drums scoured by bands like Franz Ferdinand or The Darkness; the kind of eardrum-warping bands that make the same primordial noise that a sack of cats would make if you threw it down the stairs.

The only flies in Motley's overflowing tin of ointment were the recurring nightmares (it is those with the most vivid imaginations who suffer from truly terrifying nightmares; the pale moths of symbolism testing the credulity of the sleeping mind) and the flat he was attempting to buy on Cardiff's newly developed waterfront. Buying the bay-view flat was all happening painfully slowly and he couldn't wait to move in with Rachel: "If finding a decent flat is like falling in love," Motley had said, "Then buying it is like getting married and not seeing each other for three months. It's fucking excruciating. Those solicitors move like they've been tied down with chains. Everything takes forever."

He was constantly ringing his solicitor for the latest update, constantly being disappointed as every fresh hope of moving in ended in disappointment.

"Don't worry, the time-frame is normal." his solicitor assured him.

"I fucking bet it is," he'd replied. "You bastards are paid by the hour aren't you?"

The love-lulled couple were enjoying their usual Saturday night out in the crowded and cacophonous wine-bar, and as usual Motley was completely off his face on weed and booze. One of the barmaids he had befriended came over to his table and warned him that old Jelly-Hair was saying she had it in for him: "She swears that she's going to turn your arrogant arse-hole inside-out." He just ordered another large Jack Daniels, and laughed at it.

"So what?" he said to a worried Rachel, "what's she going to do? Get her boyfriend after me? Shit, I'm a Player around here now. What can she do to me?" Then Motley fell silent. He brooded, and watched his declared adversary slowly cleaning a glass and occasionally staring shrilly at him.

"Back in a second," he whispered hoarsely to Rachel. Then he strode purposefully up to the bar. "Give me two of those pink and green cocktails," he ordered the wary and hostile barmaid. The two protagonists stared at each other piercingly for a few moments then Jelly-Hair began dilatorily mixing the cocktails.

How well do I know this girl? Motley wondered. He watched the girl's neck and back as she bent and stretched for glasses and the gleaming cocktail-making implements. How well does she know me? Where did we find this unanimity of dislike? Ah well, shit happens – Motley decided – and there's nothing anyone can do to stop it. People just take an instant dislike to each other and then one night all the boiling and coruscating and bloody-mindedness comes out. One night, they can't stop it; they just can't keep the trouble out – "That's it! I'm fucking sorting this once and for all."

Motley really didn't want to start trouble in the wine-bar, but everyone knows that sometimes you just can't keep it out. It wasn't that he minded starting trouble, fuck no, are you kidding, haven't you been paying attention? Jesus, his entire life had been a running battle with troubles and infamies; and he hadn't solved it yet either. Hell, let's be honest here: Motley loved starting trouble. It usually opened up opportunities, but Motley didn't want to start trouble in the wine-bar. Christ no, he was making too much money out of the place.

The barmaid ambled up and down the bar, reaching for various bottles and pouring the liquids they contained into a stainless-steel shaker. Finally, two glasses filled with the expensive drinks were placed on the bar in front of Motley. He took the slightest sip from one of them.

"Mm," he smacked his lips favourably, "Perhaps you can make a cocktail after all." Jelly-Hair's face instantly softened into something less adamantine than it had been a moment ago. The makings of a smile were teasing at the corners of her usually down-turned mouth. Then Motley took a second sip from the glass. Placing the glass carefully back on the bar, Motley pushed the drink towards the barmaid, "Nah," he spat, "That cocktail's shit. You'll never make a decent barmaid as long as you've got a hole in your arse." Jelly Hair's face broke into a frenzy of seething rage and humiliation. For a moment, Motley thought her pink psychodrama face might explode. "You're making a big mistake fucking with me," he hissed at the girl, "a big mistake." His voice was resonant with something barely repressed – all the more frightening for being repressed.

Motley could feel the crackle of the stunned barmaid's radioactivity, her wrecked force field. Her face looked like the eastern sky after the crucifixion of a demi-god, all darkness, lightning flashes and biblical fury. Motley couldn't understand the inordinateness of his misogyny towards her. His normal instincts towards women were helpfulness and kindness, but every look or gesture from this woman mangled his normal instincts. What was it that caused the havoc of mischief making in him? What was Jelly-Hair's power? What power did she have that made him feel so bad? Between you and me, there was a reason she made Motley feel bad. His instincts were in control; they were telling him that she was asking for it.

As he walked away from the bar, he could feel the stabbing gestures swarming across his back. He swivelled his shoulder and faced her. Jelly-Hair needed all her courage to hold his fiery gaze. Her mind struggled to find the words she wanted to say, anything, any old words would do, but her throat had swollen with contorting anger and it would take a few minutes for it to clear. She wasn't listening to the unfortunate guy who now stood hopefully at the bar in front of her.

"Two Stellas please love…love?" The rebuked barmaid wasn't listening to the thirsty bar-fly, "Two Stellas love…please. Hello?"

"I'm sorry…what was it?" she said, relaxing her stiffened face and putting her self forward deceptively again, in her 'nice person' disguise – milder, sweeter, and saner.

39

How could Jelly-Hair put up with Motley's obnoxious, vindictive behaviour, without screaming or crying or running from the room? The answer's that Jelly-Hair herself spent most of her life being obnoxious and vindictive, her real job almost demanded it. That's why she could take it: because she gave it out – all of the time. If someone made a film about the jelly-haired barmaid's life, it would need lots of sinister, menacing music to underscore her aggrievement at the blood-sport hands of Motley. But as the plot of the movie unfolded, you would see Jelly-Hair gaining ground fast over her persecutor. Ironically, the female bar-person enjoyed certain advantages over the drug dealer. The police-ID card that she kept in a secret pocket of her handbag meant that she could do things that Motley couldn't do. Just as an example of what the undercover policewoman could do, Detective Sergeant Wendy Westerby of the National Crime Squad could have Motley arrested and SENT TO JAIL for a painfully long time.

40

It was one of those nights when every lame tosser seemed to creep out of the woodwork: even one of the adenoidal students wanted a piece of Motley. The smart-arsed, rich-kid student decided to have a go at him because of his service in Iraq. Someone must have told the student that Motley had done some soldiering out there, so the guy came on with: "The UN should have been left to sort that one out. Your lot have killed more civilians than you have insurgents."

Motley automatically went into Airborne fighting mode as soon as he heard that crap. "Of course we killed civilians, pin-dick. The bastards shooting at us were dressed up as civilians; that's why. And if any civilian-dressed fedayeen rag-head wants to point a weapon at a Para, he should know that he's taking on the best, the economy-sized, the new-and-improved meanest bunch of arse-kickers that ever pulled on a British Army uniform. Airborne tab further, carry more kit, fight longer, kill more of the enemy and fuck more things than you can put a fucking name to. The Regiment eats little countries like Iraq for breakfast and then shits them out before lunch." Motley was almost foaming at the mouth.

Rachel tried to pull Motley away but he shook her hand from his arm. The tact-deficient student was paralysed with fear. He was standing there with his mouth hanging open. Rachel started pulling on Motley's sleeve again. "Leave it sweetheart," she was yelping, "he's not worth it."

But Motley was just getting warmed up. After his confrontation with the barmaid, he was definitely cruising for a bruising. He grabbed a fist-full of the student's shirt and pulled the guy's face to within an inch of his. He was getting ready to nut the little shite. "So you think our boys shouldn't be out there, yeah? Well I agree. You're right, shit-for-brains, they shouldn't be. But I'll tell you just one little thing that an Iraqi civilian said to me. He said, 'There's only one thing wrong with you British. You won't let us go and live in your country.' Get it? Now fuck off before I lose my temper."

Motley threw the young guy away from him. At that point, the student should have jumped back and punched Motley's lights out. But he just smiled his superior, studenty smile and left. The rest of the bar had gone very quiet. Motley suddenly realised he'd been shouting his head off. Everyone, including Rachel, thought he'd gone nuts, and they were probably right. That toe-rag student had made him angrier than a bag full of snakes.

"Those fucking students, eh?" Motley grumbled to Rachel, "They really piss me off with their peace-nick anxieties. They're lost in the pointlessness of 'Do They Know It's Christmas' videos and they know diddly-squat about fuck-all going on in the real world. Yet they all want to tell us war heroes what's-fucking-what in countries they've never even heard of."

Yes, Motley, you're right. I'm afraid it's true. It seems to be an unhappy fact of life that for students, nothing boils their blood or foams their brain like a soldier returning from a war – it's guaranteed to bring out the placards. Motley is still going on to Rachel about students: "What the fuck do they think we've got an army for, to keep it sitting around barracks playing snakes and ladders? If we're at the mercy of nutters who like to land passenger aircraft in the middle of our cities, then what's our army for? Oh, excuse me, I forgot. The entire purpose of the highly trained, highly paid

British Army is to sand-bag swollen rivers and drive Green Goddesses when the firemen decide to strike."

41

Okay. We know that Motley hated the Army, but he still believed that it's there to fight our battles and kill our enemies. But he also thought that political correctness would soon change all that. Motley found it easy to imagine, in the drift and flux of the near-future, a British Army made up of social-work experts; uniformed men and women, pacing up and down the parade grounds, wringing their hands and saying over and over, 'It's terrible. Something ought to be done!' And meanwhile, in some baleful African country, an envenomed dictator massacres millions of his own people. Motley supposed that the politicians would react by sending over an SAS (Soothing And Solace) team of fast-response anger-management councillors.

Oh, and by the way, here's a useful tip from Motley to those young guys who fancy the pay and uniform but have an aversion to going to war and getting shot at...

"Get a job with the girlies serving up Big Macs and fries, and DON'T JOIN THE ARMY! It's for valorous men and women who want to kill the mad bastards who are trying to kill our people." As Motley used to drunkenly maunder amongst his Airborne comrades, "Dulce et decorum est pro patria mori." As though anyone knows what the fuck that means any more.

On those boozy nights in the wine-bar, when Motley was belligerently loud and rumbling, the ex-paratrooper's uber-confidence would forcefully and arse-kickingly return, as mean and contentious as ever. On those ego-deep-diving occasions, he would re-unite himself with the idea that he was a man who had nothing to lose. But that idea wasn't strictly true any more, was it? Motley did have something to lose: something big.

— 79 —

42

Anne Tremblett was fetching the kids from school, as usual. As she drove her two boys home she was feeling tired; the kind of tiredness that a good night's sleep might lighten – "Will you two please calm down! Can't you just be quiet for a minute? I've got a splitting headache." But there was another tiredness that wormed within her, above and below the sleep-deprivation tiredness. It was the tiredness of depression, the kind of cosh-wielding depression whose gravitational pull wants to drag you down into the centre of the earth.

No amount of sleep or restoring afternoon naps would lighten the tiredness of Anne's depression. She couldn't remember the last time a full day had passed without her crying. Crying with her eyes wide open in that terrible state of hyper-consciousness, when she just couldn't stop thinking. A long time ago she had lost the knack of not thinking; she slipped out of bed in the middle of the night to make a cup of tea, and to make herself stop thinking. Thinking about betrayal. Thinking about deceitfulness. Anne Tremblett not only suffered from depression, she wore it; in her red-rimmed eyes, on her waxen face, around her listing shoulders. Anne was forty-three tomorrow, and she'd been married to Rod Tremblett for thirteen years.

How broadly her husband Rod had roamed with his excuses for betraying her: unhappy childhood, pressures of work, mid-life crisis, bad back. The bad back excuse never really got off the ground. Rod didn't know why, but he couldn't seriously bring himself to blame a bad back for his extra-marital vicissitudes. On the other hand, a bad back might have saved him. Very soon after Anne had found out about his playing away from home, Rod was dejectedly wondering: how come women are so good with words? How can a woman rip a man's balls off with just words? In the hands of an angry woman, words become weapons of extreme prejudice. A sustained barrage of Anne's angry words always made Rod feel like he was starring in a connoisseur's Snuff movie.

And then – there's the tears. It was during those terrible rows that Rod learned that it's impossible to gauge the prognosis of an argument by the volume of tears a woman sheds: the lexicon of female tears is unavailable to mortal man. Women's crying-stratagems are indecipherable to men, though it is painfully apparent that female tears have skilfully evolved far beyond those of the male. Female tears are aimed at telling a more single-minded story: hour-long extravaganzas of weeping can concuss the male target into a coma of regret and numbing contrition.

During those arguments, it became cap-in-hand clear to Rod that women have far more knowledge of tears than men; they know how tears work. That's why women don't just cry with their eyes; they cry with their whole bodies: for women, tears are a whole-body force.

Naturally, while he'd been having the affair – like most married men who indulge themselves – Rod believed that his marriage would benefit from it. He believed he was screwing around for the good of his marriage. For Rod, like most married men having an affair, it is a parallax exercise; focusing and re-focusing between the marital bed and the lover's bed – and that's where the real treachery lies. Rod Tremblett believed that the benefits of his increased libido would, of course, be passed on to his wife, in the marital bed.

43

The traffic lights had changed to red, and Anne was sitting listening to her five-year-old telling a story about a railway tank-engine that talked (what kind of hallucinogenic shit are those kids on?). Then some boy-racer screeched up beside her at the traffic lights. "Hey missus." Anne looked across through the open passenger seat window. "You drive like a twat."

The front passenger was leaning out of his window and howling at her, a couple more drunken dildos were giving her the finger from their back window. Anne, had put her hand to her mouth, hardly believing what she'd just heard, then she screamed at the hooligans: "I've got kids in the car."

"Fuck you," was the instantaneous reply. "And fuck your kids."

Right then, the lights changed and they shot off in a cloud of burning rubber, lobbing an empty beer can back in her direction. Anne turned around and looked at her two boys. They were sat there like a couple of owls caught in a searchlight, trembling and close to tears. Anne was near to tears herself, forlornly asking herself the question; why is everyone so obnoxious these days, so predisposed, so prone to anger and violence?

And there doesn't seem to be a violent 'type', anymore, does there? It's not just the boy-racers; everyone seems to be ready to explode into instantaneous violence. And it's not just men, either. The sisters are getting in on it too – thin-hipped schoolgirls, spartan-thighed teenagers, broad-shouldered Amazons; there is a new pluralism, a new promiscuity towards violence. No one is averse to violence anymore – even the politicians are punching out people in the street! Perhaps it's all those soap operas (those shabby domestic tutors), like maggots in the nation's brain they teach people how to behave – their daily screamings, the flash-point confrontations and jovial slappings. Week after distraught week, festering anger is resolved into overworked violence. The tele-visual belligerence has proved eminently exportable to our schools, our pavements and our roads. Perhaps, Anne was thinking; people have become tired with the fear of violence, because the fear of violence is a violent fear. They've given up being afraid of violence because they've immunised themselves, and so now they've started dishing it out. The sad truth is that we're all susceptible to violence now, you, me, Anne – everyone.

…"Hey, missus, what's with the sparkly hat? And that gold carriage is some fucking bling. Now let's get a fucking move on, eh?"

Boy, that violence really likes to get around, doesn't it?

Now Anne was standing in her kitchen at home, a cartoon of impatient anger, vibrating with rage. After telling her husband about the drunken youths who had terrorised her and the kids, she handed him the registration number of the hooligan-crammed car. "Ring your friends down at the station," she barked, the strain cracking her voice.

"No need. We've got his number. I'll look it up," was all Rod said.

Rod Tremblett was a sixteen-year on-the-job traffic cop, and he had just promised himself: "I'll catch up with those bastards – and soon."

44

The following week, when Andrew and Trudy, Rod's brother and his sister-in-law came over for lunch, Anne told them about the road rage thing. After they'd eaten, his brother nodded to Rod to take their beers out into the garden.

"Just going out the back to smoke a panatella love," he'd said casually, and then he followed Andrew out.

"What are you doing about that shit?" his brother asked. "You must have got their number." There was venom in his voice.

"Yeah, I got it."

"So. What are you doing about it?"

"Leave it to me, Andrew. I'll catch up with them."

"Have you looked it up on the computer? Where does the fucker live?"

"Andy, I can handle it."

Andrew was a Drug Squad detective. His brother had been trying for a transfer to the same squad for two years but wasn't getting anywhere. It was a sore point between them. Andy reckoned his brother was better off nicking motorway pranksters and drunk-drivers... "Trust me, Rod," he'd said, "you don't want to be dropped into the stinking menagerie I have to immerse myself in every day. Chasing those shit-head dealers can get dangerous. Those fuckers will shred your face with a broken bottle just for giggles."

Of course, Rod had heard all this before. But he'd told his brother, "It's okay Andy, I've seen the Serpico movies too. I know what I'd be getting into."

"No, you don't fucking know." Andy had snarled.

Rod always had the feeling that if his brother had wanted to, he could have moved a few of the obstacles that seemed to be preventing him getting his transfer to the squad. But Rod never pressed the point.

Now, standing in his garden, he was watching a forest-fire of anger blazing in his brother's eyes. "Okay Andy, what do you think I should do about those pin-dicks?"

"Not here Bro. Not today. We'll talk next week, when you come over to us. I want you to meet a couple of friends of mine. They're on the squad."

"What friends? What's all this about?"

"It's about getting those morons off the street for a while. We'll teach those bastards to start in on your wife and kids."

"Shit, Andy. What the hell are you into?"

"Just come with an open mind next Sunday. We'll have a barbie. Okay?"

"Yeah...okay...next Sunday."

"Good. Let's go back inside."

45

The brothers were sitting out in the garden, sipping a couple of ice-cold beers. Suddenly Rod heard some strange voices. Looking back at the house, he saw Andy's patio was filling up with five burly guys, each clutching a can of booze to their generous bellies.

"Andy, the boys are here," shouted Trudy.

"Hiya lads. Holy Jesus, Terry!" Andrew yelled, "I forgot I invited you!"

Andy jumped up and called the guys over.

"Come and meet my Bro lads. These are the guys I work with Rod. Except for Terry, he's something else." He laughed wickedly when he said that last sentence.

"Something else?" Rod repeated, warily.

"Tell you later," his brother smirked.

After five bone-crushing handshakes, the guys spread themselves out on the grass, sitting around Rod and Andy like a circled wagon train.

For the first five minutes, Andrew did all the talking, mostly shop stuff, moaning about the drug squad superior officers, the avalanches of paperwork they were tied down with, and other standard cop-whinges. The guys eyed him warily as Andy prattled on. Finally, the blonde guy that Andy had introduced as Fritzy – Rod discovered later, that his name was Van Oostenberger: the guy's parents were Dutch, but everyone called him Fritzy. The corrupt and vigorous Fritzy, whose cynical brain was already nurturing the inoperable tumour that would kill him within a year-and-a -half, his wife would swear – even as he moaned and died – that the cancer was a result of too many hours of urgent conversations on his mobile phone (notandum: the miracles that we hope for so rarely happen, but the disasters we dread so often do). Perhaps, after one of his fateful conversations, the phone's radiation had re-folded Fritzy's stirred and rippled brain the wrong way. The big, blonde, half-Dutchman asked Rod, "You're with Traffic aren't you?"

"Yeah, that's right. But I've been trying to transfer to your mob."

Fritzy just pursed his lips, and nodded.

Then Andy piped up, "You're probably wondering why I asked you to come to my house are you, Ter?" Andy was talking to the one guy who looked out of place amongst the spectacularly obvious gang of policemen. He was only about five-six tall, but he had the Taurean build of a prize-winning bull. He also sported a retrogressive ponytail. Terry just shrugged his massive shoulders.

"Ter doesn't say much." Andy said, turning to Terry, "He's a man of action, aren't you, Ter?"

Terry nodded, and a smile struggled to form itself on his massive face, but only managed to trudge its way to the corners of his mouth before giving up the ghost; his facial muscles had forgotten how to perform such a complicated manoeuvre. Ter just dumbly shrugged his cliff-face shoulders again.

"So, what's happening?" Rod asked no one in particular.

"All will be revealed," Andy laughed, trying, and failing, to sound enigmatic. "Fritzy, why don't you tell Rod about what's happening on the squad."

Fritzy inched himself a little closer towards Rod.

"I'm going to tell you a little story, Rod, and it's a true story, every bloody word of it."

Rod raised his eyebrows, trying to show some anticipation. Fritzy continued to look directly into his eyes as he spoke.

"Not long ago, I asked a small-time dealer why he did it. Why was he into the drugs thing? He'd already agreed with me that he could probably have earned more working in a factory, so I was intrigued. Anyway, he told me that he did it for the status…and the protection."

"Protection from whom?" Rod asked, looking around at the other faces.

"Us, the competition, everyone." said Fritzy, leaning back on his elbows. "If you make the right connections, it's like being part of a club."

"Or a loony family." Andy piped in.

"Like the mafia," growled the sullen Terry. It was the first thing he had said. Rod had thought that Ter had the slow, uncertain drawl of the dim-witted. But then Rod thought he might be under-estimating him; maybe Ter was high on something – in the middle of a drug squad barbie!

"Rod." One of the guys sitting behind Rod had decided to chime in. "Six months ago, one of our boys nicked a supplier. He wasn't a street dealer; he was one of the big players. A few weeks later, a gang chased our boy while he was coming out of the pictures with his girlfriend. They caught him and beat the shit out of him. He almost died."

"One of the bastards bit a chunk out of his leg the size of your fist." said Andy, almost spitting blood himself. "The bastards are looking out for each other by targeting the squad."

"They're fucking cannibals," said Fritzy.

"Fucking cannibals," repeated Terry, in his pedestrian drawl. Rod was getting the certain feeling that Terry wasn't the sharpest tool in the box.

Everyone was looking at Andy's brother closely, expecting a reaction to what he'd just been told. "Jesus," Rod said, trying to force some anger into his voice, "that's madness. What are those stupid pricks thinking of? Beating the shit out of a copper and his girl is way beyond the pale."

46

Rod had a problem with showing his anger: the problem was that it took forever for him to get angry. He wasn't very good at the fly-off-the-handle thing. It took time for anger to swirl around Rod's body, gathering up energy, picking up the signals – the tightness in the throat, the loaded nerves and the shiver of mobilised adrenaline. There was only one thing that could make Rod rise to instantaneous anger: treachery. Boy, when someone backstabbed Rod, you wouldn't believe how fast that guy's fists would fly. Double-dealing and deviousness could elevate Rod to punching out teeth and breaking noses within seconds. Everyone who knew him thought that it was a good thing that Rod Tremblett was slow to anger.

47

"We have a responsibility, Rod." Fritzy was moving in closer again. "We've got to do something about it. We've got to crack down on those scum."

"We've got to protect our own, Bro." Andy was looking at him intensely.

"But what about the system? The force will take care of those bastards." Rod could tell that this wasn't what these guys wanted to hear.

"You think the system is working?" asked the guy sitting behind him. Rod turned around and asked, " Why shouldn't I?"

"Jesus, Bro. Somebody has to fight these bastards. They're taking over!" Andy had a crazy look in his eye.

Fritzy continued where Andy had left off. "It's not just us that risks violence now Rod. They're a threat to our families, our wives and kids."

Then the guy sitting behind him started up again. "The smirks on the faces of the dealers as they emerge from the courts are not just smiles of relief, Rod. They're laughing at the system. Decades of 'let's be nice to the criminals' have brought the system to its knees."

Andy leaned forward and put his hand on his brother's knee.

"Rod, we're fighting back. We're taking the fuckers on."

Just then, as if on cue, Anne came over with a tray-full of paper plates, plastic cutlery and napkins.

"Come on, Rod, Andy, get cooking. Everyone's waiting for their lunch."

Andy and Rod walked over to the barbie. Andy turned the gas up and started throwing bits of meat onto the grill. Rod was watching him closely. He didn't know what to think. Okay, there are always justifiable circumstances when you want to hit back. But without the system to look up to, what do we have? Rod knew he had to deal with psychos; anti-socials and prick-heads every day, but there are guys like that in the force too. The problem for Rod was – if he'd said anything like that to Andy and his friends, they'd have kicked him in the balls.

"So, what's Terry's story?" he asked his brother.

Rod's brother smiled an insider smile before he answered.

"Terry has a lot of talents, part-time debt-collector, part-time bouncer, and a full-time hard case. A couple of years ago, I stopped him a few times for possession, just a few spliffs, nothing serious. Anyway, so, soon after Terry comes across with some underworld intelligence. He gets to hear a lot of what's going down. And so now he's one of my paid narks."

"Bloody Hell, Andy, what's he doing here? When he first opened his mouth I thought he was on drugs. Why'd you invite him over to your home?"

Andy looked him straight in the eye.

"We sometimes use Ter as independent muscle."

"Muscle? Muscle for what?" The hair on the back of Rod's neck started to bristle when he heard the word muscle.

Andy lowered his eyes to the burger he was stabbing at. "He's going to sort out those fucking morons that gave it to you and Anne."

Rod couldn't believe what he'd just heard from the lips of his own brother, a fellow officer of the law.

"Jesus, Andy! We're cops remember, we're supposed to know the difference between the good guys and the bad guys."

"The system is on its last legs, Rod, you know that. If those dope-dealing scum are targeting us, then we're just trying to equal things up."

"Equal things up? Who the hell are you, Dirty-fucking-Harry? You know that the force likes nothing better than to shit on a copper that's gone over the line."

Rod realised that they were both shouting their heads off at each other. The guys sitting on the grass were looking at them and frowning. Fritzy put his finger to his lips.

"Hey, Ter," Andy called out, "Rod wants to know if you're doing drugs."

The guys all laughed. Except Terry. He just looked at Rod in a sad, bovine kind of way. Rod expected him to pipe up any second and say, "I smoked some marijuana once, but I didn't inhale." Instead he just looked at him with big dumb eyes. Rod didn't want to piss Terry off. Not even a little bit.

"Andy's just kidding, Ter. You know what he's like," he said, quickly.

Terry just nodded, slowly and deliberately. Then he folded his huge, wallopers' arms, looking like a seriously pissed-off Buddha.

"Prick." Rod hissed at Andy.

"It's okay, Bro, relax; the big guy's in my pocket. He only does damage to the people I tell him to. Now give me the address of the moron that fucked you over."

"I...haven't looked it up yet." Rod spluttered. He wanted to buy some time to think about what the hell was going on.

"Don't dick me around Rod. After what these guys have told you today, you're in whether you like it or not. Now give me the address."

"I've only got the driver's details." he admitted, "the passenger was the one who did the mouthing off."

"Okay. No matter. Terry will get to him after he's visited the driver."

"My note-book is in the car. I'll have to fetch it."

"Do it now." Andy insisted. He was probably afraid that if Rod had time to think, he'd change his mind. He was right too, he would have.

Two days later Rod called Andy on the phone and told him that he didn't want anything to do with his hit squad. He was backing out.

Andy had talked him around, promising him that Terry was only going to give those mouthy road-rage bastards a "mild slapping".

"He'll just put their eyes out of focus for a while," were Andy's exact words. But Rod couldn't imagine Terry doing anything 'mildly.'

48

Rod wondered if there was some universal law that describes how a minor disagreement suddenly becomes very serious indeed: something like Sod's Law or Murphy's Law? The verbal working over that the morons had given his family was suddenly metastasising into something much more pathologically sinister. He was already getting worried about what he'd got himself sucked into.

At first, Rod thought that Andy was doing all this retribution stuff as a favour to him. Then he realised that his brother was enjoying it, really enjoying it. Whenever he told Rod what he was arranging for those dick-heads, Andy's eyes would darken and his lips would pull back over his teeth. He reminded Rod of a shark getting ready for a feeding frenzy. Andy was going after those guys with the unflagging determination of a Great White. Rod had the dreadful feeling that those poor shmucks were going to suffer a bit more than a couple of black eyes and a bloody nose. He guessed that the morons were in real crowbar-wielding danger, so he decided to go and see Terry himself. Rod wanted to set out the agenda. He didn't mind the jerk-offs getting a hiding, but didn't want a massacre on his hands.

49

Walking into Terry's flat was like walking into a Natural History Museum diorama of 'The Dawn of Man'. Both Terry and his wife looked as yet untouched by the refining, humanising effects of Darwinian selection. The conjunctive-eyed couple gave the impression that they had spent a lot of time huddled over a smoky cave fire.

They were both troglodytically short and thick-set, with sallow, lardy skin stretched over big-boned frames and massive, slab-sized foreheads. His wife sported warts on her face bigger than a pregnant dog's nipples. The dank flat stank of wet dogs – despite the fact that they didn't have one. And there seemed to be an awful lot of empty banana skins lying around, the word, Neanderthal kept re-visiting Rod's forebrain as he gazed across the miasmic room at the couple. When Terry introduced him to his wife, she gave him a damp hand-shake, and gazed up at him with that dazed, happy look that you see on the faces of those Special Olympics participants when they're getting a well-fought-for medal hung around their neck. Her eyes were so darkly sunken that it looked like she was wearing a burglar's mask.

Despite his Cro-Magnon appearance – even in a freezing February he was still wearing his rubber flip-flops and a pair of exhausted jeans chopped off at the knees – Terry had a peculiar kind of dignity that could only be dealt with on its own terms. The big man was easily insulted, but could distinguish between accidental insults and the kind that are intentional. And he'd learned that instead of bashing people he took a dislike to, it was less trouble if he simply turned his wardrobe-sized back on them. Although much of Terry's talk was weird and rambling, his insights were shot through with a kind of primitive religiosity, mixed with a strong dose of prison-cell philosophy. "They're allowed one mistake," he once said, "Then I clip the fuckers." It was Terry's Cartesian summing up of his philosophical lore.

The Big Fella had an inordinate admiration for those people he thought were "intellectual" (everyone but himself) and he tried to talk as he thought "intellectuals" talked. Hence this kind of thing...

'Hey Ter, how's it going?'

"Fluctuating."

'What?'

"Everything's fluctuating, man. Nothin's crystallizing."

People spoke nervously to Terry; you really had to be on the ball when you said hi to the Big Fella. He could read, a little, but he couldn't write, at all. That's how he was always shuffling obsequiously down to the Citizen's Advice for some...well, advice. So Terry couldn't write, but get this: he wanted to be a writer. Yeah, it's true. Deep in the weird fluctuations of his massive heart, he wanted to be a writer. He didn't have any stories to tell, or adventures to relate; but he figured if he was a writer, he thought people would PAY ATTENTION to him. That poor sucker, hey, what a poor, naive, misguided sucker.

Have you noticed how people talk so loudly into their mobile phones these days; have you noticed how everyone is happy to live their private lives in the street, or in the park, or on the train? Maybe it's something to do with Terry's desire to be a writer; we all want people to PAY ATTENTION. Perhaps that's why they all talk loud enough for everyone to hear? This is a problem; we all know that. Pretty soon, we'll all be screaming our heads off in the street… "Look! Look at me! I just got fired from my job. Ain't that a fucking bitch!

Gazing ruefully around the room, Rod noticed a couple of plates on the table crouching beneath the window, smeared with some kind of travestied foodstuff – mammoth burger, or sabre-tooth rissole, a carcass of some Ice Age thing that demanded much grinding of molars. Terry's wife sat there with her arms folded over the outcrop of her stomach, cleaning her teeth with her tongue. Rod thought he was having trouble placing her ethnically, then he realised he was wrong. He was having trouble placing her as a species. The smell he had first thought was wet dog was actually the smell of blind-alley sapiens, of ruined evolution. With a fortifying swallow, he refused the cup of tea that was offered. Then he told Terry that he'd changed his mind about giving the morons a hiding. He said that he didn't want any part of the retribution thing that Andy and his drug squad friends were into.

Rod was going to file a traffic-violation report on the hooligans in the car – their behaviour was likely to cause a breach of the peace as well as being a danger to other road users – and leave it at that. As they talked, Terry just kept nodding his head, like one of those dogs in the back window of a slowly moving car. At regular intervals, he would look across at his wife, as though he was looking for some sort of constant re-assurance from her. (She never said a word to Rod the entire time he was there.) As Rod talked more about the moron thing, Terry began regularly interrupting him by asking his wife strange, un-contextual questions like, "I've never laid a finger on you. Have I love?" Terry's wife would smile her affirmation. And then, a short while later, while Rod was still in mid-sentence, he would suddenly come out with, "Not even a finger. Have I love?" She'd smile and nod

94

at him again. And then, later on Terry came out with, "Never even slapped you. Not even once, have I love?"

Rod wondered if the non-sequiturs were some kind of strange mating ritual. With all that talk of suppressed violence, maybe when he left, the Neanderthals would tear each other's clothes off in a terrifying frenzy of lust and sexual urgency. He suffered the horrible vision of their fat tongues passing back and forth into each other's wet, watermelon red mouths.

"You're a good boy, Terry. You're a good boy to your little wifey." Despite her enormous weight, her voice was surprisingly high-pitched and girlish. Rod thought her voice was strangely, improbably musical, what with all the gravity pulling down on it. The furry-grey woman began murmuring impassionedly into Terry's gnarled and battered ear.

"Jesus! – Scary Fucking Movie, eh." Rod worried to himself.

He went over the story with Terry again, just to make sure he understood that he wanted him to back off. When the copper was sure he'd got the message through, he rose to leave.

"Errr..done it, Mr Tremblett." Terry suddenly blurted out.

"What? Done what Ter?" Rod asked tremulously. He had a terrible sinking feeling in his stomach, as though his entire life was starting to flush down his trouser legs.

"Those bad guys, the ones that dissed your missus and kids? They're done."

Rod could feel the blood draining from his face.

"Oh shit! For Chrissakes Ter, where are they? What have you done to them?"

Terry's chin flopped onto his chest. He looked crestfallen. Instead of the grateful thanks he'd expected, he was having his massive head bitten off. The big guy's ruminant face took on a look of utter dejection. His eyes started to get moist and his chin sank even further into his chest; he stared dejectedly down at his feet. His lumpy wife leaned over and put her podgy arm around his shoulder. Rod thought for a moment that the powerful guy was going to start blubbing.

"Ter, look at me!" Rod demanded, "You've been to that address Andy gave you, haven't you?"

Terry nodded slowly, and continued to look down at his feet. He was still unable to look up at the fulminating copper.

"You've seen the guys that mouthed off at my wife, yeah?"

Terry nodded again, almost imperceptibly.

"What did you do to them?" Rod asked, although he didn't really want to know.

"In hospital," Terry mumbled, "broke their legs."

"Oh shit, no!" Rod slammed his right fist into the palm of his left hand in a helpless gesture of fear and frustration. What the fuck had he turned loose? What had he done? The numbed traffic cop ran from the flat without bothering with any of the niceties of saying goodbye.

50

The two brothers met in a pub car park. When Rod climbed into his brother's car he noticed a magazine that Andy had been reading, now tossed onto the dash. It was called: Police Review. But he also knew that Andy had a book in the glove compartment called: Power: And How to Use It. When a copper starts reading a book like Power, it is tantamount to making a proclamation. It's saying: beware the copper with Power in his glove compartment, beware his avid eyes, his lips parted in amusement and recognition, because those coppers don't stop, in the fights and frights those coppers are always inordinate, because when they start, they don't stop. They are the kind of coppers who know what the word loophole means. Andy was a good copper, a professional, or so he thought. A copper fit for the twenty-first century; where every rule is contingent and all validity is blurred; where every line in the sand is smeared by prejudice and expediency.

"I've just been to see the fallout from what you arranged with Terry. What the hell's happened to you, Andy? You're running around like a Mossad agent with an M16 trigger-happy attitude to enforcing the law. What kind of law enforcement is beating the crap out of people?"

"It's the law of the tooth and the fang, Bro. Those bastards sank lower than whale-shit when they picked on a woman and her kids. They only got what they deserved. Anyway, the fat is in the fire and it's too late to pull it out again."

For the next few minutes there was silence between them. They both gazed out of the car's windows at the passing traffic. Then Andy looked at his watch and opened the car door, "I'm sorry you feel that way, Rod, I had plans for you. Anyway, I'm off. I've wasted a couple of hours already." He looked at Rod with a half a grin and walked back to his own car. "Call me when you've calmed down."

51

As he drove distractedly home, Rod was wondering – why do we men like to break everything? Bones, bodies, homes, even the planet. Why do us men destroy with such fierceness, such malicious exhilaration? We've even broken the very air we breath, wrecked the dioxide-heavy, ozone-depleted sky; slashed and burned the life-giving, green lungs of the forests, soiled the inky, oil-scummy seas. He realised that humanity's destruction is almost total: no other wild animal could have been more thorough. And Rod knew, in the spongy core of his heart, that finally, when all humanity was gone, and the weeping and wailing went quiet, there would be no one left to say 'Sorry!' And would humanity have any last words? A harsh groan, a confuted, brotherly gasp? You'd swear that we hated our planet, the way that we humiliate it at every turn.

52

What a day he'd had! What the hell had happened to it? It had started out a beautiful summer's morning with a cloudless sky, 68 Fahrenheit and just a slight breeze. Whatever happened to it? After starting off as a good-to-be-alive day it had ended up a horrible ordeal: the sort of day that gives you the inkling that nothing really matters: not even life itself. On days like those, Rod couldn't stop himself thinking; how dismal if this is all there is – life's constant panic, its traps and pits and nothing-makes-any-sense. But he tried not to think too deeply about it, because if he thought about it for too long he'd lose all his strength and the stubbornness would melt from him like an ice dome on the Taj Mahal. He'd give up hoping and end up lying on the floor weeping and shouting for help.

That night, Rod told Anne about the hiding that had been arranged for the morons. She was upset that their friends might try to hit back at her family. Of course there was no way, they wouldn't even know who did it. But Anne had always been nervous about being left alone at nights; so she insisted that they had a burglar alarm fitted. As he lay in bed, Rod couldn't stop thinking about the young tearaways' broken bodies lying in the same ward of the Heath hospital. He felt bone weary. The last thing Rod thought about before he found sleep was the hiding that his brother had organised for the morons. He whispered internally to himself, 'At least there was no fucking around with paperwork. And those morons weren't worth a fart in a bottle anyway.'

Now Rod was moaning in his sleep. The woman beside him, his wife, was awakened by his vocal dredgings. She turned, and laid a hand on his bare shoulder. There was a frown on her strained face as she shook him; like the venom-spitting face of someone you've just undertaken on the inside lane of the motorway. Anne knew all about Rod's moaning in his sleep; she was a wronged woman, and she had Rod's moaning down cold. It was her husband's moaning in his sleep that had once alerted her to the heart-tearing business of his betrayal. Rod had had a brief affair with a woman police officer that had worked with him at the same station, and once alerted by his nighttime moaning, Anne had doggedly found out.

After the rows, the passionate rows with their disgraceful name-calling came the mental spitting and salivating, the silences. Oh, men do silences too. They certainly do – but women can take their silences further; silence is a natural resource for women, alongside tears and the impassioned look. In the purulent game of toxic silences, compared to men, women are natural born mutes. So, after all the screaming rows came the silences, unrolled with torn thoughts and buckled feelings, silences more dramatic than yelled words. And as Anne had consumed her brain and heart, Rod drank; managing to get through a ton of beer and whisky while her silences milled around his aching head, accompanied always by an advanced guard of extravagant tears. He swore that it wasn't worth it; those ramshackle shags in the back of his patrol car were never worth all of this agony. Anne's steady-state silences turned him into something you'd find in a black bin-bag behind the house where quintuplets had recently been brought home from the hospital.

"All this shit for one little infidelity," Rod had whined to his brother, "Why did that stupid fucking WPC have to brag to all her friends about it? Anne was bound to find out."

Rod had a habit of barging through any share of guilt that came his way: "I couldn't believe that silly bitch was spreading it all over the station." And so it was that Anne did find out. Oh, she found out all right.

Andy didn't know what to say to his brother as he moaned and writhed in his powder-keg predicament. He was unsure what to say because despite his own adoring wife, he was in love with Anne himself, and had been for a very long time. So Andy kept silent; and bided his time.

"I think she might leave me for this one," Rod morosely grumbled.

Andy's face looked up, his grey eyes brightening. There was a burble of anticipation in his throat, a low-level sensing of opportunity. He leaned back into the pub chair and began rhythmically sighing and whinnying. Fortunately, Rod couldn't see the tarnished intentions rising behind his brother's eyes. And it was a seriously good thing that he couldn't.

"Bad luck," Andy finally said.

"Bad fucking luck! Is that all you can say?"

Andy's chest rose and fell in his immaculately ironed shirt.

"She won't leave you," he said, with a crushed sigh.

And Rod knew that his brother was right; Anne would never leave him. She'd ask him to leave instead. And he would have to leave. After telling his sons that he would never, ever, ever, stop loving them, he could see himself slouching towards his car with a heavy suitcase, a feeling like sea-sickness creeping over him while he tried not to show his ready-for-bed boys that he was crying. Crying his culpable, lying heart out.

53

Rod had only recently been allowed to creep back onto the ring-road of Anne's affections, still all freezing fog, black-ice and whiplash, but at least their sex-life had been partly resuscitated. For Rod, having dreary sex with his victimised wife was like listening to piped music, close to therapy, the language of calming compliance. Even this had taken much time and stolid grovelling – with many pitiless reminders of his infraction. The sex was bad, but at least it took his mind off the fear: the fear of losing everything.

That married-sex thing works well, doesn't it? It's an excellent institution, married-sex. Because married people only have sex when they really, badly need it; when they can't have sex with anybody else. And you can tell that's the case by the quality of the sex. Married-sex is nearly always well laundered and expurgated, purposefully restrained so not to damage or injure anyone's feelings or sensitivities.

Since his little indiscretion, Anne and Rod had stayed married for the kids; meekly chalking up each passing year as a losing dart player might chalk up his pathetic scores. Anne now felt her failing marriage like mildew growing on her heart. When her eldest boy had admiringly said to her one day, "Doesn't Daddy look great in his uniform?" she had replied, "He looks okay, I suppose." Anne rendered her husband praise like a dentist pulling teeth. Whenever she thought of Rod, she always pictured him in flagrante delicto, lying on a rug in front of a log fire with his tarty girlfriend; sighing at the very limit of male sexual rapture.

Anne sometimes wished that her husband wasn't that attractive, wasn't that handsome. His smouldering good looks, dark and dangerous as a Pompeiian sky, had caused the terrible travail they were now in. These days, Anne would describe her own looks as ordinary, falling apart ordinary. And sometimes, with a horror-movie gulp, she would look at her kids and imagine her youthful good looks as a painful residue on the surface of a twice-visited birthing-pool.

Every morning, she looked into the heftily looming bathroom mirror, and swore at it. "Forty three…it's just a number. Like any other." But the implacable mirror told

Anne that she looked incredibly old, incredibly tired; her chastising reflection told her that her face was burned out, post-Apocalyptic. No matter which way she angled her head trying to catch a more easily foolable patch of light, a less cruel oval of illumination, Anne felt no connection with the visage that glowered out at her from the depths of the glass. It was a false face, an inauthentic face, and a fraudulent misrepresentation of her true looks. Anne had friends who had taken to avoiding mirrors; those people believed that they looked okay, that they could pass for normal for their age. But after just one misjudged glance in a mirror, they were suddenly spending a fortune on botox and plastic surgery.

Anne didn't really mind the number of years, but she did mind the frowning face that stared out at her from the mirror, with its straight hair, and its strict mouth; its low-lidded brown eyes. Later she would sit on the stool at her dressing table, sorting through the expensive pigments and colourings of her make-up box. As she fearfully noted the flesh of her face creeping downwards, she sorted the lambent lineaments neatly, wearily, in rising spasms of distress. When she finally roused herself to put on her make-up, she would close the curtains and put on the electric light, closing out the harsh daylight that flipped cruelly, photographically, through the bedroom window.

Anne Tremblett resented the coarsening snatch of time and the intransigent stress upon her face. But what could she do…the knife, or some mad chemist's squalid concoction? No, that wasn't really the kind of thing Anne wanted. She just wanted her peace of mind back: before it got ripped and torn, before she looked so awful.

"Rod, what's the matter?" she turned over and asked, irritably.

Rod drowsily raised an arm above his head and tousled his flattened hair. "Mmm…what?" he groaned from the shallows of arrested sleep.

"What wrong?" Anne asked again.

"Nothing. Nothing's wrong."

Anne sighed herself, then turned over again and gave her pillow a good slapping, as though it were suffering from a spontaneous attack of hysteria.

"You were moaning in your sleep," she snapped.

And there they lay, facing away from each other, disgruntled and petulant in the reproaching antipodes of the marital bed. But for all her marriage's weight and compromise, when Anne had asked Rod to leave after one of their shrapnel-whirring rows, she'd then tearfully and silently begged him – internally prompting him – "Don't leave me. Please don't leave me yet."

54

In the morning, Rod awoke at six. He needed no alarm clock: even in his sleep he was already alarmed. Looking in at the boys, he tucked his youngest lad's arm back under the bed-sheet. The boy sighed complacently and snuggled himself down, pulling the sheet over his head as though sheltering from some unexpectedly frosty breath. Then Rod made his way down to the Nordic stoicism of their new Ikea kitchen, with its beech and marble-topped deference, its bleak chrome and stainless steel shimmering. Plugging in the kettle, and then staring out at the garden through the kitchen window, he felt as though he had awoken in another country; at once very threatening and dangerous, and at the same time exciting and impulsive.

Rod was still in a kind of shock about what Terry had done, but not the kind of shock he had expected. That saying about vengeance being sweet, oh man, it's spot on. It's bang on the fucking button; vengeance is sweeter than a whole jar of honey. It dawned upon Rod that if he hadn't been scared that someone would have grassed him out, he'd have taken an axe-handle to those bastards who frightened his wife and kids himself. That was the revelationary moment for Rod Tremblett; he realised right then that he'd crossed the line. Whatever the line was.

He called Andy to smooth things over. Rod told him that he was okay with the situation, but his brother didn't want to discuss it over the phone so they arranged to meet for a few drinks down at the police club that night. When Rod got there, Andy was sat amongst a group of his drug squad cronies. They sat together squabbling companionably with the familiar assurance of men who have sat and argued many times before; the camaraderie that held them was unforced.

55

The police-club scene was a fart-powered production of matey-ness, with its implied getting in at two, three, four, in the morning; coming home pissed with the prismatic rays of a new day. Taking in the tableau vivant of bonhomie, of shiny, sweaty, laughing testosterone, Rod decided to get himself a pint and to sit down on the edge of the group. He wasn't getting into a round with that boozy lot; diving into that whirlpool of sociability would cost him a fortune in drinks. The guys were getting drunk amongst the usual cacophony of male discourse, discussing male-pattern baldness, offering pitilessly crude stories about ex-girlfriends and telling jokes about the latest politician to be caught-out over his volatile love life.

The drug squad guys that Rod had met at Andy's barbecue were all there. Fritzy was now holding forth: "He should have fucked her up the arse."

"What? Why?" laughed Andy.

"If he'd fucked up the arse she'd never have gone to the newspapers, would she? She'd have kept her whining mouth shut."

Everyone was looking at Fritzy with knotted frowns on their faces.

"Besides, he should have fucked her in the arse because it's a tradition. All politicians like to fuck people up the arse."

The betting was, that in the next parliamentary term, the prurient, priapic MP's would bring in a law that all spurned women must carry a government health warning. When the laughter had died down, Andy looked over at his brother and waved a hand, pointing to the bench seat beside him. As Rod squeezed in, Andy leaned over and asked, "Everything okay?"

Rod nodded and smiled, "Yeah. Everything's fine."

"You sure?"

Still smiling, Rod winked and took a sip from his pint.

"You're okay with it then, yeah?" Andy persisted.

"I'm very okay with it, Andy."

"Good. In that case I've got some news for you."

Andy picked up his glass and held it up as if to make a toast.

"Gentlemen, I present to you our newest colleague. My Bro is joining us on the squad."

Rod must have looked completely startled when Andy said that, because his brother followed it up with a hefty slap on his back, "Aren't you, Bro?"

"If you say so, Andy." Rod shrugged his stinging shoulders.

"I certainly do say so Bro. The word's gone in with the Boss."

Then he clapped him on the knee with the palm of his hand.

"Tomorrow your super will be getting a call to push your transfer through."

"Jesus, Andy! That's fantastic. But what about that bloody DC's exam, and the interview?"

"Come on, Rod," Andy said, irritably, "the word is going in. With a bit of luck, next month you'll be on the team. Now get the fucking drinks in."

An astonished Rod sat there for a moment, speechless. He had been working hard for over a year for that exam, and now it had just been waved away without a second thought. He couldn't help wondering why.

"Hey guys, it's Rod's round. Isn't it, Bro?"

Andy handed him his empty glass.

"Yeah, sure. The next one's on me, guys."

As a dozen empty glasses were simultaneously slammed onto the table in front of Rod, the traffic cop hoped there would be a decent salary increase as a drug squad detective constable; otherwise he couldn't afford the job. Just as he finished that thought, Andy leaned over and whispered, "Don't worry about the money, Bro. Pretty soon, you're going to be making more loot than you've ever seen" With unthinking naiveté, Rod wondered what the hell his brother was talking about.

56

Motley couldn't believe how well things were working out for everyone. Sweep was moving in with his newfound girlfriend, and he'd reluctantly agreed that his daughter could move in with Motley. Perfect.

It was astonishing to see the difference in old Sweep; he spent every minute he could with his fantastically round, deep-mouthed woman. It was almost sickening to hear him talk about her. Listening to a middle-aged guy talking about love is like listening to an outrageously over-the-top country-music album. It's so maudlingly saccharin you'll never need another sugar in your tea in your entire life.

A fortnight before Motley and Rachel moved into the flat, he and Rachel had a slap-up dinner at a restaurant over on the waterfront, and then stopped off for a few drinks at the wine-bar. He couldn't help noticing that Jelly-Hair was giving him the evil-eye, like he'd just pissed all over her french-fries. Motley just ignored her. Later on, he dropped Rachel off at her dad's and drove back to his sister's house. He went straight to bed, and thought about the first time they had made love, right there, on the single bed he was lying in. Motley always tried to think of something happy before going to sleep. It helped to keep the nightmares at bay.

As he closed his eyes on the shadowy room, Motley remembered Rachel calling him a chauvinist pig. The fact was that he'd never really minded being called a chauvinist, for one simple reason. No woman has EVER had a fantasy about being tied to a bed and sexually ravished by a pinny-wearing, duster-flicking New Man. So, in his tired mind, Motley celebrated his newfound status as a chauvinist with a satisfied chuckle.

Motley couldn't help laughing wryly to himself. Rachel was probably right about the chauvinist thing; previously, the most expensive present he had ever bought a girlfriend was a fridge magnet. And, before Rachel, he felt could shag his woman anytime, anywhere and without the bother of foreplay. With all the other women he'd known, foreplay from Motley had usually been, "Lie down, shut-the-fuck-up, and hold on tight." He remembered, with shrill clarity, asking one girl that he was trying to finish with if she'd had ever had an orgasm when they'd made love. She had replied caustically, "Yeah, but not the kind of orgasm you're thinking of."

"So what kind of orgasms were they then?" Motley had asked, stupidly.

"The kind a girl has when she doesn't actually come," she'd spat, triumphantly. That can't be true can it? Motley had asked himself disbelievingly – girls don't fake it, do they? Jesus, they'll be telling me next that professional wrestling is faked.

57

Sweep had warned his overconfident friend to be wary of
Jelly-Hair; they were doing too nicely to have it all screwed
up by her: "Whenever she looks at you she's got venom in
her face." And Motley had to admit that it was true. It's hard
to describe Jelly-Hair's face: it had subsidiary faces hidden
within it, to be shown depending on who was observing it.
Her face multiplied and bisected itself like some bacteria in
a petrie-dish. When a handsome guy came in through the
wine-bar door and approached the long, elbow-worn bar, her
face would glow and beam under the high noon of the guy's
good looks. But if a guy came in who failed to measure up
to her sexual patronage, she would fold her arms and glare
at him. Her plain-speaking face would then become
hardened and primed, like a hand-grenade that was ready to
explode.

The Friday night after Sweep had warned Motley about
Jelly-Hair, they were both at the wine-bar having an after-
work drink when he stopped Motley in mid-sentence and
nodded for him to look around. Two guys dressed in
identical ill-fitting, pinstriped BHS suits were standing at the
other end of the bar. They both had their hair cut very short
and were checking out the bar with the kind of beagle-eyed
'res judicata' of the professional pursuer.

"Fucking cops, I bet," Sweep said.

"Yeah. So?" Motley asked, "I've noticed a few of the
bastards coming in here. You can tell they're cops by the
sleazy tang they leave in the air. So, what the hell should we
care if a few cops drop in for a drink?"

"Just letting you know, that's all."

"Sod 'em. They'll probably get themselves a half of
bitter each and then leave. Those cheap bastards can't afford
the prices they charge in this place."

Sweep and Motley went back to their conversation, but Motley kept glancing over his shoulder to check what was going on down the other end of the bar. Eventually, Sweep went home to his ever-ready squeeze and Motley was left sitting at the bar alone. He gave the two coppers his full, discreet, nail gnawing attention; reminding himself that that he was a drug dealer, and that's what he was getting paid for – giving the police his full attention. He reminded himself too, that he had a great future in the pharmaceutical business: hey, it's the money, genius.

58

The two men stood at the bar. Both faces were lean and fit looking, with two sets of grey eyes feeding on the ample flesh of Jelly-Hair's ventilated cleavage. The space the policemen's bodies occupied was exaggerated by their overloaded laughter and telegraphed arm movements: they were sending out the concentrated solidity of males defining their territories. A silent "Get the Fuck Away" emanated from their every movement like the infrasound thrumming of an approaching bomber group. The pair of Alpha males hummed with an alarming, declaratory pulsation.

The two guys must be brothers, thought Motley. They had similar looks and build. One of the two was louder and more outgoing. Mr Loud seemed to know Motley's bete noire who stood behind the bar, chatting to the two cops. Mr Loud introduced the other guy to her. Then Mr Quiet leaned over the bar and offered his hand, saying "Good to meet you." The way he took Jelly-Hair's hand, there was an unmissable undertow of flustered sexual attraction.

Jelly-Hair's normally mineral-white face now glowed as though she was drunk. She shook her paw up and down enthusiastically. Then she tipped her head back and exposed her neck, pushing her pink-veined cleavage forward. It was an animal advertisement that telegraphed 'access all areas.'

Motley could feel the choppy waves of male/female desire crashing against the bar, swirling around the single-file archipelago of chrome and leatherette barstools.

"Fuck it!" Motley said to himself; "the cops are chatting up old Jelly-Hair!"

59

You can't help noticing how effortless policemen are when they're off-duty, how in control, how in tune they always are. Both coppers were gazing around the bar with those accusatory looks that seem to say, 'You're all lip, you are. All fucking mouth.' Motley couldn't help laughing to himself. Most people's usual reaction to those nostril-flared, intimidatory looks (the reaction the coppers want) was, 'You're right; I've done some awful things. I'm sorry.' But when their gaze fell upon Motley, all he wanted to say was: 'Screw you, you corrupt, mother-fucking cock-suckers!'

Motley noticed that both guys were wearing wedding rings, and yet it was obvious: the horny bastards were on the pull for some illicit pussy. Mr Loud tugged at his ear as he chatted to the barmaid; the body language told Motley that the policeman was lying his head off. The pair looked arrogant and full of themselves; they looked the sort of culpable, brutalised coppers that regard fitting up innocent people and beating the shit out of miscreants as a vital part of good police work. But then, all coppers looked like that to Motley.

"He's very witty isn't he," he heard Jelly-Hair squeaking after some quip from Mr Quiet. She gratefully took in the twin smiles of her supplicants and then added, "So what jew two do then?"

Mr Loud leaned over and whispered something into her ear, and Motley fancied that this something wasn't a proposition.

"Izzatso! Really?" Jelly-Hair chirped, "that's very interesting."

She broke off her conversation with the cops and looked over at Motley, raking him with the rat-tat-tat of her machine-gun gaze. He could feel a ridiculous noose closing around his neck. Motley was becoming deeply flustered. Flustered enough to down his drink and get the fuck out of there. As he left the bar, the two coppers were ordering more drinks and Jelly-Hair was laughing her tits off at some joke the cops were telling.

When Motley got to his car, he lit up a spliff, just to calm himself down. His mind was racing – what the fuck would Jelly-Hair say to those coppers about him and Sweep? She was obviously aware of their little pharmaceutical enterprise. Luckily, Motley was holding some excellent cocaine at his sister's; some really fucking excellent stuff. He was certainly going to need to snort a few lines of that Charlie when he got home.

Motley was feeling exposed and badly shaken. His chest hair was standing up as though he was moving about in the cross hairs of some fedayeen sniper's sights. If he'd been a fan of the sixty's Beat Poets – like me – the miscreant Motley would have felt a pang of communion with a line from an old Ginsberg poem: '…they have poured shit on you…they have built a wall of shit around you.'

Why did he have to take the piss out of her, why did he bother making an enemy of her? What had made him want to crank her up and peel away her friable feelings? If only he hadn't, if only he didn't, if only it wouldn't. He could have just returned the sanction of her un-recognition and left it at that. Motley had a really BAD feeling. Bollocks! What the hell was the Filth chatting with her for?

60

Of course Motley should have realised that when you decide to really piss someone off, you don't just piss the one person off. That one person unpacks like a series of Russian dolls, one inside the other; in effect, you piss off a whole telephone book of people. Make one cry and they all cry. Then they all become freighted with vengeance; a whole compendium of reciprocity is unwittingly produced, and everyone is suddenly hungry to chew your fucking balls off.

The coke lay on its opened foil, coolly waiting and ready to use its obsessive power to settle life's belligerent scores. As far as we know, Life is all there is, but, when cocaine shakes its head, Life goes away for a while, leaving you to your romantic notions. The Charlie was a yellow-creamy colour; its powdered granules lumped together into a tiny cairn of spontaneous convalescence. It looked good. Taking out his credit card, Motley chopped himself a couple of solid lines, rolled a Charles Darwin (a tenner), and snorted them up: "Christ! This shit makes your head reel!" Running its electric currents across his hunched and scrimmaged synapses, the coke quickly began its erasing and douching, cleaning and polishing the day's shit-ridden effluent from his mind like a neurological steam-jet. Reality was being tugged and kneaded, quickly becoming tractable, a coherent delusion providing fodder for his fantasies, technicolor screenplays for his dreams. The drug allowed him to cancel out the day's disasters. A delusion of well-being was moving rapidly across his cerebral- cortex, making life beautiful, ethereal, newborn.

Motley felt a trickle in the veins that fed his nasal cavities, a familiar pacifying movement in the vents of blood. A more joyful world seeped through a hole in the floor of his mind; a world ringed by scented candles, where knowingness was only vague, and cause and effect never came around. If love is the most you can feel, then cocaine is like falling in love 7000 times all at once – and all your loves love you back. It's no wonder that cocaine is the most popular drug.

As he lay on his bed waiting for the private language of the drugged mind to start gabbling on, Motley felt himself slipping down a tipping deck, sliding towards a raging sea of denunciation. Even as the Charlie was kicking in, he was still so twitchy that he was even tempted to put his hands together in prayer. What Motley needed to know was the inside story with those plain-clothed coppers. Who were they, and what euphemistic corner of law enforcement did they operate in? If he could get the coppers' names, Toby was the man to find out what they were into. Toby worked on the City Desk and he could certainly do the necessary digging around.

For Motley, that coke was awesome, as God-sent as Jesus, and he soon got loaded up on it. He spent the next few hours lying in his bedroom, laughing and smiling under the gaze of a happy god that he didn't even believe in. The Benign Being came down to the level of the rooftops and just stared in through the window at him. Motley was as happy as Christmas; gurgling and chuckling like a little child. The lenient god just looked at him with eyes bright as full-beam headlights, His powerful gaze reaching into corners, cleansing, divining; doing the things that are normal for gods. Then Motley saw the insubstantial Him shake his head and say: "I gave my Son, for this?"

Yeahhh…it's true…that's what He said. That's what the Divine One said to poor old shitfaced Motley! I mean can you believe that? You know what, there's just no telling with those gods, is there? First there was that apple rumpus in the Garden of Eden, and now we've got the downer on drugs! I mean…come on! Jesus, you just don't know what the fuck's going to piss those gods off next, do you?

As he snuggled into his warm inner reverie, Motley wiped away a gob of coke-shimmered mucus from the rim of his upper lip and lay there, listening to the drug-enhanced, late-night sound-track from the streets of the estate. A rumbling medley of revving car engines, air-curving stereos and police sirens drifted in through his window. Through the open window he could hear the embattled pavements getting ready to crack; whirring walls of clotted air hovered uneasily above the ground. Motley could hear the street's hysteria, feel its animus; the street's disaffected breath brushed his face like a distempered breeze.

61

The doped-up Motley could hear people arguing and shouting down in the street; going at it over half a can of Special Brew, over who's round it was to flash the ash: "Arf a mo...I flashed 'em onna fucking bus. 'S yoor turn you fuckin' wanker." Drunks were whimpering and panting their random dispensations; the feral street-kids were boiling and howling. The turbulent canyons of Canton and Ely and Grangetown were full of spectacular screams. They can't stop them, you see; they just can't keep the screams out, because it's easy to scream when you live on the breaking line, and you might break at any minute. If you live among the communal Opposition for too long, your rawness becomes numb. And like a dog panting helplessly in the hot sun you're too weary to move away from the pain, and you just want the next thing to happen quickly, whatever it is. Even if it's just another grievous gust of blast-furnace heat.

For Motley, it was only a question of returning to the iniquitous streets, a re-entry into their stratospheric harshness. But Rachel had no notion of how the streets can mangle your life and murder your soul. The stacked and staggered estates wait until you're not looking, then they ravish your innocence, do violence to you, scalloping out the bits of you that once hovered around cheerfulness. Rachel would never survive on the estates, because those embattled streets are not like other streets. Those streets are drunk: they're drunk because their nerves can't take it anymore. And like all drunks they have a habit of getting easily enraged, of boiling and screaming and taunting. Those streets think they're special, but they're wrong. They're not special at all: they're the same as all drunks.

The drunken, booming streets were as loud as a holiday hotel. Wouldn't everyone feel so much better if they were like an Ibizan hotel – drunk all the time? But it's hard going, being drunk all the time: only the alcoholic streets seem to be able to manage it. And those unfortunates who are trying to stay sober are forever trying to cope with the puzzling, out-of-control streets. Motley wanted himself and Rachel out of the contamination, out of the whole risk area. Away from the bottom-feeders, the knife-carriers and the concrete boxes full of mad people. You'd go mad yourself if you stayed too long on those atavistic streets – it happens to everyone. You would start to smash, like fragile crystal that has been struck too hard. If we all had to live on the ramshackle estates, we would all smash each other along our breaking lines – Just look! Look at what we've done to each other!

62

You know what? I suppose my generation started all that – the loutish streets, with their voided eyes and their spectral, volatile faces. In the Sixties – I am a product of the Sixties – the streets were easy, the streets were genial co-operative pussycats. Okay, they were smoggy and nicotine-soaked and everyone coughed and sneezed all the time; but you never saw today's porno-shows of people chundering up day-glo curries or pissing on the pavements. We changed all that; I changed all that. I brought the streets low with Burger Power dirt, drink-hefted violence and its partners in crime.

Oh man, you should have seen me at my best (my most suave and attractive); you should have clocked my imitation of The Omen girlie. All that acoustical puking, that dynamic pissing, you know something; changing things is a lot like being drunk all the time – it really takes it out of you. It's no wonder I'm old before my time.

Of course the streets would like to be civilized again, to regain some pride, dignity and self-discipline, but they've forgotten how. I changed the streets for the better, wouldn't you say? Look how glamorously mobile and spangled they are. They're a lot more violent now, I grant you, but violence is nothing new. The streets have always been scalded with violence and mutiny; they've always crackled with human distress and chaos. Maybe these days the violence, the carnage, the diabolism, is more randomly prompted; but if you existed on the same diet as the streets, you'd feel the same way. You just try existing for a month on a diet of pubs, drink, junk food and fighting, and see how you'd feel.

Beyond the post-apocalyptic estates, the burned-out cars and boarded-up shops, Motley's resplendent apartment waited over in the particularist Cardiff Bay, its chaste architecture patiently waited for its new master without the slightest concern. The disregarding flat was too cosseted, too protected in its gated driveway. It was too remote and uncomprehending to realise the peril that both it and its owner were in. In its comfortable enclave, it was too secure, too naive too see what was going on in the floundering world just a few blocks away. The flat was almost as close to Motley's heart as Rachel was. He had envisaged Rachel and him holed up in their love-nest forever. Friends would come and visit, Christmases and New Years would come and go, Popes would change, but Rachel and Motley would go on and on like Peter Pan and his babe in Never-never Land. Of course, life being the Great Prankster, the circumventive deceiver that it is, nothing ever goes smoothly for more than five minutes before decomposing into an extravagance of hideous carnage. Right then, Motley realised that his entire life, everything, was teetering on a knife-edge – "Life…you fucking inconsiderate, obdurate, dictatorial bastard!"

63

The next morning, when the buzz from the coke had worn off, the still-worried Motley went to the bathroom for a leak and took a glance at himself in the mirror. He felt a pang of disappointment. Motley barely recognised himself. He looked hunted and paranoiac, on the run like an intelligence-fingered terrorist. Motley looked so full of drug-dealing guilt that even he wanted to challenge himself; a few seconds more of staring into that mirror and Motley would have arrested himself.

Later that day, a counter-attacking Motley went around to the wine-bar and asked one of the girls to keep her ears open for anything Jelly-Hair might say about her two new friends. He didn't have to wait long. He popped into the bar that night and got the coppers' names, and, to his heart-stopping umbrage, he learned that they were both drug squad dicks. That put him into a filthy mood, so he decided to get pissed up. A guy Motley knew as an alcoholic, out-of-luck ex-journalist friend of Sweep's was sitting in one of the booze-blearied cubicles. That unpalatable looking guy was, me.

64

Sipping a large whisky, I was quietly sitting in one of the booths reading a two day-old copy of the South Wales Mail. Motley nodded recognition and came sauntering over. He looked like he needed someone to talk to. Maybe he was hoping for an inspirational conversation from an imaginative scribbler. Instead, he got a piss-head potboiling fabulist. Anyway, he plonked himself down at my table.

"Jesus, Lewie, what you been doin' to yourself? You look as rough as pig's breakfast." I just flashed him a thin smile and nodded lightly. "So how's it bouncing? Wanna another drunk...I'm mean, another drink?" He was slurring his words and his head swayed around unsteadily.

I shook my own head from side to side. "No, I'm fine. Thanks."

"I read one of your books the other day," he continued, "you know the one, the stories about the Cardiff drug scene. When I was reading it, I was thinking; what's all this crap, this guy's full of shit, he knows diddly-squat about the drug scene. Thought it was a bit of a shambles, really. Sorry."

He said the word 'sorry' with such obvious disdain that it left a dent in my forehead. I just smiled a weak smile, shrugged my shoulders and took another gulp from my drink. Then Motley asked me what I really thought about the all the pushers and poppers that I wrote about.

I thought for a moment then said softly, "I write what I write – that's all."

Not much of an answer for a writer, I suppose. Motley must have been disappointedly thinking – it's always the fucking same, isn't it; the ones that go on-and-bloody-on about something are always the ones who know the least about it.

For a fleeting moment, I thought about asking him: come on Taff, what's it feel like? You're young, you're making more money than you've ever seen, and you've got a great future. Come on Taff, what's it feel like? Of course I didn't need to ask, because I already knew what it felt like: it doesn't feel like anything. Because when things are looking good, it doesn't feel like anything.

Motley had a malign look in his eyes. "Hey, when I was in the slammer up in Colchester, they used to organise writers and poets to come in and give us readings. Trying to educate us I suppose. Anyway, one day this hotshot London crime writer guy came in and the first thing he said was, 'Guess what, guys? I got laid last night, when was the last time you lot got laid?' Jesus, what a stupid thing to say! There was a fucking riot. The boys wrecked the entire recreational block and put that smart-arsed prick on the critical list." I answered his unpalatable story with another weak smile.

"So, do you do readings?" He asked, as though his interest was personal.

"Only if I've got a book to launch. I try to avoid them. They can't afford me."

"Mmm…maybe someone should write a book about all the shit that I've been through." The grim faced Motley gave me a cold look, and then told me that he would bet that I hadn't smoked more than a couple of spliffs in my whole life. I couldn't be bothered to tell him that I'd been off my face last night.

"So, you used to be a journo, like Sweep."

I nodded.

"What's the difference between a writer and a journalist, then?" he pugilistically asked. And that's the problem for us writers, when it comes to conversation we can be a tad taciturn – we usually have little time for chatting, we're too busy talking to ourselves. I didn't want to get into that kind of conversation, but Motley had wound me up, so I tried to give him the most aphoristic answer I could think of.

"The difference between a writer and a journalist, is that the writer gets up in the middle of the night to write something down."

"Uh?" Motley screwed up his forehead. "What the fuck does that mean? You're not taking a liberty are you?"

"Wouldn't dream of it."

"So, what is the difference?"

I gave Motley a straight look; okay, he was asking for it.

"A writer is someone who sweats over a single word, who weeps blood to find the perfect sentence. A writer will reach down his own throat and tear out his guts in search of an original phrase."

"Yeah…so what about the journalist?"

"A journalist can write a thousand words when he's blind drunk and pissing in a pot while getting his hair cut."

"Pssh…you troubled writers, eh? You think you're as sharp as nails but you're all piss and tantrums. You're all as mad as maggots, aren't you, eh?"

Two minutes after that drunken diatribe, I got up to leave. As I mooched past him towards the door like a scuba diver sinking into a murky sea, I just caught his final words aimed at my back, "Taking a walk, eh…mopey bastard." I pulled up my coat collar and yanked cravenly at the brass door handle. (If someone ever thinks of making a film of this book – I'm a Johnny Depp look a-like; five eight short, with sad brown eyes and a gloomy-Celt look. And I'm a mean mother-fucker who don't take shit from nobody. Right?)

65

A couple of hours later Motley was off his face, leaning on the wall of the old boarded-up Royal Hotel in St Mary's Street, directly opposite the wine-bar. He stood beneath the weepy clouds and the smiting rain, amid the dirty concrete corsetry of St Mary's Street. He took a defiant suck on the spliff he was holding. The bad news he'd been given about the coppers had shattered him. He felt like screaming with bafflement and incredulity: "This isn't fair. This is not fucking happening. Why do things always happen to me," he moaned, eloquently, "Once you've got form, things always happen to you. Awful things." Motley shook his head sorrowfully from side to side, "Everything's going along fine, just fine. And then Life splits your face open with one of its fucking head-butts." The glare from the neon streetlights was no longer fixed or stable, the weed was cutting in. Everything still looked like shit, but the pile of shit didn't look so impressive as it did ten minutes ago. This is what the ganja genies do for you: 'Mmmm…shit.'

Motley silently gazed at the stream of traffic choking the cheerless street, watching its poisonous tail-to-tail snake curving away to the Hayes and on down to the waterfront. The line of traffic wore its standard sneer of self-sufficiency. Each mad-eyed driver was determined to snag a space in the line; whatever the shame attached. The air was full of engine screams, horn hoots and ozone-eating breath. The crisis-torn consciousness of the panicked drug-dealer was suddenly telling him that there was something very wrong about the way the world was revealing itself to him.

"Oh man. Everything is so fucked-over; nothing is ever what it pretends to be. How come everything is always upside down to what we all see? How can we put our trust in the future? How can we put our trust in anything?"

Convinced that nothing is ever the way it appears, Motley was beginning to think that reality itself was a bloody good joke. He was thinking that the world's rickety appearance is so cracked and flawed, so fallible and wobbly, that it's developed the habit of rendering itself into a terrible joke.

"Take me for instance," he moaned, "I'm a decent enough guy, struggling to make a new life for myself. And what happens? A couple of pussy-hungry coppers come along and screw me straight back into the slammer."

Hey, here's another good joke, Motley, it's a global one too: a commuter sits contentedly in his ozone polluting auto in Cardiff, and on the other side of the planet, a rain soaked mountainside slides into a village. The drug-dealer began moaning out loud: "Shouldn't someone feel some disquiet about all this, shouldn't someone feel ashamed? Why aren't those fucking coppers at home with their wives?"

Motley continued to mutter and swear, his temples thrummed and pounded, reverberating against the plate glass windows of the shops opposite. He felt empty inside, like he'd had his guts scalloped out of him. Just being coppers would have been bad enough, but those two words – Drug Squad - changed everything.

66

Would that little scene in the bar two nights ago be the pinpoint when everything started to go wrong, the contrived astral moment when Motley's happiness was amputated like the legs from that war-torn soldier in Iraq? Was that accidental little cameo in the wine-bar – the drug-cops chatting up the barmaid – to be the placing of the charges that would implode all his dreams, collapsing them in on themselves like a demolished block of flats? A dazed Motley looked up at the city's spangled canyons, the overhanging cliff-faces of past-its-best concrete, the sky-high windows mirroring the city's swagger. The unfeeling city gazed down on the rubble of its citizen's broken dreams and broken hearts, uncaring about their lost kisses and wasted tears. Down in the clutter and detritus of the streets, Motley could feel the city's inimical heft; he could feel its brazen indifference. The laconic, uncommunicative city just didn't give a FUCK.

67

The disembodied face of Jelly-Hair suddenly appeared before his mind's eye; her cunning eyes were boring into his, the red slash of her mouth working its jibing damage. Her indiscreet mouth opened, "There's something I think you should know about," she was saying to her police friends. A cold shiver ran down Motley's spine.

The barmaid was the dark penumbra at the edge of his sun, nibbling away at its periphery. He was afraid; afraid he'd have to pay a terrible price for Jelly-Hair's humiliation. The weed, with its numbing predictability, began to usher in a slightness of consciousness, depth charging the stream of bubbles that passed by his face as he felt his life sinking from under him. The dope deadened his senses, and made his fingertips tingle. That's the lure of the drug; it sucks you in, whispering in your ear: escape, forget about your problems.

To Motley, it felt as though he was watching a documentary of some poor sod's life unfolding before him; a fly-on-the-shit news report that was enough to make you cry, to burst out sobbing in the street. Motley blanched and sweated under the strain; he'd just spent three years inside and he had no intention of going back. And then there was Rachel.

Motley hadn't lied to Rachel about his dope-dealing business, but he hadn't told the whole truth either. The idea of her despising him almost killed him. He felt blocked, unable to decide what to do. He knew it would only be a matter of time before Jelly-Hair ratted on Sweep and himself. Motley struggled to get some perspective on what had happened, saying to himself: "She was only getting chatted-up. Nothing has happened." But he still felt like some frontal lobe fuck-up, scared of all future eventualities and unable to decide what to do. He couldn't decide whether he should just cut and run. The only thing that was certain was that he needed to talk to Toby, and soon.

68

The next day, Motley had a quiet word with Toby when he returned to the office from his delivery round. They made arrangements to have a meeting at Toby's place that night to discuss what had happened in the wine-bar. Motley must have looked very twitchy because Toby's last words to him as he left the office were: " Hey, stay cool, dude."

That night, when Motley had unloaded the entire story on to Toby, his reaction was, "Tremblett? Ha, ha ha! Fucking Tremblett!"

Toby had suddenly burst into uncontrollable laughter, throwing himself back onto his hand-stitched Italian leather sofa. "Andy-Fucking-Tremblett?" Then he let out another long, ululating, "Ha, ha, ha!" interrupted with another, whimpered, "Andy-Fucking-Tremblett".

"Bloody hell Toby, you know one of those drug dicks? Jesus, this is serious, man. God knows what that silly bitch will tell them about my operation in the wine-bar."

Toby finally managed to calm down enough to pick up a packet of Marlboros off the glass coffee table and offer Motley one. After they'd lit up Toby looked at Motley long and hard.

"Well," Motley asked, "what the hell am I going to do?"

Toby took his gaze away from Motley's face and focused it on the tip of his cigarette. He was thinking hard.

"Well?" Motley persisted.

"Look, Taff. I'm going to tell you something that you must swear stays between us, you don't even tell Sweep. No one, okay?"

It was Motley's turn to look at Toby long and hard, "Okay, I swear. Now what the fuck's going on?"

Another long silence from Toby, accompanied by some rumpled, deep-browed thinking, "I'm only telling you this so that you don't panic and completely fuck things up, okay?"

"For fuck's sake Toby, spit it out. What's going on?"

"Where do you think I've been getting all my gear from?"

Motley just shrugged his shoulders, "Never even thought about it."

Another long silence, then, shockingly, "Andy-Fucking-Tremblett." Toby spat the words from his mouth like a vivid jet of flame, igniting Motley's utter disbelief.

"What?" Motley almost fell out of his chair. "Fuck me! You're kidding? Those bastards are bent?"

"Like butcher's hooks," Toby nodded, "the fucking lot of them."

Now it was Motley's turn to fall back into his seat and laugh his head off. It felt like a huge boulder had just been lifted off his back. The thorn-in-the-flesh barmaid had suddenly lost all her afflictive power; the explosive bitch had suddenly been defused by Toby's little secret.

"Listen," Toby was now leaning forward and smiling broadly, "this stays between us, but if Tremblett or any of his boys start screwing with you, just let me know. If he finds out you're on my team, he knows he risks screwing himself. If he drops the hammer on you, he's fucking himself, okay?"

"Yeah!" Motley laughed, "Fucking okay, Tobe. You're the man, the fucking man. Outstanding! You've got the drug-dicks in your pocket? Out-fucking-standing!" Toby then gave him all the details of his wholesale operation.

After every drugs bust, after every weed-growing, ecstasy-lab and cocaine-snatching operation, Andy Tremblett and his boys would turn in only a fraction of any junk that was seized. The bulk of it would be sold on to Toby. How neat is that! It was a stroke of pure genius: a beneficent circle had been created where everyone got to make some money. The good guys and the bad guys were hand in hand, heroes and villains working together to screw the entire system. Pure genius! I mean you can't help laughing, can you? That's what you've got to call really taking the piss.

When Motley called round to Sweep's to pick up Rachel later that night, his dipso friend was lying on the sofa with his head in his girlfriend's generous lap. They were watching TV, but Sweep was obviously badly hung-over from a day in the pub. Rachel was up in the bathroom getting ready for their night out. After some brief courtesies of greeting, Motley nonchalantly gestured to Sweep, nodding his head in the direction of the kitchen.

"Sweep, can I have a word, mate?"

"Jesus," Sweep moaned, "I was just getting settled."

Motley excitedly told Sweep the entire story as given to him by Toby; he figured Sweep needed the protection that the information gave him.

"Well, I'll be buggered. You don't say?" Sweep whistled through his teeth.

"Oh yes I do say." Motley boomed, triumphantly.

"It's true? The drug squad is involved in supplying drugs?" Sweep still couldn't believe it.

"Bloody right it's true." Motley confirmed. "And thank God for it, Sweep. We're fucking bullet-proof."

"Well bugger me dead!" Sweep's face dropped into a troubled frown.

"For Christ's sake stop saying that, Sweep. It's starting to sound like a bloody invitation."

"Sorry, mate. I just can't believe it. What the hell next, eh?"

Sweep suddenly took on a distant look and began distractedly picking at his fleece jacket as though he'd decided that this was the ideal moment to give it a bloody good preening.

"What's the matter, buddy?" Motley asked. "This is all good news, isn't it?"

"Well…it…it just puts a funny light on things, doesn't it. I mean, who the hell can you trust?"

"Nobody Sweep. You can't trust anyone. And certainly not the Drug Squad."

Given Sweep's habit of twisting a drinking session into a parabola of complete abandonment of sensibility, Motley earnestly forced Sweep to swear an oath of secrecy about what he'd just told him. With a great deal of hurt pride, that he'd even mentioned it, Sweep swore that he'd never tell anyone.

Motley slapped his friend on the shoulder and led him back into the living room.

"Going somewhere nice with Rachel tonight?" Sweep's girlfriend asked, looking up reluctantly from a family-pack size bag of crisps.

"Yeah. We're celebrating tonight."

"Oh, what's that then?"

"Just a bit of luck that's come our way. That's all."

"Oh, nice."

When Rachel finally came down the stairs, she looked to Motley like sublime, fresh, unsullied femininity. Her mini-skirt was short enough to show the long thin triangle of light that started at her knees and led up to the soft curly nest at the top of her thighs. When Motley thought about her greedy little fingers, her ravenous mouth, her flexing, erectile nipples, he almost blew a fuse. The horny Motley wanted to run over to her and tear her clothes off. He wanted to penetrate her right there, right at the bottom of the stairs. Okay, it would have certainly been the last jump he'd ever have had. Sweep's knees would almost certainly have broken his humped and horny back. Motley guessed that all fathers would be a bit funny like that.

"Wow! You look great!" father and boyfriend said at exactly the same moment. The father couldn't believe that he had helped to make such a beautiful body; the boyfriend couldn't believe that within an hour he would be holding it, shuddering with pleasure beneath him.

Part Two

1

Rod Tremblett had been studying for over a year for the Drug Squad detective's examination and interview, so he knew quite a bit about the country's 'drug problem'. He knew, for example, that the use of illegal substances only became a real law enforcement issue around the mid-sixties. It was about then that marijuana and LSD became widely available. The archetypal dealer in those days was a docile, disorganised Hippy who sold on enough dope to keep himself supplied. He knew that today's drug dealers are a different kettle of fish, that they are a highly organised and dangerous fraternity of thugs and gangsters who control entire sections of the underworld.

Rod knew, too, that the dividing lines between a city's 'turfs' are always in a continuous state of flux. At any moment, one gang would 'queer' the pitch of another gang. Of course, the original owners of the pitch would feel scandalised at the encroachment on their revenue-generating streets, result – a turf war. The big dealers would constantly challenge each other's influence, until they went to jail or they earned respect from the others by the use of extreme violence. Fear was the currency the drugs trade lived by. "I don't know," said one dealer, when interviewed in custody, "it's like, if you haven't crippled someone with a baseball bat, you're like…a nobody."

There's no in-between with those gangsta guys: you're either a bloodletting psychotic or you're nothing. It's a cute business, drugs. It's no wonder Rod's brother was having so much fun.

*   *   *

It had all been arranged for Rod to skip the drug squad exam – Andy had submitted a completed exam paper on his behalf. On his first morning with the team, Rod was detailed to have an interview with the head of the drug squad, the DCI. Andy reassured him it was only a pep talk, nothing to worry about.

As it turned out, it was a desperately disappointing interview; and not on Rod's part either. The Boss was nothing like he'd anticipated. In fact, the DCI was the complete and utter opposite of what he had expected. It probably stemmed from childhood imaginativeness, but Rod expected his judges and senior law-enforcement officers to look like a modern day Socrates, to be wearing half-glasses on the ends of their noses and taking Schopenhauer, Wittgenstein and Kant to bed with them. Rod expected the finest minds that the country could produce – the crème de la crème of jurisprudence and police meritocracy – to be the carbolic-clean custodians of our law-enforcement apparatus. He wanted them to sip schooners of Oloroso sherry and discuss the novels of Thomas Mann down at the pub, to play the cello for relaxation and to be able to do the Telegraph crossword with an old-fashioned fountain pen in record time.

Instead, Rod's new boss turned out to be the most disappointing cop he'd ever seen in a uniform. For one glum, iconoclastic moment, Rod had to wonder why he'd ever joined the force. The funny thing is, he never really wanted to be a cop. Rod always thought he was too lazy to be a good one. As a schoolboy, what he really wanted was to be a scientist. But not now, not like with today's complicated science. Rod wanted to be a scientist from way, way back. Back when noticing that a stone was heavier than water got you a Nobel Prize. (Ah yes, those were the days. 'Bloody hell, that fire is hot!' – there you go, Cardiff High School's first 'A' level Physics pass.)

2

After enthusiastically shaking his hand the boss pointed Rod to a seat. His commanding officer then launched straight into an uninterruptible half-hour monologue. Rod just sat there, gazing at his boss's head, with its shock of pure-white hair. His DCI began with: "If anyone deserves promotion to the Drug Squad it's you...er...er..." The old guy began ineffectually flicking through Rod's personnel file.

"Tremblett, sir. Rod Tremblett."

"Yes, Tremblett, that's it. In fact, uh, it was probably me who requested your transfer from...er...er..." more desultory shuffling of papers.

"Traffic, sir."

"Yes, that's it, Traffic. You did a fine job over there, uh, Tremblett. The Traffic boys must have been very sorry to lose you."

"Yeah, right..." Rod whispered to himself. Despite his boss's bumbling, sanguinary manner, Rod recognised that the old git was a public relations gift to the South Wales Constabulary. Even though he was only into his early sixties, the commanding officer had lively grey-green eyes that swam with unflappable sincerity. His white-hair and calm face made him seem eternal, Jehovian even. A shimmering calmness seemed to emanate from him. Rod suddenly felt secure in the calm scrupulosity of the room, cut off from all sources of alarm and noisome disorder. His picture of himself sitting there – relaxed with a well-mannered alertness – went dim as he felt his vitality draining out of him to mix with the grey of his surroundings.

His DCI looked to be the trustworthiest person Rod had ever seen, a common perception that was a problem for the DCI's superiors, who believed that the drug squad was being run by an incompetent, shambolic fool. They couldn't understand how his department appeared to be running so efficiently. To the senior police commanders Rod's boss was a vexatious enigma.

"Now, er...Tremblett. You probably already know that I, uh, run the drug squad at the highest level. I'm an executive you see, I co-ordinate, make things run smoothly, get things done. You understand?"

"Yes, sir."

"On the other hand, it's important that you lower level people keep me, uh, informed, understand?" The detective chief inspector's voice suggested that he thought he wasn't getting through to his newest recruit.

"Yes, sir. I understand." Rod nodded his confirmation.

"Good, good. So, if you ever, uh, need anything..."

"A desk, sir," Rod piped up.

"A what?" The DCI looked perplexed at Rod's sudden request.

"A desk, sir. I'd like you to requisition a desk for me."

"A desk? What on earth do you want a desk for?"

"To sit behind, sir. I'm sharing one at the moment."

"You don't need a desk, Tremblett. I don't want my detectives sitting behind desks. I want them out on the streets arresting drug dealers. Understand?"

"Yes, sir. Sorry sir."

"Now, it says here that you have a brother on the force, is that correct?"

"Yes sir. He's on the squad too sir."

"Who is?"

" My brother sir. He's Andrew Tremblett."

"Ah, Andrew. He's, uh, your brother is he?"

"Yes sir."

"Good, good. It's important that brothers stick together, eh?"

"Yes, sir. I agree." Rod was beginning to wonder what sort of bargain-priced commander he had foisted on himself.

"I have a brother too, you know." The DCI''s face suddenly took on a thoughtful look.

"No sir. I didn't know."

"Mmm…. Yes." The DCI stared out of the window into the distance, distractedly. "Brothers should stick together, you know. Like, uh, like one big family, eh?"

"Yes sir. I agree sir."

After more gazing out of the window, the DCI murmured softly, "Mmmm, must give him a ring."

"Yes, sir. That's a good idea sir."

"What?"

"Ringing you brother, sir. It's a good idea."

"Ah yes. Now, Tremblett…what were we talking about."

"The work of the drug squad, sir."

"Ah yes, that's right."

The DCI started to ramble on about the proliferation of illegal drugs, "…and don't give me any of that, uh, bleeding-heart guff about addicts not being able to get the right treatment to come off the stuff. They say that only because they like to feel put-upon. It's the difference between them having to face up to their sorry lives or just complaining about them. You see, er…er…"

"DC Tremblett, sir."

"Ah yes, Trembles. The problem with stopping their addictions is that it allows life to come into their, uh, uh, their lives. And most addicts are terrified of life. You try asking an addict what he thinks of life: 'I'm against it!' would probably be his reply."

The hectoring DCI didn't ask Rod for any sort of professional opinion, or even if he had any ideas of his own about law enforcement or government drug policy. He just went steaming on…and…on…and…bloody…on.

While Rod's boss maundered, he was thinking: why is it that you can get a politician to admit to smoking pot (without inhaling!) but you can never get them to admit that they don't know what the fuck they're talking about when it comes to drug policy? What, for example, happened to the

Drug Czar? The truth is that the people fighting the Drugs War don't know what the fuck they're doing. The only people who know anything about it are the people doing the drugs – and they've got some serious memory problems. So it's no use asking them. If you were to ask Rod (and no one has) he would say that we should give the addicts all the drugs they need until they finally put themselves to sleep – permanently. The plain fact is, that we don't need a War on Drugs: what we need is a War on Stupid People.

Despite all this time thinking to himself, to Rod's dismay the old buffer was still droning on. "...When you're talking about addicts, you, uh, have to remember that for them the choice between drugs or no drugs is always a frying pan/fire situation. And to understand our anti-drug slogans you need a certain amount of acuity and gumption that the average druggy has never possessed in his life. "Just Say No" makes as much sense to an addict as Pythagoras's bloody theorem."

In the brief interlude the DCI needed to take a breath, Rod suddenly felt that he should say something, just to let his boss know that he was still awake. "Whatever happened to that 'Just Say No campaign sir? How successful was it?" The boss gave him an undeniably sharp look. Okay, so the DCI can't take a joke.

3

Listening to his boss's interminable diatribe began to give Rod a serious headache. He was beginning to think that maybe the dopeheads are not the ones that are screwed up after all. If we took the longest possible view of human existence, it would allow us to ignore such unpleasant details as worrying about getting a job and having to sit and listen to some old fart going on and bloody on about a subject that he obviously knows fuck all about. Poor Rod was beginning to feel like a spare dick at an orgy, so he thought it was about time that he said something again.

"I really don't get this drug thing, sir. The usual excuse that a druggy gives for his addiction is, "life is the pits," then, when he tells you he's trying to kick his habit, he says it's because when he's on drugs, "life is the pits.""

The boss's eyes lit up. Rod had obviously struck a cord. Oh fuck no! The DCI was off again…"Yes, yes. That's right…er…er…"

"Tremblett, sir."

"Yes. Yes, Tremblett. Because they have nothing else to bring joy into their lives except the, uh, drugs. It's because they have no God, you see. They're the damned, Tremblett, they are the apostate, and it's our job to cleanse our society of those godless reprobates."

Bloody hell, Rod thought, where is this rubbish going? First, der Fuhrer, now John-the-fucking-Baptist!

"Do you believe in God, Tremblett?" asked the DCI, staring Rod directly in the eyes.

Oh my God!

Rod couldn't believe his own ears. What kind of question was that? He knew he had to be careful. His answer would have to mollify his interlocutor.

"Oh yes, sir. I certainly do believe in God, and all his angels," Rod lied.

Whenever Rod – the atheist – had found himself praying for some divine favour, he always had the feeling that the god he was praying to was shamefully saying: "I really hope someone can help you with that Rod, because I can't."

"Good, good, Tremblett, very good. You know I only have believers on my team. Those dirty atheists disgust me. How can you trust anyone who doesn't believe in God, answer me that."

"You can't, sir. You can't trust them. Not one little bit, sir."

"Atheist is another word for a crook and a liar!" Rod's eyebrows shot up into his hairline with alarm. "All my men are, uh, believers, Tremblett. Believers, every one!"

"That's good, sir."

"Yes indeed it's good. It's very good. Baptists, mostly."

"Baptists, sir?"

"Baptists, Tremblett. Just like me."

"Baptists are very...trustworthy, sir." Rod said, diplomatically.

"Are you a Baptist, Tremblett?" The DCI was giving him a hopeful look.

"Er...no sir"

"Mm, pity. You're not, uh, Jewish, are you?"

Rod suddenly found himself wishing that he'd stood a little closer to his razor that morning; he was thinking that that he probably looked a little blue on the chin, a little swarthy around the jaw-line. He was also thinking about his grandfather on his mother's side: his much loved and much missed Jewish grandfather. "Er...no, sir. No. I'm not Jewish."

"Nothing wrong with Jews, mind you. They're a hard-working people. The Jews have a lot to offer this country, Tremblett. Of course you know that we fought a war to stop the Germans picking on the Jews. Our country lost a lot of good people in that war."

"Yes, sir. We did, sir."

"It's just that we all know what the Jews did, don't we Tremblett?"

"We do, sir?"

The DCI looked at his newest recruit scornfully, the lurid skin of his face stirred by little cyclones of disgust. Rod quickly recovered, "Oh, yes. Of course we know what they did, sir," he hurriedly agreed. The thunder and lighting instantly cleared from his boss's face.

"Mind you, to be fair, it wasn't all the Jews fault, was it? The, uh, Romans had a hand in it too of course."

"They did, sir? Oh, yes, sir. Of course they did, Sir. The Romans definitely had a hand in it. A very big hand if you ask me." Rod hadn't a clue what the fuck the old guy was talking about.

"But the Romans were just doing their, uh, duty, eh Tremblett?"

"They were, sir. Just doing their duty."

The DCI nodded, sagely, "Hmm, they were, Tremblett. Just like us. Just like we are doing our duty, eh?"

"Just like us, sir. Just like we are doing our duty, sir."

Rod was echoing his commander like some well-rehearsed you-call-the-tune parrot. He would never previously have admitted to racial prejudice existing in the force, but now he couldn't stop himself wondering why, in a city with a large Asian and African population, were there so few black police officers, and none above the rank of constable. Perhaps the DCI's Baptist god had created all men equal – but obviously that concept didn't apply to coppers. For some unfathomable reason, Rod suddenly found himself wishing that he'd admitted he was part Jewish, "My dear Chief Inspector (whipping out his circumcised member and landing it proudly on the DCI's desk) I'm as Jewish as my grandfather's yarmulke. I'm as kike as the fucking bagel I had for breakfast!"

Sadly – for all lovers of human rights – Rod's sublime though devilishly inadvisable thought quickly passed. Instead of exposing himself, he silently decided to send himself an internal memo: Dear Rod, it's not race that gives a person identity. It's personality that reflects identity – the brain genre, the sense of humour, the affinities. There is no homogeneity in race; race reveals nothing. Rod concluded that the obsession with race must be a Stone Age phenomenon; roaring with tribalism and disaster, beginning with bleeding fists and cut lips, ending with old ladies and children being gassed.

Dear Humankind – so used and abused yet still so cocky! We pathetic, amiably vicious creatures are foolish enough to believe in gods and shamans; and so we remain a maniac's masterpiece, too stupid to be stardust.

4

Feeling as though his mind had been sliding around on black ice for the last forty minutes, Rod was now gazing across at the DCI's benign smile; he didn't know how much more of this craziness he could take. How did an incomprehensible madman get to head up the city's drug squad? Rod decided right there and then that he would try and avoid his superior officer as much as possible. He had a disquieting suspicion that this kind of psychosis may be catching.

The DCI's eyes had glazed over and taken on a manic look. He turned and gazed out of the window. The boss had obviously taken himself off somewhere into a snug sky-gazing reverie. Rod shivered with distaste; his superior was sweating and drooling with some sort of religious fervour. It was staggeringly evident to Rod: a raving Jesus nut was in charge of the drug squad!

He had heard from Andy that despite being only a couple of years away from retirement, the Boss was still fiercely ambitious. Andy reckoned that the old guy dreamed of being promoted to Chief Constable or even Lord High Sheriff. But looking into the DCI's twinkling eyes, Rod guessed that the old dog dreamed only of his fat Baptist wife lowering herself astride his patriarchal face; her ecstatic smile glowing and her shrill voice howling at the yellow moon. The very thought sent a bashful smile skittering across Rod's face. Now the DCI had turned around from gazing out of the window and was looking at him intently with raised eyebrows. Rod guessed that his boss expected him to respond to his sanctimonious extolment. But Rod was dumbstruck, he didn't know what to think or say.

When Rod had walked into his boss's office, he'd been expecting the wisdom of Kalil Gibran, but, instead, he'd got the hubristic braggadocio of a born-again bloody fruitcake. He stroked his chin, feigning thoughtfulness. Rod was just buying some time to think. Personally, he's not of a mystical inclination. Aside from the occasional prayer when one of his kids gets really sick, Rod is rooted in the profane – he'd have been the guy at the back of the Sermon on the Mount yelling the ancient Hebrew equivalent of, "What a load of old camelshit!"

Nevertheless, he had to say something, so he agreed with his DCI that religion once did the job of giving troubled people a measure of hope, comfort, and a sense of belonging to a social structure. Now, it seemed like the drug culture was taking care of all that. Then finally, Rod spluttered diplomatically, "I agree with you sir. Drugs are impotent in the face of hope and joy."

It was exactly what his superior officer wanted to hear.

"Exactly, exactly, my boy." The DCI suddenly leapt out of his chair with the athleticism of a scalded cat and held out his hand for Rod to shake.

The interview was over. Tremblett thought he'd get a last word in, "What about my new desk, sir?"

"What, uh, desk?"

"The new desk you were going to requisition for me, sir."

"Ah yes, your new desk. Tell Wendy about it on your way out, she'll make sure I sign it off."

"Yes, sir. Thank you, sir."

"I can see you're going to fit right in with us here…er…er…son." After a huge smile and a firm handshake, Rod was standing outside the DCI's office: a newly inducted member of Cardiff city's drug squad.

Standing outside his commander's door Rod felt strangely insensate. Suddenly, the boiling chaos and magnum disorders of the world closed in on him again. As he walked back to his office, Rod felt almost paralysed by the malignity and impious madness that he knew was waiting for him out on the raging, drugs-soaked, upside-down streets.

5

That Friday evening, at about six o'clock, Andy came by the office to take Rod into town for a celebratory drink. They parked up in the Central Station car park and made their way to a nearby wine-bar. The place was a favoured watering hole for some of the squad and Andy reckoned that the place would be packed with office girls stopping off for a quick one while they waited for the Friday night traffic to clear. He was right, the place was crawling with eye-catching pussy.

They managed to push their way through to the bar, where Andy ordered two Grolsches with a couple of Stoli chasers – the crack of 40-proof alcohol. There's only one way to drink that Stoli vodka: bang shots. One after the other, Bang! Bang! Bang! It's just vodka, what harm can it do? Yeah, right! An hour later you're lying on your back with a Tasmanian Devil in your brain. You wake up the next morning with your liver lying next to you on the bed screaming, "Hey man, you're an arsehole. A dumb, suicidal fucking arsehole!"

Pulsing lights revolved in the ceiling above them like a swarm of flying saucers at take-off, miming the sonic chaos and broiling the fetid air of the overcrowded bar. The hooting and laughing women failed to drown out the trendy atonal music that thudded, shuddered and needled, its repetitiveness clutching at Rod's jangling nerves. It had been a tough day. He gulped down the ice-cold beer in one then necked the Stoli.

"Oh yeeeah! It's all over. Ya-ya-ya." The music boomed and rumbled. Again and again…"Oh yeeeah! It's all over. Ya-ya-ya." The chorus was repeated, over and over. Oh dear, Rod thought, music as a form of torture, "Ya-ya-ya." The shining faces of mini-skirted girls passed by the two men like a herd of prospective Miss Worlds, each containing the agreeable possibility, the happy congruousness of future intimacy. Perhaps one of those faces would eventually morph into some unexpected cuddles and kisses, or even extrapolate into a full-blown love affair. Both coppers were up for it.

Andy seemed to have been instantly absorbed into the wine-bar's lurid atmosphere. Rod spotted him ogling a particularly attractive girl; his eyes were bulging with sexual assiduity. Reaching around his brother, Rod clinked his glass against his.

"Hey! It's nice to be on board."

"Oh shit, yeah. Sorry, Bro. Welcome aboard."

"Thanks. I've waited a long time for this."

"So, what did the boss say?"

"Jesus, Andy what a guy! He's a lovely bloke, but how the hell did he get ever promoted to a DCI?"

"Don't worry. He's up for retirement in two years. I'm pushing hard for promotion, so if I get it they might even give me the department. I've been running the thing for the last few years anyway. Our money-making scheme was all my idea."

"Hey, that would be bloody great if you were heading up the squad."

"Yeah. Well, when the chief goes we'll have a little more leeway. Of course the Old Man knows nothing about the team's little private enterprise with all the shit we seize. Christ, he'd have a massive heart attack if he knew the half of it."

Andy was looking curiously at the clear liquid in his glass.

"You know how they make this stuff, don't you?"

"What the Stoli? No idea."

"They take girls like that blonde over there…" he pointed with a nod of his head at the girl he'd been eye-balling, "…around the back and wipe her pussy with a cloth. Then they wring the juices out into your glass."

"Shit, Andy. That's gross."

With that, Andy poured the remainder of his drink down his throat with exaggerated glugging and slurping noises. Then he rubbed his fingers around the inside of the glass and licked them furiously.

"Ha, ha, ha. That's good." Rod laughed. Andy giggled like an idiot and continued to try to attract the blonde with the electro-magnetism of his long, meaningful stares.

6

That Andy Tremblett, eh? What a prick! He's the kind of total fuck-up who prefers the "Blues Brothers 2000" version to the original, the kind of unscrupulous shit who thinks that child porn is only illegal; he's the guy who, when he first heard of it, thought that Southern Comfort was a black hooker.

Eventually, the fun-seekers and the lonely debauchees began to drift away to their distant homes. The densely packed crowd had thinned out, so the guys stood leaning against the bar, chatting about Rod's first week on the squad. And then…

"Same again?" A female voice was chirping from behind the bar.

Both men simultaneously turned around. The barmaid with the ridiculous hairstyle they had chatted to a few weeks ago was smiling at Andy. He returned her smile, and then quickly transferred his gaze to her pendulous jugs.

"Yes please, love." Andy pushed the empty glasses towards the barmaid. "How are you, sweetheart?"

"I'm okay. You?"

"Could be better."

"We all could be better, couldn't we?"

"So what's your name again?" Andy asked the still smiling girl. The barmaid put him out of his misery.

"Melanie."

"Yeah, that's right, Melanie. I knew it was an unusual name. So how's things Melanie?"

"Like I said, I'm Okay. You?"

"Yeah. Fine."

The barmaid was wearing a short black skirt and a white silky-looking blouse that barely contained her space-competing breasts. Her hair was a rigid melange of multi-coloured, spiky spearheads.

"Hey Bro, you've met my friend Melanie." Rod nodded a hello to the smiling, booze-dispensing Melanie.

"You know, I've got the feeling I've seen you before somewhere, before this place, I mean, have we met before?" asked Rod.

"The police club?" Melanie exposed the mystery with another sugary smile.

"That's it! You worked behind the bar for a while, didn't you."

"Yeah, for a little while."

Rod suddenly decided to formally introduce himself, "Hello again Melanie. I'm Rod." The barmaid leaned forwards, offering him her hand and exposing even more of her zealous, bra-bursting tits.

"Pleased to meechew again," she purred.

"Good to meet you again, too." Rod held on to her hand for a couple of seconds longer than was strictly necessary. Melanie spun Rod what she thought of as her film-star smile and held his gaze as he squeezed her hand.

Rod began to tentatively chat her up, making her laugh by telling her some corny old police jokes. But despite his half-hearted attempts at pulling her, the barmaid's gaze kept lancing across the room to a guy sitting at the other end of the bar. Her glaring at him must have pissed him off because he suddenly got up and left. Rod figured that there was some sort of history between them. He didn't recognise the guy, but his face did seem familiar.

7

The sex-pot barmaid and Rod got along like a house on fire; he thought she was hotter than a freshly-fucked fox in a forest-fire. After a few more drinks, Andy piped up, "Just gonna shake hands with shorty." Then he disappeared off to the toilets. Rod drained his glass and then pulled a sad face.

"Ah well, suppose we'll have to be going soon," he moaned. "Only popped in for a couple after work."

"Hang on a minute."

Melanie was signalling to one of the other barmaids to come over. Then she walked around the bar, took Rod's arm and edged him off towards the dimly lit corridor that led to the toilets. Halfway down the corridor, the barmaid suddenly grabbed him and pushed him up against the red-flocked wall. Her lips quickly found his. As they kissed Rod ran his fingers over her bottom; one finger on each side, he traced the soft line of her panties beneath the bum-stretched fabric of her skirt. She licked his lips lightly. Then she reached up behind his neck and pulled his face down to hers, clamping her mouth against his own lips, nuzzling her tongue at them until they parted wide enough to let her tongue inside, to entwine with his.

After penetrating each other with their taste organs, they made slithered, warm withdrawals, and then returned them with deep slurping thrusts; they were mimicking the sex act with their tongues. Rod's prong was writhing and squirming in the encompassing nest of his briefs. As she felt the erection tenting his trousers, the barmaid thrust her pelvis against his, then she backed away, her thighs ungluing themselves from Rod's own trembling legs. Through the cloth of his trousers, she wrapped her fingers around his widening girth, and then gave it a firm squeeze. This spiky-haired barmaid was as hot as a pole-dancer – 'sex on a fucking stick', as Rod would later say.

8

With rapacious haste, Rod was already imagining the barmaid's gaping sex with a fevered visualisation; he could already feel its liquidity. He felt like hooking up her skirt; throwing her on the floor and shafting her right there on the rumpled, piss-stained carpet of the toilet corridor. But she suddenly broke free from their clinch and huskily whispered in his ear, "Call me." Then she furtively pushed a small piece of paper into his hand.

To Rod, and to any hip observer, it looked exactly like she was palming Rod a wrap of cocaine – he was starting to think like a drug dick already! The door to the men's toilet at the far end of the corridor opened with a screech from the painted-over hinges.

"Hello. Hello. What do we have here then?" Andy sounded too much like a copper to be true. "You two didn't waste any time, did you?"

"Yeah, yeah. Thanks Andy." The barmaid had already broken free and retreated back behind the bar.

And there she now stood, triumphant in her encrypted terrain, her face inflamed and glowing among the glittering 'have another drink' foliage of bottles and glasses. She stood with her hands on her hips; her chin thrust forward, eyebrows raised. All whorish bitch, all brazen barmaid.

"She fancies the fuck out of you, Bro." Andy said, downing the last of his drink. Rod thought that was a pretty redundant thing to say after what his brother had just witnessed. As they sidled across the room, and out of the doors, she held him with her eyes, daring him not to ring her. She didn't bother returning his wave. Poor Rod, poor helpless, horny Rod; he already wanted to possess the ember-cheeked barmaid, with her Botticelli tits and her iceberg heart; her duplicitous, streng verboten heart. He wanted to have her; forgetting the axiom that what remains out of reach, remains perfect. Rod was already surrendering himself to the jelly-haired provocateur's vulgar charms.

9

As soon as he got home, Rod poured himself a large scotch and decided to take a long soak in the tub. "I'm going up for a bath, love. How long till food?"

"Oh, bout half an hour."

"Plenty. Give us a shout, eh?"

He revelled in the hot relaxing water, his drink in one hand and his penis puckered between forefinger and thumb in the other. His soap lubed fingers began sliding rhythmically back and forth over the purple tumescence of the glans. He was thinking about his aberrant snog with the barmaid, thinking about inserting himself into her body, lunging in and out of her, sucking and pulling viciously at her distended nipples. Rod was treating himself to a long, languid, ball-wrenching wank; the kind of jerk-off you're desperate for after being primed by some oversexed, tongue-nibbling, prick-teaser. He was just on the point of coming when, Rat, tat, tat…

"Are you okay? You've been in there for ages."

"Er, yeah. I'm fine."

"Food's ready."

"Yeah, okay. (Fuck!) Be down in a minute."

Anne's voice had blocked his vision of the barmaid; his porno-primed concentration was zapped, terminally brushed under the conceptual carpet of intruding domesticity. ... "Bollocks!" Fucking shame that, it was a virtuoso wank.

Averaged out over the last year, Rod had made love to his wife one and a half times a week. And that was all right, that was, because the relief that followed their lovemaking was partly the relief that the next few nights would be nights off for him. Whenever Rod made love to his wife, he invariably thought of someone else – anyone else. Leaving behind the moist and insouciant sheets of uxoriousness, he would think about the girl who read the TV news, or the girl on the supermarket check-out, or his wife's friends and relatives, his niece, his niece's school chums, nurses, nuns, traffic wardens, any girl, any woman.

"Oh! You're so big," he would have his wife say in his heroic imagination, "That hurts...but I like it," or "Jesus Christ! You're the best sack-artist I've ever had!" And Rod would always reply, modestly, with an almost hum-drum repetition, "Well, thanks, it's nice of you to say so."

Of course, Anne never said any of those things. To Rod's disgust, his wife never said anything as he gurgled and gasped, snorted and truffled his way towards a recalcitrant orgasm. With his elbows and knees grappling to find purchase on the slick and slippery bed sheets, and without a single molecule of genuine desire, his ejaculation would arrive, coldly, poignantly, with an imperious trickle.

When he made love to his wife, Rod's mind was a chaos of different couplings. Unsuspecting women would wander into Rod's quotidian orbit, and giving them all what he called his 'shagger's eye', one by one, he would have the lot. When Rod made love to his wife, the real action was always elsewhere. But from now on, when he made love to Anne, Rod would be thinking only about his barmaid; and the flattering noises she would make as he pumped his painfully engorged manhood into her wide and grateful mouth. He would be thinking only of Melanie's fever, her delirium. And pretty soon, Rod would be spending entire lunch hours in the back seat of his patrol car, giving himself a low five while seeing himself hysterically coming into his barmaid's mouth or ejaculating veritable fountains of sperm over her slaked and smiling face.

10

That frustrated masturbatory session in the bath had decided it. Rod was definitely going to call the barmaid. He was just bursting to give her one. Of course, he knows it's crazy for a married guy to be sleeping around these epidemiological days: you don't just risk picking up a dose of clap, you risk picking up an obituary. But this was different: for Rod, this was uncontrollable desperation.

So why, he wondered, when he was thinking about betraying his wife, did he suddenly think of his children? Why now, when he should have been able to occlude them in the blinding radiation of his lust? Why did their sleeping faces come humming into his porn-served consciousness? Their innocent sweetness converged on the pit of him, threatening to tear him inside out.

He looked across the kitchen table at Anne, who was now forking Spag Bol into her mouth in the shovelling action that only worked for her. What was he doing thinking about having another affair? If she even found out he'd snogged that girl, it would destroy her. Besides, he was probably getting too old and too prim for the exigencies of raw, vigorous, cock-powered deceit.

Anne looked up at him from under her straight fringe, eyes aglow; a weak smile was gaining purchase upon her tomato-sauced lips. We are man and wife – Rod was thinking – friends and lovers, brother and sister. We have played all our lives in the same toy-box; two people reduced to the same soul. And he wanted to risk throwing all this into the abyss, just for a few quick shags? What, is the guy nuts?

Hey, hey, take it easy!

Give the guy a break here. We're all pre-programmed that way, aren't we brothers – it's in our genes, right? Those little DNA suckers have had it easy for far too long; it's about time they started taking responsibility for their actions. Anyway, it isn't us; it's our hormones what does it. We can't even help ourselves, can we? Mother Nature made us this way. If you want to blame someone, blame that evolution guy Mr. Darwin, and his natural fucking selection.

Just a couple of hours ago, Rod was only two seconds away from raping that Melanie, throwing her down to the sticky carpet and forcing his tool between her impressive cleavage. (He was glad that he hadn't raped her, though that image was something he was looking forward to enjoying.) In his incorrigible mind, he was still pointing his rod like a rifle at her greedy mouth, his balls slapping against her tits like loaded bandoleers. The horniness of the recurring image brought beads of sweat to Rod's forehead. He wiped the wetness away with the back of his trembling hand, "Bloody hell. That bath was hot. I'm still sweating."

Anne just stared at him vacantly, chomping away at the slippery spaghetti. Rod thought that she was looking a little mousy tonight, a little fatigued. She looked the part of the weary, put-upon mother and wife. Although she was just in her early forties, the march of the years and two small, demanding children had left their brushstrokes upon her. Her face, once as clear as a windblown sky, was now clouding over with a network of lines and leaking veins. Rod couldn't help thinking about all the lukewarm, indifferent lovemaking that joined up their marriage. His eyes suddenly filled with resentment. A wife at bedtime – he couldn't think of anything less seductive, less extra-marital.

They ate their meal in silence, trying to finish off the fast-cooling pasta. Finally, Anne asked, "Are you okay?"

"Yeah, yeah. Just tired I guess. That meeting with the boss wasn't easy. The guy seems to be a total jerk-off. Turns out that it's Andy who really runs the department."

"Well it was a big week for you. Why don't we have an early night and you can tell me all about it in bed."

"Hm, hm."

Lying in bed, Rod's mind kept sliding back to the toilet corridor, and the barmaid's jellied mane. He wondered if tonight she'd round up someone else and canter him off to the toilet corridor, gathering up the guy's crotch in her hand and asking him to call her. Her near-seduction, her molestation, her scummy tongue-sucking mouth had sent Rod's whole life into a tailspin. He wanted to call her up on the phone and talk to her about sex, about fucking; above all about the parodies of fucking. It was incomprehensible to him that perhaps Melanie, aka Detective Sergeant Wendy Westerby, had no interest in listening to his slutty phone call. She was already talking on the phone, talking to her superior at the Special Investigations Branch. Wendy was taking an ideological stance; she was saying, "I don't know, sir. I'm trying not to think about it. But if it works, it will all be worth it."

When Anne turned out the light and started thumping her pillow into submission, Rod started to finger the nerve-ending G-spot at the end of his prick, just where the shaft joins the head. He was still shunting the dregs of horny memory through the doors of his mind. The last thing he thought to himself before sleep overtook him was, "She's too young for me. Way too young." Then the very last thing was: "Oh, sod it. I'll buy her a Mickey Mouse T-shirt for her birthday."

11

A week later, Rod had arranged to meet Melanie at a restaurant out in Cowbridge. It was far enough away from town for them not to be spotted by some wayward neighbour or colleague. Rod had already downed a couple of glasses of house wine before she arrived. Melanie looked fabulous. She was all woman; with her mini-skirted thighs and plump breasts barely contained in the woollen stricture of her tight sweater. When he'd recovered from the disturbing sexiness of her outfit, almost blushingly he grunted, "You like your mini-skirts, don't you?"

"You're not complaining are you?"

"Shorter the better as far as I'm concerned." The ringing memory of him once bollocking Anne for wearing her skirts too short echoed around Rod's sententious, hypocritical brain.

The food was excellent; nothing too fancy, just a couple of perfectly cooked medium/rare steaks and a tureen-full of fries. Rod was never one for desserts, but Melanie ordered a slice of chocolate gateau and took only a few desultory spoonfuls out of its sticky coagulum, so he finished it off for her. Then they polished off the bottle of wine and sipped a couple of brandies with their coffee.

Rod hadn't been to a nice restaurant for an adult's only meal in ages. If Anne and him ate out, it was usually a quick Saturday evening chicken and chips and a pint down the pub. The indifferent food scoffed amid a wrestling jumble of kids' arms and legs and Anne's frantic, "You two sit down and eat your food or we're not coming again," wasn't the same as a civilised evening in a decent restaurant.

When Melanie had finished the last of her brandy, she pushed her chair back slightly, and dabbed theatrically at the corners of her mouth with her napkin.

"So, you're married then." She suddenly quipped.

It wasn't a question she was asking; Rod had already told her over the phone that he was married. She was merely making an overfrank diagnosis, just stating an accusatory fact that needed some sort of explaining.

151

"I can't deny it." Rod tried to say it with a laugh, but it came out sounding like a half-hearted apology.

"What's her name?"

"Who?"

"Your wife, stupid."

"Why do you want to know her name?" The hackles had started to rise on Rod's back.

"Just conversation, that's all."

"It's…Anne."

Melanie shrugged her shoulders and then stooped to pick up her bag. Then she made a big production of taking out her cigarettes and lighting one up.

"You smoke?" She offered him the open packet across the table. Rod shook his head. He was starting to have serious doubts about this whole thing. Rod couldn't stand being around a smoker – filthy fucking habit that. Melanie puffed the acrid smoke into the air above her head then manipulated the grey whisps with her waving hand. Rod's glance fell to her ripe tits, jiggling about in their soft prison. He imagined their pink, bulging swellings. His rapacious dick shuffled uncomfortably in his briefs. It was then he decided to nail his colours to the mast, put his cards on the table, so to speak.

"Look, I don't quite know how to say this, but are you sure you want to start dating a married man?"

Melanie just smiled an imperious smile; her vulpine eyes had all the cunning of a vixen. Rod was already addicted to them.

"Are you the one that's sure? You're the one with everything to lose," she snorted. It was a good answer, Rod thought, and a worrying one. What the fuck did she mean by that? Was she making a threat? Nah, she was just vaunting her female power over a poor sex-helpless man.

"Take me back to your place and we'll find out," he answered, swaggeringly.

He followed the barmaid's car all the way back into Cardiff, fingering the turgid presence in his trousers the entire way. They drove along the A48 right through town, past the crouching bulk of the castle; the crenulated hunk of Victorian hubris squatting in the middle of the city like a set from a Harry Potter movie. The Scottish billionaire's misrepresenting folly had only recently been out-loomed, arrogantly eclipsed by other monumentalities; even greater concrete and steel Titanics of megalomanic delirium.

12

As soon as they got inside the door of her flat, they were gnawing hungrily at each other's mouths, and trying to loosen bits of cumbersome clothing. Rod had Melanie's bra pushed up over her tits and the spikes of her nipples between his forefingers and thumbs. He couldn't get enough of her erect nipples, sucking and pinching at them. She moaned and squirmed as he manipulated the pink, pliant protrusions.

Anne's nipples never got that hard anymore; they were inverted and temperamental; sometimes they were impossible to get erect enough to flick with his tongue. He supposed they were now just the workaday milk-teats of a wife and mother, atrophied appendages that had been too-long gummed and twanged by two hungry babies and one horny, nipple-fixated husband.

They managed to scramble out of their clothes and into bed, stroking and kissing each other all the while. For some flagellant reason, when Rod slipped his eager cock inside Melanie's wet pussy, he thought again about his children; their innocence had become caught up in their culpable father's sexual recklessness.

The sobering fact was that when Rod lay down with his barmaid, he was laying down in the impress of all the other bodies that she'd ever lain with. If only there was some embrocation, some rub-it-in cream that would eliminate all those STD risks. And don't even think about condoms, even as a teenager Rod could never use them: he could never get along with their nerve-blocking, cock-shrinking touch.

Back in the old days, everyone worried about catching a dose of clap. Now, if all you have is gonorrhoea, you're a pure, untarnished hero. "You've got a dose of clap? That's all? Fuck it, let's hit the sack!" These days Rod even washed his hands before a wank. He didn't trust anybody.

Where were his children while Rod hovered over the barmaid's quivering body? Where were they now? At home, of course, with their mother, and Rod would see them soon. When he got home, he'd subsume his guilt among their small limbs and blonde heads, burn off the layers of his accumulated deceit in the slipstream of their profligate trust. But right now, Melanie lay beneath him, uttering soft gasps of pleasure, interspersed with strangulated yelps that seemed to slide in and out of her throat, matching the machine-like thrusting of their pelvises:"Uh…Uh…Uh. Yeesss."

The soft tones of Melanie's body were bleached by the irradiating light from the hallway, the paleness of her skin provided salience by the black satin sheets shimmering below her. It was a skin that had been made purely for stroking, licking and lying on. Still the soft grunts as they lay sideways across the bed; Rod gripping the edge of the mattress beneath her head, giving him purchase for some hard thrusting. Then he was up on his elbows, gazing into the oval space of her open mouth. Her hands slid between them, and her fingers wrapped themselves around his oily penis, squeezing off the storm of blood that coursed through its veins.

"Uh…Uh…Uh. Yeesss," she growled.

Unbidden, and with a gasp of exasperation, she suddenly pulled him out of her vagina and flipped herself over onto her stomach. Rod fell back onto her and tried to insert his pulsating knob back inside her streaming pussy.

But her hand came around and grabbed his penis. Then she started rubbing it up and down the crack of her bum cheeks.

Luckily, for us guys, there's a genre of sex where the lovers strive to ravish each other. Rather than the usual self-conscious 'making love' it's a no-holds-barred assault on each other's bodies: with no areas denied access. Rod wondered should he try and stick his cock up her bum-hole? Was that the idea? Was that what she was hinting at? Melanie was flipping the head of his weapon along her arse crease, uttering grunts and moaning encouragement. Rod could no longer suspend belief. He grabbed his dick from her hand and aimed it at the pulsing caldera of her anus.

"Yes. Ow…yes," Melanie yelped, encouragingly.

He slid slowly inside her; then her moaning suddenly stopped. Melanie's mouth was just hanging open, her eyelids half-closed like in a drugged sleep. She started clutching handfuls of the sheet and pillow, contorting her face and making noiseless screams that emerged from her mouth as great wafts of warm air.

Rod started in on his rhythm with long slow strokes, oozing in and out of her with a steam-engine precision, with an oily ease. Then, having caught his beat, he started fucking her with resumed violence, urging her, zapping her into the dark trench of her bed. Yes…yes, this was further, this was more; this kind of fucking was a whole mineshaft further down. She suddenly stretched out her arms, fists clenched as if ready for a fight. Rod felt a shudder as she began to climax, a tectonic shifting deep down in the centre of her. He moved further up in the bed so that he could get his body projecting out over Melanie's head. His rapacious cock was pulling at her insides like a ship tugging at its anchor.

"I'm coming! I'm coming! I commm…" she started howling.

"Come baby. Come."

"Oh my God! Oh my…Aaaaahhhh!"

Rod's thrusting went into hyper-rhythm. Then there was a complicated thrashing and contorting. He could feel his belly pounding into the knobbed curve of her spine. It felt as though he had jumped on the back of an extremely angry crocodile. Melanie was arching her back and screaming – "Aaaaahhhh!" – pushing back against the rock-hard shaft of Rod's deeply buried cock. As his own eruption began to squidge deliciously up his dilating urethra, Rod's arms lost their lock and he collapsed onto Melanie's sweaty back, gasping as the hot come poured from him in scorching jets.

It was a long, long time before either of them could move; they were both completely and utterly shagged-out. Melanie gave a stifled grunt as Rod lifted off her and padded to the bathroom. He climbed into the shower and spun the hot-water tap right up. Standing beneath the stinging-hot cascade, he was thinking about the sex they'd just had. It was the kind of sex that most men just daydream about, but are too afraid to ask for: dirty sex, hard-core and effort-full; the kind of gut-busting sex that gets most guys horny just thinking about it.

When Melanie clambered into the shower with him, she appeared so nonchalant. She just crouched down and washed herself, soaping her bum while he vigorously scrubbed his cock. She gave him a wide grin and soaped his limp penis for him; then she popped it into her mouth. Rod nearly fainted.

She was pushing him in and out of her cloying lips, gobbling and slurping. It seemed that she could just press some secret button and the poor bastard would come skitting and bouncing into her, his prong frolicking around like a stunt cock in a porno movie. As she sucked him off his rampant prick swelled to an even greater length and girth, engorged with half the blood in his body. Melanie was playing with the lips of her vagina and sliding her slippery finger over the tiny bud of her clitoris; she was getting ready for another orgasm. In the bent pipe of her throat his cock began to romp and jar as it felt another surge of semen ungumming its flattened eye. He felt as helpless before this woman as Adam did before Eve in that scary orchard.

Sliding down the tiled waterfall at the back of the shower, Rod's chest was pumping and heaving, his wet eyelids flickering oddly as he tried to blink away the water in his eyes. For a brief moment he wondered if all this was a dream? A dream sent to debase all other reality – meant to break and fling its value. His life outside the shower cubicle suddenly seemed worthless, meaningless, and easily shattered.

It's hard to believe how delicate our lives are, how pitifully breakable. Everything about us is so easy to break, the heart, the nerves, the promises. Everything about us is much too delicate. A sudden CRACK! – And look…it's all gone. It's all in tiny pieces.

13

The lovers had made love as though they were starring in a hard-core porno movie; a movie that demonstrated the excruciating availability of a woman's orifices; a video-tape that covered every loathsome misconduct, every looping, overstrained cum-shot. Is there a return to a normal life after that kind of sex: that kind of ne plus ultra humping? Who knows? Actually it would be just like life to have that kind of trick up its sleeve, wouldn't it? "Life is ONLY for fucking, and nothing else" And it must be true: because there you are and here I am. And we all got to be here because…"Life is ONLY for fucking."

14

As Rod drove home, he could almost taste Melanie in his mouth: the essence of her, her body's pheromonal quiddity. He wiped his still sweating forehead with the back of his hand, and opened the car window to let in some cooling air. The thought of her clitoris wobbling about on the end of his tongue opened every artery and vein in his body, sending the blood pounding through him in a series of visceral thuds. Rod's mind palped and his cock spasmed, he couldn't release her from his mind; couldn't let her go. As he walked into the house, Tyson, the ex-police dog, came whuffling up the passage and instantly buried his muzzle in Rod's crotch. A great draught of human sex had caused the dog's nose to almost fall off its face. The old German Shepherd was still worrying at Rod's cock area when he walked into the lounge. Anne was watching TV.

"So, how was Andy?"

"Fine. Had a good night."

Rod had told her that he was going to the Police Club for a drink with his brother and a few of the lads. It was a cast-iron alibi. Andy would cover for him, as Rod always did for him. He thanked God that Anne didn't have the olfactory precision of a police canine. The poor bugger couldn't take his nose away from his master's crotch.

"Put him out in the kitchen, Rod." Anne scowled at Tyson with a disgusted look. "Yeah, okay, love. Fancy a cuppa?"

"Ooh, yes please."

In the kitchen Rod administered a salutary slap to Tyson's nose, and sighed a deep sigh of relief. Trying to masquerade a semblance of normal life wasn't going to be easy when he felt as though he was bouncing around like a horny cherub on cloud nine. Throwing a couple of tea bags into two bone-china mugs, he pushed the replay button of his memory bank and conjured up the vision of Melanie's welcoming thighs. As he gratefully immersed himself in his porno daydream, Rod suddenly realised that he didn't care what was happening at home; he didn't care about the dog sniffing his groin, he didn't care about Anne or the kids. Because what was happening at home wasn't really happening to him, it was happening to someone else, on another planet, in some other universe. It wasn't happening to him, because he was falling in love.

Strangely, it had been just a few weeks ago, after another bruising marital twelve-rounder, that Rod had been moodily thinking…so, what the hell do I need love for? Why is love so important? Now, he suddenly found himself thinking…love can teach us so many things about ourselves. Without love our inner selves are like alien beings. Without love our souls are strangers to us.

Oh, no! Rod, please, no! That's all bullshit. Not with that Melanie, pleeease. Don't fall in love with her. Not with her of all people.

15

Motley awoke with a convulsion from another nightmare. He lay there trying to recover some composure. The nightmares still came to find him in his sleep, their elliptical mouths open, their bloodied teeth glinting; thrusting their snouts up from his deep sub-conscience. Again, he was reliving the Iraqi suicide bombing, the stormy red core of energy, extravagant and fat with horror. He saw his friends seething in the irresistible surging and drifting, lost in a white shawl of broken everything. He saw his men giving up their spirits with sudden helplessness, without struggle; their ghosts racing away, warping upward from the great globed Earth. The volume of nightmares still tumbled into his consciousness, weighted with obscenity and filth like a bag-full of tipped rubbish. Awaking from those nightmares, it was always difficult for Motley to tell to what extent they were excluded from reality. Perhaps the horror of the dream was as alive as he was. He shook his head to clear the terrible images and leaned across to Rachel, cushioning his throbbing head against her breast.

In his soul-shattering dreams, Motley was meticulous, capable, brisk – but completely powerless. His world was split; he was aware of two realities. The reality of his day-to-day happenings, and the even more dazzling reality of his nightmares. He feared that his dual realities were a forerunner of creeping insanity. Motley often wondered, in this cause and effect world, could it be that his nightmares affected his daytime reality? The nightmares had possessed him in his sleep – would they not tell sometime later, when he was fully awake? Were his bad dreams capable of tampering with his fate? Can a nebulae of nightmares give birth to reality?

Sighing with relief, Motley burrowed down into the warm sweetness of his girlfriend. The cadences of her breathing rose and fell like the distant swishing of a tropical sea. Cuddling up to her cancelled out the worst of the bad dream – and his turbo-charged hangover. His head hurt badly; this morning, his head couldn't take living with his sins. That's what Motley needed, a nice cuddle a large glass of freshly squeezed orange juice and then bucketfuls of strong coffee. But for now, he couldn't leave Rachel's lovely smell; the remnants of the Ferragamo perfume she always wore and the more erotic smell of her sweat-infused body; the damp, musky deposit of the previous night's lovemaking. She wriggled her backside into his pelvis and pulled the sheet away from her shoulder. Her body lay in a foetal attitude, arms together in front, her long legs bent at the knees, ankles touching. Their two bodies were locked together like a couple of spoons in a drawer. Rachel's sleep-flattened hair stuck to her neck, damp with sweat. Motley reached across and stroked her bare arm, her baby-smooth, loveable arm. He nuzzled at the nape of her neck, her loveable neck, and kissed it with infinite tenderness. Where did I find you? He asked himself. How did I find you? He was convinced that their inexhaustible sexual ardour would some day dissolve them into one single being, a single self-marvelling entity. How this would happen, he didn't know; but he was convinced it would. Motley could no longer envision himself without Rachel; her starburst radiance and her voodoo power were slowly subsuming his desire to be someone else.

16

"My head hurts," Rachel mumbled into her pillow.

"Mine too." Motley's mouth tasted metallic, his tongue felt like a roll of flocked wallpaper. The previous night had seen their flat-warming party. This morning was their first day in the new pad and the sun's rays were creeping over the windowsill, silvering the freshly painted ivory-coloured walls. Except for the pain from his hangover, Motley felt like he had awoken to a bright mirage; a sunlit heaven where happiness was stuffed into his skull until it burst its bony walls.

"I need some aspirin." Rachel moaned. It was the after-effects of the champagne. She'd drunk far more last night than she usually did. Her dad would have been proud of her if he hadn't fallen over unconscious-drunk in the kitchen halfway through the party. They sent the comatose Sweep and his girlfriend home in a taxi; then they all got down to some serious partying. All his ex-Para friends were there, and some friends they'd made over at the wine-bar. Motley had even invited Toby, who turned up with a case of champagne for everyone's enjoyment.

"I need some aspirin." Rachel moaned again.

"I'll get them. I need some too." Motley dragged himself away from his girlfriend's warm body and rolled out of bed. Then he tripped arse over tit on the long loops of the carpet that Rachel had chosen for their bedroom. He fell heavily against the windowsill. The shock of wood against bone displaced the throbbing in his head. "Shit…that hurt!" Motley rubbed his side with the palm of his hand. "That's probably going to mean a hip replacement in thirty years time."

"Better get your name down now then," Rachel quipped. Motley thought that was pretty funny, coming from a half-comatose girl with a terminal hangover.

An hour later, they were just sitting down to some scrambled eggs and toast when Motley's mobile rang. He thought it might have been Sweep, apologising for fading so early the previous night.

"Yello." He mumbled into the tiny plastic voice-carrier.

"Hey, Taff! You fucking old jailbird! Howyadoin? Jesus, you sound awful. Gotta cold or sommat?"

As soon as Motley heard that word 'Taff' spoken with an English accent he froze. It was a word lifted from the past. Every Welshman in the Regiment had carried the nickname, Taff.

"Who's this?"

"Jesus, mate. You wouldn't believe the trouble I've gone to trying to get hold of your number. How are you?"

"Fine. Fine."

A second later a guffaw came from the other end of the phone.

"Bloody hell Taff, you really don't know who it is, do you?"

He didn't even try racking his brains; it would have hurt too much.

"Nope."

"Jesus, don't try thinking too hard, you'll pull a fucking muscle."

After another few seconds of silence, came: "Oh, Christ! Tenerife, ninety-seven. The two Geordie girls."

Motley's mind raced back – nineteen ninety-seven, Tenerife? Then it clicked. He'd had a boozy holiday in Tenerife with a mate from the Paras. Later, they'd been badged into the SAS at the same time: it was Micky Benning. "Jesus, Bennie!" Motley yelped.

"Yours fucking truly, mate."

"Hey, buddy, what's happening? Are you still with the mob?"

"Nah…well. Tell you later. Listen, there's lots happening, mate, lots. But we can't talk on the phone. I need to meet up with you pretty quickly. Can we fix something up ASAP?"

"Yeah, sure. When?"

"I'm in only Cardiff for today and tomorrow."

Motley thought for a moment, then realised it was Saturday: it wasn't a working day for him. "Yeah, okay, how about later today? Where're you staying?"

"I'm at the Saint David's Hotel."

"What? Jesus, have you won the lottery or something?"

"Better than that. Can you meet me at midday, in the bar here? Okay?"

Motley looked up at the clock on his kitchen wall.

"Yeah, okay Bennie. That's good for me."

"You fucking old jailbird!" Bennie's laugh was loud and genuine.

When Motley put the phone down, Rachel was looking across the table at him with raised eyebrows, "Well?" she asked.

"It was Bennie. An old mate from the army."

"And you're meeting him later?"

"Hm, hm…is that okay?"

"I thought you were going to take me shopping for curtains."

"Want to come and meet Bennie? He's over at the Saint David's."

"No thanks. I'd rather go shopping." Rachel's voice was weighted with consternation at the sudden change of plan.

"You sure? I know Bennie would love to meet you."

"There are still lots of things we need for the flat. You know that. Have you got to meet him today?"

"He's only in town for a couple of days, and it sounded really important."

He tried not to show it, but Motley was grateful that Rachel had something else to do. His meeting up with pals from the Regiment invariably dissolved into a drinking session that ended with him sleeping in some urine-smelling bus shelter or on some windblown railway station, wondering what fucking planet he was on. Despite his pulverising hangover, Motley was looking forward to seeing Bennie again. And the subsequent drinking session.

17

The ex-para Sergeant was standing at the bar when Motley arrived. His massive shoulders looked uncomfortable and out of place in his obviously expensive suit. As Motley stood a few feet behind him, it felt like he was standing beneath an overhanging cliff-face. Bennie's instincts must have told him to turn around. His wide face cracked into a huge grin. "Fuck me, Taff!"

Bennie grabbed Motley in a bear hug and then started pumping his hand. "The last time I saw you, you were being carted off in handcuffs, mate. You had a couple of crap-hats hanging onto each arm."

When Motley finally retrieved his mauled hand, he replied, "Well thanks for reminding me of that happy occasion Bennie."

"Sorry mate. Anyway it's great to see you. You look fit, you still working out? Still tabbing twenty kliks a day?"

"Yeah, you're bloody joking, of course. I did enough of that fitness shit in the slammer. I don't want to lift another weight in my entire bloody life."

Bennie was indicating to the barman with his fingers that he wanted two more of what was in his snifter glass. Motley's ex-Para and SAS comrade was a chunky, well-built guy with an appealing look – in a stereotypical sun-blond, stunt-man rugged kind of way. He had a chin like a great hairy bum, with a deep fissure right down the middle. In the past, Bennie had pulled as many girls as Motley; now, looking at his lop-sided smile, Motley guessed that he still did.

The trouble with Bennie had always been his temper. He could transpose from a composed, intelligent, easy-going bloke into a raving nutter in a nano-second. This guy didn't have a short fuse: he had an instantaneous one. Maybe that's why Bennie and Motley had got along so well; they recognised the same shortcomings in each other.

"What's that?" Motley asked, nodding at his friend's glass and plonking himself on top of one of the barstools.

"Remy, of course. Triples. Started at breakfast. Fucking great stuff. Love it."

Motley's mate had always been an accomplished boozer. But so was everyone else in the mob. He grabbed both the fresh drinks in one of his huge paws and nodded to a couple of leather armchairs, "Let's talk over there."

When the two men sat down they got straight into the Iraq thing, "You know that the battalion came home three months after they shipped you out don't you?" Motley just nodded. "Okay, look. First off, I'm sorry you lost those three guys, yeah? But we all knew it wasn't your fault, so let's just get that out of the way."

Motley held up his hand, "Bennie, it doesn't matter whose fault it was. Those poor bastards are gone."

"Yeah, right. Anyway, at least half-a-dozen senior NCOs bought themselves out when we got back. And then they immediately signed up with American companies as bodyguards back in country. They call themselves Security Operatives or some such bullshit. They're pulling down more than five grand a week on the circuit, babysitting oil and construction workers."

"Yeah. I heard. But we've lost a couple of good guys doing that bodyguard crap. It's not worth getting yourself blown to bits for five grand a week, is it?"

"Bloody hell Taff! We were doing it for a lot less than that when we wore the Queen's uniform."

"Yeah, well. That was different."

Motley didn't know how it was different. He just felt as though it had to be. Otherwise, nothing made any sense at all. After catching up on the news, the two men got down to talking about the madness and defective thinking behind the entire war. Then they came to talking about the squaddie's war – the combat soldier's take on the whole business. Bennie started going on about the idea that if young guys knew what combat was really like; there'd be no wars. "The fighting soldier's breakfast, eh, Taff. A yawn a piss and a good look around."

But Motley knew that Bennie was wrong. Motley actually believed that young men love to shoot guns and kill the enemy; it puts a smile on their aggressive faces. Especially if a paratrooper's red beret is sitting above their infuriated faces. He also thought that the only shabby little secret of combat that would actually put young men off going to war is about how miserable and dirty it all is. The sleeping on rocks, eating shit food, crapping in a hole in the ground, washing your balls in cold water, sitting around bored silly for weeks on end, and then suddenly you're pissing in your pants because you're so fucking scared you lose control of your bodily functions. What kind of job is that for a youngster?

And then there's the sheer silliness of war. You won't believe this, but the sand in Iraq was the wrong kind of sand for fighting in. It's too fine for sandbags – it doesn't have the stopping power to soak up the energy of a high-velocity round. At one point, the Army had to use a fleet of lorries to import sandbags from Kuwait and Saudi Arabia. How daft is that? Finally, after all the reminiscing, Bennie concluded: "That's why every squaddie who fought out there in the desert hoped that Israel would get a nervous breakdown and nuke the sands of Iraq into one big sheet of fucking glass. Of course, that's not going to happen now. And that's why Brit and Yank kids are still going to be dying in Iraq for the next ten years."

"Blood for oil, brother. Blood for oil." Motley intoned. It was the squaddie's favourite hymn out there.

18

Motley was no dupe as far as international politics were concerned; for him the objectives of America's post-9/11 foreign policy seemed to be to snag control over near-eastern oil. He remembered sitting in a desert mess hall watching a televised broadcast just before the troops advanced into Iraq. Motley enjoyed decoding the crude attempts at disinformation – "My fellow Americanists. Today I'd like to talk to you about being…greedy and self-righteous…at all times. Now I've got nothing against those Eye-raqis…they're nice folks…it's just a damn pity they're sitting on all that oil." Then Motley remembered laughing out loud when he heard… "So if Saddam won't come out, we'll go in and get him." A few hours later, Motley's arse was bumping across the southern Iraq desert at the head of a para recon patrol.

19

Motley took a great gulp from his glass of Remy. His hangover was starting to dissolve into another boozing session.

"Anyway…" Bennie sat up in his chair, "…to business, Taff. Word is, that you've landed on your feet back here in Cardiff." Motley just smiled at his inquisitive friend. Bennie continued. "…Got yourself a nice little Pepsi business going. Yeah?"

"Uh…Pepsi?" Motley didn't know what the hell his friend was talking about.

"You know, Pepsi."

"Jesus, what the hell are you talking about Bennie?"

His grinning friend looked around the bar then said quietly. "We don't call it coke anymore Taff, too many electronic ears around."

Then the penny dropped. Pepsi…Coke! "Bloody hell, Bennie, who've you been talking to about me?" Motley's voice suddenly had a righteous buzz to it.

"Come on, Taff, the Regiment's a very small family, remember. We all stay in touch, right? Anyway, street Intel is that you're set up with a guy called Toby Stevens. He's your supplier, right?"

"Christ! What the hell are you doing that kind of digging around for?" Motley was getting worried, "If you can find all that shit out about me, the cops can do the same."

"Forget the blue-meanies, Taff, they don't have the kind of Intel we get."

Motley sat back in the soft leather of the hotel armchair, and racked his brain for an idea of where this conversation was going. He wanted it to get to the point, fast.

"Put your cards on the table, Bennie. I think you should tell me what the hell this is about." A slight edge had crept into Motley's voice. Bennie raised up his palms in his friend's direction, trying to placate him.

"Relax, buddy. All I'm here for is to make you a proposition. A business proposition." Motley did start to relax, but only slightly. He was still feeling very exposed. He nodded and moved forward in his seat. "So, what's the deal?" he asked.

"You want to talk about it in here?" Bennie looked around at the bustle going on in the fast filling-up bar. The lunchtime crowd was piling in. Security-wise, it wasn't a good idea to be prattling on about the drug trade with a couple of hundred business bozos passing by their shoulders.

"Let's take a little walk," Bennie threw the last mouthful of his drink down his neck and got up from his chair. "You can show me the sights. Looks like they've done a nice job on the waterfront. Those new buildings look great. What about that big curved copper roof, eh? What's that? "

"It's the Millennium Centre. It's an opera house."

"O dear. It looks like the humped back of a horny animal, screwing the living shit out of that old red-brick building."

"Jesus Bennie, what the hell do you know about architecture, you're from Milton-fucking-Keynes, for Christ's sake!"

20

The two men strolled along the windy promenade that ensnares the deep scallop of Cardiff Bay. They looked around at the immodest steel and glass structures that triumphantly unreeled themselves around the veranda-pocked waterfront. The unimaginative blocks of expensive apartments pseudonymously denied the fact that the area was once a mighty coal exporting port. Cardiff's dockland was a place of dusty embarkation for millions of tons of ozone-trouncing coal dug by hand from holes in the crudely slashed, pit-hooter thrumming valleys of south Wales.

Bennie kept glancing over his shoulder occasionally, checking to see if they were being followed. He spoke in almost a whisper, "Right. For the sake of our own security, I'm only going to talk to you in general terms, okay? And it goes without saying that everything I tell you is strictly confidential, yeah?" Motley nodded agreement. "But when I've finished, if you say yes to coming on board, I'll tell you everything you need to know. Agreed"

"Sure," Motley nodded again.

"Okay. Now you know from your time at Hereford that there's an affinity between government covert operations and the drug syndicates. Both are practitioners of 'the clandestine arts,' so to speak." Bennie held up a couple of fingers on both hands and wiggled them in the air in that horrible quote/unquote fashion. Motley hated that stupid affectation. It seemed to have caught on with every pretentious wannabe twat on the planet, along with that cringingly misunderstood phrase 'per se'. He ignored his mate's 'faux pas', so to speak.

Bennie went quiet for a moment as a young couple walked past. Then, after looking over his shoulder, he continued. "If I just call them, 'The Company', you know which intelligence organisation I'm talking about, yeah?"

"Course I do. Everybody in the Intel game calls them that anyway."

"Okay. Well, The Company has been deeply involved in the world drug markets as an extension of American foreign policy for more than thirty years. Yeah?" He looked at Motley for a reaction.

Motley just nodded in agreement, "Tell me something I don't already know, Bennie."

"So, you know that the world-wide drug trade is the most profitable of all criminal enterprises. Like the man

170

said, drugs are the ultimate merchandise. You also know about The Company's covert involvement, yeah?"

"Yeah, yeah. For Christ's sake get on with it."

"Sorry Taff. I know you you're up to speed on most of this. Anyway, the intelligence community and the criminal gangs run the same kind of ops. We both maintain organisations that carry out operations on a global scale without being detected."

"Yeah, I know all of that shit."

Bennie suddenly stopped walking and held out both his hands, "For Christ's Sake, buddy! Wake up and smell the profit. It's a natural symbiosis…the government trained us, and now we're using our Special Forces skills to get rich. Ha-ha-ha! It's a fucking joke innit."

Motley turned to look Bennie in the eyes. "Yeah. And they trained us to get very nasty when we need to. But we've left all that shit behind. Right?"

Bennie's smile suddenly dropped from his face. "Er…look. Before we go any further. I suppose I should tell you. Our business expansion plans recently meant that we had to go to war with a couple of Yardie gangs up in Birmingham. You might have seen it on the TV news."

Motley shook his head. He didn't bother telling his friend that he made a point of avoiding the TV news. That crappy business over in Iraq made him lose his rag every time he watched it. "A couple of their top guys got slotted," Bennie continued, "bad news that, but it had to be done. By the way, we can get you tooled up with any hardware you might need."

"Jesus, Bennie! You've been watching too many Godfather movies. There's nothing like that kind of action in Cardiff. They've never had a drive-by shooting or any of that shit. God-fucking-forbid!"

"Oh," Bennie grunted, with some surprise. Motley thought he detected a note of disappointment.

"Well there might be pretty soon, Taff, when we start to take people's business away from them. It's entirely up to you. If you agree to come in with us, you'll run the entire retail end in south Wales. However you run it, it's your business. Just as long as we get our margins every month."

"So, what exactly are you offering me? A drugs deal?"

Bennie stopped and took a long look into his face.

"More than that buddy: much more than that. The drugs business in the UK is worth about eight billion a year. If you take the heroin and crack out of that, I'd say there was still seven billion. We're not interested in the smack heads and those other mainline losers. That's not where the big money is. Weed and Coke is the future, my friend. Weed and cocaine are the smiling faces of the well-dressed future. And that's where we're at."

"Suits me fine." Motley never had any intentions of getting into the mainline gear anyway.

"Okay. Let me tell you a bit more about our set up. How deep do you think The Company is into supporting drug cartels with protection and logistics?"

He was asking Motley for a history of Company complicity in the worldwide drug trade. Jesus, it would have taken all bloody day! Motley decided to give him the potted-history, as he understood it.

"It started in the sixties. Everyone knew that south-east Asian politics were being dominated by the narcotics trade, so The Company got involved trying to further the US's strategic goals in the region. Company planes were used to transport raw opium from the poppy fields in the Golden Triangle to the Thai/Burma border for shipment to the heroin labs. With the supply of arms, this gave them some authority over the warlords and drug barons."

Bennie was nodding as Motley stopped for breath.

"Okay. You're up to speed on the heroin trade." he interrupted, "But we're not involved with the Far East connection. Our sphere of influence is the Caribbean cocaine trade." He pulled Motley's arm to get them moving again. "Keep walking, Taff." Bennie was obviously very twitchy about surveillance. He even lowered his voice, talking almost in a whisper. "After the cold war ended, the covert ops guys were sitting around with very little to do. So some of them decided to use their drug cartel connections to go into business for themselves. Now, tell me what you know about the South American theatre."

"Bloody hell, Bennie, what is this? Some sort of exam?"

"I just want to know how much I need to fill you in on, Buddy."

Motley decided to play along with his ex-comrade's little narco/politico quiz. He struggled to recall all the gen he'd been given while up at Hereford.

"The Colombian cartels around Medellin expanded in the early eighties when the Company was smuggling arms to the Contras down in Nicaragua. Planes would fly south from Florida loaded up with guns and under Company protection, they'd return to the States loaded up with cocaine. That's the thumbnail sketch, yeah?"

"Spot on. I don't really have to tell you much more. So, what are you earning right now?" he suddenly asked.

"What?" Motley's friend's final question had startled him. For his own operation's security, he didn't really want to get into telling Bennie anything about his own business, so he decided to be oblique with him. "Listen mate, I'm doing okay right now. I've got a nice little number going here and I don't want to fuck it up."

"How much?" Bennie insisted.

"It isn't the money. I can't say too much, but the way things are down here I'm pretty much bulletproof regarding the cops. It's a nice situation to be in."

21

Motley and Bennie kept walking along the gusty waterfront; occasionally stopping to monitor the performance of the Bay's dancing Millennium waters. Fat ribs of water fell and broke with a splat against the stone walls of the embankment. The elliptical, steel-caged pond was wind-rippled and turgid. Bennie still kept glancing furtively over his shoulders.

"Mm…so you've got a couple of Drugs Dicks in your pocket, eh. Jesus Taff, our guys are buying government fucking ministers over in the Islands. Coast Guard Admirals, and that kind of shit. After a couple of years with me you could buy yourself a Chief Constable here if you wanted to. Now for the last time how much?"

"I make about a grand a week."

"Oh shit! You're dicking around over peanuts! If you come on board with us, and run our Welsh operation, you can multiply that by ten. That's just for Cardiff. Twenty when you've got Swansea and Newport in the bag."

Motley couldn't help laughing at Bennie's talent for inducing people to agree to spend the rest of their natural in a prison cell – given the rules of the drug-dealing game.

"I don't know Bennie, the bigger the profile, the bigger the risk, yeah? It's a risk versus opportunity thing isn't it? I don't want to get too bloody greedy and end up back in the slammer."

Bennie was nodding. He didn't say anything for a minute, and then he asked, "You've got a girl, right?"

"Jesus, mate. Leave her out of this."

"It's just that you were never this timid before. I know you were always careful, and that's good. But hell, I'd thought you'd jump at this deal."

"It isn't the girl, Bennie. Okay?"

"Sure. No problem, Buddy," he slapped Motley hard on the back, almost winding him, "so what products are you moving right now?"

Again, Motley didn't want to answer. Then Bennie answered the question for him, "Some coke, some 'E', a bit of weed. Any Horse?"

"No, I won't touch heroin. It's disgusting. Who needs to be around those ratty-looking junkies? They all end up dying in some shivering doorway from an OD-cancellation of breath."

"Good. That's not our product anyway. The Colombian connection is our business: the fruit of the coca leaf, God bless it. You know that in thirty years time, they'll have banned tobacco completely and they'll be selling government-taxed cocaine from street-corner kiosks, just like the old tobacconists did. Coke is the coming thing, my friend. It's the happy-time drug of the future."

22

Once again, the two men stopped and gazed across the Bay at the incongruous white wooden shack that is the Norwegian church. It looked so aloof, so out of place amongst all the soaring glass and concrete that it seemed like a building from another planet, instead of just another century. Its pale, fragile beauty reminded Motley of Rachel. It was then that he started thinking about their future together. The last thing he wanted was to jeopardise that. Maybe it was then that Bennie sensed he was losing him.

"All right Taff. I'll tell you what. Take the job just for a year or two, yeah? Get it up and running for us and then you can retire. I promise you'll have made enough loot in a couple of years to live it up in the South of France until your pension days. What do you say?"

It sounded tempting. Motley was beginning to waver. Bennie had made him an offer he knew Motley couldn't refuse. But before he agreed, Motley wanted to talk to Rachel. "Let me have it for tonight, Bennie. I'll call you in the morning with a simple yes or no."

"Can't do it," Bennie shook his head and sank his hands into his coat pockets, "I need to know now, Taff. If you're out, I need to find someone else down here PDQ."

"For Christ's sake Bennie. I need time to think." He just needed an hour with Rachel, but Motley wasn't going to tell Bennie that.

"You don't have it my friend. In or out?"

"Fuck that shit, Bennie. That's not the way I do things." Recognising that he couldn't rush his friend into a decision, Bennie backed off. He decided to come at it again from a different direction. After a few moments, in a slow and level voice, he said to his friend, "I just want to tell you, Taff, that the guys who were killed over there on your road-block are in on the deal. They're part of your team." Motley looked at him like he was from another planet.

"What the hell are you talking about?"

It was crunch time; and Bennie had decided to play his trump card, "Their families get a cut of your action, okay. Straight off the top." Bennie smiled lavishly at his friend, pleased with what he thought would be a masterstroke. He followed up,

"Those boys' families will get a share of your operation."

Motley gulped back a gut-curling curse. He saw his mind's eye filled with flag-draped coffins being carefully lowered from the transport plane. Shaking his head from side to side, he growled, "It's no fucking good to them now, Bennie!"

"It's the right thing Taff. It's loyalty to mens' families. We'll take care of them. Two of the lads had kids didn't they?" Motley just nodded, turning away in anguish. "Well, then," Bennie continued. "They'll need the money, won't they?"

The memory of the men's ugly deaths bludgeoned at Motley's forebrain like a hideous hammer. To die so young was bad enough, but to die so disgustingly and unnecessarily was something that made him feel sick with grief. "They're fucking dead, Bennie! So stop using them to get what you want."

"Jesus, Taff, stop shouting. Calm down. I was only trying to do the right thing. That's all."

"Yeah, well. We will help their families, but stop trying to use them."

"Sorry, mate. It just came out the wrong way."

Motley nodded lightly. He felt the anger and suffocation slowly rising from his chest, "Okay. Let's go back and get some scoff."

23

After lunch Bennie pressed him for a straight answer. Motley took a deep breath, he was thinking, maybe two years and then off to somewhere warm. You can live like a king over in those tropical paradises, and he knew that if he said no, Bennie would find someone else. It also occurred to him that eventually he'd end up fighting the bastard Bennie took on just to hang on to his own patch. It would have to be a go-er. He'd explain to Rachel later. "Okay, Bennie. I'm in."

"Great!" His bear-like ex-comrade slipped an arm around his shoulder, "Let's shake on it."

Motley swept Bennie's arm from his shoulder and pushed his hand away. "Jesus, Bennie. We could be under surveillance right now. No handshakes, you daft bugger."

Bennie quickly realised his mistake, "Oh yeah, sorry mate. So let's down a few cold ones, then we'll take another walk and I'll fill you in on some of the other details."

24

They strolled around the encircled waters of the Bay once again; the hissing, murmuring waters; the conspiracy of waters. The murky green surface of the Bay stirred and recomposed itself according to the revisions of the wind. Bennie explained to Motley the drug supply line. The operation concentrated on the cocaine trade because of their contacts in South America. The deal was: that the old anti-communist organisation kept their spheres of influence, the far east drug trade was still run by The Company but now, instead of fighting communism, they were using their contacts to make billions of dollars in profit for themselves. The Drugs War thing was a complete hoax. It wasn't a Drug War: it was a Greed War.

The south American cocaine supply chain worked like this. The nose-candy was flown up from Medellin to Honduras. It was then flown across the Caribbean to Barbados where it was loaded into containers for shipment to Marseilles. Bennie's operation had bought a couple of customs officials down in the south of France who made sure that they didn't lose more than one container in ten of the shipments.

The coke was then transported across Europe by a maze of routes. Each region of the UK had its own set-up to import the stuff from the continent. Bennie reckoned that all he needed to know about the Welsh operation was that the merchandise was brought over from France by a fishing-trawler that was met by a receiving boat out at sea. The supply line was secure; they hadn't been stopped once since they'd started test-running some weed three months ago.

"Sounds tight. Very tight," Motley said.

Bennie had tried to re-assure him about the security of the organisation. They had a long conversation about personnel set-up. Motley liked what he heard.

"We try to recruit only ex-Special Forces or ex-army Intel types to run our ops. You spent a couple of years at Hereford, so you'd be a natural for us."

"Sounds good. But how did you know I'd be interested? You were taking a bit of a risk, weren't you?"

"Not really. The truth is we first approached Barry Bolly, you know him, yeah? He's ex-SBS but he told us he didn't think he had the experience or the brains to run the ops. He also said that you were already into the business, and that if you came on board he'd be happy to work for you."

"Barry Bolger told you that? Jesus, BB's the guy that gave me the driving job over at the Mail."

"That's right. BB's a good man, considering he's half shark, half fucking seagull, but he's not a real organiser. You're the man with all the skills we need for this operation, Taff. We're all going to make a bloody fortune out it."

Motley hoped that Bennie was right. Just a year or two of making the kind of money he was expecting would set him and Rache up for buying a bar down on the Costas, and a life of sunshine and Sangria.

"Come on Taff, we're sorted here. Let's get back to the hotel and down a few Remys. On me." Over a couple of millionaire measures of expensive cognac, they talked through some of the details of the supply operation. Bennie made Motley memorise a contact number, and told him to call him in a couple of days. He would transfer strategic funds to an offshore bank account in Motley's name. A figure of $250,000 US was mentioned as a start-up fund. Motley was also was told to get Barry Bolger on board and use his Royal Marines experience to buy a fast sea-going boat to make the French trawler rendezvous.

Setting up a drugs empire is a lot like setting up a Hollywood deal for a blockbuster movie: it's a typical capitalist adventure. And every investor thinks that it's a breeze. At that level it's all about financial security, business confidence and the passionate connoisseurship of money. It's about crime and insider knowledge, about advantage and privilege. The anonymous investors are handsome fathers and nervous mothers with growing assets and two freckled kids, constantly shepherded by a beautiful Swedish au pair. The drugs business is about making money work; the entire drugs problem is about the genius of money.

Bennie was hot on security, stressing that Motley should only use random phone-boxes for all his calls to him. After outlining their immediate plans for the business, the ex-paras got back to their army days. They talked about all the great guys they'd served with, the good times they'd had, and the bad. They laughed, smoked a couple of fat cigars, and drank a whole bottle of Remy. All the while, Motley was trying to figure out how he'd tell Rachel and Sweep about their new lives. This was going to be the big time for all of them. He was going to have to give up the driving job at the Mail, and Sweep was going to have to come into the import business with him. They needed to set up a company as a front for the real smuggling operation.

Meanwhile, gnawing at the back of his brain was a strategy to get Toby to come in with him. Toby was the key to going up against the Drug Squad dicks. Toby would have to bring tangible evidence of police corruption with him when he came over to Motley. That would be everyone's insurance when the turf war started. If they were going into competition with the bent coppers of the Drug Squad, they'd need all the leverage they could get, and some prejudicial muscle. Motley needed to pull in a couple of old mates from the Regiment. Up until now, Motley had treated his drug-dealing activities as an important hobby. But now he was going to have to get a lot more serious about money and time. It's like with so much else in life, if you want to make it big you have to get a lot more serious. Motley started by calling Barry Bolger, the ex-SBS guy, and offered him the job of Head of Security for the new operation. BB was famous among Special Ops people for killing more of the enemy with his bare hands than anyone else in the history of the Special Boat Section. BB seemed to have a knack for ending a man's life with nothing more than his steel-like fingers.

I suppose that everyone has a different theory about what 'getting serious' means, but usually it's accepted that 'getting serious' ends up with someone getting hurt. And with Motley's new security chief, 'getting serious' meant busy hands wielding broken chains, crowbars and baseball bats. It's a good thing that 'getting serious' doesn't cross all our minds, a good thing it doesn't catch on. That would make life too bloody interesting by half.

25

Have you ever seen those pictures on the TV of men getting ready to go to war? The ones where they're cleaning their weapons and then loading them up with ammunition; getting themselves tooled up for unleashing an extravagance of fury, for doing homicidal harm? It's the same when men prepare for any war: including a turf war. They arm themselves with the necessary, and then they make bombastic jokes about each other, the enemy, and about Death: especially about Death. They insult Death, call him silly names; but their jokes are subconsciously fraught with fear. Oh no, not the fear of Death; but of coming apart when the fighting starts, of coming apart at the seams and breaking unstoppably.

26

Motley was in a unique position to know what was coming, what would happen next. He knew that when men go to war, they're suddenly not men anymore. They become trembling fingers on triggers, sweating Pavlovian bodies holding a weapon, vulnerable shapes standing up fighting or lying down on the ground nauseous and cold with fear. The only thing that stops them breaking and running is the respect of their comrades. They'd rather die than face the shame of letting their mates down. Motley also knew, that you really need to be young to fight a war, very young, fearlessly young.

You and I are too old to fight a war, we know too much: we're too full of imagination and fear. Maybe you have a younger brother, a teenaged son – they should be the ones to fight our wars. No…even they are too old to fight a war. In fact everyone is too old to fight a war. Perhaps the unconceived don't have so much to lose as the living, but even they, the unborn, are too old to fight a war.

The frowning ex-soldier was thinking these thoughts because he was starting to get old, and old men start to think upon their dying. Come on, admit it, we're all scared of dying, right? …I'm scared of dying. I'll be truthful with you: death scares the shit out of me. I'm afraid of death because Death takes your life and throws it away like a bag of old rubbish, like a piece of useless junk, that's fucking why. That's what scares me. It is Death who decides which of us is a bag of old rubbish; who's just a piece of useless junk. And who the hell is Death to decide? What the fuck does Death know about any of us?

27

"I want you to call Andy Tremblett and tell him that you're cancelling your contract with him," Motley told a disbelieving Toby.

"But he'll kill me," Toby had whined, "He'll kill me!"

Now Motley was sitting in Toby's flat with BB, they were waiting for Tremblett to arrive. Toby was sitting on an armchair in the corner, almost wetting himself with fear and trepidation.

When the doorbell rang, Motley got up and answered it, preparing himself by flexing his fists and hunching his shoulders. When he saw Motley, Tremblett's face was a picture of confusion and alarm – you know the picture I mean, the scary one with the guy holding his hands to the sides of his face and screaming his head off.

"Who…who the fuck are you?" Tremblett managed to stammer.

"Me? Oh, I'm just your worst nightmare," Motley answered, pointing at his own chest. Terry was standing behind the astonished Tremblett, and instantly moved forward at the provocation. The copper raised his hand in restraint.

"Hang on, Ter. Let's see what's going on first." Brushing past Motley, Tremblett marched down the short hallway into the lounge. Terry and Motley followed, eyeing each other warily. "Didn't you used to be in the movies?" Motley asked Terry as he followed him into the lounge, "Didn't you used to be Godzilla? What happened to your rubber tail?" Terry's face remained as expressionless as a stone fossil.

Toby almost let out a scream when he saw Tremblett. BB was just sitting with his arms stretched out across the back of the sofa; he smiled broadly at the stony-faced policeman. Tremblett weighed up the scene.

"So, you two are the new guys on the block, eh?" The detective was nodding at BB and Motley as he spat the words, "Well, here's the deal. You've got two days to disappear from my patch, or you'll find yourselves bounced into one of my cells so fast it'll make your fucking heads reel."

Motley leaned down and picked up his drink from the coffee table. After, taking a slow sip, he said, "You're reading from the wrong page, friend. I'm here to tell you what the deal is." He glared provocatively at Tremblett over his brandy glass.

The copper's head fell slightly to one side as he looked at Motley, "Don't I know you from somewhere? Where is it, eh? Have I ever nicked you for something?"

Motley laughed and took another sip from his drink. Meanwhile, Terry and BB were eyeing each other with evaluatory glances. The ex-SBS guy thought that Terry looked like a super-embellished breezeblock: he was as wide as he was tall. The two hard-men had already recognised each other as the designated enforcer for their organisation.

"I'm taking over your turf," Motley suddenly announced, "And there's nothing you can do to stop me."

"Oh, yeah," Tremblett laughed sarcastically, "I'm just going to let you kick my arse and do nothing about it, am I?"

"That's it," replied Motley, "You and your corrupt coppers are going to go quietly and let us take over your business."

"You fucking moron," Tremblett almost jumped at Motley, but managed to restrain himself enough to launch a stream of fierce invective at him, "What kind of pussy do you think you're dealing with here? I'll have you and your dip-shit pal wishing both your dad's had settled for a blow-job. I'll kick your arses back to the shit-hole you crawled out of. You pricks are making a... "

Motley suddenly held up his hand, "Not that old cliché, please."

Tremblett turned purple with rage, his eyes bulging, his hands shaking. Toby was already curled up in a ball, his knees pulled up to his chest, his hands over his ears. BB was sitting forward in his seat, ready to launch himself at Terry if the big guy made a move towards Motley.

"So, why can't I stop you?" Tremblett finally calmed down enough to ask, "What do you think you have that's going to stop me from dumping you two in the fucking river?"

"Him," Motley, jerked his head backward towards Toby sitting behind him.

"That little queer?" Tremblett laughed, "What the fuck can he do?"

"Oh, my queer friend here can fuck this city's entire drug squad up the arse, that's what he can do." Motley said, the satisfaction dripping from his lips.

Tremblett looked stunned. He leaned around Motley and jabbed a finger at the terrified Toby. "You little prick. You keep your mouth shut!" he snarled.

Toby couldn't prevent a sob escaping from his convulsing, on-the-run mouth.

Motley stepped into the visual line between Tremblett and Toby. Terry leaned forward on his toes as BB simultaneously rose from his seat, taking a step to stand beside Motley. The two men now formed a blocking wall between Tremblett, Terry and the whimpering Toby.

"Just to let you know the score," Motley's voice was weighted with threat, "Toby's given me a signed affidavit of all his business activities with you and your boys. I've got names, places, dates, and amounts of money, goods that were exchanged. The document's now sitting safely with a solicitor, you know what I'm saying."

"You little shit!" Tremblett screamed at Toby, while trying to push past Motley to get at him. "You fucking double-crossing little shit!"

The agonised Toby cowered in his armchair, crying and whimpering. The two ex-Special Forces guys closed up together, holding up their hands towards their opponents, ready to go to war. Terry reached out to grab at BB, but his hand was expertly slapped away at the same time a size eleven boot crashed into his groin at excruciating speed. The big guy made a sound like high-pressure steam escaping from a locomotive then sank slowly to the floor. That well-aimed kick seemed to stop everything in its tracks. Tremblett froze then began struggling to help a still moaning

Terry up from the slippery laminate floor. They backed away from the confrontation, retreating towards the door.

"You shits are going to be sorry you were ever born!" the policeman yelped as he practically carried his wounded hireling out of the flat.

"Jesus. Not another old movie cliché, please," Motley jibbed. "You sound cornier than Steven Segal. I'll give you the number of a script-writer friend of mine."

As Tremblett dragged the groaning Terry through the front door, BB called after his opposite number, "Be seeing you, big guy." But Terry's ears were deaf to taunts; his ears were full of a high-pitched sound, like dolphins laughing. Terry was in a world of his own, a malevolent world of searing pain and broken testicles. Now Motley had another war to deal with; he hadn't wanted another war, he didn't need it. But licking his dry lips he announced with a laugh, "That was fun!"

He knew that in the drugs game, brutality never does you in; it's being nice that does you in. Yeah, it's all wrong, I know, but that's the drugs game for you. BB just smiled and nodded, while Toby continued to cry with renewed exertion. He was pawing pathetically at a patch of spreading wetness staining the crotch of his Ralph Lauren chinos. That was the only discernable sign that a war had just started.

28

With BB's help, Motley quickly assembled a strong team of ex-Special Forces sinners. And soon there was a fast, sea-going launch moored in Swansea marina, ready to meet up with the French trawler bringing the merchandise from France. Sweep and a couple of the guys would then meet the launch at one of the many remote inlets along the west Wales coast and drive the tightly wrapped bundles of cocaine and bales of weed to a garage that Motley rented under a false name on the outskirts of Cardiff.

The entire operation was up and running surprisingly quickly, and the six-man team, especially Motley and Sweep, already had a lot of fellow feeling for achieving their objective: to make as much loot as possible and retire from the drugs business before their luck ran out. Toby's expanded customer network and Motley's old wine-bar operation were already providing a return on Bennie's original investment. But Bennie reserved his happy smile-down-the-telephone for each time Motley called him with details of the scaled up army of pushers and the escalating profit figures.

Although pleased with the way things were going, Bennie kept warning Motley to prepare for the backlash from the recently ruined Drug Squad operation. But Motley was already prepared. It wouldn't be true to say that he was looking forward to the confrontation he knew was coming, but he couldn't help smiling to himself whenever he thought about asserting his right as a businessman to protect his legitimate interests. He was ready to injure the heads of anyone who was dumb enough to try and snatch his new entrepreneurial, moneymaking scheme away from him.

In recent days, several recalcitrant dealers loyal to the Trembletts had regrettably had their toenails clipped – with a pair of rusty pliers. BB was atavistically adept at persuading those freelancers to go quietly. The work of controlling any grievances was, of course, given to BB. But as the weeks and then the months rolled by, nothing terrible happened on the Drug Squad front. There were no visits from balaclava'd figures in the depths of the night, no snarling baseball bats or screaming machetes. Motley's anxiety about an all-out turf war was slowly receding. Perhaps, he thought, the shuddering kick in the balls that BB had given Terry had knocked the fight out of the entire bent-copper operation.

It was only when he was lying awake in bed at night, with the peacefully sleeping Rachel at his side that Motley

twisted and squirmed with worry. He knew in his heart that
the Trembletts and their corrupt friends were coming for
him. When he closed his eyes, he could see blood being
spilt, bones being snapped, heads hitting concrete. He saw
faces showing fear, terror, then horror, forcing more
sleepless convulsions from him. The ruined bodies that
littered his mind's eye caused him to wince and writhe,
drenched in the sweat that comes at such times. And then,
when he'd finally fallen asleep, the ghosts would come:
"Boys…boys? I'm sorry."

Poor Motley, you had to feel sorry for him. He was a
young, getting-rich businessman with a beautiful girlfriend.
But he was also a helpless victim of the impeaching,
antipathetic dead.

29

It was Saturday night in the wine-bar, and Motley was there
with his entire team, including Sweep. They were discussing
what had happened when Motley had confronted Andy
Tremblett, and BB downed Terry with a ball-crusher.

"That Terry's easy to handle," BB was saying matter-
of-factly in his raw Glaswegian accent, "He's a bulldozer
type, no finesse. He just tries to use his size to overwhelm
you."

"Well, if you meet that human rhino again, I don't want
you to underestimate him," Motley advised his friend, "He
looks a right bloody handful to me."

That's exactly what Motley told BB. And it didn't
occur to him that it was hypocritical nonsense: because
Motley himself was underestimating the Tremblett brothers.
He didn't realise how truly, breathtakingly nasty sold-out
coppers can be.

30

If you looked into Andy Tremblett's eyes, you would see no shame: his eyes were only another concealment. If you met his family they would all tell you what a good, caring and generous man he was; like so much glorifying bullshit. The truth was; that Andy Tremblett didn't have any time for snowjobs about being good and caring: he was a man of action, and right now, it was determined and violent action that was required. Detective Sergeant Tremblett's favourite saying as he briefed his team before an early morning raid was: "The task, gentlemen. Nothing but the task."

Ah, yes – Andy Tremblett was a guy who could focus down, a man who was able to cut through all the cluttered confusions and identify the solution to a problem. He had already identified the solution to his present problem with Motley. The task he now set himself was daring, unconventional and unbelievably immoral. It was way outside the conventional rules of war, even for an impure turf war: he was going after Motley's woman.

When he told his brother Rod, and then Terry and the rest of his drug squad conspirators, no one flinched. No one so much as blinked. Nobody, including the once dissenting Rod, groped for words of objection, or whistled through their teeth, or jabbered on at a mile a minute at the outrage. They looked one another right in the eyes, and didn't even raise an eyebrow – proving conclusively that there are no 'civilians' in a drug turf-war. The thinking is this; if you're going after maximum shock value, maximum scare tactics, you do violence to the women.

After that meeting it was all unflagging activity; reconnoitring the routes Rachel walked, observing her routines, assigning tasks, planning. Not until the night before the operation did Rod Tremblett sit at his kitchen table and down a half bottle of whisky. With his head in his hands, he wailed, "What am I doing? I can't go through with this!" But that was a lie. Because the following evening, he found he could go through with it. So he did.

To be fair, when Rod had driven the car into Rachel, he didn't have actual murder on his mind. The ghostly potential for murder had been on his mind, but not the actual. All he was thinking about when he aimed the bonnet of the speeding car at the girl was; don't fuck it up, don't miss her. All he needed to do was drive into her and, well…after that, it was all down to her, wasn't it? It was only the next day that Rod's mind became creased and puckered with some massive scene shifting, some colossal re-arrangements. The re-ordered motes of his brain were telling him that he could never have murdered anyone – no, not him, never, never in a million years.

31

If you had seen Rachel moments before the stolen car broke her body, you would have said that she looked stunning, in her navy blue slacks, her crisp white blouse and fitted jacket. Earlier in the day, she had attended an interview for a job on the make-up counter at Boots the chemists. Rachel had quit school a while back, and now wanted a little job of her own. She didn't need to work; Motley took care of her; and he didn't want her working for what he condescendingly called 'pin money'. But Rachel's independent streak made her think that it would be nice to have her own income. She was eighteen now and hormonal eighteen-year-olds are like that. Aren't they? Jesus, to be truthful, I can't remember. I don't think I was ever a teenager.

Of course, looking as good as she did, Rachel got the job, and she was walking home from her father's to her new apartment when a different destiny was made for her. How easily life can be one thing, and then moments later, something totally different. That's exactly what Motley was thinking as he raced across the city to the A+E department, nestled heavy-eyed and groggy at the bottom of the sky-eclipsing tower of the Heath hospital.

Motley understood nothing about destiny, or fate. That's to say, that he understood nothing about life's stubborn determination to seize upon his heart like a wounded lion, and tear it into tiny pieces. As he ran through the hospital corridors, he was yelling into his mobile at Sweep, and then at BB. At the same time, his blood-swollen heart was yelling at him a confession: "Well, that's that then. I shouldn't have bothered you, should I? Making you fall in love, I mean. You fell in love, and now you have to pay the price. Oh well, take care…be seeing you."

We told you Motley, didn't we, me and Sweep. Remember, that night in the wine-bar, we told you. We said, "Don't decide to fall in love with Rachel, not yet. If it happens, it happens. If it's meant to be, it's meant to be. Love is all ready out there waiting for you, so relax. Just enjoy. But don't fall in love, not yet. She's too young."

And what did you say?

…"You guys. You fucking guys."

Yeah, well. You learned the hard way, didn't you tough guy.

32

I shouldn't really say anything about what followed, when Motley burst into the Intensive Therapy Unit and saw Rachel lying fractured and misshapen in a nurse-encircled bed. I should really have Motley's permission to say anything about that, because that kind of mind-numbing scene ought to be licensed. To write about it without permission is impinging on privacy, scandalously disregarding of people's feelings. What I will say – in the parlance of the moment – is that Motley was 'absolutely gutted' when he saw what that speeding car had done to his girlfriend. When he looked at the bandage-swathed, pathetic figure lying in her labyrinthine bed, Motley almost fell to his knees howling with pain. It was as though his heart had been thrown into a huge blender: he felt every bloodied spin of the blades, every ripping, tearing turn of the stainless steel fingers.

That old love, eh, Motley, with its dangers and addictions; it's acid rains. How much do you know about love now, eh? More than me, I'll bet: a lot more than me. Even though I'm sitting here giving half-arsed advice about it, everyone knows more about love than I do. So, Taff, answer me this…why does love have to punish us like that? Why does love so often feel like pain? They're definitely in the same family, aren't they, love and pain? Oh, yes. Love and pain are like a brother and sister who can't get along, a pair of tearful siblings constantly going at it. Or maybe they're not like brother and sister after all; maybe they're more like bloodbrothers. That pair, huh? Those guys, eh? Excruciating pair of bastards, I bet they don't even concern themselves with the suffering they've caused.

Those two berks must be having a joke, aren't they, those piss-taking bloodbrothers? They must be having a larf, kicking us around like that. But they'd better watch out, those two, 'cos their joke is wearing a bit thin, isn't it? I bet you've had enough of it, with their droll wit, their screams of laughter? I'm tired of them too, punching me in the heart and poking their fingers in my eyes. I swear, if I ever get my hands on…but those brothers know that they're on safe ground, because despite our pouts and panic-attacks we're always boomeranging back to them, breaking all the speed limits. We come roaring and clattering back with our arms open wide; because we're weak and raw, and we can never keep away from them for long. Those love/pain twins: those vain, wire-pulling, propagandist bastards.

To be truthful, Taff, my old buddy, to be perfectly honest, my old mate, if you're really looking for some candour from me, here it comes – I sometimes think that perhaps it isn't love that's the fuck-up. Maybe it isn't love that's full of trickery, hazardry and jagged lies. Maybe it's just me. Yeah, I've thought about that one too…maybe it's me that's the bile-filled, vituperative, emotionally crippled fuck-up. What a scream, eh? What a real piss-taker. Christ, I need a drink…and yeah, I know what you're thinking…and ten years of full-on therapy.

<h2 style="text-align:center">33</h2>

Hey people, have you ever seen one those intensive care beds? Oh, jeez, those intensive care beds aren't like any other beds you've ever seen. There's so much life-saving paraphernalia hanging from them that they look like some kind of reef-building organism. Things are constantly being added to them; billowing bags of blood and saline are hung from poles, ringlets of coloured wires dangle and trail, thickets of plastic tubes throb and pulse, gleaming banks of electronic devices fuss and fibrillate. Every machine is metronomically beeping with electrical distress.

The bed was so cluttered that Motley could hardly see Rachel's face. Bandages swathed her head, plastic tubes emerged implausibly from her nose and mouth. Motley constantly strutted around the bed like an expectant father, wringing his hands (yes, people really do that on the ITU ward) and asking the intensively caring nurses whether Rachel was going to be okay.

Then the heavily sweating Sweep swept in with his heavily sweating girlfriend. He instantly dissolved into a river of tears as soon as he saw his daughter.

"They said that a car hit her…sob…sob…a hit-and-run car hit her…sniffle…sniffle…mounted the pavement…and…sob…hit her." Sweep's face, normally torn with larval angers was a mosaic of cold yellow and baby-arse white. It was a Dead End face. It was a face of wasted time and washed away humanity, a face of shadow and darkness and out-of-control eyes. Sweep looked like a ghost, wanting what all ghosts want: a life. Even before Sweep had finished speaking, Motley's face turned as white as fresh snow, signalling the quantum chaos, the split-second adjustments, the unstable convolutions. He knew what hit-and-run cars mounting pavements usually meant. As it sunk in, Motley came close to exploding all over the highly polished floor. But, for now, he was too concerned about Rachel to think about anything else. For now, everything else was meaningless.

34

Of course, Motley understood that the things you dread most you have to let happen. You just have to sit back and let them go ahead – because you'd been expecting it; because we're always expecting the worst to happen, aren't we? And then we rudely chortle through all the hideousness because we'd been expecting it. And that's all we can do; because when the worst finally happens we concede, and we can't contribute. Hey folks, welcome to the ITU – The Intensive Therapy Unit.

Are you prepared for this scene of unparalleled horror, because you'll see things here that you've never seen before? For example, you'll see none of the patients talking or reading here. Most of them are not even thinking. There's an almost total absence of human nostalgia on the ITU, an absence of cerebral contact. It's as if all the patients are taking a rest from the life process – catatonia doesn't impose contact, only life's addiction insists upon that. (That's the only angle that life insists upon: contact.)

Life is a drugs high on the ITU; because on the ITU life is just an observation. When those ITU patients start in on the morphine, their lives become a contraindication, an improbable, vaporous principle. What's instantly noticeable in this forewarned place of the dying is that there are no human cries here, no autonomic struggling to breathe or pulmonary churning. The ITU patients are forced to breathe reconditioned air. Not ordinary reconditioned air; but horrible, man-made air that knows the price of every cough and gasp; knows the trumped-up cost of oxygen, nitrogen and all the other bump and grind molecules that are needed to keep a human-being alive. Oh yes, the air that's breathed on the ITU has its hierarchy of shakers and movers, its battalions of shareholders, profit-makers and undertakers. On the ITU the wolf pack is always profitably closing in for the kill.

35

The two men sat at Rachel's bedside all night, taking turns to wet her lips with cotton-wool buds dipped in water. She remained stubbornly unconscious, and despite the constant pestering from Sweep and Motley, none of the doctors could tell them when or if Rachel would come out of her trauma-enforced sleep. Motley gnawed at his fingernails, while Sweep took deep and surreptitious swigs from a half bottle of scotch he kept in the inside pocket of his beer-stained, dandruff-flecked jacket.

"Jesus, Sweep. Don't you ever think about the damage you're doing to your charred liver anymore?" Motley asked his friend, wedged between the landslide of machinery that slaved away, trying for all it was worth to keep a faltering life advancing.

Sweep looked at Motley as though he had just committed a crime against their friendship. He lifted the bottle of booze to his lips and took another huge slug. Then he looked down at his pot-bellied mid-rift and said: "There you go you wobbly bastard. Sort that lot out." Motley shook his head with dismay.

"Just letting the bugger know who's boss," Sweep snorted.

"What did you have for breakfast this morning?" Motley asked.

"Scotch."

"And for lunch?"

"Beer…and scotch."

"How about dinner tonight?"

"Some wine, maybe…and scotch."

"You're a very sick man, my friend."

Sweep gave his friend a wicked smile. Then he dropped his smile and said, "When Rache's mum left me," he paused and sniffed heavily, "I decided to drink myself to death. But maybe a bottle of scotch and a few beers a day isn't enough. It's taking forever. Maybe I should be drinking ten bottles of scotch a day, or maybe there isn't enough scotch in Scotland for me to drink myself to death. Jesus, maybe I don't have enough time to drink myself to death."

Motley shook his head sadly, and pursed his lips with a weary knowing. He knew in his heart, that there's always time for dying: because it's always time that kills you in the end.

36

The two men watched with quiet admiration as the nurses, those elite trench-fighters in the life-or-death battles that raged around them, went efficiently about their business. The thing you should know about those intensive-care nurses is that they are angels locked up in human bodies. Maybe you are an intensive care nurse yourself…if you are, do you ever feel like breaking out and flying away? Who do you talk to about the awful things you have to look upon? I mean, how can you take it when they come with their steel box to collect your heroic failures, the ones your angel's skills can't save? When Motley and Sweep gazed upon the nurses, they realised that they were looking at battling angels, sent straight from heaven.

Rachel's father did not hold out much hope for his broken daughter: broken femurs, broken pelvis, broken clavicles. That vindictive car had beaten the shit out of her. Her multiple injuries were like a ghastly shopping list of anatomical spoliation. While Sweep wept softly, Motley stroked his girlfriend's uncomprehending forehead with the back of his index finger. "They tried to kill her," he moaned to himself," The bastards tried to kill her!"

That was the moment when Motley lost the plot. That was when it happened, the moment when derangement saw its opportunity. Whatever catastrophes were to happen next, it would all just be cannon fodder for his revenge. So, Motley sat at Rachel's bedside and planned a future of prodigal violence – sans consequence, sans caring, sans mercy, sans everything.

37

Well? Did you see it coming? The shit storm, I mean. Everything's changed, hasn't it? All of it: there's nothing left of the people we knew a couple of days ago. You wouldn't know Motley anymore: you wouldn't want to know him. Unless you need your head examined, unless you're some suicidal frontal-lobe fuck-up, you wouldn't want to know ANYONE like Motley.

He had called a war-council; and now his team sat around him in his flat overlooking the danse-macabre waters of the Bay. Motley was tied and bound by his rage; he could feel its intensity driving out all sense and demanding immediate action.

"Right. We go all out for the bastards! We go to the fucking wall," he was saying to his team.

It seems that at a certain age – my age, for instance – a man's outlook is best tempered by moderation, resignation even. At a certain age one shouldn't look back to grievances or invite challenges from the mean powers that inflicted them. But Motley was far from my capitulating age. And so he wanted vengeance, with all its requisite ruthlessness.

"We'll do whatever you want us to, Taff." BB was speaking for all the men, "But before we strike back we need to draw up a plan, based on logic not blind anger."

"Blind anger? Jesus fucking Christ, BB, she's still unconscious!" Motley slammed his fist down onto the table, rattling the array of coffee mugs, "Two days and she's still unconscious!" Sweep just shook his head sorrowfully, and reached again into his pocket for his already soaking wet handkerchief.

"Those bastards will get what they deserve," one of the three ex-SAS boys that BB had recruited piped up, "but Barry is right. We don't want to be rushing around like a bunch of amateurs. We need to plan an effective response, organise a punitive strike."

The "boys" I refer to are a particularly odd trio. Two of them are broad-shouldered and ox-like, the third is as thin as a pipe cleaner. When not 'active' these boys are agreeable enough, self-mocking and quick to smile. These boys are all literate and self-educated; they are familiar with the works of Shakespeare and the world-changing theories of Einstein. But when they are on a mission, these boys seem to impersonate human sub-species: more repellent, fiercer, with more of the capacity for animal ferocity.

Can you understand these men? Because I can't, I could never understand these men. With all their fierceness and fluency in taking away lives, they still suffer the same anguish, the same emotional destruction that we do. They still weep with their heads in their hands crying out silently, "She can't die! She just can't!" In his incredulous despair,

Motley, the professional soldier, the trained killer, managed to box in his sorrow, and planned with his men what was the best way of handling what would happen next. He could be sobbing vinegary tears one moment, and then, like a baby who suddenly stepped from infancy into adulthood, he was cunningly plotting a pandemonium of violence.

38

Poor Terry...he had been a successful hard man for quite a long time. And he'd done his very best to be a hard man on his very last night on earth. But there was no way he was going to walk away from a punishment by four Ministry of Defence trained professionals. Although Terry didn't really have a neck, it had broken like puny matchwood when they threw him down the stairs. Well, they hadn't actually thrown him down the stairs. It was an accident really, but no one would have believed that. Motley's crew had only thrown the big guy out onto the landing to give themselves more room, but he'd bounced off the wall and fallen headfirst down the concrete stairs. You should have heard his lavish vertebra snap. It was like breaking a stick over your knee. Snap! – it went. And everyone knew that the big guy was dead.

Terry's unfortunate wife had already been knocked out cold, suffering a bashed-in nose and a matched pair of black eyes. But that too was purely accidental; she had answered the door to the flat and so BB had had to deck her to get to Terry. You should have seen them ten minutes later, trying to carry Terry's carpet-wrapped body down the urine swathed, high-rise stairs (well they couldn't just leave him on the stairs could they, and no one wanted to carry him back up the stairs). It was a full, back breaking fifteen minutes before they were stuffing the big guy's carcass into the back of their transit. Half an hour after that, the green bellies of the river Taff's eel population were being swollen by eighteen-and-a-half stones of what must have tasted like adrenaline infused play dough. Poor Terry. Poor bloody eels.

39

Of the four men directly involved with Terry's demise, Motley was the only one who didn't feel any erosion of conscience. The shrinks all talk about feelings of guilt, and, of course, Motley knew all about guilt; he knew guilt like the back of his hand. He knew guilt inside and out; but he didn't feel guilt about this one. In fact, he felt the other thing: he felt acquitted. The next day, as he sat beside Rachel's bed, amongst the pain-encoded noises and smells, he took her hand in his and satisfyingly whispered in her ear, "Rache, we got him. We got the swine who did this to you."

But, unknowingly, Motley was telling a terrible untruth: because he was wrong about the big guy. It wasn't Terry who had been behind the wheel of the speeding car that had turned Rachel into a cataleptic token of her former, unblemished self.

40

Andy Tremblett's mobile phone suddenly chimed into life, "Tremblett here."

"Andy – gulp – Andy – deep breath – he's dead!"

"Jesus, calm down, Rod. Who's dead?"

"Terry! He's dead!"

"Shit! What…but…how?"

"He's dead Andy!"

"Rod…for fuck's sake calm down. What happened to Terry?"

"I don't know the details. I just picked it up over the net. The medics fished his body out of the river lunchtime, and his wife's in hospital."

"Shit! Shit! Shit!"

"Its out of control, Andy. It's gone way too far. We've got to put a stop to this madness. People are dying!"

"Shut the fuck up! Meet me at the usual place, and don't tell anyone else about what's happened."

As soon as Rod jumped into Andy's car in the pub car-park he started babbling, "It's gone way over the top. I didn't sign up for any of this craziness."

"Shut up, Rod. Shut up!" His brother yelled at him. "I need time to think." Rod visibly crumpled into his seat, buckling under the weight of the awful news.

"Andy. The wheels are falling off," he muttered. But Andy wasn't listening to his brother's stumbling metaphor; he was thinking too hard.

Looking up at the back door to the pub, Rod saw two punters emerge into the car-park. One of them was methodically tearing up a betting slip, letting the tragic snowflakes flutter to his feet. The other took a last swig from a bottle before starting to juggle it, flipping it into somersaults and catching it by its neck. The ex-traffic cop watched them climb into their car and drive off into the fizzing traffic that pounded along the littered North Road. I'd be breathalysing that bozo if I were still in Traffic – he was thinking. He stared down at his pinstriped suit, missing the primacy of the uniform he once wore: the declatory uniform that was no longer the uniform of the good.

The thumping traffic caught Rod's attention; he suddenly realised that all traffic is the same – the same in its heterogeneity. A line of traffic farting out its nauseous humours is exactly the same as any other line of traffic. With a leaden depression settling on him, Rod realised that he missed his old job. He missed sitting in lay-bys dutifully observing the traffic's ugly language, decoding its baneful narrative. "I should have said no when you asked me to drive that car. It was sickening," Rod moaned.

Yes! He said it!

Rod admitted that he was driving the car, but his brother still wasn't listening. Andy suddenly looked over at Rod with a smile of happy discovery upon his face. "We've been lazy!" he yelped, "What's our business, Rod? We're coppers for Chrissakes. We should start thinking like coppers instead of drug barons."

Andy gave his brother a sardonic smile, and reached for his mobile. Thirty minutes later, Rod and Andy were standing outside the late and sadly missed Terry's block of flats, talking to an unpleasant looking young man named Mick the Snake.

"I was 'ere, Mr. Tremblett! Fact, I saw em comin' out o' the flats. I was down in the alley see, where I keep me stash. Then I see these four fuckers carrying out a carpet. I was finking, fuck me, it takes four of em fuckers to nick a fucking carpet!"

"Go on." Andy sounded only mildly piqued with his constantly effing and twitching snake-tattooed grass.

"Well, s'all it was, really. S'all I saw."

"Did you see their faces, catch any names. Did they say anything?"

"I was too far away. Didn't ear 'em say anyfink."

"What did they look like? What were they wearing?"

The grass shrugged his narrow shoulders, "Dark stuff. All fuckin' dark. Wiv black caps pulled down."

Andy placed his arm around his snitches' shoulder. He hissed menacingly into the man's shivering ear, "You've got to do better than that my old son, that shit is about as useful to me as a nun's cunt. There's no reward for that useless crap. That's not even worth a kick in the arse."

"Aw, Jesus, Mr Tremblett. It's worth a little somfin' innit? Just a little somfin'. Please, Mr. Tremblett, I ain't well."

Andy dipped one hand into his jacket-pocket, and then deftly palmed his desperate informer the fix of heroin he'd brought with him.

"Fanks, Mr. Tremblett. Fanks."

"Go on, fuck off," Tremblett snapped. As the snitch sloped off, the drug squad copper called after him, "Keep your ears open. Let me know if you hear anything."

The disappointed Detective Sergeant felt sick to his stomach. His face gave off a pale glow; a thin rain was falling and his pasta-coloured face seemed to be spotted with sweat, "Don't worry, we'll get those bastards, Rod. We'll get 'em. I'll put a tail on that shit Toby, and I've got snitches all over this city. We'll track em down, and then we'll nail em."

41

Andy couldn't have known it, but his words to his brother were superfluous. Because Rod wasn't worried about 'nailing' anyone: his world had already been turned upside-down, and his attention was now elsewhere. Rod's head was full of sex, as it always was; but not his wife's sex, oh no. It was full of Melanie's sex. At that moment he was watching himself having contortionist sex with the barmaid, stretching his imagination until it twanged. It was like watching a DVD of him fucking her. His carnal imagination gave him a power over time; he was reliving every sexual move he'd made on the voluptuous barmaid; replaying, fast-forwarding, freeze-framing. In his porno-inflamed imagination his porno-star face was smiling, with rivulets of porno-star sweat dripping from it.

"Rod? Rod! For Christ's sake. I said get in the fucking car."

With a disquieted sense of himself, Rod pressed the 'eject' button on the remote control of his imagination; with the informed certainty that the porno-DVD would make its contents available for later delectation.

"I've been doing a bit of thinking Andy. Shouldn't we try and talk to the other lot. You know, try and make a deal with them?" Rod was staring straight ahead at the road as he spoke. Despite the car just starting to move off, it suddenly shuddered to a screeching halt. Andy stared at his brother with mad eyes.

"Was that meant to be serious or what?"

"I suppose." Rod continued to look straight ahead. "It's just that…well, you know I deplore violence."

Jesus! Can you believe that? Can you believe that guy?

Of course it wasn't true. Even as a young man, one of Rod Tremblett's nicknames was 'Belter'. Andy shook his head vigorously from side to side.

"Nah, it was a fucking joke, Rod. Trust me, that was a complete fucking joke. Don't even think about it. Okay?"

As they drove back to the pub car park to pick up Rod's car, Andy kept glancing over at his brother provocatively. Rod kept avoiding his gaze, looking down at his watch and pretending to yawn. He didn't seem to be able to think logically or consecutively anymore. All his imagination could do was groan and sigh. He thought that perhaps his mental stasis was a function of his moral decline.

42

Motley was alone at Rachel's bedside. "When you come home, sweetheart, I'm going to cook you your favourite supper. And I'll give you lots of back rubs. That'll be nice, won't it? You like me rubbing your back don't you?"

Motley sat for hours chatting to his comatose girlfriend. He wanted to be alone with Rachel, to stroke her face with his lips, and to tell her how much he loved her. He wanted to say secret things to her, things that he'd never thought of saying before. But there is no place for secrets on the intensive therapy ward. As soon as you enter the ITU they strip you of all your secrets; and sometimes your secrets are never returned. Never.

Whenever he walked from the ITU, Motley left slowly, agonisingly slowly, his presence reluctantly receding from Rachel. When he walked from the hospital foyer into the revenue-generating car park, his head dropped suddenly like a heavy weight. It hung, at right angles to the black sheen of his leather coat. Only by dropping his head could he manage to take himself away from her.

Despite spending the entire day with his girlfriend; sitting in the plastic covered armchair; sitting on the floor; staring out of the window; he turned in the car park and stared up at the sixth floor window with apologetic tenderness. Then he dipped his head again, with futile and painful weight.

43

Have you ever been in one of those temples of faultless treatment; have you ever been on an ITU ward? Have you ever seen all the beeping and flashing machines arrayed in there? It looks and sounds like an amusement arcade, a repressed fun-palace whose comatose funsters are languorously loitering between life and death. If you're the kind of person who harbours admiration for high-tech stuff, for unstinting high-tech instrumentation, or your soul melts to the gifted rhythms of well-behaved electronics, your ardour would be unusually sated in the ITU. You see the truth is, that none of the intensive-care doctors believe in that myth about the body healing itself. They know that a badly broken body needs lots of faultless treatment, lots of outside help; because a badly broken body is like a bad husband, a nightmare husband. When the going gets tough, the badly broken body just decides to pack it in; it takes the easy way out, suddenly disappearing in a swoon of indignation.

<h1 style="text-align:center">44</h1>

Three days later, Motley was seated at Rachel's bedside, gazing up at her with his head resting on the plaster cast of one of her mangled legs – and then she opened her eyes. "Oh!...ah!...oh my God! Nurse, she's awake! She's back! N-U-R-S-E!"

Motley had jumped to his feet, and was pointing and smiling at Rachel, "You're back, sweetheart! Thank God you're back! Thank God!" Even though he didn't believe in the God he was thanking, he thanked Him profusely anyway.

After calling for the doctor, the nurse was suddenly at Rachel's bedside, pushing Motley aside and shining a small metal torch into the bewildered girl's eyes: "Rachel...Rachel. My name is Colleen. I am a nurse. You're at the Heath hospital. Can you hear me? You've had an accident Rachel."

The nurse was gently tapping the back of Rachel's hand. Motley's heart was overflowing; he desperately wanted to hug his girlfriend, to kiss her face, to take her home. The tears of relief streamed down his cheeks and fell noiselessly into the tangle of sky-blue bedclothes. "Thank God," he kept saying like an assenting communicant, "Thank God."

The doctor arrived and quickly checked Rachel's vital signs; then he dragged Motley back up to the bed: "Talk...talk to her. Let's see if she recognises you."

Motley smiled down at Rachel, the tears still flowing. "Look at you," he smiled, "You're back." Motley took her hand in his and squeezed it gently. Rachel blinked and then gazed up at him, "Look! She's trying to smile," Motley gasped. But it was just the weakened mesh of Rachel's facial muscles giving off a few arthritic twitches.

"Look," he yelled again, "She's blinking!" And this time Motley was right, she was blinking rapidly. "She recognises me!" he yelped. And he was right again, she did. And even though Rachel couldn't say anything, in that moment of recognition, both of them knew that their passions for each other had survived. The nurse began fussing over Rachel again: "Hello Rachel..." Now conscious Rachel moved her eyes to look at the nurse's face. "...You've had an accident, Rachel. You're in the Heath hospital."

Motley stepped back from the bed, suddenly swarming with feelings unconnected with his present surroundings. The warmth of Rachel's recovery had been drawn out of him by what the nurse had just said: it was a lie. What had happened to Rachel was no accident. His fevered mind thought again about the Tremblett's, and his blood began to boil: all the blood within him began to boil. His face contained a Richter-scale tremor of agitation; but for the first time in days, there was no despair in it. For the time being, he would try not to think about the Trembletts. It was enough that Rachel had emerged from her coma, and now he wanted to protect her. So, for the time being, he would remain passive.

45

And Motley did remain passive for the next couple of months. Until BB discovered that it wasn't Terry who had been driving the car that broke Rachel. In fact, his informant told him that Terry hadn't even been out of the flat that night. When Motley guessed who had been in the pavement-mounting car, his blood instantly boiled again. But this time it didn't just boil: it came out in a florid riot. His blow-torched corpuscles mutinied; they made their base on the roof of his rage and started throwing down slates at anything that moved.

46

Dear Reader...have you ever killed anyone? Suppose not, eh? Suppose it's a silly question, really. But I bet you've thought about it, haven't you? Oh yeah, we all think about it. But that's not like doing it, is it? Oh no. Thinking about it isn't like doing it. Otherwise we'd all be in jail, wouldn't we? Motley was thinking about killing someone. The trouble was, he didn't know whom he wanted to kill. And there's really no point in killing someone if they're the wrong one, is there? Although Motley had a great eagerness to kill, he didn't want to kill the wrong one; that just wouldn't be fair. First, he had to find out exactly who was driving the car, Rod or Andy Tremblett; then it would be fair. Then he'd be killing the right one.

47

His discovery that Terry wasn't the person driving the car was only made slightly easier by the timing: he found out on the day that Rachel was being brought home from hospital. It had taken more than three months of consummate NHS care, and she was still in a hip-to-knee plaster cast, but now she could be cared for at home.

Bennie had become alarmed at the news of Rachel's mortifying skirmish with the stolen car, and had especially flown in from the Caribbean for the weekly team meeting. He, and some of the sterner members of the team, told Motley that for the time being he couldn't touch the two coppers – the heat that kind of action would pull down would almost certainly be the end of their money-making operation. What came to pass was a decision that Motley would have to wait another year – until he retired from the business – before he could take his revenge. The team agreed that the Trembletts had to be a personal matter for Motley to resolve. And then, on that day…Oh, on that heart-churning, Carpe Diem day!

As the team meeting broke up, Bennie took Motley to one side.

"Thanks for going along with the vote, Taff. I know what it takes for you to sit tight on this." Motley nodded, and put his hand on his friend's shoulder.

"I want you to get hold of a piece for me, Bennie. Something small that I can keep in a jacket pocket." Avoiding his friend's concerned gaze, he added, softly, "I'm going to take them both down. I'm going to slot both of them." The raging fire in Motley's voice almost seared his friend's face.

"I know you will, Taff," Bennie said, looking into the gritty hatred in Motley's eyes, "I know you will."

Although neither of the brothers knew it yet, the Tremblett's lives were already tapering off. Neither did their families know it, or their friends, or colleagues, or accomplices. But from that moment, the spin of their lives had started to slow; and it was just a matter of time before the gravity of Motley's wrath stopped it altogether. At the thought of the corrupt policemen's shrinking future, Motley couldn't help smiling an anticipative smile. Unreservedly and inexpediently he smiled his grim smile – and was answered by a roaring in his veins.

Part Three

1

If you peeled away the layers of Rod Tremblett's fall from grace, you'd be left with an updated version of The Catcher in the Rye: a failed quest for authenticity and honour in a world full of every kind of fraud and lies. Only unlike Holden Caulfield, Rod had abandoned his quest, and was now participating in the phoniness and fraud himself. He had sold out to universal venality and treachery, and his conscience was no longer fighting it out with the fact that he loved the illicit sex, the money and power. Rod was irredeemably hooked on all the unstable things that corruption affords a man.

After a few drinks and an hour of titillating chat with Melanie in the wine-bar, Rod turned around and looked behind him at the guy his girlfriend was now staring at.

Rod narrowed his eyes as he gazed at Motley, "What is it with you and that guy?" he couldn't stop himself asking.

"Oh, he just pisses me off, that's all. I'd love to kick the stupid sod in balls," Melanie replied, with a hint of hoarseness in her voice.

2

Well, you're probably wondering why Melanie – aka Detective Sergeant Wendy Westerby – didn't tell her drug squad boyfriend about the drug-dealing activities of the man who annoyed her so much. I mean, now is the time isn't it? With Motley sitting right there with his boozy friend Sweep. She had her chance, didn't she? But the fact was that all Melanie knew of Motley was that he was a small-time, smart-arsed dealer in soft drugs. And as a member of the elite National Crime Squad, Westerby wasn't interested in small-time dealers. Oh, no...Detective Westerby was after much bigger fish.

The under-cover policewoman had been called in a year ago by the Assistant Chief Constable of the South Wales Police to investigate allegations of corruption in the city's drug squad. Her jobs at the police club and at the wine-bar were arranged so that she could mix with the suspected police miscreants. And now DS Westerby was hot on the trail of the Trembletts and their bent colleagues.

In all fairness, the Melanie we know – the jelly-haired, hot-arsed barmaid – hadn't roused herself to the affair with Rod only to get inside information; she did actually fancy the pants off him. She had, admittedly, already used him to gain a great deal of incriminating evidence by asking discreet and seemingly innocuous questions. But now that she had most of what wanted to know, she had decided that she had little use for the sex-panting Rod. Besides, the trap she was carefully setting for the Tremblett brothers and their entire gang was almost ready to snap shut. So now she thought that the time had come to gradually distance herself from the corrupt and infidelitous copper. With an involuntary frown, Melanie realised that although Rod was looking at Motley, he was speaking to her. "He keeps staring at us. Fuck it, I'm going to have a word with him."

The disgruntled copper stood up from his barstool and strolled across to the table where Motley and Sweep were sitting. He pulled up a chair and plonked himself down with an accusatory, "We know each other, don't we?" His robust words were aimed at the top of Motley's head as he steadfastly stared down into his drink.

What bliss it would have been for Motley to send his fist right through the face of this man like a piece of throbbing shrapnel. Motley's fists were tensed; he could barely keep his hands off Tremblett. Of course, he had the advantage of knowing whom Rod was without the policeman-cum-attempted-murderer knowing who the hell he was. Motley stolidly forced himself to shake his head from side to side, trying to remember his promise to Bennie and his team about biding his time before going after the Trembletts.

"I'm off." Sweep said, with a quivering voice, and rose from the table. He looked at Rod with blazing eyes and then headed for the door. Even the out-of-condition Sweep was only a breath away from launching himself at his daughter's suspected attacker.

"What's your friend's problem?" Rod asked, nodding after Sweep.

"Maybe he doesn't like the smell of steaming shit," Motley replied.

Surprisingly, Rod was unfazed by Motley's scatological jibe, "Listen, I don't think you want talk to a copper like that. You could be making a big mistake."

Motley almost let out a laugh, "Jesus. You must use the same corny script-writer your brother does."

"Oh. You know Andy do you? Nicked you sometime, did he? Well, you should behave yourself then, shouldn't you?"

The simmering Motley could no longer contain himself, "Go fuck yourself Tremblett, and fuck your gutless cock-sucking brother."

Dropping his glass to the table, Rod suddenly leapt to his feet at the grave insult. He hovered menacingly over Motley with clenched fists, "I don't think you know who you're talking to," the apoplectic copper seethed.

Motley gave Rod Tremblett a bone-piercing look of utter detestation, and hissed at him through clenched teeth, "No. I don't think you know who you're talking to you, scumbag." He stood up, and spat at Tremblett's feet. Then, trying desperately to control his metal-smelting temper he walked slowly and determinedly towards the door.

"I'll be seeing you again," Tremblett called after him. Motley turned and raised one fist, pointing an extended index finger at the policeman, then flicking his thumb up and down several times; Motley had satisfyingly pulled on an imaginary trigger, emptying an imaginary magazine. The ego-spanked copper could hardly believe what had just happened. "The next time I see you, I'll fucking nick you," he snarled.

3

Tremblett's threat was shouted with a crumbling authority. What Rod had said about seeing Motley again was just a load of old bollocks. If Motley had his way, the next time Rod Tremblett saw him, the policeman-cum-criminal would be floundering on the ground breathing in the acrid smell of cordite, and swimming in the sticky horror of his own blood.

It was a plain fact that Rod Tremblett's future no longer unreeled itself towards infinity, because infinity for Rod had suddenly got very near. The bent policeman's want of future was a sternly pointed finger, a painful jab of reproach. So it's no wonder that his future had its head dipped, its mouth stretched into an uncertain grin. His future had become a matter of suspense, and though much had been planned for his life, his plans no longer had any solidarity.

4

Later that night, when Rod crept into his darkened bedroom, he was desperately in need of some solace. Melanie had turned down his supplicatory request for a date, and his frustrated porno-expectations were seeking an alternative acquiescence. The rejection had hurt him deeply; Rod's lust for the barmaid had finally morphed into what he now called 'love'. But he was embarrassingly learning that love is a lot like religion; it's just a wilful smugness, a wishful interpretation that we force upon the world. Personally, I've never felt the itching complicity of religious smugness, but I've certainly enjoyed the spells and curses of love-smugness.

And so Rod was learning that when a man's illicit lust turns to love, it's all about impossible dreams, it's all about unreality; and it has nothing to do with practicality. He was discovering that love is all surface, an all-encompassing, all subsuming surface. That's what love is for a man like Rod; and that kind of surface-love does its best to submerge you. But he had prepared himself mentally for falling in love, like a boxer prepares himself for a fight: Rod was determined to do all of love's hitting. And he was determined not to get beaten down himself.

He gazed at his wife's sleeping form, her nakedness stretched invitingly across the bed like a valentine greeting. Rob stared hornily down at Anne's bare breasts, and her bosom-pal nipples stared culpably back at him. Then he moved his gaze down to look upon the filigreed triangle of light-brown pubic hair. Rod stood beside the bed, stroking the hot length of his burgeoning penis and purring like a cat. Then he slipped in beside his wife and began lapping at her nipples with the tip of his tongue. After a few seconds of serious tonguing, Anne roused herself with a moan, and turned sleepily onto her side. Rod nestled in behind her, pulling her warm backside into his groin. Then he gingerly eased his thoroughly swollen cock inside her somnolent vagina.

Once he began the familiar rhythm of slow thrusting, the urgency in him started to seep away, and surprisingly, he felt no real desire. He was simply overtaken by the familiarity of weekly, mechanistic marital-lovemaking. It was only because Rod was desperate for release that he didn't just turn over and go to sleep.

Feeling boredom closing in on him, Rod rolled his wife over onto her stomach and lay on top of her, his elbows taking his weight. The rigid tent-pole of his member lay in the crease of her buttocks. His penis's tiny mouth was almost barking at her, "Open the cheeks of your bum. Open up for me!"

In the orange-hued dimness that crept into the bedroom from the streetlights, Rod sensed his wife tensing as he nosed his glans into her most private of places. He pawed at her dry vagina with proficient fingers, trying to gain a few drops of cognisant wetness; an acknowledging flow of moisture from her insouciant vaginal glands. Pulling the butterfly-wings of her labia apart with deft digits, he slipped his middle finger inside her. Anne wriggled uncomfortably beneath him, imperceptibly pulling away from his pleasure-seeking fingers – she was about as responsive as an acquiescing nun.

The sleep-distracted Anne lay spread-eagled between Rod's legs, naked and sweaty, looking as though some wild animal had just torn her clothes from her; and now she was about to be ravished by the glowering beast. Her husband pulled her hand around behind her, placing it forcefully on his cock. She slid the oval of her fingers up and down its shaft with a desultory rhythm. But tonight, she wasn't interested in lovemaking. Besides, she was almost as bored with the scenario as her husband; he had made love to her while she lay on her tummy a thousand times before. But – horror of horrors – tonight, Anne was in for a very unpleasant surprise.

5

Rod seized two generous handfuls of his sleeping wife's bum-cheeks and parted them; then releasing one hand he spat into its palm and rubbed the lubricating spittle into the maraschino cherry of his throbbing cock. Lodging its glistening head right into the tight pucker of Anne's anus, he leaned forward. Rod was trying to force a breach in the heroically resisting anal-sphincter of his confused wife. She started to pull away from him, but before she could wriggle up the bed he had forced his overindulged cock into her fundament, deep into the very core of her.

Anne let out a sickening scream and bucked from under him like a wounded animal struggling to tear itself free from a trap. Jumping from the bed, she now stood at its side, trembling and grabbing at handfuls of her hair; pulling them down around her exposed neck as though the fibrous strands could protect her. Anne was quivering from head to toe as tears began to stream down her face. Rod had never seen his wife look so vulnerable, so exposed: he'd never seen her look so frightened.

"I'm sorry," he grovelled, "I'm so sorry. I won't do that again." Rod felt stupid and cruel, kneeling on the bed with his fast-shrinking dick in his hand. "Please come back to bed. I promise I won't do that again."

The digital clock on the bedside table read 12.15 am. By the time he'd talked Anne back into bed it was 12.58 am. Rod had completely blown their lovemaking. Neither of them attempted to sleep; they just lay there with their backs towards each other, a chasm between them as wide as the Grand Canyon. The recriminatory couple were only separated by two feet of stretched cotton, and an insurmountable mistake: "You fucking pervert!" screamed and echoed across the abyss between them.

Rod quickly realised that he had broken some sort of major taboo with Anne; breached some sort of behavioural limit. The realisation dawned upon him that it would be a very long time before she'd trust him in bed again, before his love-snake would be allowed to slither across the fitted sheet and turn up the hem of her nightie.

He told himself self-pityingly: You can't blame me! I can't help my tastes in sex, can I? I can't do anything about it. And he was right; there is nothing we can do about our sexual proclivities (ask your internet provider about the concealed hyperborea of our sexual proclivities). The fact is that for most of us, our sex lives are a fiction, an incontinent fantasy. We all have our dilectorial preferences, our perilous and morbid perversions, and that's it.

6

When Anne finally fell asleep, she was whimpering oddly, in an animal way, low-pitched and growly. Her legs were concertinairing beneath her, thighs and ankles tightly curling and uncurling, as though she were in the throes of a seizure. Rod guessed that her mind was negotiating the shock of what had just happened – trying to recapture a steady, before-the-event state. Her shoulders suddenly hunched and quivered; it was a cowering device; her sub-conscious was admitting that the awful thing that had just happened to her could happen again.

In the claustrophobic vestibule of her dream, Anne was involuntarily re-living the dreadful assault upon her person, the terrible thing that had happened in her own marital nest. Some invisible force field that protected her had been breached: she had been raped in her own bed. In the deepest corners of her feminine mind, her libido was being dragged down by a huge weight. Anne's sex drive was going catatonic.

As the guilt-ridden Rod lay beside her, he felt a terrible coldness. He knew he would have to struggle to shift it, to give some movement that would lessen its dead weight upon them both. He knew that there was going to have to be some serious grovelling done. He continued to stare at the back of his wife's sleeping head, trying to enter the bricked up passages of her dream. Perhaps she was fast-forwarding what had happened on the video screen of her sub consciousness, trying to make the next thing happen sooner, trying to get to a happier place: trying to get past Rod's tearing, spiky rod.

Anne's breath lurched and her body began to quiver; the pain of unwanted bodily piercing burst through the tight crux of her body. Involuntary sounds squeezed through her lips; Rod guessed that her eyes were leaking tears into the swelling of her pillow. The bedroom air hummed with molten iron and sparks of flame; Rod knew in his heart that, if his wife had any love left for him, one by one their spangled points of light were going out. Now he was desperately wishing that he hadn't even bothered his wife, wishing instead that he'd just sloped off to the bathroom and spent five minutes burping the snake instead.

Something started griping in his stomach, as though something was beginning to gnaw at him. He wondered if the thing being devoured was what linked him to Anne and the kids, what bound him as a husband and a father. He began to freeze with self-loathing, like one of Brueghel's wintry little figures stilled beneath layers of yellowing lacquer.

7

You know what? I'd take a bet round about now that you're thinking: that Rod Tremblett used to be a pretty nice guy; but he's changed a lot, hasn't he. And you'd be right. But you haven't seen the greatest change in our friend Rod. Not yet. Oh, no. What? You think he's changed for the worst already? Oh hell...you're going to be disappointed then. The life-shattering change that turns everything upside down for Rod Tremblett and his entire family is just about to happen. And it happens when his wife finds out that he's been banging the arse off Melanie, the spiky-haired barmaid. So, who do you think was the mean bastard who told Rod's wife about his turgid love affair? Can you guess? Go on, you're pretty smart, aren't you? I'm sure you can guess.

Hey, congratulations...you're right! It was his brother, Andy, who told Rod's wife about Melanie. Yeah, the slimy little rat! He also answered her tentative questions about where Rod had been getting so much extra cash from lately. Andy told his sister-in-law all this one illicit afternoon as a means of persuading her that what was good for the goose, well, you know the rest. And now they were lying in bed naked together, fucking each other's brains out. Well, it happens, doesn't it? It's not very nice I know; but it happens. Hey, don't be so prudish about it; sometimes a guy finally gets around to screwing his brother's attractive wife. And you can't really blame Anne can you? After all, she wasn't getting anything in the bedroom department any more, was she?

When Anne sprang out of bed and stumbled towards the bathroom for her post-coital piss, Andy couldn't help noticing her dappled thighs, the stringy lines on the undercurve of her belly and the crater-like indents on her backside. With his ardour grimly retreating, he winced as he listened to her peeing. It sounded like she was peeing like a bloke; standing up. Afterwards, Andy watched disinterestedly as Anne dressed herself. For all her charms, she was a disappointment in the sack, he thought. She had fucked like she was having a nervous breakdown; scared eyes, uncontrollable twitching, verging constantly on the brink of tears (muffled sobs). What Andy wanted in bed was a sexual equal, someone who was as revoltingly experienced as he was (when on dazzling form, he was quite prepared for instance, to put on a PVC hood, a black cape and wear a studded-leather collar around his cock). Anne was too timid, too nervous. She wasn't rude enough. Turns out, that in the sack, Anne wasn't bitch enough for Andy. With a token of reflexive pity, he felt sorry for his brother – it was no wonder Rod was always so keen to swell the blankets with another woman.

As Andy Tremblett drove home to his own wife, he didn't give his brother's wife a second thought; other than chuckling at the memory of leaving a wet-patch of sexual effluvium in his brother's bed. Later, as he lay in the tub at home sipping a cup of tea handed to him by his felicitous wife, he realised that screwing his brother's wife had already got boring – a pleasureless promiscuity. And that's the trouble for the really serious sack-artist, isn't it? That's the snag for the guy who takes his humping to the extraordinary…after the first few thousand fucks it all gets a bit boring. Andy couldn't even remember half the fucks he'd had. But then, he didn't want to much.

8

Detective Sergeant Andy Tremblett was a shrewd policeman, all corruption and contingency. He understood human behaviour. Paradoxically, he thought it was a cute trick to be screwing his brother's wife. For such a smart guy he should have known better – he'd met enough mad pricks with vengeance on their minds.

There are some men that never make allowances for the liberty takers. They will get up in the middle of the night and call a taxi, or get on a plane, or wait in an alley with a sawn-off, or go berserk with a blade in the middle of the street. Those men suffer from a terrible psychic incapacity: you just try telling one of them to put out a cigarette, or try taking his glass from him, saying 'you're banned'. If you're a liberty taker, those men – the hurters and do-ers – are usually your fellow inmates, your fellow Winson Greeners. And if you're a liberty taker, God help you: because those men of principle will have you, they'll vengeance you, and it's never over. Those dumb-fucks will always keep coming back at you; they'll keep coming at you with Payback like some unstoppable raging comet.

9

Rod Tremblett's discovery that he was a mendacious, philandering bastard didn't come as much of a surprise to him (he'd worked that one out a long time ago). But his discovery that he was a potential killer did come as a shock. He would gasp, spontaneously, whenever he thought about that horrific night; when he had deliberately broken Rachel's youthful body. He gasped at the unconcealed viciousness of it. Rod's excuse to himself for his savagery and callousness was that his persuasive brother had coerced him, n'est-ce-pas? Poor choice-less Rod had been inescapably sucked into things.

Rod knew that there was a turf-war still going on, but it didn't occur to him that he was going to have to pay the ultimate price for his part in it. However, the agony of that inexorable defeat still lay in the future. Meanwhile, Rod had the colossal problem of his unappeasable (and as we now know) hypocritical wife to deal with.

10

For those of you who tenaciously believe that love can survive anything (a truly pious, unrealistic belief) it will disappoint you to discover that Rod's wife instantly and irrevocably fell out of love with him the moment she learned of his second infidelity. Even though she had been unfaithful herself (and with Rod's own brother!) Anne's fourteen-year-old love for her husband was gone in a moment. Now the immediate task for her was to get Rod out of the house as quickly as possible. With a forthright calculation, Anne was contemplating a quick and (for Rod) a very costly divorce. Like all wronged wives, Anne had suddenly become a great believer in the curative powers of a costly divorce. But, before taking her marital woes to the solicitors, there were the estranging, pillorying arguments to take care of.

When Rod returned home from the one-day course that Andy had cynically sent away him on so that he could spend time with his sister-in-law, it seemed to him that the house was unusually quiet and unwelcoming; it had an intransigently un-domestic feel to it. Looking down the hallway into the kitchen, he could see Anne's slippered feet protruding from under the kitchen table.

"Hello. Anyone home?" he called.

There was no reply; only a cold astronomic silence radiated out from the kitchen. "Anne?" Rod called out, placing his briefcase under the stairs in the hall while staring at his wife's unmoving feet. After a few moments, Anne's querulous voice emerged like a choric for whom the bell tolls.

"Why? Why did you do it?" she intoned, her voice almost breaking, "Why did you...do it again?"

Rod's thinking instantly went into denial mode. He began to hone all the tired and overused Shibboleths of the deceitful – it's a lie, it wasn't my fault, you don't understand. "What are you talking about? Why did I do what?" The clockwork of Rod's mind again swept into hyper-drive – "What? Why...did what?"

"You must have known that one day I'd find out," the clapper of Anne's voice rang out again. The house suddenly gained another magnitude of hostility. Rod stumbled into the brightly lit kitchen, his face a mask of barely concealed terror.

"What's the matter? What the bloody Hell are you talking about?"

His wife's eyes were wet and red-rimmed, her eyelashes matted and sticky. "You're such a...such a..." Anne had to stop to pull a disgusted face in mid-sentence.

"Jesus, sweetheart," Rod moved towards his her with open hands, "What the hell are you so upset about?"

Anne pulled away from his touch. "Don't call me sweetheart, you…you lying, cheating bastard!"

'UH!' Oh, no. Please no! Not that fucking nightmare again!

11

At that moment Rod realised that he loved his wife more than he ever knew. But of course, those kinds of discoveries are always made too late. The haunted orbits of Anne's eyes, the sharpness of her mouth, the conspicuous venom in her face told him that he'd already renounced everything he cared about: wife, family, home. The long videotape of his losses spooled on and on. Rod suddenly grabbed his seated wife by the arms and lifted her to her feet, "What's happened?" He yelled at her, "What the fuck's happened?"

"You've been screwing that dirty bitch of a barmaid, that's what's happened!" Anne screamed back at him. For a moment, Rod thought about deploying his skills at circumvention, using his newly acquired art for unaffected sophistry, but he quickly realised that lies and fraudulent denials would get him nowhere.

"Who told you that!" Rod was shaking his wife by her shoulders. His internal alarm system was all screaming sirens and flashing red lights, violently pulsing like the seam of fluttering LCDs on the front of his stereo.

"You're not going to deny it are you?" his wife snarled, "That's just like you isn't it?"

Rod was already conducting two or three different conversations in his head, and could probably have conducted many more, as many as were necessary. "No. I'm not denying it," he whined, "but it's all over now."

"Oh, you've had your fun and so you've dumped her now, have you?"

"It wasn't like that."

"So, what was it like? Was it all the crooked money you were making that made you decide to flush your entire life down the toilet, or was it something else?"

Rod was stunned. He had only told his wife that he and Andy had a profitable sideline going at work, but she was better off not knowing anything more about it. Now he didn't know exactly what Anne was getting at, but he knew that he had to defend himself.

"Look. I realise that I've been full of bullshit lately. I've been into some bad things. But everyone's been at it, okay. It just got to the point where I thought that right and wrong were two sides of the same bloody coin."

Anne blew a deep sigh and folded her trembling arms defensively. There was a long silence. Rod knew that he had to be the one to break the silence, "Anne...?"

"I'm listening."

"There's so much going on, love. Stuff you don't even know about."

"I know all about what's going on."

What the hell was she talking about? Rod wondered. His embarrassingly blameworthy wife sat on the arm of the chair opposite him, looking straight into his eyes like an angry iridologist trying to diagnose some lying, deceitful pathology. While condemning her husband, Anne could blamelessly, and with Machiavellian deviousness, ignore her own recent fall from grace.

"I admit we've got a lot to talk about," Rod said.

"Oh yes, we do have a lot to talk about."

Rod realised that Anne had something else besides the Melanie thing, some information that he didn't even know she had. He knew too that it was probably something really BAD. A horrible feeling washed over him, a feeling that he was on the edge of something: that he was staring helplessly over some vertiginous precipice. He reached over to take her hand but she quickly snatched it away, her face a freeze-frame of pathos and enmity.

"You and Andy must be looking at ten years in jail. At least."

"What?" Rod almost screamed. "What did you say?"

"I know all about how you've been putting so much money away. You and Andy have been selling the drugs you impounded."

...Screaming Fucking Shit! This can't be happening!

12

Rod felt as though his whole life had suddenly been surrounded by police crime-scene tape, its garish chevrons dancing and wriggling in the breeze. What had once been his life was now a heap of nuclear waste, the lamentable effluvium, the quantum chaos of a Chernobyl-style meltdown. He grabbed Anne by her wrist and painfully twisted her arm sideways. With fury leaching out of his eyes he growled at her, "Tell me who the hell you've been talking to or I'll break your arm."

"You did it to that dirty bitch, didn't you?" Anne screamed at him, "You fucked her up the arse, didn't you! And then you tried to do it to me. You...you...animal!"

Rod nearly had a heart attack. He couldn't believe what he'd just heard. The poor guy wanted the floor to open up and swallow him. Who could have told her? How could she have guessed? "You bastard. You...you...creep." Anne was swinging at Rod's head with her one free fist. "You'd have given us all up for that...that sodding tart." Every beat of her outraged heart throbbed with burning rivers of hatred and contempt. Rod grabbed his struggling wife and wrapped her in his arms, squeezing her to his chest.

"Who told you about her...who told you?"

Anne continued to struggle and twist to free herself, but Rod managed to wrestle her to the ground. He ended up lying on top of her, pinning her shoulders to the floor. "Who told you?" he was yelling. He raised his hand up from one of

Anne's shoulders, setting himself up to slap his prostrate wife.

"Mummeee!"

The warring couple's youngest son was standing in the doorway to the lounge, tears were streaming from his bulging eyes, and a look of absolute terror mangled his six-year-old face. Rod let his struggling wife up from the floor. Anne rushed over to her child, picking up the terrified boy. Then she ran upstairs sobbing and screaming.

"You've lost everything you bastard. I hate you. I hate you!"

The exaggerated click of the bedroom door-lock being thrown signalled to Rod that Anne meant every word she'd said.

13

Boy! Have you ever had that kind of pain? Do you know it – that really bad kind of pain that's right up there with the top two or three worst things that can happen to you? The trouble with that kind of pain is that it hurts so BAD.

Ouch, ow…it hurts!

After a scene like that you can hear the hurricane of blood wrenching at your temples, you can feel the tornado of air whirring in your lungs, your teeth vibrating and loosening in your gums. Everything hurts; every flustering, searing breath wields a knife; every thought carries a bloodied stick. When the truth starts to fall down on your head like a shower of sulphuric rain, you can feel its terrible burning. You can see the stark facts of your loathsomeness, the hunched Hell of your hideousness. And yes, it's true: losing the ones you love because you betrayed them renders you hideous. When the truth falls, and all your lies are washed out of you, you can feel their blistering resonance. You can feel their bitter unguents haemorrhaging fear and pain, and nothing can save you: not remorse, nor penitence, nor regret. Nothing can save you.

Okay, we've all had our share of tragedies and grief, right? Of course we have: God knows we've all had our share of grief. The tragic deaths of our parents and friends for instance, our kids' grievous illnesses and the days spent in worry-soaked hospital wards. And then there's that eye-gouging kind of suffering from the relegation of our favourite footy team or when we lose a rugby game to England. But you need to combine all of those blitzkrieging-wraths into one single torment to know what kind of pain Rod Tremblett was feeling.

So, who did all those heinous things to Rod? Well, it wasn't really a 'who' was it? It was, perhaps more accurately, a 'what'. It was drugs, wasn't it? Drugs did it, and the unrestrained greed and untrammelled power that drugs bring with them. Yep – even though Rod had never used drugs in his entire his life, it was the infamy of drugs that did those awful things to him: and his inherent horniness. But don't worry about Rod. Rod is up to it. Because right now, sex and torture occupy the same places in his heart; and they both rely on an intimate knowledge of the quagmire of his inner self. Meanwhile, the tape of his losses spools on, and on. Of course, as with all great losers, Rod Tremblett firmly believes that none of it is his fault.

14

Well, brothers and sisters, doesn't Time change everything? Can you believe how much Time can fuck things up? Even a little bit of Time has turned Rod Tremblett's entire life upside down. Time, that perishable minute by minute ooze we're all thrashing about on, stoically trying to stay on the surface while watching a matrix of faces and unfurling lives pass by as though seen from a bus window. Rod has learned that we are all Time's slaves, even the mountains that surround us. It's Time that crushes everything in its senile hand, huge, blind, inanimate, prayer-denying Time. Everything sinks beneath its surface in the end.

15

When Motley lay in bed at night, his survivor's guilt cut through his mind like a scalpel. The survivors of life-taking catastrophes sometimes believe that they must have special powers. And they do. When the traumatised survivors of the London Underground bombings talked on the television, you could see them drifting away on a lake of magical powers, drenched in the animate chemicals of survivor mind-damage. But even if they survived that particular outrage without a scratch, they still suffered the head-piercing wound of a ruined mind. Because the gift of survival comes at a price – they know that whatever magical powers they possess, were bought at the expense of others.

The car bomb in Iraq and now the violence against his girlfriend was constantly doing combat with Motley's conscience. He had been responsible for his men's safety at the roadblock and he had been responsible for Rachel's immunity during his drug hostilities; and had scandalously failed in his duty on both occasions. When the turbulence in his head became too much, Motley would get up from the bed and walk out on to the bedroom balcony. Dressed only in his overcoat of guilt, he would gaze out at the post midnight skies that hung over the Bristol Channel, with their star-crammed incandescences. The element-birthing stars reminded Motley that his eyes had once as contained as much twinkle in them as the Milky Way. But his eyes now contained only the dullness that comes when a man contemplates his own dull purpose: when he contemplates some inflationary revenge. And that's all very well, that is. Because it's as it should be when the wound is in a man. When that kind of reprisal-demanding wound is in you there's no use looking up at the skies for help, because there's nobody can sort it out but yourself.

He liked standing out on his late-night balcony looking eastwards towards Somerset's pinpoints of light. Standing up on his seventh-floor vantage point built upon the pregnant belly of the south Wales coast, the infallible Westerlies ripped at his ears and slid chilly fingers beneath his invisible overcoat. The April winds, fresh off the North Atlantic, were colder than a cock-sucker's knees. They committed indecent assault upon his nakedness; supplemented by a ball-freezing booster called 'wind-chill'. Standing alone on the apartment's mega-expensive promontory, Motley could hear the groaning of his subconscious mind. He could hear it sighing, "I know, mate. There's going to be a lot more grief, isn't there? And it's all going to end in tears, isn't it" And the grief, and tears, were getting nearer all the time.

As he conversed with himself, Motley couldn't deny himself a wince of fear and regret. Because he could see the descending future, hear its explosive anger, its napalm doom. In an attempt at clearing his head, he would breath in salt-tanged lungfulls of the city's wronged air, with its smutty undertaste, its devalued wholesomeness. It was as if all the restorative oxygen had been sucked out of it.

The city air was a lot like his own life: a thing of obscenification. They were trussed up together with barbed wire, naked and face-to face, him and the dilapidated, dumped-on city air: both abused suckers, both out-in-the-cold losers. But they both survived its horrors and vivisections didn't they? Survived the city's hauntings, its force fields of violence and outlandish hatreds? When the wind off the Bay picked up and the yellow air fled, taking with it its carcinogen-hefted genies, Motley would return to bed and chase illusive sleep, until morning crept groggily through the bedroom's sliding doors.

16

While Rachel had been in hospital, Motley had become dependent on frequent inhalations of cocaine to keep him from sinking into despair. Until very recently, every time he picked his nose he came away with half a gram of coke tucked under his fingernail. But in an effort to please his recuperating girlfriend and to aid in his pandering care for her, Motley now decided to give up the booze and drugs.

After lovingly tucking Rachel into bed at ten o'clock each night, he would then drive down to the wine-bar for a couple of hours. There, he would celebrate his giving up the booze and drugs with a few large Jack Daniels, a couple of loaded spliffs and a snort or two of coke. Unsurprisingly, Motley thought that abstinence was easy; just so long as it didn't go on for too long – 'now I'm off it…now I'm on it' seemed the best way forwards with all those giving-it-up scenarios. He knew that he couldn't give up the twin pruriences – drink and drugs – for good, but he held no grievance against his will power, because it wasn't a willpower thing. The idea that he should deny himself something that he really wanted was simply an alien concept.

He often said to a disapproving Rachel, "Booze and drugs are only a problem if you can't afford them. So where's the problem?"

17

After midnight, when he returned home from the wine-bar, Motley would pad softly into the bedroom of the apartment and gaze down at his sleeping girlfriend, vigorously lapping up the vestiges of her beauty with inflammable eyes. There was her youthful body with its familiar form, its placid circles and half-circles, its mesh of feminine symmetries. But now it included something that had not been there before. A buzz-cut of scars and welts signalled the great trauma that Rachel's body had been through. The girl that Motley was gazing down at was the same girl he had loved before the car had mown her down, but her body had suffered a discontinuity, a radical re-shaping.

The couple had often discussed the pursuit of offspring. Rachel had been happily enthusiastic about having Motley's baby, his child: their child. She believed that a baby would have proclaimed their love for each other, their entwining genetic commitment. But those fanciful ideas were now harshly delusional; Rachel's shattered pelvic girdle meant that childbearing would be at best a painful, and, at worst, a dangerous endeavour. Motley didn't want to chance it; his girlfriend had already been through enough. The severity of her leg and pelvic injuries meant that for the rest of her life, Rachel would be walking with a pronounced limp.

18

Now – girls and boys, respected readers – you really need to pay attention here; because what happens next is…well, before I tell about what happens next, I want you to know, that even as Sweep was telling me, I found it quite unbelievable. I mean, when Sweep first told me about what happened next, I was agog. And I even did my best to look agog. Letting my mouth gape open, I said… "Oh, come on Sweep! Come on! Are you serious?"

"Abso-fucking-lutely. It's all true," he said, "its all bloody true!"

So as Sweep is telling me, I'm thinking, "What a twist, what a bloody corkscrew!"

Just remember what Jelly-Hair thought of Motley, right. Just think about how much she detested his quick-off-the-mark insults and all his big-guy braggadocio. Because what happens next is…is just…un-fucking-believable!

Get this…Old Jelly-Hair – aka Detective Wendy Westerby – asked our boy Motley to help her to nail the Tremblett brothers on corruption charges. Can you believe that? Jesus H. Christ! Talk about an undercover expose; talk about a diamond-studded denouement. Talk about an outrageous bloody yarn!

19

Motley was in the packed-out wine-bar for his usual ten-o'clock relaxation, when Jelly-Hair just walked over to his table and said, "We should talk."

Oh boy! You should have seen his face. Shit, you should have seen it! Motley couldn't have looked more surprised if the barmaid had walked over and punched him in the mouth. Sounding like some half-arsed Bobby DeNiro from the movie Taxi Driver, Motley pointed at his chest and mumbled, "You talkin' to me? Are you talkin' to me?"

Later, in the Central Station car park, the undercover policewoman explained to an incredulous Motley that she was a Detective Sergeant with the National Crime Squad and that she was working on a special assignment. She also told him that she had known about his drug dealing in the wine-bar from the very first night he'd started. But then came the haymaker; then she hit Motley with something that almost knocked him off his feet.

The woman detective announced, "I've been working for over a year to bring down the city's bent police drug-enforcement team." Christ! You could have knocked Motley down with a plumber's spanner. He'd always known that there was a reason for his intense dislike for the spiky-haired barmaid. Now he patted himself on the back for his subconscious intuitiveness, and then the conversation came to the hilarious, rib-tickling, pants-pissing bit.

Jelly-Hair told Motley that her boss was prepared to offer him an amnesty on his drug-dealing activities, if he agreed to help her in a sting to trap the Trembletts. Motley couldn't get a handle on what he was hearing; it was all too preposterous, too far-fetched. Then, an on-his-toes clarity struck him, it was so obvious: Jelly-Hair was working with the Tremblett brothers in an attempt to trap him. In chess terms, it was a knight's move – strange, asymmetrical, and completely unexpected.

"So what drug dealing activities are you talking about then?" he blithely asked, with feigned solemnity. "I really don't know what you're talking about."

"Don't try and piss around with me, Motley," Jelly-Hair said in a steely tone. Then she unslung her bag from her shoulder and after a few seconds of rummaging around in its depths, she produced a police ID-card. Moltey took a long, nauseated look at it – he read its blue-coloured intonation, Special Investigations Team.

"I could have you lifted tonight if I wanted to," the policewoman threatened.

"So, what kind of deal are you offering?" Motley painfully asked.

"Immunity from prosecution for all your drug related activities. I should warn you that we have plenty of evidence on your little pharmaceutical business at the wine-bar. And that includes your piss-artist friend."

Instead of being dismayed at the policewoman's revelation, Motley suddenly felt elated; the under-cover cop obviously had no idea that for most of the past year he'd been the kingpin supplier of most of the illegal drugs being used in the South Wales coastal cities.

"If I do get involved with your sting, I want the same deal for my mate Sweep; immunity from prosecution for all our past drug-related activities. Agreed?"

"Not my decision. I'd have to sort that one out with my boss, but I'll get back to you in a couple of days with an answer. I think we might manage it."

"And I want to see all the evidence that you say you've got on me and my friend. Just to make sure you're not bluffing." Motley wanted to be sure that she didn't have any police Intel on Bennie or the rest of his team. "Can you fix it?"

"Why not? I was the one who sent in the report, I'll make you a copy." Jelly-Hair then pressed a folded piece of paper into Motley's hand, "My mobile number. Call me when you want to talk."

As the unlikely-looking, mini-skirted policewoman climbed into her car, Motley had to bite his lip hard to stop himself from laughing out loud. It was a grim ordeal to watch the double-dealing barmaid preen and swank at her own self-applause; she was already giving herself a standing ovation for the subtlety and cleverness of her scheme – ensnaring the Trembletts and putting Motley in his place with one intrepid stroke.

Motley shuddered when he saw Jelly-Hair's shimmering, heavily-lipsticked mouth open into a too-wide-for-her-face smile. He could see past her bared teeth, past the sourness of her breath; he could feel her posturing heartbeat; hear the beat of her play-it-to-the-gallery pulse. When she flipped him a raised hand from the steering wheel as she drove off, he made a theatrical play of waving like a madman at the illicit, ID card-carrying barmaid. But for Motley, Jelly-Hair was no longer just a contentious barmaid: she was his ticket to the future. A future bereft of the threat of violence and many years behind bars. Tonight would be the very last time that Motley thought of DS Wendy Westerby as 'Old Jelly-Hair'.

20

The confused and contemplative Motley stood in the rain-puddled car park for a long time afterwards, trying to consider the capsizal madness of the new situation. He looked at what had happened with a glorious, head-back guffaw; it was almost operatic in its suddenly exposed secrets, its dramatic storyline changes and unexpected enlargement of the plot.

He was being offered a satisfying chance to square it with the Trembletts and their colleagues, using the very police force they were working for. And to top it off, there was an opportunity to settle his own execrable past with the law, and to make a fresh start. He'd already managed to salt away a decent wedge from the drug-dealing profits in an offshore account; it would be enough to set him and Rachel up with a beach-bar somewhere far away from the minatory streets of Cardiff. As long as that somewhere was cheap.

Besides, he was becoming expediently enthusiastic about putting the city's entire drug squad in the slammer. They were bad people, he reasoned, they were traitors, rotten and polluting; he'd be doing the entire world a favour. Motley was slowly inducting himself into the policewoman's break-with-the-past plan. But he would still carry the Walther PPK he'd ordered from Bennie; just in case he decided on a more conclusive, a more culminating solution to the Tremblett problem.

21

Over the following week, after a confused series of cautious stops and starts, and talking it over several times with Sweep, Motley settled positively on the idea and phoned DS Westerby to set up a meet. He had decided that it was the best thing to do. Because obviously that's what you always try and do - the best thing. And when you go down that best-thing road, you're choosing to play the game. Hopefully, when you try and do the best thing, you're placing yourself in another dimension, where you're staying one step ahead of the ones who are after you.

Nevertheless, Motley still felt a sense of failure. "I should take the bastards down," he would say aloud to himself. "I should smoke the pair of 'em, " he'd snarl, as he thoughtfully fingered the cold, black metal of his loaded piece. But, imperceptibly, the massive blocks of his revenge were slowly shifting, involuntarily lurching and pitching like the rumbling plates of the world's tectonic body-armour.

22

So what can I say about Cardiff's leafy bowers, the city's munificent, tree-bearing parks? In October they turn a golden yellow: oak and elm, maple and willow. Filaments of weakened sunshine spangle the nervous leaves preparing for their autumnal surrender. The mulching smells seize like childhood memories. I knew the parkland's genial secrets once, and have forgotten.

Motley and Westerby were sitting amongst the dog-shit garnished grass and wind-hissing trees of Bute Park. The drug-dealer and the policewoman spent an hour talking through their entrapment plan. Like two angry wasps with convergent vindictiveness, the ironical couple weaved and feinted, meandering towards a workable and effective sting. When they had begun their plotting, Motley's voice had been fierce and nasal as the words of retribution flowed. He mentally sorted through the tray of injurious implements at his feet, skewers and chisels, hacksaws and hammers. He reached down for each flesh-tearing tool with a frown and a fraught thought. Finally, after much argument and forceful disagreement, they settled on a plan. "Are you sure it will work?" asked a still unsure Westerby.

"It'll work alright," Motley intoned with bravura persuasion, "it'll work because those greedy bastards won't be able to resist it."

Westerby bit her lip apprehensively, but nodded her assent. "Listen, I've got the report I sent in on you and your friend's dealing activities in the wine-bar." She laid the newspaper she had been holding in her lap next to Motley. "My chief has agreed immunity from prosecution for you both, so this plan of yours had better bloody well work."

"Don't worry," Motley smiled, picking up the newspaper as he rose to leave, "You'll probably earn yourself a commendation for this one." He smiled grimly as he turned and strolled off through the trees.

As he walked through the refuge of the city's green lung, nestled snugly amongst the arid urban bergs, the cox-combed, dun-coloured castle jealously vied for Motley's attention with the anarchic modernism of Cardiff's new architecture. He remembered walking these parks as a teenager, with a smiling, teenaged girl hanging on his arm. Then, these city parks were like a welcoming lover; they enveloped you in their euphoria, indulged you with their unaffected naturalness. But these days the parks have become as strong-arm as the city: hair-triggered and ready to start a fight, ready to break your innocent, smiling face. Those verdant municipal Edens, with their disaffected cherry-blossoms and roiling flowerbeds, are now exactly like the city: they just can't stand a smiling face.

As Westerby nodded him a discreet goodbye, Motley realised that he was feeling a slight arrhythmia in his enmity towards the policewoman he'd suddenly found himself teamed up with. There was a definite softening in his belligerence towards her. In fact, a meagre admiration for her nerve and courage was beginning to displace some of the animosity he had once felt. Almost shamefacedly, he couldn't stop himself thinking about those burlesque breasts that extended out towards the world like a pair of highly kissable binoculars. "Thank God for a nice pair of tits," he rhapsodically intoned, with the clarity and accuracy of an epigrammatist.

23

Motley and Rachel were sitting out on the apartment's lounge balcony, watching an atom-trouncing ball of fire sinking into the haze of an expectant sea. Rachel reached across the table and poured out two glasses of tongue-chilling white wine. She was wearing the blue linen dress that Motley had recently bought as a surprise present for her. "Do you think it makes my breasts look small?" She now asked, smoothing down the front of the garment.

"No I don't." Motley got up and kissed his girlfriend's breasts. "You've got the biggest tits in the world," he laughed. (No, she hasn't.) His all-consuming love for Rachel fell from him as effortlessly as a tumbling asteroid.

"So, the first thing you'll have to learn is how to mix a decent cocktail," he began enthusiastically saying, "When girls are on holiday somewhere hot, they like nothing better than sitting in a shady beach-bar lapping up an exotic cocktail." Rachel smiled, and nodded indulgently at her boyfriend's prospectus for their Utopian future.

His love for his wounded girlfriend seemed to have a life outside of Motley; it was the thing that distinguished him from afar. Rachel's love for him presented him with options and choices, together with opposing emotions of peaceful joy and abject terror. More than anything, he now wanted to protect their love from all things – especially himself.

24

Have you noticed how fear always gets you where you're weakest? Fear, with its watchful cruelty, never gets you where you're strong and bold. It always gets you where you're weakest, always finds the gap in your defences.

"Intensive Care – Yes! That's it!" That's what the fear centre in Motley's brain was telling him. The dense knot of neurones at the ventricled core of his brain, where he stored all his fears and anxieties about Rachel, was telling him that from now on, he would have to dedicate himself to protecting her. "Keeping her safe from the violators," was to be his life's work, more important than anything else he could think of.

As he sipped his wine and gulped in his girlfriend's smile, he wanted to pounce on her, to thrillingly bury her under a protective barrage of kisses and hugs. A flow of enveloping love came streaming into his brain, rearranging its electrical currents and changing its temperature from lava-red to cool blue.

"Better put this on," Motley placed Rachel's sweater around her bare shoulders, "It's a chilly breeze." As he placed the garment around her he patted her arms, and then he softly clasped her head in his hands and kissed her hair. "I'll go on kissing you until you tell me to stop," he said. After four or five minutes of kisses he wearily hinted, "I'm still here."

Rachel turned her face up to him, "I love you," she sighed.

It was the first time that she had said those words since she had been hit by the car. Tears began to loom in Motley's eyes; he had feared that he'd never hear her say those words again.

25

That's something they don't normally tell you in those books about hard-men, those books about flawed soldiers and unlikeable drug-dealers. They don't tell you that even tough guys sometimes have to turn away because they can't stop the flow of their tears. "Jesus, Rachel," was all Motley could say through his constricted throat.

He wiped his face with the back of his hand then he kissed the back of his girlfriend's wonderful, forgiving neck. Time passed...and slowly, without even the slightest whisper, the roaring ball of the sun disappeared into an incendiary sea. The swollen sky still vibrated with light and magic...and Motley went on kissing Rachel's beautiful, redeeming neck, until she told him to stop.

Part Four

1

The month of August had been grievously hot, and the heat had given Sweep a villainous thirst. Naturally, Sweep took his thirst VERY seriously, and every morning as soon as he got up, he poured himself a tumbler of scotch, adding a single ice-cube as a ratifying nod to the scorching temperatures. Before downing his reviver in an uninterrupted series of heroic glugs, he would shake his head slowly from side to side – once, twice, three times, as if he was performing a religious rite. As a failed acolyte of the Church of Rome, Sweep was attracted to the solemnity of ritual. Within seconds of throwing the scotch down his experienced throat, Sweep's blood would accelerate off the speedo, hitting his brain with alcohol molecules at a hundred miles-an-hour. Then he would take a deep breath and say something relevant to the ritualistic ceremony; "Fuck," or "Shit," was the usual fervent invocation. Then the thanks-giving alcoholic would slide himself into an armchair, listening for the frantic message from his jeopardised liver to his celebrant brain, "We have a big problem here Houston!"

Sweep was feeling quite ill; he wasn't really up to it. The will shrinking, brute-power of unflagging stress had made him feel like he was looking at himself down the wrong end of a telescope; he felt shrunken and shrivelled. There were the anxieties over Rachel's injuries to worry about, and (even though he hadn't been directly involved) there were the sweat-trickling worries about Terry's murder. And then there was the bone-breaking turf-war. There were all those terrible happenings and more to fret over, and the strain of the weekly midnight runs to the sequestered bays of

Pembrokeshire had been enough to overloaded Sweep's nerves, without all the other disruptive imperatives. Now he found that he was worrying over everything, agonising about everything. He was relieved that Motley had decided to get out of the drugs racket, because he was ready to get out of…well, everything.

2

Loosening the knot in his tie, and unbuttoning his shirt-collar, the shaggy-faced Sweep pushed his empty glass across the polished bar towards his ample, amiable lover. He was now in the Sportsman's bar at lunchtime, paying his devotions to his spirit-raising girlfriend. "Didn't I have enough to worry about, without all that other shit happening?" he whined. "If only Taff hadn't bowed to his mate's pressure to join him in the big-time," he was now disingenuously saying, juggling with the truth of the matter. Sweep's girlfriend nodded supportively.

"Your so-called friend nearly got Rachel killed."

Well, you've probably heard that old saying; to become wise, a man has to learn that a truth is worth more than a lie; especially when a man is lying to himself. Feeling that he had to come to his friend's rescue, Sweep shook his head at his girlfriend's inflammatory suggestion. "Oh, I wouldn't go that far, it wasn't only Taff's fault. It was just as much my fault for not protecting her against all the crap we'd got ourselves into. Nah, it was just as much my decision, just as much my fault."

And it hadn't been Motley's fault that he'd met Rachel just as she had reached the age when girls complete their journey from childhood-princess to womanhood. When young women fall in love for the first time, they whisper goodbye to their fathers: God be with you – they say – because I won't be. It's usually a survivable misfortune for most fathers, and yet this was not so in Sweep's case. He was a highly dependent man, and he knew that he needed his daughter; she was a lode star point of guiding fixity, a see-in-the-dark compass needle unerringly pointing him in the right direction. Rachel's setting up home with Motley had definitely been a moment of Sweep's leave-taking, a Station of the Cross on his way to ghostdom. As he sat at the beer-spilled bar, he remembered his daughter as a little girl; before she became bigged-up, before she owned such a lot of physical space. Tall, leggy, with long thick hair and eyes that contained such sparkle in them. Rachel's face now had a womanly sheen to it, a hope-for-the-future glow. And most satisfyingly for Sweep, she was of his blood; she was of him! His daughter had been his only hope of leaving behind something of worth from his ragged and bestial life. Placing another large Laphroiag in front of her boyfriend, Sweep's blame-seeking girlfriend couldn't resist improvidently pointing out the fact, "Just remember, it was your friend Taff who started all this trouble. You were happy when you just worked for the Mail. You know what I think? I think it's a pity that you ever met him."

3

Perhaps that was very the moment, the start-a-fight moment when Sweep's girlfriend first thought about getting Motley out of the way. And the big problem with that kind of thinking was that even a truly lugubrious and mild-mannered friend, if he's an unstable alcoholic, could easily become an un-friend, an irreconcilable ill-wisher. At this point, Sweep was managing to avoid blaming Motley directly for what happened to his daughter; though he was only a thought away from a fever of blame. But for now he was thinking, "Just one mental-breakdown at a time, thank you very much."

He had to make sure that Rachel, his adorable Princess, was fully recovered before he could blow a valve about whose fault it all was. After downing a packet of pork scratchings and a good half of the Sportsman's bottle of Islay malt, Sweep sloped off home again, smelling of shorted-out electricity and the peaty, twelve-year-old aromas of Scotland's Inner Hebrides.

4

There was a week's hiatus in Motley setting up the sting with Westerby, while he flew out to the beautiful villa that Bennie owned on one of the smaller, lusher Caribbean islands. He was going to talk the whole deal over with his ex-Special Forces friend – no secrets, no double-dealing. Motley was going to be up-front about all his discussions with the under-cover cop.

It was an epiphanic week for Motley. Late at night, he would lay in his bed listening to the comforting swish of the fan above his head while the night-winds drummed up a tune from the palm trees bordering the nearby beach. He fell instantly and irrevocably in love with the Islands. He loved the scent of flowers in the perfumed air, the heady fragrances of frangipani, oleander and the glorious fragrance of the night-blooming jasmine. He loved the Islanders' friendly, china-white smiles that flickered in and out of his eyes like cool quanta of light. The warm sands and opal seas, the clear mountain streams and the Wedgwood-blue skies were easily the closest thing Motley had ever seen to paradise. Sitting in a local harbour-front restaurant on his last night with his friend, the two men raised their glasses simultaneously.

"You're a clever fuck, Taff" Bennie exclaimed, "killing coppers is always a shitty idea. I think your plan with the under-cover cop is a good one. Just so long as it doesn't harm our business investment over there."

"You can count on it," Motley reassured his friend, "I wouldn't even have thought about it if it had compromised anything we had going on. The beauty of it is, the cops only know about my old wine-bar gig, they have nothing on the bigger picture." Bennie took a deep draw on the huge spliff he'd just been passed by the restaurant's owner as an after-dinner smoke. Two large glasses of Remy were also placed on the table in front of them – gratis.

"That's cool with me, Taff. When are you going to move on the sting, then?"

"That depends on when you can get things set up over here for me."

"Yeah, well. That's one of the big problems with living in paradise; things take forever to happen. But if I apply some pressure in the right places, I should think about a month to six weeks should see the deal done. Two months at most."

"Great. Rachel's gonna love it."

"So she should, mate. That's the best damn beach bar on the entire island. You only got a grab at it because the retiring owner is a friend of mine."

"Yeah, I know. Thanks for getting me such a good deal on it."

" No sweat, Taff. Besides, there's a bit of self-interest involved here, isn't there?" Motley looked at his friend quizzically, "Well, think about it. I'd much rather have you over here where I can keep an eye on you, rather than have you running around the streets of Cardiff slotting coppers like a homicidal maniac. Be bad for business that kind of stuff, wouldn't it?" Bennie smiled broadly as he took another drag at the spliff; then he handed the smoko over to Motley. Draining his glass, Bennie began rubbing his distended stomach. "So, what do you think of the sea-food platter over here, pretty good, huh?"

"Brilliant," Motley agreed, "I'm as full as fat lady's knickers."

After several pulls on the marijuana-rammed joint, Motley noticed that the humidity had suddenly become more emphatic, more ticklish. There was lightning dancing and flickering away, miles out over the moon-shimmering sea. It looked like rain was on its way. But Motley even loved the Caribbean rain. For him, standing in its cooling, caressing effervescence was just like taking a refreshing shower. In these holiday latitudes, where summer is always just outside the louvered doors, the rain falls in corpulent tears on the land's green-swathed shoulders, and the beach-kids continue to play through the downpours; as happy as a steel band, they laugh and play, their occasional shout of 'Owzat!' lost to the sea's background commentary. And then the sun faithfully returns, catching the rain in the children's tight-curled hair, beading it like spider webs.

5

While Motley was away from home, and much to Sweep's girlfriend's jealous consternation, Sweep had temporarily moved into the apartment down in the Bay to look after his daughter. He was sitting on her rumpled, mid-morning bed, still dressed in his pyjamas. The familial pair were drinking tea and playing a desultory game of 'snap'. Sweep had been up for two hours already and he still hadn't had a drink. One o'clock came and went without him reaching for one of the many expensive bottles in Motley's drinks cabinet. While he prepared a light lunch for them both, the cirrhotic Sweep admitted to a trembling in the hands; but then he put the kettle on for more tea. At about three-thirty he was saying to himself – I wonder if I can go another ten minutes. He still had four minutes to go when he reached for the handle on the drinks-cabinet.

Whenever the booze closed in, and the alco-hit closed his eyes, Sweep could feel himself tumbling away, falling backwards towards his childhood and its smug happiness and security, when people admired his sporting prowess and he liked them in return. Whatever happened to me? he would ask himself. Sometimes he would get a repeating dream of himself running towards a try-line, clad in his school's colours, the oval ball tucked under his arm, his face fresh and try-umphant. That was the last time he could have sworn that he was alive.

But his childhood had vanished, along with happiness and smiles and everything else; replaced by the unsmiling dourness, the woundings and goings-on of adulthood. He'd awake from his dreams coiled in a tight foetal curl, his cheeks sticky with tears, wondering if death began a long time before life ended. Then he'd wonder what death would be like – and knew at once, with abrupt certainty, that it would be bearable. It was during those terrifying four a.m. moments that Sweep could see himself as others saw him – a drunken bum, drowning in black water.

Nevertheless, Sweep's first ever attempt at moderation had filled his daughter with pride and affectionate amazement. To Rachel, Sweep's effort at restraint had made some form of intermittent sobriety just a matter of time. The next time, he'd get through those extra minutes, those extra moments. And that's all sobriety is for an alcoholic; it's just a matter of increasing the number of moments between drinks.

As Sweep sat down on the bed again, guiltily holding his whisky, Rachel stroked his furry cheek: "You're very brave, Dad. That's the longest I've seen you go without it."

The complimented father looked down at his glass, and had to fight back the tears. "I wish I could do it. I wish I could give it up. For your sake, Rache, for you."

He placed the untouched drink down on the beside-table and lowered his monolithic head into his daughter's lap. She stroked her father's crew-cut hair, as he began to weep into her towelling bathrobe. "Don't cry Dad, you did good. You deserve that drink."

Rachel reached out and timidly offered her father the scotch. Sweep took the glass from her hand, but still didn't take any of the assailing liquid it contained. "By Christ, did you see that, Rache? Did you see that? I was almost compos mentis. For a few hours there, I was very nearly sober!" He said it with a broad grin, and Rachel nodded eagerly.

"You could do it again if you wanted to, Dad. Anytime."

Sweep downed the whisky in one go, but Rachel still couldn't wait to break the happy news of her father's six hours of quenched thirst to Motley when he returned.

6

When Motley did return from his tropical sojourn, after telling Rachel all about the beach-bar, the first thing he did was to call Wendy Westerby on her mobile. "You can start the clock for the photo finish," he'd said cryptically, "Conditions should be perfect in about six weeks."

The detective knew exactly what Motley meant. Their blueprinted plan entailed Motley setting up a meeting with the Trembletts at which he would declare his retirement from the drugs game, suggesting the battering that Rachel had received as his reason for him wanting to get out. He was going to tell the two brothers that they had won the turf war; and that all he wanted now was to get away to protect his girlfriend. If they agreed to buy him out, at a sum that would secure his future, he would turn over his newly acquired business to the Trembletts.

Of course the meeting was to be monitored by Westerby's anti-corruption colleagues through a wire that Motley would be wearing and through long-range microphones and video. As soon as Westerby's surveillance detail had got enough confessional evidence on tape, the heavy mob would move in to arrest the rotten policemen. After the arrests, Motley would then hand over to Westerby a copy of Toby's affidavit, outlining his previous business dealings with the Trembletts. Naturally, Toby would have already left the country for Thailand with a bag-full of cash, so there would be no danger of him spilling the beans about Bennie's new set-up.

And then, finally, when the whole shabby melodrama had been played out, Motley would be allowed to slip away quietly to begin a new life – in the tropical paradise of St. Lucia. Good plan that. Jesus, I bet you wouldn't mind a plan like that, eh? I know I wouldn't! – except for the part about wearing a wire and all that other Bruce-Willis-fortitude stuff. All that stuff sounds a tad tricky to me. Maybe a bit dangerous, even. Oh, bugger that intrepid beau sabreur stuff; sod that big-cojones bravery thing. I think I'll just stick to beating the shit out of a typewriter. Okay, it's a tame, excitement-free way to make a living…but it's as physically safe as ride in a top-of-the-range Range Rover. Although, thinking about the dangers of being a writer, I did mange to drunkenly stab myself in the thigh with a biro once. Shit, that hurt! I bet even Bruce Willis would have yelped at that one.

7

Even I, his oldest friend, couldn't imagine what Sweep was thinking of when he told me he was getting married again. The irritating woman that he was already calling his 'next ex-wife' had told Sweep that she loved him.

"Oh, I love you!" she'd cried out during one of their elaborate and arduous sex sessions. "I love you too." Sweep had distractedly moaned, wiping the sweat away from his overexerted brow.

And that was it! Marriage plans were suddenly being drawn up. When my friend told me in the pub that he was to be married in three weeks time, instead of congratulating him, I'd slipped my arm around his shoulder and quietly asked, "Is this a good idea? After all, you haven't known her that long."

But Sweep was adamant. Perhaps his Viagra powered old-fart virility was blinding his judgement. Now, you may think I was being hard on Sweep's girlfriend, being 'not nice' even. But what Sweep didn't know was that his girlfriend was already trying to betray his friend Motley.

So, despite his first marriage being a total failure, Sweep was preparing to make another bad deal. Even though he couldn't see it, Motley and I knew what his girlfriend was really like, what she was really trying to do. And I did try to tell him. Oh yeah, I didn't mince a single cautionary word either.

"Give up the idea of marrying her," I said, "I don't think she'd be good for you, mate. And anyway, what the hell have you got to gain by it?"

But it seems Sweep hadn't been diminished enough by marriage. Like someone who is addicted to physical abuse, he was in pursuit of a final, malicious assault, an ultimate injustice that would validate his aggrievement forever. Perhaps it was his embattled self-image, his gnarled ego, or perhaps it was something more mundane. Whatever it was, my friend was on the brink of turning a wrong-headed mistake into a catastrophe, until Motley reigned him in. I had tried, but I failed.

I couldn't tell him about what I'd seen in the wine-bar one night. Perhaps it was the fact that I felt slightly intimidated by him. Well? You never knew Sweep when he was a player, did you? He was good: a hard-as-nails hooker who could run like a wing-forward. And even today, you can still feel his physical presence, you can still see why all the other rugby playing 'hard men' were intimidated by him. Even now, if you see Sweep sitting at the bar, you know that somebody is sitting there. So I couldn't save him from himself; but Motley could. And he did.

8

Motley told Sweep about what his girlfriend had been doing in the wine-bar the night I saw her. I had told Motley that I'd seen her having a long and agitated conversation with the barmaid he called Jelly-Hair. And then, apparently, he'd got a secret call from the barmaid herself, warning him of an attempted betrayal.

Sweep later found out that his girlfriend had recently read a piece in a magazine that posited the emergence of a new kind of woman: the uncompromising go-getter who knows her personal goals and isn't afraid to rattle a few cages to achieve them. It seems this new kind of woman is also supercontemporary in her acceptance of change, isn't afraid of being a life-altering force, and so on.

So, unflinching and unsmiling, she set out to achieve her own personal goals. Sweep's girlfriend had already visited the wine-bar many times with him, and she knew all about the weight of animosity between Motley and the barmaid. So she decided that she had found an ally in getting Motley out of the way. Having seen Jelly-Hair canoodling with her policeman boyfriend, one night she decided that she would let the barmaid into the secret of Motley's wine-bar drug-dealing enterprise, while still trying to retain her anonymity with the police.

"No…see," said Sweep's girlfriend leaning across the bar, "I don't want your boyfriend to know who told you. I don't want anyone to know where you got the information from, see. No, I don't want my Sweep ever to find out who told on his friend. But Sweep's easily led, see. It's that bloody Motley who's telling him to do it. You can tell that, can't you?"

"Oh, I guessed that," the barmaid had said, vauntingly, "thank you for telling me about that swine Motley." Jelly-Hair then said with collegiate spirit, "I'll pass that information on to my friend. He'll be very interested in that.

And don't worry, I promise not to say anything about who told me. But you mustn't say anything about it to anyone else. Understand? It's our little secret now."

Standing back from the oaken bulk of the bar, and with her heavy bosoms heaving in her dynamic brassiere, Sweep's stool-pigeon girlfriend nodded, and breathed a huge sigh of relief after being so destructively communicative. In her New Woman's mind, she was just protecting her man, while at the same time covering her own treacherous tracks. For her, grassing out Motley was just a means of achieving her personal goals. Leaving the women's magazine's journalistic theory behind, she was turning the 'New Woman' idea into eviscerating practice.

9

The DCI in charge of the drug squad was at home, just finishing his evening meal. His wife rose from the neatly laid table to answer the unexpected ring at the doorbell. When she returned to the dining room: "Darling, the Assistant Chief Constable and another gentleman are here to see you."

The DCI's wife called him darling all the time. And they held hands, with interwoven fingers, all the time. They were very fond, the ideal couple – they were the dream marriage; childless through choice, they were each other's children. She said the following words to her husband with a thud of temple-to-temple fear upon her face. "They said they must see you tonight. They're waiting in the sitting room."

Fifteen minutes after the Assistant Chief Constable had entered his home, and with a sound like tinnitus ringing in his ears, the shell-shocked DCI was putting his signature to a form requesting early retirement. Instead of describing the anti-corruption investigation into the DCI's department in soft, forgiving tones, the silver-braided Assistant Chief Constable was almost gurgling with sadistic satisfaction. In monotonous, declarative sentences, he rendered a discreditable précis of the drug squad's illegal activities, a rigorous catalogue of its endemic corruption.

Corruption…this was a disastrous word to say to a man who bore his life gripped by belief and religious observance. The Assistant Chief Constable knew that the DCI was innocent of corruption, as innocent as early morning mist, but his face was still all rancorous glint and animosity. He saw the DCI as a patchwork of weaknesses – a bad joke copper.

"We know that you weren't involved in any of the corruption," the ACC finally said, redeemingly. "But at the end of the day, you were responsible for the running of the department. You failed to impose your authority over your men. It was a bloody disorganised free-for-all, wasn't it? You were indulgent and neglectful beyond belief, bordering on abrogation of duty."

The DCI nodded in weary agreement, his leonine head lowering by degree until finally his chin was resting on his chest. There would be no disciplinary charges brought against him; but quite possibly, the weight of failure and shame he now felt was an even greater price to pay. At least he was told, with malevolent generosity, that they were going to let him keep his pension. Finally, when the ACC had exhausted himself, the ruined DCI had something to say. "I trusted them," he simpered, "I trusted those boys, and they let me down."

The Assistant Chief Constable gazed without trace of pity at the pious old man sitting opposite him, a glint of pleasure still coruscating in his infidel's eyes.

"Can you do me one favour?" The DCI asked, softly, apologetically.

"What's that?"

"Let me be the one to arrest them."

"What? …Why?"

The DCI answered him with a scrupulous archaism –
"Because they chose to follow the path of evil," he quivered,
his hand toying with the pocket bible sitting on the table
next to his armchair, "Let me be the Lord's instrument of
retribution."

The next morning, the vengeful instrument of the Lord
was sitting in an unmarked police van, waiting. The
surveillance team sitting hunched in the back of the van with
him, encumbered by their microphones, cameras and VCR's
must have been used to seeing some good acting from their
victims. How many times had they admiringly witnessed
their target's slobberingly proficient arts of faultless lying
and deceit? But today they were in for a real treat.

10

Under Motley's instruction, Toby had rung the drug squad
detective to set up the meet. Andy Tremblett didn't believe a
word of it. "What kind of shit are you trying to pull now,
eh?" he'd said. But he was still intrigued enough to agree to
the rendezvous. Unknown to the rapturous Westerby though,
Motley had changed their plan slightly: he'd insisted that
Toby would tell Andy Tremblett to show up for the meet
alone, without his brother. He had other plans for Rod, more
representational, more proportionate for the man who had
almost killed his girlfriend. Toby was almost shitting his
pants when he made the call, but he was now more afraid of
Motley's crew than of Tremblett's.

Motley stood waiting by his car. Across the other side
of the car park, the plain white van sat unobtrusively
between a couple of steroid-pumped-up Japanese 4 by 4s.
When Andy Tremblett drove into the car park he circled
around a couple of times before driving out again. The
surveillance team told Motley not to move; Tremblett was
just trying to flush out any trickery that had been set up.
Five minutes later, Tremblett returned, and parked in a space

a few cars away from Motley's. Again, through his earpiece, the surveillance team told Motley not to move. After a further five minutes, the drug squad detective emerged from his car wearing an artificial smile. "No reception committee, I hope," he shouted. Motley continued to stare down at the ground immediately in font of him. He picked at his teeth for a few seconds. Then, shaking his head from side to side, he muttered, "Let's get this over with, Tremblett."

The quivering DCI watched Andy Tremblett through the windscreen of the van with bulging eyes, his once-lenient face glowing as red as a traffic light.

"What I don't understand," he hissed, "is why those people did it."

"Oh come on, sir. Don't be a hermit. They're bad coppers. Just bad people, that's all." The overalled policeman sitting next to the DCI wondered how the ill-informed old guy had made it to such an exalted rank. Then he thought to himself: well, at least the old bugger is honest.

Andy Tremblett took a three-hundred-and-sixty-degree look around the car park as he cautiously walked towards Motley. "So, what sort of bullshit racket are you trying now?" he goaded. Motley remained silent until the policeman came within a couple of yards of him.

"It's time to make a deal. Put an end to this turf war," he said, still looking at the ground. Finally, Motley managed to bring himself to look up at his declared enemy. "I want out. But it's gonna cost you to get your business back."

"Fuck you, arse-hole."

Motley shook his head disappointingly, and returned his gaze to the ground in front of him, "Jesus, Tremblett, can't you say anything that isn't a worn-out cliché? You're as bad as your scum-bag hit-and-run brother."

"Yeah, he told me about your little tête-à-tête in the wine-bar," Tremblett laughed, "and he's going to do you for that. You're going to spend some time in hospital for that, just like your fucking girlfriend did."

Motley sprang towards the grinning copper like a wounded tiger. The surveillance guy was screaming at him to stay calm as he charged forwards. Tremblett danced backwards half a dozen paces, and then held his hands up. "Whoa, hard guy! Why don't you just say what you've got to say? Then I can get the fuck out of here."

Biting into his lower lip until he could taste his own blood, Motley calmed down enough to say, "It's up to you Tremblett. I'm getting out of the drugs business, but if you want your old patch back, together with the copies of Toby's affidavit, it's gonna cost you. And your bent colleagues."

"So, it's forgive and forget, eh?" Tremblett sneered, grimly.

"Yeah, if you like. Put it behind you. It's only business, right?"

"Hey, shithead. You're getting out, aren't you? That means we've won. So why should we give you anything? You're running away, and if you come back or you show that pack of lies you forced out of Toby to someone you shouldn't, your crippled girlfriend might not be so lucky next time." The adrenaline-pumping exertion of controlling his temper was causing the sweat to stream down Motley's body. He wanted to launch himself at the self-satisfied cop and strangle the living shit out of him.

"Use your head for a change, Tremblett. You can easily afford to pay me off if you get your team to stump up a slice each. Your squad has made enough loot over the years to buy me out with their loose change. Why don't you take it to back them to think over? They might be a bit smarter than you."

"They'll think what I tell them to fucking think. We're going to take back what's ours, so you can shove your deal up your jacksy." The policeman turned to leave, but then spun on his heel and growled, "Oh, and by the way, if you don't fuck off out of it soon, you're likely to end up in the river. Just like our friend Terry did."

Motley suddenly heard a voice shouting into his earpiece: "That's it we've got enough. Move, move, move." The back of the white van suddenly burst open and four blue-overalled policemen ran towards an astonished Tremblett, followed sedately by his own uniformed chief. Simultaneously, an unmarked police-car came racing into the car park. Two plain-clothes detectives jumped out and approached their cursing colleague, followed by a smiling DS Wendy Westerby.

The DCI's eyes glittered with moisture as he stared into his subordinate's bulging, unbelieving eyes: "You're under arrest, Tremblett, on suspicion of corruption." Before turning his face away from his ex-protégé, he said: "May God forgive you, because your colleagues and their families certainly won't." He delivered his speech without talent, unsatirically, like a distraught accountant. Then he turned and walked away with infinite grief, and started thinking about a different life.

"Where's your brother, Tremblett?" Westerby demanded. "Where's Rod?"

The expected, "Fuck you, you treacherous bitch," instantly flew across Andy Tremblett's wronged lips. Motley walked towards the tight scrum of officers as they patted down their spread-eagled prisoner. When Tremblett turned around from the body search, Motley had barged through the wall of policemen. The good news is that Motley's iron-tight fist smashed into Tremblett's jaw, shattering it like crystal. The jail-bound copper was spun around by the punch like a kid's top; and then he crumpled, unconscious, to the oil-prismed tarmac.

"Get out of here Motley." Westerby was screaming, "We've nicked him. Now get the hell out here or I'll bloody-well lock you up as well!" Two officers grabbed Motley by the arms and led him back to his car.

"You'll bugger off now if you know what's good for you," one of the overalled coppers barked at him before pushing him into his top-down motor, "you don't want to piss her off, believe me."

Part one of Motley's secret plan had worked. Now he was looking forward to part two – the part that his erstwhile partner, DS Westerby had no idea about. Part two of his plan was the delicious, pleasurable, unbalanced part that was going to avenge all of Rachel's pain and crippling injuries. Part two was to be a fever of reparation; part two was to be Rachel's assailant's curtain call; the visitation of his lacerating dueness. For Rod Tremblett, part two of Motley's plan was to be a full semi-automatic magazine of .79-caliber Nemesis.

11

As soon as Motley drove out of the car park after Andy Tremblett's arrest he stopped his car and called the police HQ from the nearest call box. He was put straight through to the drug squad office. "Could I speak to Detective Constable Rod Tremblett right away. Tell him it's an urgent family matter."

"Just a second," a female voice replied. Motley could hear the raucous sounds of office banter in the background, then suddenly the banter stopped. A tremulous voice then came on the line.

"Yes? DC Tremblett speaking."

"Your girlfriend just nicked your brother on corruption charges. Your fucking barmaid is an undercover cop, dickhead. She's on her way over there right now to nick the fucking lot of you." There was a stunned silence at the other end of the phone.

Then a panicky, "Who is this? Who the hell is this?"

"If I were you, I'd get out of your office right now. Get out of there right now or you'll be spending the night in the next cell to your brother." Motley then hung up the phone and drove home; he wanted to spend some time with Rachel before the next part of his plan kicked in. A few days before he had flown out to the Caribbean to talk things over with Bennie, Motley had followed Westerby home from the wine bar. He knew exactly where she lived. He now figured that he had three or four hours before he needed to be hidden in the shrubbery opposite her apartment building.

12

Motley was standing at the table with his hands full of dirty dishes; they had just finished eating. Rachel rose from the table and moved unsteadily onto the large beige carpet that spanned the lounge area. She held out her arms invitingly, "Come on. Let's dance!"

"What?" Motley looked askance at her.

"Come and dance with me. We haven't danced in ages."

Motley's favourite Dido album was playing on the stereo...soft music...easy listening. "You sure? I mean...your legs, are they are okay?"

Rachel was smiling and nodding. Her face was cushioned by the candlelight, the coils of her hair resting upon her shoulders. As he looked at her, Motley thought he was going to faint with love. He took her gently in his arms. Rachel placed her arms around his neck and began stepping awkwardly around in a small circle, trying to ignore her pain-ridden legs, her gnawing ankles and her vehemently protesting hips. She placed her head on Motley's shoulder, and broadened her smile – even though there were tears of pain streaming down her cheeks. She was dancing again! The moment was an assurance that she was going to make it – despite her aggrievement at having to live the rest of her life inefficiently moving about, walking precariously as if on moving sand. She was smiling because she knew that she was going to make it.

As he held his slowly turning girlfriend, Motley could feel her taut body beneath her dress, smell her familiar smell drifting up from her shoulders. He slid his fingers from around her back and began stroking the smoothness of her neck. From there his fingers moved slowly to her cheek, her lips, and then to the tangle of her hair. His fingers were in no hurry; it's the journey that makes it fun. Rachel turns her head, and now he is looking into her face. He is seeing her...every particle of her. And she knows it. He is seeing her, and they are connected. She knows that he wants her; she knows that he wants to claim something. And she wants him to claim it. She moves, taking his hand, and the transfer of love begins. They walk towards the bedroom. Soon the dance will become another kind of dance – the high-voltage stuff of elongated bodies rhythmically moving, the sinuous swirling of arms and legs clasping and stretching across the rumpled wavelets of bed-sheets. Later, Motley lovingly holds her face in his hands. "I see you," he says, softly.

"Do you?"

"You want to know how I see you?"

Rachel nods, suspecting that this is a secret moment.

"I see you because I can't see anything else."

"Good. That's the deal," Rachel smiles.

"When I look at you, I don't see or think of anything else. It's just you...and me...and here." Rachel reaches up her hand and touches Motley's face.

"Well, that's all the important stuff then."

Is Rachel right, do you think? Is that the deal? ...Does love kill off everything else? If that's the deal, then you'd better know that when you fall in love it's going be taking a huge bite out of your life. Love takes away your fantasies, your future, it takes everything: until love finally owns you.

"Have you ever wondered why it's me?" Rachel asked.

"What? What do you mean?"

"Why me? Why this face? I mean it could have been anyone, couldn't it?"

Motley remained silent; he was too confused to provide his girlfriend with an answer. Rachel snuggled up even closer into Motley's body.

"I bumped into my ex-boyfriend the other day, the one I told you about."

"Who…the weeper? The wimp?" Motley almost snarled, "What did you talk about?" he asked, giving his girlfriend a steady, unblinking look.

A slight frown had creased Rachel's forehead, "You. Us."

His lower lip bulging aggressively, Motley grunted, "Hmm."

"You know what he asked me? He asked me why you, instead of him?"

Motley stared down at Rachel, "What did you say?" For a moment it seemed to him like he was asking a stranger an awkward personal question. A question he wasn't sure he wanted answered.

"I can't tell you."

Surprised and disappointed at the answer, Motley almost shouted when he asked, "Why not?"

After a moment, Rachel replied warily, "Well, you know what you're like."

"Jesus, Rache. What the hell does that mean?" Motley rotated Rachel's head so that she was looking up at him. "Tell me. What did you say?"

Her eyes falling away from Motley's face, Rachel still didn't reply.

"Tell me what you said to him, Rache. Please." By repeating the question, Motley suddenly felt like he was surrendering something. Something Stone Age old, like macho power: like male identity. Rachel turned her head away, sheepishly.

"I, I just told him that for the first time in my life I felt safe. With you."

Motley was almost crushed by the irony. Even though he'd almost got her killed, Rachel could still say that she felt safe with him.

"Then I told him…" before Rachel could finish Motley had put his finger gently to her lips.

"Shhhh…don't say any more. That's enough "

He wrapped his arms around her, and kissed the back of her neck. "I'm sorry," he whispered. Rachel snuggled securely into the hardness of his body.

"They say that love means you don't have to say sorry," she murmured.

"Yeah, well. What do they know?"

13

Later that evening, Motley set off to complete the second part of his plan. Striking out from the light and space of the Bay, with its ongoing banter of machinery. He left behind the large-scale, cathartic reconstruction, where builders had been fucking around for years with their Tonka cement trucks, their diggers and cranes. Builders usually imply construction, but around the Bay area builders meant destruction, raising nothing but people's expectations.

As he headed in a northeasterly direction, Motley entered the lumpen network of undeveloped roads leading away from the 're-developed' waterfront. He stop-start motored his way through the Victorian squatness of terraced houses, the don't-give-a-fuck streets of Adamstown and Splott, with their crouching people, the frowning, headlong, fucked-up-postured people. He began passing walls and the flanks of bridges that bore the spray-canned names of personages like COOLIO and BANJAX and BOOMY. Then came a lexicon of assiduously sprayed injunctions like, FUCK THE FUZZ and E IS BRILL. Further along the ravaged streets, he began to notice little troupes of ferrety-faced young women coalescing under street-lamps, clutching paper cups of supermarket's-own gin, or teetering in solitary impropriety on the pug-nosed edges of pavement kerbs. As he passed them by, he thought, as he always did: You lot must be taking the piss…you lot have got to be fucking joking!

Some of these girls were doing what their mothers and grandmothers had done before them, when the Nazi bombs had been falling on the docks and rubble was bouncing around in the streets. The spell of selling their underprivileged bodies on the streets was still fast, still good. These girls charged a little more than their mothers and grandmothers did, but that's inflation for you. None of these working girls made their futures; their futures came at them. Their futures were already out there, already formed in their shrugging vulnerability, in their mothers' tired and fulminating wombs.

He had never paid for sex in his life, now Motley wondered what kind of man went with these winter-faced girls. Maybe that's what keeps some guys going: the sex you have to pay for, the improper fucks. Maybe that's what keeps some guys interested, keeps their whore-mongering peckers alive and working. In grim joggers, crayon-coloured leggings and lime coloured puff-jackets, in lumpy fleeces and tired jeans, chain-smoking and wind-chilled, the girls offered themselves to leering men as they solemnly commuted home in the evening gloom. It was hard-earned money, keeping the lid on men in cars; nauseatingly breathing in their meaty breath – their rancid breath was just another way of doing down the helpless – suffering their pythonic embraces, listening to them croaking their pathetic excuses for penile dysfunction (naturally, always the very first time it had ever happened).

All the neon-drearied street-girls talked Cardiff (Care-diff), but for some, there were inherited memories of potato-famine Ireland or parched Horn of Africa in them, though colourfully denied by the blonde tints of home-rinsed hair, now elliptically flattened to their heads by the press of the wind. Every one of the teenaged girl's faces was stiff with cold and defiance (a defiance discarded when necessary).

"Sometimes you don't have to do nuffing. Sometimes all they wants is the smell of a woman."

Sometimes, all they wanted was the reek of a woman: to sort out the stress of work and the loneliness of unworkable marriages. And the young women's eyes were bright and shining, but the blood in them was cold; their mouths a hardened pucker of indignation that contained volumes of swallowed insult.

Unlike most gatherings of young women, these girls never talked about men. Neither was there talk of music or make-up or television soaps: these girls talked only of affliction. Endometriosis, poor circulation, haemophilia and sexually transmitted infections: disease-rich talk, reeling and retching. No. There was never any talk of social justice or de-forestation or ozone depletion, only of pain. Apart, that is, from a very great deal of talk about the police vice squad: another affliction, another of life's painful maulings.

Suddenly Motley felt his head incline towards them, as though braced for some revelation, as though these nothing girls, with their stunned and bewildered-infant gaze could tell him something that he really needed to know. He turned his stare away from them, suddenly feeling wincingly self-conscious and clandestine. The faces of these street-walking girls forbade inspection; these depthless faces were shorn of everything unnecessary for business – they were just two dimensions of injury and defiance. Motley thought that they wore the faces of soldiers lost behind enemy lines.

He drove on, gazing out at the damp deaf-and-dumb streets, and the streets stared accusingly back at him – sitting in the business-class comfort of his German auto, with his adjustable climate, digital speedo, and his sordidly cruising

266

cruise control. Beyond the importuning working-girls, in the disfavoured, anti-utopian streets bordering the away-with-the-old-on-with-the-new waterfront, the ancient divisions of class and race were giving way to the new divisions: good jobs versus bad jobs, certainty versus uncertainty, preparedness versus un-preparedness for the different forms of urban life that were taking over.

14

As Motley nosed his car towards the Roath Park area of the city, he was trying to weigh up every nuance of his intended actions. He was thinking that perhaps he had lost his peripheral vision: he could only see the long awaited revenge directly in front of him, but nothing else. He could see no other options out of the corners of his eyes.

"How can I know? How can I know, when I don't know anything?" Motley was looking within himself for dispassionate guidance; for dispassion and guidance that was no longer there. He knew that it was a mistake to focus down too tightly on a plan; in the army, a lack of peripheral vision could get you killed. He tried in his imagination to broaden his perspectives, to try to get an objective overview of his intentions: "If I do this, I have to give up everything: Rachel, the beach-bar, everything. Everything that I love."

Then he asked himself a will-sapping question: "Why doesn't someone stop me for Christ's sake? Why doesn't someone say something?" Of course Motley was forgetting that someone had said something. His trusted friend Bennie had very recently said, "Killing coppers is always a shitty idea." And that's what Motley had chosen to forget.

15

After failing to get his brother on his mobile, Rod Tremblett had fled from his office as soon as he had put the phone down. Instead of going home to say a heart-cracking goodbye to his kids, he drove to the Central Station car park and abandoned his car there. Then he got a taxi across town to Roath Park. His life, he felt, was approaching its final-act climax. What sort of genre did his life belong to? That was the question. Was it comedy or tragedy? Rod decided that it was inglorious comedy, which is a kind of tragedy.

Rod was intent on something more consummate than saying goodbyes to his kids, something more vengeful, more insane. As he sat in the back of the lurching taxi, his mind seethed and flamed with all the misfortunes that had befallen him – and now, his inexorable coup-de-grace at the hands of his double-dealing mistress. How did it all happen, how did it all go so badly wrong? As he staggered around the Edwardian park with its ruffled lake its child-sized lighthouse and its motionless time, Rod Tremblett's mind spiralled into the unreasoning obtuseness of blind hatred. No clear thinking is possible when someone is seized by that kind of loathing, no circumspection. Only further derangement is possible.

He closed his eyes as he began his third turn around the lake, hoping that the entire, fucked-up horror of his life would just go away. But instead, his eyes began to explode beneath his eyelids; tears began to roll down his cheeks in unstoppable rivulets. He was still sobbing when he lifted his mobile phone from his pocket and pressed the quick-dial key for his home number.

"Hello? Rod?" He recognised that Anne's voice was taught with tension. There were probably police officers sitting in his lounge right now, drinking endless cups of Anne's cheerlessly made tea and waiting for him to call.

"Anne. I...I'm..." mesmerised by his wife's familiar voice, Rod couldn't speak. He was trying to say he was sorry, but he couldn't get past his throat-clenching sobs. Then his youngest son's voice chirruped across the airwaves.

"Is it Daddy, Mummy? Is it Daddy?"

Astronomically speaking, we know that everything is flying apart: and right then, that's what Rod's mind felt like. It was right then that Rod felt a billion light years away from the things he loved. His heart split asunder in that terrible moment, screaming in horror at the hideous things he'd done to his family. Every pain-thrumming molecule inside his body groaned and sighed.

"Hush sweetheart, Rod? Rod, please come home. Are you still there?"

The agony he felt in his chest was almost crippling. He'd always kissed and hugged his boys as often as he could; because he'd once read somewhere that fathers should kiss and hug their sons, otherwise they grow up to be mutilated psychos. Rod was aware that we should be careful about what we do to our children; because what we do to them we do to ourselves; when our children grow up, they always become us. Anne hugged and kissed her boys as often as she could, too; but she hugged and kissed them because she needed to. She needed their love; she needed their valiant, thoroughgoing love like she needed the air in her lungs. When she hugged her children it helped combat the depression. When she hugged them, she didn't feel happy or sad: she just felt authentic, validated: which is the opposite of neglected.

"Rod? Rod, are you still there?" Anne was asking. "Come home, sweetheart, please. They're here waiting for you, but they've said it will only make it worse if you run away."

269

Rod managed to whisper what he had to say to his wife, and she whispered back that she understood he didn't mean for it to happen. Then he let the tiny plastic voice carrier slip from his hand, terminally crashing onto the concrete path. His mobile must have previously heard countless squalid conversations, but it trembled and smarted with electronic indignation at what it had just heard. When it hit the hard ground, the phone shattered into ragged pieces, its innards still tenaciously vibrating, still scandalised at what it had just had to listen to.

16

Tremblett's white face was turning slowly grey in the city's Dostoyevskian gloom; a withering wind whipped across the park from the Bay.

"Nearly sixteen years. I put in nearly sixteen years. And then fucked it all up."

Rod's cancelled eyes closed at the thought of it. Every mote of age was highlighted in his sullen face; every nasal hair bristled with indignation. It had all happened like a chain reaction; first it was just the one step over the line; then came another, and another. Now he felt like he was a thousand miles away from the Rod Tremblett he had been three years ago. For the last few years he had been imitating himself; his expressions, his mannerisms; all his old persona. But the fact was that he had become an entirely different person. He had no old self left. He was an exactly-alike Rod Tremblett; but a fake one, a poisoned parody wearing Rod's old clothes.

Just look at his expression, just look! The dishonest grey face, the cold-grey eyes, and derogatory grey-lips greying even more in the forbidding dimness. Rod Tremblett was already a ghost, an incredulous chimera, wounded and fading into approaching night.

Suddenly, Rod throws back his head, and lets out a long mournful, animal cry; the sort of spine-tingling scream that's normally only heard on the moon-lit African savannah. The tortured ululation ripples across the candle-smooth lake in a series of sonic waves, across the moored rowing boats and out of the park, on and on through the frantic rush-hour streets, unnoticed and unheeded into the city's rackety maw. The throaty sough was a vocal representation of his terminally shambolic, Gordian-Knot life, with its inescapable falsities and denunciatory lies.

An evening mist begins to surround Rod as he heads for the big iron gates at the entrance to the park, his blank eyes darting and jerking like a reptiles eyes. His tongue moves around inside his mouth, moulding an arabesque of words that he can't speak. "I…I…" Rod is attempting to express something like a self-apology; but he has lost his voice. It had fallen, broken and clanking to the ground with his mobile phone. He knew that he was running out of time, and that it was now time to make his intrusion into someone else's time: Melanie's time. The same time that Wendy Westerby was occupying.

Poor Rod, he felt like he had awoken this morning to find himself in Hell. Tortured, battered and annihilated. But there was one creature whose banishment to the nether regions would justify his own diabolical suffering. The jerking extinction of a certain malefic person would be his own misery's justification.

17

Ladies and gentlemen – patient reader – when you think about it, "rationality" is almost a miraculous exception, isn't it? Most of us are readily capable of believing known lies, of denying obvious truths; confounding and confirming all kinds of irrational things like a bunch of mad, hallucinogenic Charlie Mansons. Look how easily we mistake cunning for cleverness, mistake self-interested sophistry for wisdom. We easily forget that clever, with its intellectual insight, always thwarts cunning, and lies are always exposed by well-exercised memory.

The unkind truth is that most people exemplify self-ignorance, and are capable of justifying everything they do – probably because there are no longer any "absolute" truths, no verifiable rights or wrongs. Or maybe it's just because human existence itself lacks veracity. The thing is, with our own lives constantly teetering on the verge of extinction, it's quite a miracle that we can ever care about somebody else's life, isn't it? Why are other people's lives so precious to us when our own are so stricken with uncertainty? With Rod Tremblett's life so fatally stricken, why should he care about taking the life of the person that struck it?

18

Motley had already got to Westerby's apartment building and settled himself down to wait: in the words of the American Civil War general, he'd got there...fustest, and with the mostest. He had the loaded PPK, with its full clip of death, tucked into the expensively tailored waistband of his Hugo Boss jeans. He was now sitting with his back leaning against the trunk of a half grown tree, surrounded by the litter-endowed shrubbery that lined one side of the avenue upon which Westerby's apartment building stood. He was waiting for the policewoman to arrive home after her triumphal day's work; and he was waiting for someone else too.

Motley's secret plan was relying on the poisonous reaction that his brother's arrest would ignite in Rod Tremblett's panicked brain, the reaction that would draw out the harassed and humiliated drug squad detective to exact his revenge upon his treacherous ex-lover. Fingering the butt of his semi-automatic, Motley remembered from his time spent in combat that it was often a fit of madness that provided the geometry for decisive action. He realised that he would have to be insane to kill the police detective; so he readied himself to take advantage of his own moment of insanity when it came. Sitting on his haunches in the growing darkness, Motley must have looked like an intrepid ghost, a ghost torn with disembodied rage and unspeakable anger.

As darkness settled like volcanic sediment over him, he realised that, to the casual observer, he could be mistaken for a peeping tom, or some drug-hungry burglar casing out his next job. He shook the thought from his head and stood up to take a badly needed piss. After just a few bladder-relieving squirts, he painfully squeezed off the flow when he saw a man's figure turning into the street. Quickly hefting his unnerved penis back into his boxers, Motley dropped back into his squatting position. Peering out through the bushes he saw the darkly dressed man approaching. He immediately recognised his indistinct prey; the shadowy figure was none other than Detective Constable Rod Tremblett: the erstwhile lover of DS Wendy Westerby.

The street was sickly-hued, wet and glossy, with a noir-ish look. But for Tremblett, the street was agitated, sweating, howling. As he shuffled along he felt a momentary pang of regret, like he felt when sending his kids to bed without a goodnight kiss. He seemed to be smiling gauntly. With a gulp of effort he growled huskily, "Come on bitch. I'm dying here. And you are too."

Yesterday, he cared more about Melanie than any other person on earth. But today, he was going to kill her: quid pro quo. Rod looked around warily, then he ducked into the dark vestibule of a doorway.

Motley knew exactly what Tremblett was feeling at that moment. "Numb," he said to himself, "Numb. No emotion. No heartbeat. Numbed out." Then he tried to guess at what Tremblett was thinking: "Payback. Payback!" That's it!

That's the answer. The primal answer to everything. Motley got really close to understanding Rod Tremblett's thinking – What else is there for him? Disgrace? Jail? Then the years of crying and screaming, wanting to smash everything. And always the question: 'Why?' It has to be Payback, then suicide. There's no alternative. He wondered if those people who kill ever see themselves as murderers? Maybe the murderers are like people in the pornography industry; those people never see themselves as porno stars simply fucking for a living. They see themselves as actors and actresses. And there's a reason for that. It's because fucking for money is beyond the moral order; it's atavistic and blameworthy. Just like murder.

For over an hour, the two men skulked in their respective hiding places. Two desperate men, concealing themselves in the darkness within yards of each other, both with one single thought on their unbending minds: vengeance. They were like a union of angry revengers; a brotherhood of two held in tight orbit by the gravitational pull of monstrous intent. They levitated in a paradise for angry men, a more angrier than thou heaven of outrage and perceived wrongs, of unprovoked attacks and uncalled-for betrayals. Both men sized up their retaliation-demanding defilements, their individual teach-em-a-lesson complaints. Retribution swirled around the neutral streets of Roath like a flood of foul water.

Rod stood in the dank doorway, a hole-in-the-wall crowded with dark vapours, breathing in the steaming breath of traffic with its respiratory betrayals. He looked down at his dully-shining shoes and thought to himself: this is terrible. A voice in his head was telling him to stop: now. But he'd gone too far. Retribution and then death: eternity's endless night, with its wealth of time, its torrent of discontinuity.

When he saw his girlfriend pulling into her driveway, Rod's face seemed to take on a new coating, a different kind of cladding – without vigour and light. It also had something of the top-of-the-food-chain about it. This new face feared nothing, and no one. His eyes gave a freshened bulge, new bravado and new defiance forming in the brain: actual, grievous, and homicidal. Someone was going to have to pay for her past; someone was going to have to be made a victim of her mistakes, her own mired schemes. And then DS Wendy Westerby stepped from her car.

The sight of his lover sucked the remaining colour out of Rod's face; and bared his teeth. But, strangely, Rod is uncannily calm, and he's had the shit kicked out of him too. He's lost his wife, his kids, and his career – not to mention his girlfriend. And pretty soon he will lose his freedom. And yet, he's calm. All he has to do is step from the shadows and keep moving towards her. He is going to pretend that it's happening to someone else, that Melanie is someone else. He's not going to strangle his lover, the woman he'd fallen in love with. This woman is a stranger. That makes it a lot simpler; it's the simplest thing he's ever done. Don't fuck it up by thinking about her. Don't fuck it up! His eyes are now red with tears. It's not about you; it's not about her.

He caught up with Westerby as she walked around her car towards the door of her apartment block. She reeled backwards when she saw him, the requisite stunned look upon her face. "Rod!"

A tremor ran through her, as of a gazelle scenting a lion. Her whole face was blinking at him. Rod closed the distance between them.

"You're dead! You're fucking dead!"

Westerby was suddenly reeling backwards towards her car.

"No. Don't do this! Don't please!"

Rod ran towards her and pushed her back against the side of her auto. The policewoman's thinking had now shut down. She was too terrified to think of anything.

"It's Payback time," Rod hissed, his hands on her shoulders.

"Don't…don't. Please, don't," was all Westerby could say.

How many times had Rod heard a woman say those words before? They usually said it as one word…"Pleasedon't." He'd thought that they said it because that's what they were supposed to say. It was no more than that; it was just a part of the game before they hopped gleefully into the sack. At least that's what he'd told himself at the time. He grabbed his betraying girlfriend by the shoulders and pushed her firmly against the wind-efficient curve of the car window.

"You know what?" he asked softly, "You taught me so much. But now I'm going to teach you something." Then he stepped in closer towards her.

"Don't. Please, Rod. Don't."

Rod's mind was spinning like a kid's top, quivering with centrifugal force. "I doubt you've ever said that to a guy before, have you?" he sneered, with a cold laugh. Then he reached for the policewoman's throat.

Westerby struggled to free herself from Tremblett's grip, grabbing him by his wrists and writhing to get away. "…Argh! Let me go!"

But the six-foot-one copper was too strong for her. He squeezed her throat tightly, his mind blundering and stumbling about, looking for what he wanted to say. He hissed into her ear, "When we're both dead, what does anything matter, eh?"

Still she struggled, trying to force his hands away from her windpipe. But again, he tightened his grip on her neck even harder. Westerby was very close to passing out. "I wanted you, but it doesn't matter now, does it?" Tremblett was snarling, "Nothing matters now, does it?" Finally, the struggling policewoman went completely limp in his hands, and passed mercifully into unconsciousness. "Die, you bitch," Rod snarled, "Die!"

He lowered the dead weight of his girlfriend onto the tarmac and sat astride her, still with his hands held around her throat. All the anger and shame that had simmered and boiled inside him was now pouring through the muscled conduits of his arms. His emotions had lost all lucidity; become something toxic, something rancid and pulmonary – an exhalation of hate and grief. Rod put his emotions on Auto, as a pilot might when wanting to land his plane without thinking about it, without imagining its terrors. At the same time he felt the clarity of perception that every artist knows, when everything becomes crystallised, clear. Overhead hung the crescent moon, a bright trigger looming – but not yet ready to bark into the night, booming into the deep blue yonder, not yet. Not yet.

Why does the bark of a pulled trigger so often come at night, the grim echo of its pre-historic thunder echoing down the labyrinthine streets? Is it because everyone is so afraid at night, afraid and fearful in the gun-barrel dark? Maybe if he'd looked around just then, maybe if he'd just glanced up momentarily from his brutal work, Rod Tremblett would have seen something happening behind him, something huge that was roaring down on him. He would have seen

Motley flying out of the bushes, a weapon in his hand and his head full of Payback. But Rod, poor Rod, he couldn't see anything: he was blinded by rage. He couldn't see the fretful moon gazing down in horror, or the clouds foaming with outrage in the wind-dishevelled sky. He couldn't see the long line of beech trees raising their leaf-stripped branches into the crackling air, appealing to some arboreal deity to intervene in the life-or-death struggle that was taking place beneath their quivering arms.

The blood throbbed in Tremblett's temples; he couldn't see or feel. He relaxed his grip on his girlfriend's throat, letting his arms fall limply to his sides. He looked serene, but that was just faking it. He'd already made up his mind – take her out, then take himself out...."Got nothing to lose." He had been on a suicide mission. Now he would head for the river; no more words, no more thoughts, no seeing, no hearing, no tasting or smelling. The only thing he could feel now was anger, adrenaline and resignation. Rod believed that his treacherous girlfriend was dead.

21

He had been afraid that he'd feel too much to kill her, but he didn't feel anything now; except for the cold muzzle of the Walther PPK that was suddenly jammed into the nape of his neck.

"Did you think it would make you feel better?" a voice behind him breathlessly asked. Tremblett tried to turn his head around, but the pistol was shoved even harder into his neck. "Uh, uh. Don't turn around."

There was a kind of relief in his face when Tremblett recognised the voice of the man holding the gun. "Pull the trigger," he moaned, "Pull it!"

"What about your wife and kids, eh? Not thinking of them now, are you?"

"She might just as well have killed my kids," Tremblett sobbed, still sitting astride his unconscious ex-lover.

"And you almost killed my Rachel," the voice behind him snarled.

"Please, do it! Pull the trigger!"

Motley's finger began to squeeze on the small quarter-moon curve of the pistol's slender trigger.

"Don't. Don't do it!" Westerby was leaning up on one elbow, coughing and gasping for air, "No. Don't. That's what he wants." Motley looked down at her with gleaming, determined eyes.

"Well, let's give him what he wants, shall we?"

"Don't be stupid. Think about it!" Westerby pleaded.

"This piece of shit tried to kill my girlfriend. And he just tried to kill you. Why shouldn't I waste him?"

Westerby desperately gasped for breath as she tried to speak, "Don't do it, Motley. You said he tried to kill your girlfriend. Do you think she'd want this? Is this what she would want?"

Tremblett had turned around, and was screaming up at Motley, his face a contorted mask of sweat and tears. "Pull the trigger you gutless bastard. Pull it. I'm dead already. Shoot me you gutless cunt!" Motley grabbed Tremblett by the hair and forced the muzzle of his gun into the policeman's contemptuous mouth.

"Don't be a fool Motley!" Westerby was gasping.

All at once the ruthlessness disappeared from Motley's face, and something emerged both stronger and milder – his intelligence. "No, I'm not a cunt," he said calmly, "but you're right about one thing. You are dead already!" And he smashed the butt of his piece down hard into Tremblett's skull. The stunned copper fell to the ground like a two tonne sack of cement.

22

Now what you need to remember is that Motley knew all about killing. That had once been his job hadn't it? That's what the government had trained him to do; they had trained him for years to kill his country's enemies, to kill them so fast that they wouldn't know what the fuck had hit them. And he did his job as a soldier. Oh, he did what he was trained to do all right, but he had managed to avoid killing anybody. And he still couldn't kill. Well, it wasn't that he couldn't kill. Don't get me wrong; he would have given anything to have slotted Rod Tremblett. He would have given anything – but not everything. In his deranging surge of fury, Motley had stepped up to the line and looked back at all that he had. And then he had looked over at the other side, and seen all that he would lose.

23

The half-choked policewoman had sunk back onto the tarmac, coughing and spluttering. Motley dropped to one knee beside her. Lifting her head into his lap he patted her cheek gently, "Wendy…Wendy. Try and breathe slowly and deeply. You're hyperventilating."

Coming around again, she looked up at Motley and weakly murmured, "You knew he'd try this didn't you?"

Motley nodded apologetically, "I had a good idea."

"Bastard! You could have warned me!"

"Yeah. I'm a bastard all right. I'm the bastard that just saved your life."

Westerby nodded lightly.

"By the way," Motley vigorously stroked Westerby's arm as he spoke, trying to keep her warm, "thanks again for warning me about Sweep's girlfriend. He's finished with all that now. And she's history too."

"And you'll be history if you don't get out of here. Somebody must have rung the police by now. You'd better go, I'll be okay." Westerby was seized by another coughing fit as she spoke, so she waved Motley away with her hand. He suddenly became aware of a crowd of people standing around him. A Philippino-looking girl walked warily over to stand beside him, "I'm a nurse...can I help?"

Pointing to the spread-eagled form of Rod Tremblett, Motley answered, "That man tried to strangle her. He's unconscious now, but make sure the police know about that when they arrive. Take care of her, she needs to breathe deeply and slowly."

As Motley handed Westerby over to the nurse, he could hear the air-curving ululations of the approaching sirens. He walked back towards his car lurching and weaving, as if impeded by unseen obstacles: "Christ, I need a drink."

As he approached his car, a cellophaned parking ticket waved bashfully at him from beneath the near-side wiper. Removing it from its plastic nest, Motley carefully and deliberately tore it into two, four, eight pieces, letting the pale confetti flutter to the ground; turning the annoyance over to the simple-minded laughter of the wind. He hated the idea of an unyielding parking warden mixing uniformed authority with gleeful misanthropy: "The fucking wankers."

Despite his antipathy, an impenetrable darkness seemed to be lifting away from Motley. The accident that wasn't an accident, and the vision of Rachel's mangled body – her cracked skull and ripped flesh, her broken legs and her outraged womb still tore at him like a blunt knife. But the insatiable drive for revenge that had almost broken him had begun to crumble like eggshells. Motley drove home, his aching bladder still telling him that he was in desperate need of a Chinese singing lesson. He was also longing for a stiff drink, and a rib-bursting cuddle.

24

So, now you know what happened to Sweep's girlfriend's plan to get her boyfriend away from Motley. She had unsuspectingly gone around to Sweep's house on the night he found out about her talk with Jelly-Hair, expecting to settle down for another of their usual evenings of drink, TV and fifteen minutes of the straining, wheezing fiasco that was their lovemaking. But all that was over. When Motley had told Sweep what she had tried to do, he made no allowances. When she knocked at his front door, he kept her standing on the doorstep. "That was a stupid, totally unforgivable thing to do. That's the last," he yelled at her. Then he went to shut the door in her face.

"May I say something?" she had asked in her most gracious tone, her head lolled at a dogged angle as she brushed her ash-blonde quiff from her face. Sweep remained silent. "I only did it for you," she said, folding her arms defensively.

Yes! Can you believe that...that's exactly what she said! And she said it with her fractional eyes stacked with sanctimonious tears. Sweep just held up his hands as if to say, enough! And then asked her to leave. Well, what he actually said was, "Get the fuck out of here!" Then he looked at her as though she was a stranger, before he slammed the door on their eighteen-month relationship.

Leaning against the inside of the door, the trembling Sweep felt as though a thousand butterflies were mating in his stomach. No, make that a flock of vultures; and they were feeding upon his heart. It was the worst night of Sweep's life, and he'd had a lot of BAD nights. Later on, he got more pissed than the time his wife had walked out on him. But the next day, Motley had come around with the revivifying news about the beach-bar, and Sweep was all for it: "Count me in on that, Taff m' boy! I'm badly in need a change of scenery right now."

"You're gonna love it, Sweep. This ain't no beach shack you know what I mean? This is proper, mate. And it's only a few yards off the main beach-road into town. It's a bloody gold mine."

Even just thinking about the beach-bar facing out towards a turquoise sea made Sweep feel slightly less winter-cold, less glacial. "Jesus, Taff. I can't wait to get my arse parked on one of your bar stools."

"Our bar stools, Sweep. Our stools, mate." Motley smiled broadly and clasped his friend's shoulder.

25

In the southern Caribbean, there's a short time after the setting sun dips into the sea when the burnished water and the fire-streaked sky seem on the verge of saying something to you: something you are anxious to hear. They never do; or perhaps they do but we don't understand it. Perhaps what they say is as untranslatable as birdsong. They may simply be saying something about the end of the day; or maybe the rubric skies are telling us something about the end of everything.

Motley sat back on his stool and leaned one elbow on the bar: his bar. With the work of vengeance done, he now felt that he was a nobody. Or rather, he was another incarnation: he'd become someone else. And since identity is based on memory, Motley's new identity means that his memories of Iraq have become small and fleeting. These days there are no séances with dead comrades; the word nightmare means nothing more than a word to him. It's as if the old Motley is separated from the new one by a pane of dream-proof glass; the old, nostalgic Motley had lived in successive time, while the new Motley lives in the present, in the eternity of the instant. No one from the past had come to him to say farewell; there were no goodbye dreams.

"I'll tell Rachel you'll be up in a while, yeah?"

"Yeah. Thanks Sweep. I'll just lock it all up. See you back at the house."

Sweep gave his newly acquired son-in-law an affectionate slap on the back, "That's another day in paradise taken care of, and another day I've been off the booze."

Motley turned around to look at his friend and father-in-law with a raised and questioning eyebrow, "Sweep?"

"Well?" said Sweep almost apologetically. "...You can't call just six beers in a day a drink can you?"

"Okay. And what about the bottles of wine you'll be having with us at dinner tonight, eh? And then the bottle of rum we'll down afterwards?"

"Jesus, Taff," Sweep said with a smile, "drop the logic, you're a much nicer guy without it. You know, I've never worked out what Rachel sees in you."

Sweep waved a hand to Motley as he walked along the beach towards the white painted, open-veranda'd house that the three of them happily shared. The house was actually large enough for four or five people, and that was a good thing: because Rachel was pregnant. Oh, it wasn't an accident or anything like that. Motley had taken Rachel to a specialist gynaecological centre in New York, and they had given the couple the go-ahead for having kids. Apparently, with the right specialist care, Rachel would be okay on the baby-making front.

Emotionally, the Big Apple had taken possession of Rachel as she advanced from one stupendous sight to another; Manhattan's skyscrapers, with their layered windows looming with reflections, the commanding Art Deco spire of the Empire State thrusting skyward as proud as a Viagra-pumped erection. The famous New York yellow cabs staggered about in their military-style phalanxes, wholly preoccupied, it seemed, with the task of ignoring the prospective fares desperately tying to wave them down.

Coping with her aches and pains, Rachel had been constantly excited: "Oh my God, look! Look! It's just like it is in the movies!"

Motley's silhouette-prowling eyes were drawn upward to the re-aligned skyline, with its catastrophic bald-spot plangent with vestigial grief. He still carried the incarnadine images of 9/11 in his head. The entire world had re-arranged itself on that September day, but the brutally wounded city had briefly paused, missed a beat, and then began its life again, as though it were used to dealing with even greater prodigies of horror and aggrievement.

"They're using airline tickets as smart-bombs," Motley had said, blinking and swallowing hard as he watched his blighted television screen. It took his breath away. It was as though Hollywood fiction had suddenly got big ideas; but this was actually happening. He had been a combat soldier for nearly a decade, but what he saw that day was the worst thing he had ever seen. Motley stood in the grimly flickering television glow, stalled and disbelieving, watching the thwarted escapees; the jumpers, the thrashers, the blameless head-first renouncers, falling through layers of smoke and insult – falling, falling, interminably falling, terror-crazed and voiceless through the defiled and shamefaced air; like killer rain. And when, finally, the doomed reached the end of their falling, the bloodbath of sunset is daubed over the pavements. The traffic lights continue to flash their arterial warnings, hardly daring to change colour to kinetic green. Soon, the outraged streets will be wrapped in an impatient white shawl, as preposterous and impenetrable as night.

And now Motley stands on the streets of the indomitable city, remembering the fallen. Of course he knew that New York's streets weren't always filled with such necrotic rage, such pathos and disgrace. They were once filled with wolves and bears and Red Indians, and before that the streets had been filled with sabre-toothed tigers and woolly mammoth. Even further back, there were the downwardly mobile dinosaurs, once infinite in their powers. After going through all that, the streets of New York must be wondering where they're going to end up. They'll end up like all dead things, I'm afraid – primal and embittered, weeping unheard into the vast nucleic chaos.

One evening, the couple shouldered their way through the partying whores and gaping fatsos that cluttered the sidewalks around Times Square. Seeing the gaudy array of sex-shops and video-parlours, Motley was simply thinking – America…the Land of Opportunity, and the stupendous aberrations of dick-wiping porn. He couldn't help checking over the Square's constantly changing troop of streetwalkers. Motley concluded that American hookers are not so docile as their Brit counterparts; "Hey honey, you looking for me?" or "Hey sweetie, you and your pretty girl lookin to party?" He imagined that these working girls' conversations were different too; they talked only of movie stars and money. And he imagined that when they talked to the tricks, they said things like – "Hey, let's do it," or, "Hey, you got it." And they probably said it in that tough, corporate, yankee-doodle way that makes you think that you can't even afford them. But Motley thought that the biggest difference between Brit and American hookers was the look in their eyes; there was no bafflement in the American girl's eyes, their eyes beamed-back untapped resources of intellect and articulation.

It must be New York's kick-ass way, Motley thought, because none of these girls looked like victims. There was no sense of stooping or floundering here; the victims didn't believe they were being victimized. Even the whores stand tall in New York, thinking that they're up there with the skyscrapers. Motley's guess was that American hookers didn't see themselves as whores; they were businesswomen, and they welcomed all major credit cards. That's the other difference between Brit whores and American whores; a Brit whore thinks of herself as having been raped ten thousand times; an American whore thinks she's had a glittering career in the service industry.

A few blocks from Times Square, the couple suddenly found themselves thinking once again; America...where homicidal maniacs poleaxe sky-towers with fully fuelled-up passenger planes. They had stumbled upon Ground Zero – that rancid, emotive battlefield where the unavoidable, shelterless war on terrorism had started. The surrounding buildings stood with blind erectness, backward-leaning, as though they'd been through some intolerable stress; they no longer felt as though they were above it all. Terror had seen to that.

"That's where the towers used to be." Rachel gripped Motley's arm as she spoke, almost whispering the ugly truth, "People went off to work, but they never came home."

The tears flowed easily down her cheeks; Motley took out his handkerchief and held it gently to her nose. "Blow," he said, while sniffing heavily himself.

"What else can we do but cry?" Rachel asked.

Before he answered, Motley took a long look around at the heart-burning scene. "Prevail," he finally growled, "We prevail."

Over the following days they went to the museums, to the galleries; and the Statue of Liberty, and they shrank back from the vertiginous view at the top of the Empire State. They went to the movies where Rachel wept over a sentimental love story. In part, she had gone to America to rescue a portion of her own love story. In the gynaecologist's office she watched the silver-haired, bespectacled doctor quietly read through the results of all her tests. She was hopeful that something good was about to happen. And it did. "Well, I think we have some good news for you, Mrs. Motley," the doctor had said, "with the right specialist care..."

That afternoon, back at their hotel, Rachel and Motley showered and ordered a bottle of champagne from room service. When Motley emerged from the bathroom, he saw a naked Rachel already stretched out on the bed, arms and legs akimbo. "Now, make us a baby!" she laughed.

"Well here it comes," he eagerly cried, diving onto the bed beside her, "One beautiful baby. Coming right up!"

Of course they didn't know it at the time, but Rachel would be leaving New York with something she didn't bring with her: something very precious. Unsurprisingly, when Rachel had given them the good news, Motley and Sweep had both got drunker than a pair of rats in a vat of cider.

Then, a few weeks later, it was Sweep who brought some good news to Motley and Rachel: he'd fallen in love with their next-door neighbour. Carmen was a petite and friendly American widow who had sought refuge in the Islands from the crime wave that had engulfed some of the larger American cities. Her sixties-style bouffant hair was entirely grey, but that was okay, because Sweep's hair was greying along the sides too, and she had soft and generous blue eyes. All year round, she bore a red noose of sunburn around her shoulders, freckled and peeling from working in her garden wearing a peasant blouse and straw hat.

"You know that you've got old when you notice that men have stopped looking at you," Carmen had said to Sweep, shortly after they met. He didn't say anything at the time, but he suddenly realised that from the very moment he had met her, he couldn't take his eyes away from her.

So, Sweep fell head-over-heels in love again, and it happened on the night of a terrible tropical storm. Carmen and Sweep were sat on the balcony of her bungalow, sipping cocktails and playing a two-hander game of poker. As always, Carmen was winning hand after hand; probably because Sweep's mind was on courting the Mid-Western lady instead of counting the cards. As the rain rattled against the corrugated roof of the bungalow like a fantastical drumbeat, Sweep's hand reached out for Carmen's hand. Then the words came from his lips that would decide their future.

"I think I've fallen in love with you," he murmured. And wouldn't you know, they had decided to fall in love just as the violent storm was hitting the Islands with its full force. The rain entered the veranda horizontally, like soft dum-dum bullets of water, the wind snuffled and woofed around their bare legs like an old family dog. As he sat holding Carmen's hand, sitting on the wet balcony, Sweep stared menacingly at the blustering storm that was threatening to ruin his moment of triumph. He looked at the storm, and the storm looked at him. He didn't like the storm, and the storm didn't like him. They were a pair of pugnacious tempers trying to stare each other down.

The tropical storms were definitely getting more intense each year, as if you could hear the polluted atmosphere's exhalations, its roaring, resentful struggle for breath. Sweep's lips moved soundlessly, mouthing the words, "Bloody global warming."

Pretty soon, he thought, the entire planet was going to be downgraded to a tropical storm, a low-barometer collector's piece. He wondered why those TV documentaries made the effects of global warming sound so complicated, because they're not; the effects of global warming are dead simple. It's all about Payback. The fucked-up weather is Payback for global warming: Payback for screwing the planet. Sweep suddenly thought of that famous picture of the earth taken from the moon; how fragile our celestial home looked, how amazingly fragile.

26

Further north, category five hurricanes are just routine now: stock, steady, and entrenched. More and more it's becoming obvious that the studies and stats are right – when someone told the weather about global warming, it went fucking insane. It seems that when global warming moves in, the hurricanes move out. Sweep thinks that the weather has overreacted, but he's a man of the world, and so it's natural that he should feel sorry for the state the world is in: its green and blue beauty pouting under a thick blanket of greenhouse gas, it's heavenly face slashed with glutinous tears, toxic tears, sulphuric tears. The World is weeping, weeping, weeping. He guesses that the weather is getting its own back, doing it to the Caribbean first, but eventually it will get around to spanking the rest of the World too. Then the idea occurs to him: a roaring hurricane is what the Earth would sound like if could protest at its treatment.

So, the World is suffering along with the rest of us. Though its shortness of breath comes not from the effort of its cosmic convolutions, but from the smell of exhaust gases. The planet is starting to realise that the human gorillas that infest its dirt-encrusted skin are actually human guerrillas; suicidally intent on becoming the World's governing force. And now a crisis is coming: the World's rage is gathering against the guerrillas' plundering actions.

27

But despite the awful weather, Carmen's smile was radiant – luscious, even; her crinkled mouth giving ground in its battle against the recklessness of time. Set in the glowing oval of her face, the smile outlined by her lipstick was so dark it appeared black in the half-light. Sweep could imagine that smile lighting up rooms, glancing skittingly, teasingly, from face to admiring face. For a moment Sweep thought about his own rumpled smile, his much-patched teeth and the stale taste that lingered between the cavities. He wondered what the lovely lady sitting opposite him was seeing in his monstrously creased and craggy face, and in that moment Sweep never felt so old, or so young.

How lovely, how adorably alight Carmen's face had been in its girlish confusion when Sweep had taken her hand, and what a beautiful hand; elegant and round, corpulent with feminine expressiveness. She looked happy and fulfilled. Perhaps the world of human affairs can be deconstructed into those two basic needs – happiness and fulfilment – the one chasing the other.

"You are so beautiful," Sweep gasped, "you take my breath away." She looked at him starry-eyed; Sweep had never encountered starry-eyed before. "Well, you're not bad," he bluffed, "don't want you getting big headed, do I?"

In her flat Great Plains accent, Carmen said, "Oh, my dear Sweep. I've fallen in love with you too." Sweep bent his head and kissed the palm of her hand.

"So what happens next?" He asked, tremulously, wondering…

"We get married." Carmen half proclaimed and half-asked. The widow was a respectable lady, and wanted to retain her respectability.

"Is that a proposal?" Before she could answer, Sweep rose from the table and crossed the planked floor to kiss her. Carmen kissed back her wordless answer, wordless and yearning, her heart pounding in her chest as if to break her ribs. Later, when Sweep made ready to leave, she said in an almost fainting, little girl voice, "Oh, don't go!" The buzz from the cocktails she had drunk allowed her to give Sweep's hand a connubial squeeze.

Adjusting his eyes to the dimness while emerging from the tiled brightness of the bathroom, Sweep slid into bed beside the expectant Carmen. She wound her arms around his neck like a long, smooth, shivering puppy. "Well, we're almost married, aren't we?" she whispered into his ear.

Touching her lips with his own, Sweep murmured, "I can't wait to be your husband." He could have said, "Because you make me want to live longer. You make me want to cut down on the boozing." But there were many things he could have said to the beautiful woman wrapped in his arms wearing only a dazzling smile.

Sweep gazed down into Carmen's eyes; the beckoning bowls of dreams that were her eyes. Carmen's trusting eyes were where her strength and virtue lived, and they were now only inches from Sweep's own eyes. He was dazzled by the gleam of her smile, her teeth still tight-bound from teenage braces; teeth so fantastically perfect that her lips could barely cling to them. He wondered what Carmen was seeing in his own rheumy eyes, ragged and deep-set in his gnarled face, with its hairy shrubbery and mild reek of desperation, all topped off by a curt haircut. He wondered if she could see the famine in his eyes, the plight of failed love and the scoured grooves of hard-learned epiphanies. He wondered if the vibrant widow saw a comatose life of heart-breaking descents, a boneless ego dissolved in alcohol and unrelenting remorse.

When Carmen reached down towards Sweep's groin, he could hear the blood beating in his ears, feel the gurgle of its pulsing bulk in his veins. With nerve-ripping, cock-shrinking waves of anxiety, he wondered whether he could come up with the goods. As Carmen's hand closed around his manhood, she began stroking. One…Two…Three…Bingo! Hard-on. (Phew!) It had been a dangerous moment for Sweep's sexual confidence, but once ignited, his passion for the modest Mid-Westerner would continue to roar and flare like a burning oil well.

In their later years, Carmen and Sweep will take their minds back to that magical night, when they sat on the veranda; when the tree-tearing winds, the thunder, and the lightning-scorched shadows provided a dramatic backdrop to their declaration of love. In the years to come, they will smile whenever the tropical rain belly flops onto the iron roof and the flattening storm returns to claim its privileges. Like two grateful refugees, they will hold each other's hands, and reclaim their love with laughing authority over the hissing tide and slanting wreckage. This, this wicker-chair present, this shawl of love, was as much happiness as Sweep could ever imagine.

28

...And what do we have here?

Over at the Motleys' house, the much-awaited baby is here at last; lying on its baby-mat on the kitchen floor, being unwrapped by Motley for its imminent nappy change, its arms waving and legs flailing in response to Motley's earlobe-to-earlobe smile. Feeling happier than a flea in a honeymooner's bed, the ex-soldier is struck by a sudden swelling of protectiveness that threatens to completely overwhelm him.

"Pass the powder please, love."

Rachel looks up from her coffee mug and pushes the requested container across the kitchen table towards him. As Motley gropes warily around inside his daughter's romper he feels a fatherly love drenching his heart: his heart so hugely enlarged, so deep-encased in love. A camera clicks behind him. Rachel is beaming down at them.

"One for the record. You look so sweet changing her nappy."

"Nah," Motley says, with an avoiding eureka, "I don't look half as sweet as you do when you're doing it."

And look...there he is again.

He's locking up his beach-bar at the end of another day. There Motley stands in the viscous evening gloom; gazing with satisfaction over his new business; little by little it comes to him that from now on his life will be about enjoying simple, ordinary things. Motley relaxes into a bliss of inflated hopefulness. He had been begging for forgiveness for the last few years, and now someone has given it, and much more besides. He hears the soft murmur of music coming from further along the beach, a faint strumming of guitar strings. The lilting reggae chords of a Bob Marley song are tangling and untangling on the warm wind, reaching out their impromptu arms to the far-from-home Cardiff boy. Broken rhythms dip and whorl, vibrating on the breeze the way music does when it's looking for a listener. Marley's mournful melody transmits its hauntingly predictive, "no woman…no cry" – advertising the vulnerability of the Rasta-man that ran out of time. Marley: the jubilate Rastafarian, the rock icon, the Main Man, lives on in his potent music, and the devoted ears of a million dope-heads.

The tremor of descending evening – night smoke is already creeping over the sea – brings the legendary colours of a Caribbean sunset, filling the sky like a huge hosanna. Low clouds hang over the horizon in faint phosphorescence, like streaks of radioactive aftermath. Further around the bay, the small harbour is lit up like a shrine, with its neon signs and strings of streetlamps picking nervously at the patient night. A sultry blackness begins spreading shadowy shapes across the white sands, over the smiling owner of the palm-thatched, dream-come-true beach-bar and up towards the mountains of the island's interior. The great dome of the sky is filling with a million stars' visitant light; and as Motley looks up at the rising moon, he reflects that the ring surrounding the disc like a halo is a sign of rain. By morning, the air will be filled with interwoven fragrances, and everything will be fresh and new, the future continually forking into countless other futures. Motley wears a satisfied smile, because he knows that by renouncing the role of executioner, he's won all of those futures.

29

Beyond the sun-mirrored moon, the sky opens out into the black hole of space. Motley is thanking his god, his indeterminate god – any god, for the miracle of a beautiful daughter. And he realises that all his previous tortures and trials, all the hoops of flame that he's had to pass through, were simply preparing him for this miracle. He tells his gurgling baby a thousand times a day that he loves her, and her infant smile tells him that he is immortal; that he will live forever. Taff Motley smiles his broad smile, and puts out the final lamp above the doorway of his beach-bar.

THE END

DENNIS LEWIS

Dennis Lewis was a Rhys Davies winner in 2003 with his story Love's Ligature which is published in Ghosts of the Old Year (Parthian). He is a professional writer and lives near Cardiff.

Also by Dennis Lewis published by Accent Press

THE FEVERED HIVE

"High octane prose – fast and genuinely furious…" CATHERINE MERRIMAN

"A south Wales Bukowski without the gambling – where has he been hiding all this time?" PETER FINCH

ISBN 095486736X   Price £7.99